Early Praise for Stephanie Combs

Stephanie has crafted a world I could happily get lost in for ages. With seamless fairytale vibes and a classic romantasy feel, The Sun and Her Shadow is steeped in old magic, filled with missing gods and memories, and is one I won't soon forget.

— M.A. BROWN, AUTHOR OF THE SEVENTH SISTER

Combs weaves a magical tale that will leave you begging to find out what is on the next page! This is a must read for romantasy lovers who crave a slow burn with the best banter and mysteries that will leave you speechless once solved!

— WILLOW ASTERIA, AUTHOR OF THE REALMS OF ELSWYTH SERIES

THE SUN AND HER SHADOW

TALES OF THE FORSAKEN REALM

STEPHANIE COMBS

Midnight Tide
PUBLISHING

Published by Midnight Tide Publishing

www.midnighttidepublishing.com

Cover design by @selkkiedesigns

Character art by @koijix; @theesamevi; @delilahsdrawings

Map by @julsiji

Developmental/Copy/Line Editor - Rachel Bunner

Email: rachels.top.edits@gmail.com

Instagram: @rachels.top.edits

Proofreading by Rachel L. Schade

1st edition 2025

Paperback ISBN: 978-1-964655-57-4

Content Note

This story contains content that could be sensitive for some readers. There are scenes/mentions of violence, blood, torture, death, miscarriage for a side character, and loss of loved ones along with blood play, victim shaming, familial emotional abuse, and attempted assault. There is also on-page intimacy.

If you have specific questions about any of these, or any you do not see listed here, please reach out to the author at steph@silverflamebooks.com

Pronunciation Guide

CHARACTERS:
Raelyn Astoria - RAY-lin uh-STOR-ee-uh
Kian D'Amaris - KEE-in duh-MAR-iss

PLACES:
City of Elsmont - ELLS-mont
Kingdom of Maardune - mar-DOON
Kingdom of Rakveren - ROCK-vair-in
Kingdom of Sillamae - SILL-uh-may
Town of Narvae - NAR-vay
Town of Paiden - PAY-den
Liial - LIE-ell

DEITIES:
Kyros - KEER-oh-ss - god of the sun
Galyna - guh-LEE-nuh - goddess of healing
Luna - LOO-nuh - goddess of the moon
Veritius - vair-IT-ee-us - god of truth

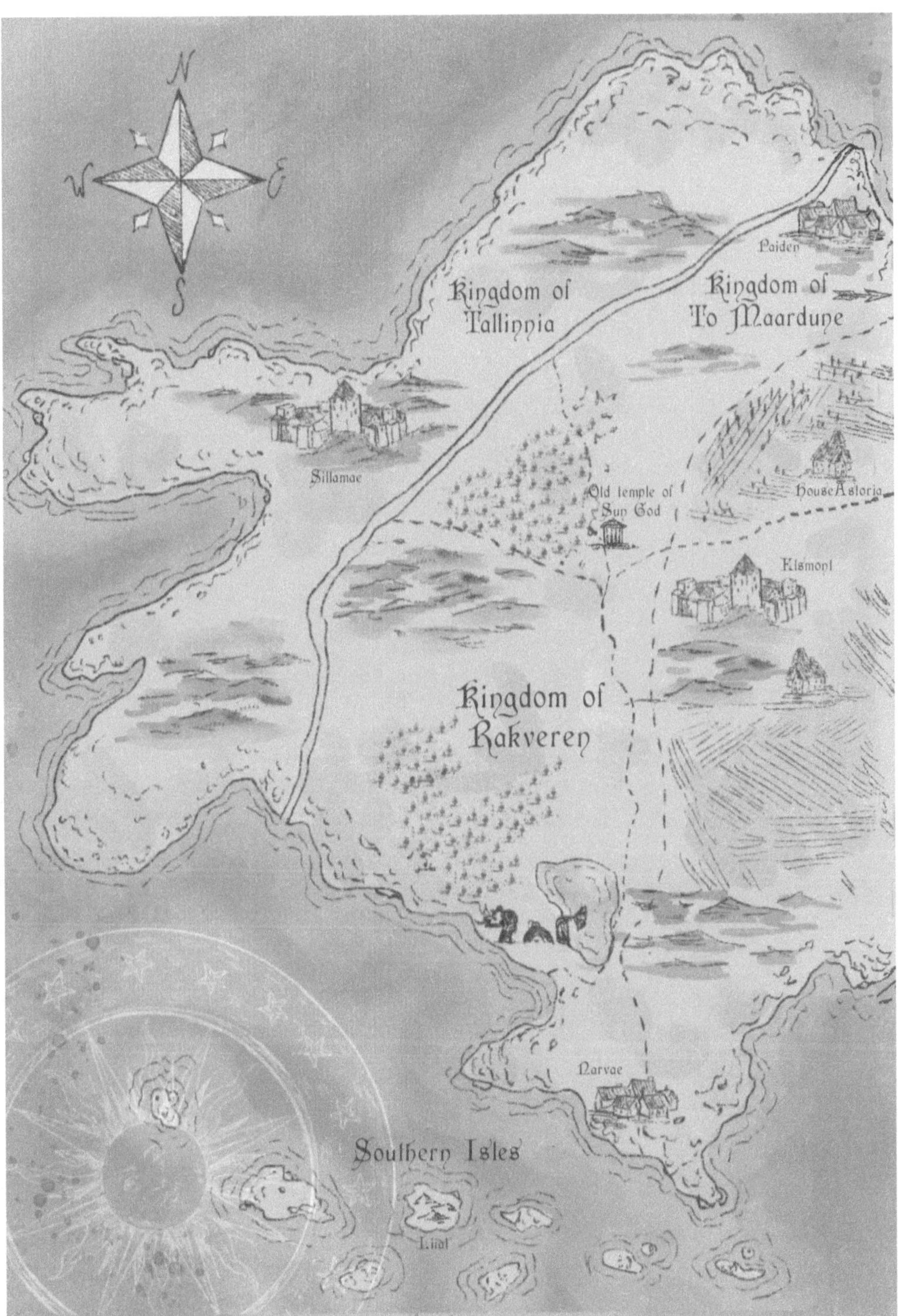

N
W
E
S
Kingdom of
Tallinnia
Kingdom of
To Maardune
Paiden
Sillamae
Old temple of
Sun God
House Astoria
Kismopl
Kingdom of
Rakveren
Narvae
Southern Isles
Liiat

Chapter One

RAELYN

The ancient grandfather clock's jarring chimes announce the late hour, though considering I live my life in the dark, the night is still full of possibility.

Stretching from my curled-up position on the chair, I stifle a yawn. Perhaps not so full. Father told us at dinner that he had an important announcement for us in the morning, which piqued my curiosity, but I'm prepared to be disappointed. Regardless, I'm going to regret staying up—skipping breakfast is not an option.

After returning my books to their shelves, I fold my blanket over the chair and open the door to the hallway. Most of the lamps are out, with the exception of one or two turned extremely low, and the house is silent but for the subtle tick of the clock. I'm the only person awake as far as I can tell. Tiptoeing down the hallway, I try to avoid the creaky floorboards. I've spent enough nights staying up later than Father likes to know how to be quiet.

Just as I'm about to step onto the staircase, the floorboards creak. I whip my head around. Who else is awake at this ungodly hour? My eyes try to pierce through the dim light, but I see nothing. Did I imagine it? Another creak. Should I call out? *No.* I bite my lip. The smart move would be to run up to my bed.

I take a deep breath and blow it out slowly. Damn me for being the responsible and nosy eldest sibling.

Could it be Chessa snooping where she doesn't belong? I can admit the thought of catching her and having something to hold over her is very appealing.

The creak sounded like it came from the hall near Father's study, so that's where I go. I'm fairly certain I'm the only one who knows how to avoid the noisy spots. She'll never hear me coming.

I creep down the hall toward the study, and sure enough, his door is cracked. I can't wait to see the look on her face when I catch her.

Without pausing to think, I push the door open and dart across the threshold. "Chess—"

Her name fizzles out on my tongue as I look around the room and find it empty. What in the gods' names?

I walk around, looking for something out of place in Father's usually immaculate study, but as far as I can tell, nothing is. A sigh leaves me as I turn to go, until the kiss of a draft followed by the whisper of a breath turns my blood to ice.

I freeze.

"Who's there?" I speak and whirl back around. "Show yourself," I command.

A figure drops from the ceiling, and before a scream can leave my lips, I'm pulled into a rock-solid chest and a gloved hand covers my mouth, blocking my cry.

"Uh-uh-uh. Do not make a sound."

I squirm as a chill snakes through me at the vibrations of my captor's low dulcet tone.

"I will let go of your pretty mouth as soon as you stop moving," he purrs.

The hint of amusement in his voice gives me pause. I reposition my feet and still my body, curious to let this play out. When my breathing slows, he relaxes his hold and his hand drops away from my mouth.

"Who are you? What do you think you're doing here?" I ask.

He murmurs against the back of my head, "Nothing that concerns you, my lady."

"Let me go. Please."

His arm tightens around me. "I don't know. Perhaps I enjoy having a beautiful woman captive in my arms."

That's it. I've had enough of him. Who does he think he is, coming into my home to steal from my father?

With a quick, practiced move, I grab his arms, tuck a foot behind his leg, and use my weight to knock him off balance, flipping him onto the floor.

A surprised grunt comes out of his mouth, and before he can move, I straddle his torso, pinning his arms with my knees.

My hand darts down to pull one of the blades from his thigh, and I hold it to his throat. "Who's captive now?"

A delighted chuckle escapes him, and his full lips twist into a grin. The dim light doesn't reveal much and an onyx mask covers most of this face, but I can see a chiseled jaw covered in a light dusting of stubble.

The thief relaxes under me. It's almost insulting. As if he thinks I couldn't possibly be a threat.

I position the blade under his chin and tilt it toward myself. "I'll ask one more time. What do you think you're doing here?" The dagger digs into his skin, and a drop of blood wells up. The scent of something rich and woodsy fills my nose, and I find myself salivating, my jaw aching. I shake my head. My eyes bore into his despite being obscured by the mask. His are dark, like thick, black smoke. I press in closer. "What is your business here, thief?"

His eyes practically smolder as they pierce right back into mine. "The lord of this house has something of value to me."

I roll my eyes. "Obviously, or you wouldn't be here in the middle of the night, trying to steal from him."

A dark laugh bursts out of him. "You amuse me. Now be a good girl and get off me."

"Or what?" I dig the blade a little farther, and another drop of blood trickles down his neck. My tongue darts out to wet my lips, and the thief's eyes follow the movement. *What in the realms is wrong with me?* I shift uncomfortably, and his grin only widens.

"Don't get me wrong, my lady. There is nothing I love more than having a beautiful woman on top of me." He winks. "But . . ."

Before I can think of a retort, he lurches forward and rolls me so that our positions are reversed. The dagger I held to his throat clatters to the floor, and he pins my shoulders down with an arm, his legs on either side of my waist. I glare up at him, more angry at myself than anything for allowing him to get the better of me again.

He leans forward and moves his lips to my ear. "It's best I be going now. It was lovely to make your acquaintance. Be good and don't scream, all right? Unless we meet again . . . under different circumstances."

"You cad," I grit out. Anger writhes inside me at the audacity of this stranger with the smoky eyes and cocky grins.

He jumps up and blows me a kiss before pulling back the curtain and leaping out the open window into the dim light of Luna's embrace.

I push myself to sit, and a drop of something glides down my cheek. Reaching up, I wipe the liquid off my face, holding it up to the moonlight that shines through the open window. The drop of ruby blood glimmers, and before I can stop myself, I suck it off my finger.

The smoky, spicy taste explodes in my mouth, making it water. I must be losing my mind. I've never tasted someone else's blood before, but a sudden craving overwhelms me. *What in the realms?*

Dusting myself off and shoving the thought of blood to the back of my mind to unpack later, I get to my feet and do a quick scan of the room, looking for some kind of disturbance or a clue as to what the thief was after. Once again, nothing looks out of place, but I haven't spent much time in here lately, so perhaps it isn't obvious. The shelves look undisturbed, and Father's desk is as tidy as he likes it.

Perhaps I will never know who the mysterious thief is or what he was after. I stifle a yawn as I close and lock the window, then peer out into the night—no sign of him anywhere. My eyes drift to the moon, and I throw up a quick thanks to Luna that the man didn't actually seem to wish me harm.

Will he return? I should probably tell Father. He'll know what to do.

Chapter Two

A sliver of rare sunlight slips through the drawn curtains—a beckoning call, a siren song meant to lure me toward something that can only do me harm. The rebellious side of me wonders what would happen if I were to stick my toe in that bright beam of light. Would I burn? Father never specified, but I trust he's not lying when he tells me how ill I would get as a child, so I live in darkness. Not completely, but I stay out of the sun. Father's efforts at finding a cure for me have gone nowhere.

I stretch my pale arm in front of me in the dim light, not for the first time wishing my skin matched the sun-kissed hue of the rest of my family's. Perhaps that's what's wrong with me, why I can never touch the sun. Perhaps my mother passed this affliction on through her family line or ate something she wasn't supposed to while carrying me. At least that's the story I prefer instead of the rumors that I'm not my father's daughter. Surely he would have told me if there was any truth to that.

Mother never spoke of it, and I can barely remember her now. Funny how eighteen years can erase a person from one's memories. I vaguely remember raven hair and eyes like the deepest pools of water, but still, she feels foreign to me. She rarely doted on me or had a pleasant thing to say.

Sometimes, I have dreams of a green-eyed woman singing lullabies over me with the kindest smile. However, despite all my searching, I have yet to find someone in our family—or even a previous servant—who matches the description. More affection flows from those dreams than I ever remember receiving from my mother. Perhaps this mystery woman is merely a figment of my overactive imagination stemming from my lack of love at home.

"Raelyn, darling, why ever aren't you dressed yet?"

I groan as I lie back on my bed, reaching for a pillow to cover my face and ears from my sister Erika's obnoxious voice.

"Leave me alone." The few hours of sleep I managed to get were far from enough to be awake right now—my entire body aches. My tumble with the handsome thief didn't help either.

Who was he? What was he looking for? I really ought to tell Father about him at breakfast, but then I'd have to admit how he got the better of me and Father would likely take his unbearable disappointment out on me at our next training session. Not to mention, I'd have to deal with my siblings' mockery . . .

"Father will kill you if you're not down to breakfast on time," Erika says in a sing-song voice, and I wince at the grating scrape of the curtains opening. "You know he has news he wants to share, so we really mustn't be late."

I peek my head out from under the pillow, noting that the light shining into the room won't touch me as long as I stay on the right side of the bed.

"Fine. I'm up," I say with a huff.

Erika lets herself into my dressing room and swiftly re-emerges with an emerald day gown draped over her arm. "Now, Raelyn."

I roll my eyes. She's so bossy, one might think she's the older sister. Dropping my feet onto the chilly stone floor, I yelp.

"I don't understand how you bear this darkness," she says morosely.

"You just opened the damned curtains, Erika. Stop complaining." It's not as if she actually cares how isolating it is, how it forever sets me apart.

She throws the dress at me, and I catch it, making my way behind the green-and-gold dressing screen.

"Do you have any idea what his news might be?" I ask as I strip off my cotton nightgown and throw it onto a chair.

"Wouldn't you like to know," the snide voice of my other sister, Chessa, rings out.

"You could knock first," I mutter under my breath. I have absolutely no privacy with the twins walking around like they own the place.

"As if you have anything to hide," Chess croons.

The derision in her tone makes me want to claw her eyeballs out. How I loathe this *dear* sister of mine. She acts as if the entire realm revolves around her, and if for one moment she feels it doesn't, she throws a fit. It's embarrassing, really. She's twenty years old, for Luna's sake.

"It's a good thing I'm behind the dressing screen. Unlike you, I prefer not to show off my body to anyone who will look."

"Trust me, no one would care if you did, Raelyn," she retorts, ignoring my comment. "Or have you forgotten your lack of suitors? Always so forgetful . . ."

I shrug off her comments and stride out to my mirror so I can fix my hair. Chessa's dark, judgmental eyes mock me in the reflection as she twists a piece of her black, silken strands around her finger.

"You look terrible," she says.

"Thank you. You're so kind."

I glance at Erika, and sure enough, she's trying to hold back a smile. She's slightly more bearable than Chess. While the twins have their obnoxious similarities, Erika is quieter than Chessa, a little bit softer, and perhaps a touch kinder. There have even been moments when I thought we might be friends.

"You're practically an old maid now," Chessa prattles on. "Father has completely given up on arranging a marriage for you. Clearly, no one is interested in you, especially not with this being *my* season."

My eyes nearly roll out of my head as I drag the hairbrush through my long, wavy hair, wincing as it snags on a tangle. It's Erika's season too, and Chess thinks far too highly of herself. I pity the man who ends up saddled to her for eternity.

A screech drags me out of my thoughts, and I whip my head around to look at Chess. "What in the realms?"

"My nail is broken! This is all your fault."

My brow wrinkles. "How do you figure?"

"If I hadn't been sent to fetch you, I never would have broken this nail!"

I have no words. When I glance at Erika with a "can you believe her?" look, she gives a shrug and smirks in response.

"Time to go, girls," Erika commands, tossing her pin-straight onyx hair over her shoulder as she ushers Chessa out of the room.

I tie off the ribbon holding my hair back and pinch my cheeks. Good enough. After sliding on my satin slippers, I run after them, knowing that angering Father is the last thing I want to do. Ever since our mother died, his temper is one to be feared, but he still seems to have a soft spot for me. He treats me somewhat like a prized possession, which has only created more friction between my siblings and me. I've always had the best healers and teachers, and many plans or appearances at court have been declined due to my affliction.

My sisters' chattering ceases once I catch up, and we walk together down the grand staircase toward the dining room.

Their silence makes me feel unwanted, reminding me of how I've never quite fit in. As much as I want to pretend Chessa's words didn't hurt, she wasn't wrong. Perhaps Father truly has given up on trying to find me a match. Is it my fault that I've managed to scare off all my suitors? A wife with my affliction isn't the greatest prize, but my father is well-respected at court and a close friend of the king. Surely, that has to count for something.

The intoxicating scent of bacon wafts through the air, making my mouth water as we enter the formal dining room.

"Girls, so nice of you to finally make an appearance," Father says from his seat at the head of the table.

Sunlight pours into the room from the wall of windows, and I stick to the opposite side, looking for a safe place to sit.

Father notices me, then glances at the windows, an aggravated look crossing his face as he signals to one of the servants. "Pull the curtains. It's far too bright in here for Raelyn."

Guilt over the accommodations I need is a sinking stone in my gut. I don't miss the annoyed looks of my siblings at the lack of natural light in our home when I'm in the room or the muttered curses Father throws at Kyros, the sun god.

"The dark is so depressing, Father," Chessa complains. "We so rarely get to experience the sun!"

"Hold your tongue, girl," Father spits out. "I'll have none of that from you."

She bows her head, staring at her empty gold-rimmed plate. "Yes, sir."

"Now, eat up, children. We have much to discuss," Father says, turning his attention back to his breakfast.

Just as I reach for the last croissant, Charlie, my baby brother, snatches it from the plate. "Too slow, *Ratlyn*," he taunts.

"You're such a child."

Father always wanted a son, and tragically, his birth stole our mother from us. As the baby of the family, he is spoiled rotten, and he acts more like a ten-year-old boy than a man of eighteen years.

I fill my plate with a heaping pile of fruit and a large serving of eggs. Who needs a croissant anyway? *Me. I really wanted that croissant.* I glare across the table at my brother.

"You've kept us in suspense long enough, Father," Erika speaks up. "What is this news you have?"

Father wipes his mouth and sets his napkin down as we all wait with bated breath.

"There is to be a wedding in a fortnight."

Chessa claps excitedly. "How fabulous! Did my first choice accept your proposal? Though, does it really have to be a fortnight? Two weeks is not nearly enough time for me to have a dress made," she rambles.

"That's enough, child," Father shushes her. "This wedding is not about you."

The clatter of silverware hitting her plate drags all of our eyes to Chess. She looks like she's either going to cry or scream.

"Let me make myself crystal clear," Father continues. "*I* am to be married in a fortnight to Lady Olivia Carlisle."

Chapter Three

RAELYN

"*You*?" Chessa's lip quivers.

I gaze around the table and take in Erika's surprised expression while Charlie looks bored out of his mind.

The scrape of Chessa's chair across the hardwood floor grates on my ears as she stands and throws her napkin.

"How *dare* you? This is supposed to be *my* year. I can't believe you're making this season about *you*!"

"You will leave my sight this instant before I have you removed, you spoiled, selfish brat," Father yells, spittle flying from his mouth.

Chess screams before turning and rushing out of the dining room.

Erika clears her throat. "This is certainly surprising but happy news." Always the diplomat. "I had no idea you were looking for a new wife."

Father lifts his goblet of sparkling juice to his mouth, drinking deeply before responding, "Yes. It comes as a surprise to me too, but the match is most advantageous for both of us."

"When will we meet our soon-to-be stepmother?" I ask.

His eyes dart over to mine. "She'll be arriving before dinner, and I expect you all to be on your best behavior."

Whether a new stepmother is good or bad news will only be seen in time. I want to hope for the best; perhaps she will soften some of Father's hardened edges, and maybe having a maternal figure around won't be so bad.

I struggle to recall what Father was like before Mother passed, but the memories are blurry, like looking into a fogged mirror. One would think a nine-year-old would make more visceral memories with their own mother, but she was always distant and uninvolved. My sisters and I were raised to be proper ladies by countless governesses. Every once in a while, guilt eats away at me that I hardly miss her. What a terrible daughter I must be.

Just as I'm about to leave the table, Father clears his throat. "Raelyn."

What in the realms have I done now? "Yes, Father?"

"You didn't drink your tonic."

I glance down at the table, and sure enough, the golden elixir remains full next to my plate. I've been taking it every day for as long as I can remember. Father once explained that after my affliction made itself known as a child, I was prescribed the daily dose of nutrients to keep me healthy and strong. Distracted by his upcoming nuptials, I completely forgot to drink it.

"Thanks," I reply before knocking back the sweet, citrus-flavored tonic.

His nod is dismissal enough, and I make my escape. My embroidery project is calling my name.

A tiny bit of guilt at not informing Father about the masked man pricks at my conscience, but it was clear he no longer wished to be disturbed. I can always tell him later . . .

I wander to the cozy sitting room in the center of our manor. I like to think of it as mine, as it's my safe haven filled with all my favorite things. A fire is already burning in the hearth, and the soft glow of the lamps brightens the space as much as it can in a windowless room.

Bookshelves span two of the walls, and I briefly consider pulling out one of my favorite tomes until I spot my unfinished project waiting for me on the small table next to my favorite chaise.

Kicking off my slippers, I curl my feet up under me and reach for the needlepoint. The project features a mountainous island with a bright yellow sun blazing in the corner. I'm in the middle of adding a lion with golden eyes creeping out of the emerald jungle and have been itching to finish it. Where the idea for my art comes from, I'm not entirely sure. Sometimes, it feels as if my fingers have a mind of their own as I create little vignettes of places I have never seen before. Because of my affliction, travel is quite challenging, and I find myself confined to our manor a majority of the time.

Massaging the back of my neck with one hand, I groan as I stretch my feet out in front of me. A soft knock followed by the creak of the door grabs my attention.

"Sorry to bother you, Raelyn." Sera, my lady's maid and my only true friend, pokes her blonde head in. "Lady Carlisle will be arriving soon."

"Oh hells!" I jump out of my seat. "Where did all the time go?"

I didn't even realize how late it was, and my stomach starts to growl.

Sera shrugs sheepishly. "You do get so engrossed in your projects. One might almost think you were a vampire with how you hide away in here all day."

"Don't be ridiculous, Sera." I laugh. "Vampires aren't real."

She raises a delicate brow, her violet eyes sparkling with mischief. "Maybe not in this realm."

Trying to ignore her implication and the nagging memory of the drop of blood I tasted the night before, I continue, "I'm almost done with this one, and I like to finish once I really get into it."

A knowing smile on her face, she shoos me toward the back staircase. "Your soon-to-be stepmother will be here any moment. You need to get dressed!"

I can't stop my eye roll and exaggerated sigh as I trudge toward the stairs. "What's wrong with *this* dress?"

"Come now, *my lady*," she drawls sarcastically. "You know better than to ask. Your father wants everything to be perfect for his new bride. We've been re-polishing the silver all day."

Rolling my aching shoulders back, I march up the stairs to my rooms. I don't always bother changing into an evening gown for dinner, and Father usually lets it go, but I have a feeling Sera is right that it wouldn't go over well tonight.

I breeze in and make straight for the dressing room. My favorite lavender evening gown catches my eye, and I pull it off the hanger.

"Let me," Sera demands, reaching for it.

"I am perfectly capable of getting myself dressed."

She motions for me to turn around, and I do so begrudgingly.

"That explains the mismatched buttons I'm looking at," Sera says smugly as she unfastens my dress.

I throw my hands up. "What do you expect when there are hundreds of those tiny things?"

She chuckles. "That's what I'm here for. It's a wonder your father didn't have me dismissed for not attending to you this morning—clearly evident by your disheveled state."

I frown. "Where *were* you? I was rudely awoken by Erika and Chess."

Sera's fingers freeze on my lower back for a moment before she continues, "I'm afraid I woke up feeling quite ill this morning. I over-slept . . . I promise it won't happen again."

My dress falls to the ground, and I turn, taking one of Sera's hands in mine. "Please don't feel bad. It sounds like Father has been working you all extra hard lately. Are you sure you're all right? I truly can manage to get myself dressed."

She gives me a look.

"I can *mostly* get myself dressed." I smile.

"Well, I'm here now."

She helps me step into the diaphanous gown and pulls it up over my slender hips. While fitted snugly at the waist, it falls in beautiful layers to the ground. It always makes me feel like a princess when I wear it.

At my dressing table, Sera goes to work taming my dark locks into an appropriate evening style. Using a heated wand, she curls some face-framing pieces and smudges kohl on my lids, all while regaling me with her stories about other realms. They're my favorite—especially the ones about the fae. When the gods walked our realm, they brought tales from other places, and those stories were passed down. By now, I doubt the tales hold even an ounce of truth, as they've been retold and embellished, but Sera's stories are always so vivid, I almost feel like I'm there. Her imagination knows no bounds.

"My work here is done," she says, stepping back to admire the look.

"You really ought to write a book or something," I muse. "I never tire of your stories."

She tsks, brushing a thick strand of blonde hair behind her ear, and waves me off. "I love to read, but that doesn't qualify me to write, now, does it?"

I shrug, then drop into a curtsy, fluttering my dark, curled lashes. "I meet your approval then?"

She opens her mouth to reply, but her eyes catch on the clock and she blurts out, "You better hurry. Time to go!"

Right as I make it to the bottom of the stairs, my father walks in from the direction of his study.

"Just in time. Barely." He gives me a once-over and nods his approval before walking to the front door, which our butler swings wide, and Father motions for me to join him.

I follow him to the front courtyard, where my siblings are already lined up. Chessa gives me a dirty look and turns her head away while I take my place next to her.

Erika reaches behind Chess and pokes me in the side. "Cutting it close, aren't you? I can't fathom why Father puts up with you, honestly. Your head is always up in the clouds, doing unladylike training or buried in some new piece of needlework."

"Your jealousy is showing, Erika," I retort under my breath.

"As if," she huffs.

I can't stop the eye roll, even though she's not looking. My occasional evening training sessions with Father are some of the only times I spend outdoors, unless it's extremely overcast. With colder weather approaching, those days will be even farther apart. Perhaps I can convince Father to work with me on my sword skills later this evening.

"You're just mad that Father lets me get away with more than you."

"That's just because he's given up on you," Erika whispers harshly. "It's like Chessa said, you're an old maid."

"Low blow, sister," I say with mock sadness, trying to ignore the bite of her words.

The clopping of horses' hooves draws my attention to the front gate, and I look up. Father turns to face us, giving us one final appraisal.

"Do not embarrass me," he reiterates, his gaze fixed on Chessa, and I snicker softly.

A breeze whips by, and I shiver. The evenings are getting chillier, and this gown is not meant to be worn outside without a cloak. The sun has just set, the sky a pretty purple as the final rays of sunlight dip below the horizon of the rolling hills that surround us. Glancing toward Father's vineyards, I can't help but notice they're not as abundant as in previous years. The vines look almost sickly, and the scent of ripening grapes is missing. He hasn't said anything, so perhaps I worry for nothing. Taking a deep breath, I soak in the only amount of sunlight I can tolerate, sad that the dark is so quickly approaching.

A white-and-gold carriage comes up the long drive, and I glance over at my siblings. Even they look impressed. It pulls up in front of us, and a coachman jumps off the back to open the door.

An elegant lady descends, gripping the hand of her coachman, her blonde hair piled high on her head in the latest style. The gravel crunches beneath her jeweled cane topped with a ruby the size of an egg, and her travel clothes are over the top with so many ruffles, she almost looks like a layered cake.

Cake. Ugh. My stomach grumbles. Missing lunch has me starving, but we won't be eating any time soon if Father wants to give her a tour of the manor first.

"My darling Olivia," Father says, walking over to kiss her gloved hand. "I hope your travel wasn't too taxing."

Our soon-to-be stepmother looks up at the manor, raising a brow. "Your home is so quaint, Cary darling. I had no idea."

Lovely. She's going to be *that* way. I bite down on my tongue to keep from saying something offensive to this snobby woman.

Father ignores her statement and turns around, sweeping an arm in our direction. "Children, let me introduce you to my soon-to-be wife, Lady Olivia Carlisle."

Lady Carlisle's stormy grey eyes look over us critically. I wonder what she makes of our family.

The four of us are fairly close in age. My three younger siblings all have my father's raven-black hair and dark brown eyes, so deep, they appear almost black at times. I, on the other hand, stand out like a sore thumb with my reddish-brown hair and vivid green eyes.

Father points toward me. "This is my eldest, Raelyn, then we have the twins, Chessa and Erika, and finally, last but not least, Charlie."

"I so look forward to making your acquaintance," Lady Carlisle purrs demurely.

I'll believe that when the sun shines at night.

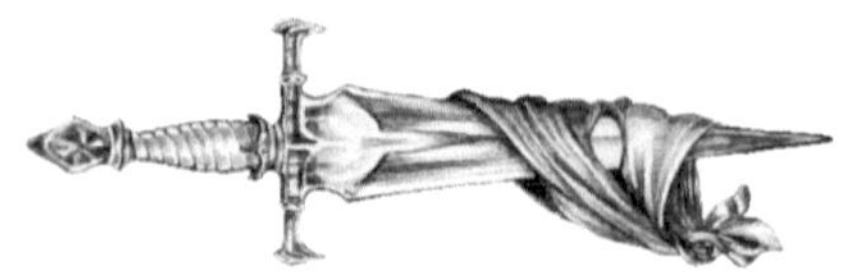

Chapter Four

KIAN

"You have got to start taking your role as prince seriously, Kian," my father, the king, drones on in his condescending manner. "If you won't settle down, I'll make you."

"You can't be serious, Father." I groan, covering my face with my hand.

"I'm dead serious. You've had your fun—you've traveled the realm —now it's your turn to fulfill your duty to the crown."

I sit up straighter, uncovering my face, and glare at him across the table overladen with delicacies. "I'm just the spare, Father. What duties could I possibly have?"

His dark grey eyes meet mine as he spears a piece of fruit. "You may not be my heir, but to keep our kingdom strong, you will do your part."

My eyes follow the fruit as Father gestures at me with his fork. It's just about to fall off when he shovels it into his mouth; the disgusting slurp makes me want to flee the table.

"I'm not convinced your brother will provide an heir, so we need backup. Just be glad I'm not shipping you off to another kingdom," he says with his mouth full. "Thank the gods our alliances hold strong."

I'm going to be ill. Everything about this man sickens me—from his eating habits, to his policies, to the cavalier way he discusses my brother's painful lack of living heirs, though he and his wife have been trying for the past eleven years. I'm glad Colin's not present to hear it. Father adds another pile of food onto his plate, and I bite my tongue. Doesn't he realize our people are suffering while he has a meal large enough for twenty laid out on this table? My stomach flips unhappily. Maybe I really am going to be sick. I push my plate away.

"Just spit it out, Father. Do you have someone in mind?"

"Cary Astoria is hosting a ball in celebration of his latest *conquest*. I'd like you to attend in my stead and survey your prospects. I believe his daughters have yet to be bound."

A painful ache in my chest distracts me from my upset stomach, and I rub at it, as if the touch could somehow soothe it.

"Oh, so you're saying I get a choice in who I wed?"

The king points his fork at me again. "Don't you get ahead of yourself, my boy. I will step in if you fail to do what I ask. You must be bound by the end of the season."

My jaw drops. That's not nearly enough time.

Trying to appeal to his rational side—if ever he did have one—I soften my shoulders, hoping to appear less intimidating. "Father, are you certain it must be so soon? Colin and Juliana *are* about to have their first child, and I would not want to take away from that grand celebration."

The king snorts while some of the juice slides down his chin. "We'll see."

Unable to stop myself, I start to reprimand, "Fath—"

The word fizzles out as he fixes me with a glare. "I'll consider it, but you *will* attend that ball and you *will* dance with all of the eligible maidens there. Understood?"

I clench my teeth to keep the snarky response inside and give him a curt nod instead. "May I be excused, Father?"

He waves his fork at me again, and I rush out of the room. How my mother ever put up with him is beyond me.

I make my way to the training yard, hoping to work off some of my pent-up frustration.

"In a rush, aren't we?" I pull up short and turn to my best friend, Alex, who is leaning against the side of the courtyard wall, his dark skin gleaming under the lamps.

"Perfect timing," I drawl. "Ready for an ass-kicking?"

"You wish," he retorts, examining his nails. "I have a little time before my next engagement though, so I'm happy to watch Master Waylen kick yours."

"Remind me why we're friends?" I tease as I continue toward the training room. We've been thick as thieves ever since his father, the ambassador from Maardune, came to court five years ago.

Alex catches up and matches my stride. "Because I'm so incredibly charming and your best excuse whenever you need one." I think there's a note of hurt in his voice, but I shake it off. Surely I'm imagining it.

Jabbing him with my elbow, I joke, "Sure you don't want to reconsider? You're getting a little soft."

A gleam of challenge lights up his eyes, and he flexes his arm. "You jest. I trained just last week."

I roll my eyes. "Exactly. Consistency is key, Alex."

"Not everyone wants to have rock-solid abs like you, Kian."

"Just keep telling yourself that."

AFTER A GRUELING TRAINING session with Master Waylen and even convincing Alex to get sweaty, I make my way back to my wing to freshen up. I have important plans, and it's going to be a late night.

After my failure at House Astoria, I'm more than anxious to find another lead. Gods willing, I'll find *something* to guide me to the next step in my quest, but first, I have a small caravan to rob.

Clad from head to toe in black, I take the servants' passages out to the stables without seeing a soul. My glorious onyx stallion nickers happily as I sneak him a treat before readying him for the evening ahead.

Phantom's coloring is dark as night but for the white crescent moon on his forehead. I dip my fingers into a pot of kohl, covering up his distinctive mark as always. Thankfully, Father has a stable full of black horses, and no one will be the wiser if we're spotted.

Once Phantom is bridled, saddled, and ready to go, I mount up and race off into the night.

Father let slip that a small caravan of grain, fruits, and vegetables is arriving tonight, so I just need to catch it before they make it here. There are so many starving families in our city, and if he isn't going to do anything about it, I sure will.

I have to admit, I'm slightly angry my brother, Colin, doesn't seem to care about the people he will eventually rule. He appears happy to enjoy all the wealth our kingdom has to offer and ignore the plight of those he considers beneath him. I had high hopes his wife would be a good influence on him, but so far, nothing has changed.

Why do I have to care? Life would be so much easier if I could just enjoy the privilege I was born with and spend my days in the company of good women, fine food, and drink, but no. Something within me says, *"Kian, you must do more."*

The darkest part of me wonders if an "accident" should befall my father or brother so our kingdom could be in better hands. Perhaps Colin's child will grow up wiser.

I shake my head. *Regicide? Really? I'm not that horrible of a person, am I?* No. Killing must be a last resort.

I gallop down the king's road and into the forest, hoping it's not too late. I have very little time to get into position before the caravan is supposed to arrive. The forest is eerily dark and quiet when I slow Phantom to a walk. Perhaps I'm an utter fool to attempt this thievery all on my own, but the last thing I want to do is bring someone else into it who could possibly be caught and put to death. Nor am I willing to trust someone else to keep this secret. I made sure to spread rumors about a party I'd be "attending" this evening to avoid any suspicion. Luna willing, my ruse will hold.

Pulling out a long skein of fishing wire, I string it across the road. It's practically invisible in the dark, and the wagon's lanterns are not likely to catch it. Step one complete.

I retreat to Phantom and settle in to wait, pulling out my water flagon and drinking deeply. A yawn escapes me, and I reach into my saddle bag for some of my herbs. Chewing the somewhat spicy blend, I'm instantly more alert when they kick in. Thank the goddess Galyna that Margot, my favorite healer, told me about this stuff.

Before long, the rumble of the caravan filters through the trees. It's small enough that I should be able to handle it on my own—*should* being the operative word. Two wagons pass by, and I tie my black mask around my head. Immediately, I'm more at peace. I'm ready.

There are four guards accompanying the wagons, two of them riding ahead and two behind. They should reach the trap in . . .

Three.

Two.

One.

The first two horses neigh as their riders are flung off their backs, the invisible wire taking them out. Just as I planned, the horses take off into the night, spooked by their invisible foe. I chuckle to myself. Like taking candy from a baby.

The wagons rumble to a stop, their drivers looking around frantically. I jump off Phantom and silently stalk toward the fallen guards. Stunned and disoriented, they don't even put up a fight as I slam my fist into their temples one by one, knocking them out.

Now for the other two. Shouts ring out through the forest as I sneak between the wagons. One guard's back is to me, and I leap onto it, throwing my arm around his throat and pulling tight. He slumps to the ground, and I duck as the almost silent *zing* of a sword zips over my head. Shit. That was way too close for comfort. I roll to my feet while pulling out my own sword, and it meets the guard's with a clang.

"You're not gonna get the better of me, you thieving piece of filth," the guard taunts as we parry. His blade slices toward me and nicks my arm. I hiss at the sting but then quickly spin and have my blade to his throat before he can blink.

"Should I let you wake up with a roaring headache, or do you want to die tonight?" I ask, lowering my voice to a growl. He doesn't need to know I'll do everything I can to avoid the latter, but I have a reputation to uphold.

When he refuses to answer, merely glowering at me in the moonlight, I scoff. "All talk and nothing to back it up, eh?" I slam the hilt of my sword into his temple, and he crumples to the ground.

All in an evening's work. Now the fun part.

"It's him, I tell you," one of the drivers says excitedly. "It's the Shadow!"

I make my way toward the front of the wagons, my sword casually in hand. "Gentlemen, would you like to fight me before giving up your goods or just hand them over?"

"We don't want any trouble," one driver says, "but we can't just give them up. We have families to think of. If we just let you take them, the king will punish us at best . . ."

My face splits into a grin, but I continue, "Here's my offer. Help me load up the biggest wagon with as much variety as it can hold before I tie you up with the king's imbeciles, who don't have to know you helped me, or—"

"We'll take the offer," the drivers say in unison. Throwing nervous glances my way, they hop down and get to work. We move quickly and quietly, transferring as many supplies as we can into the lead wagon. My job is significantly easier when the drivers cooperate. Especially when they help me drag the heavy guards and tie them to a large tree. I instruct them to muss their clothes and appearances to give the impression they put up somewhat of a fight.

After I tighten the rope around the last driver, my heart warms when he whispers, "Thank you, Shadow. We won't forget what you've done. May the gods bless you."

I tip my head at them, slice through the invisible wire, and hop into the loaded wagon. A shrill whistle calls Phantom, and he obediently trots behind as we take off toward the outskirts of the city of Elsmont.

There is something incredibly gratifying about stealing right from under my father's nose. But enjoyment aside, I will do whatever it takes to make sure my people are cared for, even if it means beating the hells out of some of the guards. Most of them are selfish assholes, only out for themselves. I have caught more than one lining their own pockets and bellies with the excess at the palace.

As the Shadow, I try to right wrongs, but I've made mistakes. My mind flashes back to Mateo, the guard who drowned because of my miscalculation. He was one of the few decent men working for my father, and I carry the guilt with me every time I go out . . . every time I see the pain in his widow's eyes or his smile lighting up the face of his child. Ever since that night, I do my best not to kill unless they leave me no choice . . . but there's almost always a choice.

Once I leave the wagon at one of my random drop points, I hop back onto Phantom and start toward my next stop. All my research has led me to one name. Cary Astoria. The laughable part is, I'm not completely sure *what* I'm looking for other than information, and with Lady Raelyn catching me last night, I was unable to complete my search.

Gods, I hope she didn't recognize me. If she did, I'm in deep, deep shit. The absolute last thing I need is for Cary to have something to hold over me. His finances are in shambles, and I know he's looking for a way out. It appears said way out is marrying Lady Carlisle, if the marriage agreement I saw is any indication. She's a power-hungry widow, clearly unaware of the Astorias' financial status, and I shudder at the thought of her digging her claws into that family, especially the green-eyed beauty I had on her back.

Lady Raelyn. I grin thinking of the soft feel of her curves beneath me. Will I be so lucky to see her again tonight? No. I shouldn't tempt fate. I have a mission to accomplish, and she would only get in the way again.

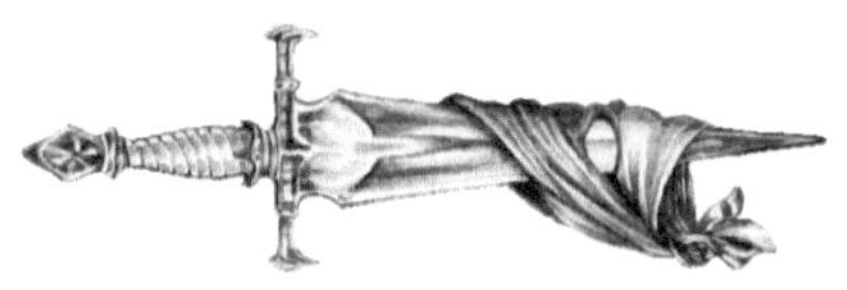

Chapter Five

KIAN

A light flares as I walk into my bedroom, causing me to draw a blade.

"Where have you been, Ki?" Alex drawls from where he's seated in the corner, one leg propped up on the other, a tumbler of golden liquor in hand.

"Gods, Alex. What are you doing sitting here in the dark? You nearly stopped my heart." I re-sheathe my blade.

A dry chuckle comes out of him. "How else am I supposed to find out what you've been up to? You've been shutting me out for months." He eyes me suspiciously. "Nice outfit."

"This old thing? I was just out for a midnight stroll and didn't want to be bothered."

"I wouldn't believe you if Luna came down and told me herself. What aren't you telling me?"

I sigh and sink into the chair next to his. Every part of me wants to keep this to myself. Trust doesn't come easy to me.

"I'm sorry, Alex. I just don't want you to get mixed up in my shit." I grab the bottle of liquor off the small table between our chairs and pour a generous portion.

"That, or you expect me to keep covering for you without knowing what's going on. It feels like you're just using me, Ki. You're hardly around anymore, but I keep hearing stories about us partying together." He raises a brow. "What parties are they speaking of? I surely have no clue. Strange, considering I've supposedly attended them."

I palm my face and lean back in my chair. "I'm sorry. I'm the absolute worst. Can you forgive me?"

"Forgive you for what, exactly? For sneaking around and not telling me about it? Or for using me as your alibi without informing me in advance?"

I throw back the glass, enjoying the burn of the alcohol as it slides down my throat. "Both, Alex. Both."

It's clear from his expression that he's not going to let it go this time, nor can I ignore the hurt in his voice. Alex can be like a dog with a bone when he wants to be; perhaps it's time to come clean.

He leans forward in his seat, his hazel eyes widening. "What happened to your arm?"

I reach for it and frown, realizing the temporary bandage I threw on has come undone. Fresh blood coats my fingers when I pull them away. Great.

"Ah, nothing to worry about. Just a little consequence of my actions."

"What in the realms have you gotten yourself into?

I blow out a breath. *I guess I'm doing this.* "Have you heard rumors of the masked man—the Shadow—running around Elsmont?"

A burst of nervous laughter leaves Alex and he stares up at the ceiling. "Shit, that's you?"

Gods, I hope telling him wasn't a mistake. I reach for the bottle, pouring myself another glass.

Alex drags a hand over his face before sitting up and glaring at me. "How could you be so damned reckless? And why in the hells did you wait this long to tell me about it?"

I clench my jaw, my hand squeezing into a fist at my side. "I didn't dare put your life at risk for my vendetta. You know your life would be forfeit if I ever got caught and you were implicated. You don't have the privilege of my station to protect you."

Alex grimaces and picks up his glass again. "You're not wrong. But what makes you think *you'd* be safe? You're only the spare, after all."

"Don't remind me. My father has complained of my uselessness plenty of times, but I don't think he'd ever actually harm me . . . at least I hope he wouldn't."

"Your father and all the lords have been losing their minds about the Shadow's thievery," Alex says, shaking his head.

I can't stop my grin. "As they should." As scary as it is, I have to admit it feels good to let someone in, to share this burden.

"I still can't believe it." Alex takes a sip of his drink before setting it on the table and getting up to pace. "I've also heard tales of this 'Shadow' doling out punishments to the usually untouchable lords. Why would you take such a risk, Ki? You're practically enemy number one in the kingdom of Rakveren."

"Something had to change. There are so many people in need, and my father has done nothing to help. He's happy to just sit on his throne and watch people starve. The majority of his lords are no better. I'm only taking the excess he has no need of . . . and trying to 'encourage' the lords to take better care of their people."

"What about the innocent people you've attacked during these thefts?"

A pang of guilt makes my stomach queasy when I'm once again reminded of Mateo, but I try to brush it off. "Most of Father's guards are far from innocent. As far as everyone else, it's only ever been a little bump to the head or a minor stab wound . . . nothing that can't easily be taken care of by one of the healers. I've never meant to kill anyone . . ."

Alex laughs again. "What a vigilante you are."

"I try," I say dryly, glad he's not prying further.

"How can I help?" he asks.

I raise a brow. The absolute last thing I want is to drag him into this.

I work alone. It's safer that way. "Well, technically, you keeping your mouth shut and letting people think I'm with you is a help."

Alex groans. "That's not what I mean, Ki."

I wave a hand at him. "Yeah, yeah, I know, but I'm worried what my father would do to you if he suspected your involvement. I'd never forgive myself if something happened to you."

"Typical Kian," Alex mutters, leaning against the wall. "Have to do everything yourself."

"Alex—"

"Don't you trust me?" he blurts out.

Of course I trust him . . . but I will not be responsible for his death. "It's not that simple."

"It absolutely is. We simply do not get caught."

"I wish I had your optimism." I scoff.

"I'll be optimistic for the both of us then."

I shake my head. "That's why I love you, Alex." *And why you're definitely not coming along.*

He grimaces. "Shut up. Don't get all sentimental on me now."

I blow him a kiss, and he rolls his eyes before dropping back into his seat and knocking back the remainder of his drink.

"For real though, I've missed spending time with you, Ki," he says sincerely. "You've been off vigilante-ing and I've had to entertain all the ladies on my own."

"You poor sod." I gasp. "However have you survived it?"

He frowns. "I can't keep up, that's for sure."

I laugh at him and finish off my own drink. "I'll join you one of these nights, I promise."

"You better," he insists. "Now, tell me, what else have you been up to?"

My heartbeat quickens at the sudden flash of green eyes that takes up my thoughts, and while my instinct is to stay quiet and keep everything else to myself, I fight against it, trying to let Alex in. "Well, I might have paid Lord Astoria's home a visit the last two nights."

"Whatever for?" Alex frowns. "According to rumors, he doesn't have much worth stealing."

"True as that may be, my research led me to him."

"Research on what?" he asks.

"Kyros, the lost sun god."

"Kyros, the lost sun god?"

"Are you just going to repeat everything I say?" I sigh in exasperation, looking up at the ceiling.

"Apologies, my prince. I may have had too much of your fine liquor while waiting for you in the dark."

I snort. "Clearly."

"What kind of research has you looking into the lost sun god?"

I blow out a breath. "The highly treasonous kind."

"More treasonous than your vigilante-ing?"

"You know that's not even a word, right?"

He grins. "So what? I like it."

"You idiot."

He snickers.

"I've been chasing stories of him—of Kyros. Trying to figure out the reason for his unexpected appearance and then disappearance a few decades ago."

"Sounds like you have a death wish with your vigilante-ing and 'treasonous' research." He snorts. "You know I'm not devout. Luna, Galyna, Veritius . . . they are as good as missing too with how they abandoned our realm centuries ago. We're on our own here."

"Fair, but I believe something else is amiss," I say, rising and walking to my desk. "If Kyros were merely in Celestia with the other gods, our realm wouldn't have faced all the famine and lack of sunlight for the past few decades. He was here, and then he disappeared, sending our realm into chaos that's only getting worse."

"That might be true, but even if you prove the correlation, what do you think you can do about it?" Alex asks.

I flip through some of my notes. Despite all his questions, it feels freeing to have someone to talk about this with. Maybe he'll see something I missed. "I have to find him or find out what happened to him. Resources are getting thinner. One wouldn't know at the palace with our overabundance of stores, but even with the famine, the king steals portions of crops from all the surrounding farms. Despite the lack, he hasn't lowered the tithe. He continues to demand his share, even though our people are dying. If I weren't 'vigilante-ing,' as you put it, my people wouldn't make it through the coming season."

"I respect that, but do you realize how much pressure you're putting on yourself to solve an entire realm's problem?"

"It might be our only hope of things going back to normal around here. It's not like I can travel to Celestia and ask the other gods for help. Surely, Kyros must be somewhere on this plane. If I can find him, maybe he can put things back. I have to at least try."

Alex arches a brow. "But if Kyros *is* here, why hasn't he done anything to help us?"

"That's a damn good question, and one I am trying to find the answer to. I have the feeling that something is wrong . . . something is preventing him from acting."

The frown on Alex's face reeks of skepticism, but I appreciate that he hasn't completely shut me down like Father has.

"Why Lord Astoria's house?" he asks.

I grab my notes and retake my seat. "My research led me to some old stories of his connection with Kyros. Apparently, they were rivals. Both in love with the same woman."

Alex snorts a laugh. "That seems unlikely."

"That's what I thought, but I had to know for sure."

"Did you find anything?"

I grimace. "No, I couldn't find a thing in his study tonight, and his daughter interrupted me the night before."

Alex waggles a brow. "Daughter? Which one? Was it the lovely Lady Erika?"

I shake my head.

"Ugh, don't tell me it was Chessa. Stories of her make me never want to cross her path."

I snort. "No, not her either. I'm fairly certain it was Lady Raelyn."

"Ah, the mysterious beauty who never leaves the house?"

"I suppose."

My mind flashes back to her warm body seated atop mine, and I harden at the thought. Hells. The last thing I need is the distraction of a beautiful woman, as intriguing as I might find her. She's already broken my heart once; I can't let her in again.

Chapter Six

RAELYN

"Sit up straight, Raelyn," Lady Carlisle admonishes. "Stop daydreaming and focus on eating your meal like a lady."

Who does she think she is? My mother? I'm twenty-seven years old.

I do my best to hide my annoyance as I roll my shoulders back and nod politely at her. "Thank you for the reminder, Lady Carlisle."

"Chessa, I love what you've done with your hair," Lady Carlisle compliments.

"It's the latest fashion," Chess gushes before she twists and turns her nose up at me. I fight the urge to roll my eyes. It's not as if she had anything to do with her hair. She has her lady's maid to thank.

For some reason I do not understand, Lady Carlisle has taken an extreme liking in Chessa ever since arriving a week and a half ago. The attention has Chess brimming with pride, making her even more unpleasant to be around. Father's choice in a new wife leaves much to be desired.

She has shown plenty of interest in Chess and Erika, but I, on the other hand, have become the focus of her criticism and ire. Charlie is, as always, the most doted on of us all. Apparently, having a dick in his pants is all he needs to inherit the family estate and earn Lady Carlisle's favor.

"Lady Carlisle, are you excited about the wedding ball tomorrow evening?" Erika asks demurely.

"More than you know," she replies before pointedly fixing her eyes back on me.

My shoulders roll back as I straighten my posture once again.

"Once I'm officially the lady of the house, I plan to make some changes around here."

"What kind of changes?" Chessa asks.

"Your father has done an admirable job of raising you all without a mother during some of your most formative years, but it is quite clear to me that *some* of you need a little more work than others in etiquette and decorum."

"Some of you" meaning me, obviously.

"It's not right for a woman to sit around all day and shirk her duty to the family. If you're to remain here under this roof, you will have to earn your stay."

I almost spit out my wine at Lady Carlisle's words. What in the gods' names is she implying?

Chessa sits up straighter and gives me a wicked smile. "Sounds like she's talking about you, Raelyn."

"I beg your finest pardon?" The words fly out of my mouth before I can pull them back.

Lady Carlisle looks down her pointed nose at me. "If you are unwilling to marry, Raelyn, surely you can find a way to make yourself more useful. Needlepoint and reading are hardly valuable uses of your time."

I hate to think what she'd make of the sword skills. Even more worthless, I'm sure.

My eyes dart from hers to where my father is engrossed in the paper. "Father, you agree with this?"

He waves a hand, brushing me off. "I'm sure whatever Lady Carlisle has in mind is a wonderful plan."

Has he even been listening? What is she planning? Having me scrub chamber pots? I shudder.

"Erika and Chessa aren't married yet—do they need to earn their keep as well?" I ask.

Lady Carlisle turns to look at the twins, her finger tapping her chin. "They will spend their time making themselves as attractive as possible to lure potential matches."

I think I might be sick.

Chessa gloats. "We appreciate all of your attention, Lady Carlisle."

Lady Carlisle gently pats her shoulder. "Feel free to call me Mother, Chessa. I will be soon enough. And of course I'll ensure you both make advantageous matches this season."

I would call her "Mother" over my dead body, not that she offered.

With each condescending glance and every demeaning word out of Lady Carlisle's mouth, my unadulterated loathing for her grows.

THE ENTIRE MANOR is aflutter with preparations for the wedding ball tonight. I try to stifle a yawn as I stand on the small pedestal while the seamstress tugs and pulls at my dress.

"Stand still, Lady Raelyn. I swear to Luna, if you don't stop fidgeting, I will poke you with my needle," the seamstress reprimands.

I bite my tongue to keep from snapping at her, but she's practically family, and I don't really mind her snark. It just feels like I've been standing here for hours, and I'm exhausted.

"Better do as she says," Erika comments from the corner, where she and Chessa are seated in front of a large mirror, their lady's maids trying to force their pin-straight hair into curls.

"Father will have your head if you ruin his important night," Chessa adds.

"I don't understand why it's such a big deal," I retort. "It's not like he hasn't been married before. It's all happening so fast."

Erika turns her head and gives me a haughty look. "Just because you don't care about it doesn't mean it's not important. Father has been alone since Mother died. Why can't you let him be happy?"

"Why is he so set on impressing Lady Carlisle? She already agreed to marry him, did she not?"

"Because she's perfect and deserves the best," Chessa says dreamily. "I plan to be just like her someday."

It takes everything within me to bite my tongue.

The seamstress looks at me and lowers her voice to a whisper. "I've heard talk that your father would be financially ruined if not for Lady Carlisle. You might want to try harder to get on her good side."

I hold in a gasp, trying to hide my shock. "Are you certain?" I consider Father's recent behavior, and it starts making sense. A good number of our servants have been dismissed, and our meals haven't been quite as lavish. Every time Chess orders a new dress, Father nearly loses it.

"What are you two whispering about?" Erika calls out, her lips twisting into an unattractive pout in the mirror.

"Nothing for you to worry about," I say as I continue to ponder this new revelation.

What if the lack of funds is precisely why Father hasn't pressured me to find a match? For all I know, he doesn't have a dowry available . . . I thought I'd just been lucky that he hadn't forced me to marry one of the many stuffy lords I'd been introduced to.

"How do you know?" I whisper under my breath.

The seamstress looks up from her position at my feet, armed to the teeth with pins. "Servants talk."

I shake my head. For Father's sake, I hope the marriage isn't one purely of convenience—I want him to be happy—but my first impressions of Lady Carlisle haven't been the best. Over the last two weeks, she's moved all her belongings in and commandeered our staff to prepare the most lavish wedding ball our manor has ever hosted. There is even talk that some of the royal family might attend tonight.

"Turn for me, dear," the seamstress says.

When I face the floor-length mirror, I can't stop the grin from forming despite the shocking information I've just received. The seamstress has completely outdone herself with my ballgown. The emerald satin shimmers in the glow of the lamps, mixed with fine swirls of gold filigree.

"Incredible," I breathe. "Are we almost done here?"

"Almost," the seamstress mumbles around the pins in her mouth. "Okay, done. Now step out and go get your hair done so I can make these final adjustments."

I wince as one of the pins pokes me. "Ouch. Okay, fine, I got it. You don't need to keep torturing me," I joke.

"Lady Erika, get your arse over here," the seamstress calls out. "Your hair will never curl—you might as well just give up now."

I hold back a laugh as my sister huffs and gets to her feet, and we switch places.

Sera comes over and gets to work on my hair. Unlike my sisters', my hair curls like a dream.

"Sometimes I swear Mother must have had an affair," Chessa complains. "You look nothing like the rest of us."

Her words hit me where it hurts, like they usually do. One would think I'd be used to the unkind comments about my parentage, but I struggle to feel like I belong as it is. The nasty insinuations are the absolute last thing I need.

I straighten my shoulders and look at Chessa through the mirror. "Don't be jealous that I got all the good genetics."

She rolls her eyes, and I look away. I can't let her see how much her words get to me, or she'll never stop.

Is there truth to them? Am I proof of Mother's infidelity? Surely not. Father would have never stood for it . . . and yet the vague memories I have of her are not filled with love and care . . . I felt unwanted.

The sooner the twins are married off and out of the manor, the better. Despite Lady Carlisle's threats, I have no desire to be married. I want more out of life than becoming some lord's wife and birthing heirs who could potentially carry my affliction.

While I've never told anyone, I long to travel to far-off kingdoms—perhaps someone somewhere has a cure that could set me free from the dark. Marriage to one of Rakveren's lords would only keep me trapped in an endless cycle of loneliness. If that is my lot, I might as well remain here.

THE BONDING CEREMONY for Father and Lady Carlisle was short and private, which is honestly almost shocking to me. Apparently, her children from a previous marriage are too busy with their families to deign to visit, so it was just us along with the priestess. Thankfully, we were dismissed after the ceremony for a few hours until we have to change into our ballgowns.

Lady Carlisle had not one but two elaborate gowns made for today. Personally, I think it the biggest waste, considering the first one was only seen by our small immediate family. I always thought of our family as wealthy, but Lady Carlisle's spending habits give new meaning to the word. The way she flaunts her countless jewels at every opportunity seems frivolous at best. Who needs to wear diamonds dripping down one's ears at the breakfast table? Lady Carlisle, apparently . . . though I guess she's Lady Astoria now.

Chessa and Erika wanted two gowns as well, but Father put a stop to that. We had to make do with less formal dresses we already owned for the bonding ceremony.

My stomach roils as I walk through the main hall of our manor. The entire place is covered almost floor-to-ceiling with lilies and a wide array of gourds—it smells like death. I need to get out of here just to breathe.

Bursting out the front doors, I'm immediately hit by unexpected sunlight and flinch as its warm rays caress the bare skin of my arms. They tingle in an almost pleasant way.

Dear gods, am I starting to burn? I don't know what I was thinking, coming out here this time of day, even though it's usually overcast. I *never* come out until the sun has almost set, just to be extra cautious.

Icy fear hits me, and I step back into the shade of the manor. I'm not supposed to be out here. Am I going to be sick? What's going to happen to me?

The crisp, cool air fills my lungs, and I breathe in deeply. The dichotomy of the sun's warmth and the colder weather is deliciously invigorating. What if something has changed? Has my affliction lessened?

Excitement starts to overpower my fear, and I take a small step back into the sun. When I don't burst into flame, I begin to wander the grounds, enjoying the tranquility and quiet after the hustle and bustle of the preparations for tonight's ball. I almost want to cry.

I need to tell Father immediately! But no . . . Father is supposedly consummating his marriage. My entire body shudders at the thought.

Considering I have nowhere to be and no one demanding my time for a few hours, I choose to enjoy this moment of solitude and awe. Perhaps Galyna, the goddess of healing, finally answered my pleas and I no longer need to spend my days in the dark.

My skin prickles once again, and I get the feeling someone is watching, but when I look around and no one's there, I shake it off. Must be my overactive imagination playing tricks on me . . . not that I don't have reason to suspect anything. After the break-in the other night, I keep wondering if the masked man will return to continue his search for whatever it is he was looking for. I never did tell Father about him, and the more time that passes, the more I worry he'll be angry about the omission. For now, it'll remain my secret.

A sudden rush of energy bursts through my body, and a laugh bubbles out of me. I find myself running. Exhilarated, I race down the path, tiny stones kicking up beneath my feet. The heel of my shoe snags on a rock, so I kick them off and keep running in my stockings.

The new Lady Astoria would be aghast, but I can't bring myself to care. I'm so tired of her and her demands already, and it's only been a couple weeks; I hate to think what she could possibly do once this wedding is over. I'm slightly worried, but for now, I'm running. My hair trails out behind me, and for a second, I wonder: if I leap, could I possibly fly?

All too soon, the sun dips below the horizon, and a chill breezes through me. Time has flown by, and I'm a complete disaster. I have no idea where my shoes are, and my stockings are in ribbons. Wrapping my arms around myself to keep warm now that the rush of adrenaline has faded, I trudge back to the manor.

What felt like the most refreshing run of my life has been reduced to aching feet and my heart beating frantically in my chest. Gods, I hope nothing is wrong with me.

I turn a corner and bump into Sera.

"Raelyn! I've been looking all over for you. Where have you been? You look like a mess."

I smile sheepishly. "I kind of went for a run. The house was overwhelming and I needed some fresh air."

Sera's eyes dart around frantically, as if looking for someone. "Have you lost your mind? It's not safe! You can't be seen like this. Your father would have my head."

I frown at her worry. Surely my father wouldn't blame her for my jaunt around the grounds.

"Come, come. Let's get you inside before anyone sees you." Sera practically drags me through a side door and up the servants' stairs toward my room.

When we finally make it inside, she helps peel me out of my sweat-ruined dress and stockings and into the quickest bath of my life. She frets over my hair, but there's no time for it to fully dry before the ball is to begin.

Wringing her hands, she looks me up and down as I stand before her in my frilly undergarments.

"Gods, what am I going to do with your hair? I spent so much time on it earlier."

"I'm sorry, Sera. I don't know what I was thinking. I made it outside, and I just found myself running and running and couldn't stop!"

Sera frowns and turns away so I can't see her face. "That is strange."

"Sera, what aren't you telling me?" I demand. Her anxious behavior isn't making sense.

She turns around but won't meet my gaze, keeping her blonde head down. "It's nothing . . . I'm just under strict orders to keep you confined to the house, and I failed. Your father will punish me if he finds out."

I balk. Orders? The rational side of my brain says that it's only for my safety, but why can't he trust me to do so on my own? I'm aware of my condition. And yet . . . didn't I do exactly what he feared and run outside without thinking? But nothing happened. Wouldn't he be thrilled to learn that the sun had no effect on me?

"Listen, Sera, the last thing you need to worry about is me telling on you to my father, but it irks me to no end that he has given you orders I knew nothing about."

"Yes, Raelyn." She bows meekly, which is so unlike her.

"I would love it if you could inform me of any other orders my father has given you regarding me."

Sera's skin blanches, her posture tense. "You know I am loyal to you . . ."

"But?" I bristle.

"But . . ." She struggles to get words out before finally shaking her head. "Your father gave me this position, and I need the coin to help take care of my family. I can't risk that."

I soften. I truly don't want to do anything to harm her, but the betrayal stings.

"Perhaps this is not the time, but we will revisit this later."

Sera bobs her head.

I hate that things are uncomfortable between us. I always thought I could trust her, but now . . . I'm impossibly alone in my own home.

My sisters are insufferable and my little brother a pain in my rear. Father has also become a completely different person since Lady Astoria arrived. Sera has been my closest friend for as long as I can remember—we practically grew up together, ignoring the typical formalities—but perhaps I'm fooling myself and she means more to me than I do to her. If I'm merely a job . . . I choke back the hurt. There's no time for this. I'll figure it out later.

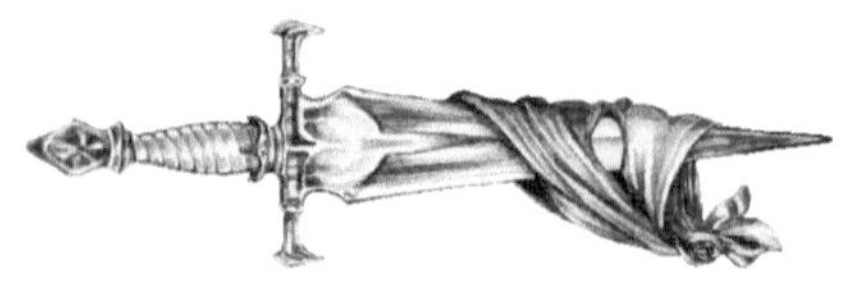

Chapter Seven

KIAN

"Please, don't make me attend this on my own," I beg Alex as my valet, Giles, fixes my cravat.

"You expect me to miss watching you suffer through a miserable ball?" Alex quips from where he lounges in my dressing room.

"I wouldn't blame you for leaving me hanging after . . . everything."

He laughs. "I'm not that petty, my friend."

"Good, good." I grin.

"Plus, I'm dying to see the Astoria girl who's gotten you all tied up in knots."

"Don't be ridiculous."

"Me? Ridiculous? Uncalled for, Ki. Don't even try to pretend you haven't been thinking of her. I've seen you staring longingly into nothing."

I snort and roll my eyes, trying to change the subject. "I still can't believe our king is forcing me to get married this season."

"All the more reason for me to check out Lady Raelyn and make sure she passes muster," Alex says, bringing it right back to her as Giles finishes up and I dismiss him.

"I can't risk her recognizing me." I grunt my reply after double-checking to make sure my valet has left, even as my mind drifts back to the green-eyed beauty. Alex doesn't know about our history, and while she didn't show any signs of recognition that night, I need to be careful.

Alex laughs. "Weren't you in a dark room wearing a mask? How could she?"

I shrug, reminding myself it's okay to share details with him—though I'm hardly used to speaking freely. "It's not as if I was fully hidden from her. She did practically sit on me."

Alex chokes on his drink, and I pat him on the back.

"You didn't tell me that!" he sputters.

"It didn't seem necessary."

"Necessary, my ass. I had no idea you got that close to her."

"Did I mention she got close enough to cut me? And with my own blade?" I mutter. It was one of my favorites, and I miss the damn thing; it had perfect balance and was wickedly sharp.

Alex shakes his head. "Well, since you want to keep your distance, you wouldn't mind if I took her for a turn around the dance floor?"

All the muscles in my body tense, but I try to shake it off. Of course I mind, but I really shouldn't. I refuse to be hurt again.

"She doesn't belong to me. Do whatever you want." I hate myself for lying to him, but I'm fairly certain he's only baiting me.

"Maybe I will." He winks.

"I thought you were interested in Lady Erika," I say as I grab my navy evening jacket.

"I guess I'll have to wait and see which one catches my eye."

My possessiveness over Lady Raelyn irritates me to no end. I want to forget and move on, get back to focusing on what matters most.

"Horses or carriage?" Alex asks.

I groan, palming my face. "I'd love nothing more than to get a good ride in, but—"

"I bet you would," Alex retorts under his breath.

"Hey, I heard that," I snap.

"If the shoe fits."

Maybe that *is* what I need. My vigilante-ing, as Alex calls it, has kept me from seeking out any female companionship for quite a while.

"Father would disown me if I didn't show up with all the pomp and circumstance. Honestly, I think he's using my need to find a bride as an excuse not to attend Lord Astoria's wedding celebration himself."

"Didn't they use to be fairly close?" Alex quirks a thick brow.

"Yes, but I get the impression things have been a little strained between them," I confess.

Alex shrugs. "Well, I guess it's up to us to make up for it then."

I snort. "I have the feeling Lord Astoria will be quite disappointed."

THE LUSH, rolling hills of the countryside whisk by as our carriage rumbles down the wide road leading out of the city of Elsmont. When we finally approach House Astoria, nestled in a valley that once boasted flourishing acres of vineyards and farmland, I'm reminded once again how much the estate has fallen into disrepair. The hardship is evident despite the glowing torches and abundance of flowers and greenery that attempt to hide it. Is this the cause of tension between our families? Did Lord Astoria request help and my father denied it? It wouldn't surprise me, but at the same time, Lord Astoria seems far too prideful to ask.

Alex and I are ushered in through the manor's front doors, the scent of lilies so overpowering that Alex sneezes.

"You think they have enough flowers?" he complains.

I wrinkle my nose, sidestepping to avoid squashing one of many small pumpkins beneath my feet. "Definitely feels like they're compensating for something."

We follow the steady flow of partygoers toward the ballroom's entrance, where an announcer is shouting lords' and ladies' names before they enter. As we approach, I shake my head firmly. No. I will pay my respects to the newly bound Lord and Lady Astoria, but I don't want to make a big deal out of my presence.

"I owe you one," I say to the announcer as we sweep into the room without a fuss.

I snag a drink off a tray, and Alex rubs his hands together. "Divide and conquer?" he asks, his hazel eyes gleaming.

"If you insist. Make note of any 'eligible' ladies I need to check out."

The sarcasm in my voice elicits a bright laugh out of Alex, and a few heads turn in our direction. I give him a *Thanks for that* look before making my way toward the happy couple. It feels somewhat frivolous to make such a big deal out of his second marriage—her third or fourth—but if this is how he wants to spend his newly acquired money, that's up to him.

"Lord and Lady Astoria," I say smoothly as I approach.

"Your Highness," Lord Astoria replies, dipping his head in an insulting mockery of a bow.

"How wonderful of you to come tonight," Lady Astoria croons. "Is your father here as well?" She looks behind me, as if expecting him to pop up out of nowhere.

Pompous ass that he is, he never arrives anywhere without the entire realm being made aware of it.

"He sends his regards," I say diplomatically.

I don't miss the twitch of annoyance that crosses Lord Astoria's face at my response.

"I do hope he is in good health," he replies.

"Yes, he is quite well."

"Wonderful," Lord Astoria says through gritted teeth.

"Perhaps we can arrange a visit in the near future," Lady Astoria says demurely. "It's been oh-so-long since I've had a chance to visit court."

"I'll let him know," I reply before tossing back my drink. "Now, if you wouldn't mind excusing me, I must find myself some dance partners."

Lady Astoria beams and turns to her side, pulling at a young woman's arm. I hadn't even noticed her, I was so focused on paying my respects and getting out of there.

"Lady Erika would love to dance," Lady Astoria announces, placing her hand on my arm in a way that makes me cringe. She's being quite forward, and I don't like it. Unfortunately, I don't think my father would approve of me embarrassing his old friend's daughter in a room filled with people, so I nod in agreement, even as I immediately dread the time I'll spend with this woman.

It isn't that she's unattractive—her dark hair cascades down her back like a sheet of the deepest waters, her heart-shaped face pleasant enough to look at—but I will never see her as more than Lady Raelyn's annoying little sister.

I lead her out to the dance floor, and she beams happily, gushing. "Your Highness, thank you so much for the honor."

"It's my pleasure," I lie.

As we spin, I spy another woman with dark hair glaring straight at us. Her beauty is harsh, the malice in her eyes taking away from it, but the similarities to the woman currently in my arms leaves no question. Of course. Lady Chessa. I quickly look away, not wanting to give her any encouragement to try dancing with me as well.

Despite everything in me telling me it's a terrible idea, I can't help but search the rest of the room as we glide around the dance floor. Where is the woman who haunts my dreams? I briefly stiffen at the thought that Alex might have already gotten his hands on her, but no. He's my friend, and he's watching me dance with an amused expression.

"You're a wonderful dancer, Your Highness," Lady Erika says.

"Thanks," I mutter, really not wanting to chat.

"I am so looking forward to this season's balls," she chatters on.

I can't say I am. Especially not with the sudden mandate to find myself a wife. I sigh.

"Are you all right, Your Highness?" she asks, biting her lip in what I'd guess she thinks is a seductive move.

It takes everything within me to hold back a snort. "Quite all right, Lady Erika."

She lets out an awkward chuckle. "Oh good. I was afraid I might have stepped on your toes."

I can't stop the grin from forming, and she immediately blushes. Hells. I really don't want to give her the wrong impression.

The song mercifully ends, and I give her a bow as she curtsies.

"Thank you for the dance, Lady Erika."

I make my exit before she can respond and push through the throng of people to Alex's side.

"Shit, Ki, you work fast," he teases. "I told you Lady Erika was a looker."

I roll my eyes. "She was quite literally thrust upon me."

Alex chokes. "You can't help yourself tonight, can you?"

I frown. "Really not trying here."

"Riiiight," Alex drawls before dropping his voice to a whisper. "Any sign of the reclusive Astoria—the woman who almost managed to best the Shadow?"

I stiffen, wishing for a moment that I could take back the knowledge I'd shared. "Be glad it's loud in here or else we'd be having some serious words," I bite out. "You can't be making jokes about that."

"Lighten up a little, Ki," Alex replies, grabbing another drink off a passing waiter's tray. "Anyway, back to the question at hand . . . have you seen her?"

"I've been here all of ten minutes and you expect me to have immediately sought her out after I told you it's a bad idea?"

Alex hides a grin behind his drink. "Just want to make sure I get my chance to make an impression before you sweep her off her feet with your broody looks and grunts."

"Shut up, Alex."

But then I see her. Across the room. Unwittingly, I take a step toward her, admiring how the emerald dress matches her eyes and drapes over her figure perfectly. The swirling gold detail draws my attention, and I can't help but take in every glorious inch of her. What in the hells is wrong with me? I step back. Am I a glutton for punishment? I promised myself I'd stay away.

Her eyes meet mine from across the room and I hate the way my heart stutters in my chest. I'm in deep shit.

Chapter Eight

RAELYN

Smoky grey eyes look me up and down, and the stranger's lips quirk into the hint of a smile. Do I know him? Not that I know many people, thanks to my hermit-like habits. Still, there's an odd pang of familiarity, but when I grasp for it, it slips away like ash on the wind.

For a moment, I wonder if he's even looking at me. I glance to my left and right and then over my shoulder, but when I turn back, he tilts his head and gives me a slight nod. Almost as if to say, *Yes, it's you I'm staring at.* A blush creeps up my neck, heat engulfing my body. I take a sip of my sparkling wine, but when I look back, he's gone.

My shoulders droop after scanning the room and not seeing him. I didn't expect anyone to catch my eye, and that glance made me feel alive, made me think that perhaps I'm not a completely lost cause. What a shame. Would it be so terrible to find a handsome lord to dance with? If I'm all dressed up, I might as well take advantage of it.

My skin is still buzzing from my afternoon run. The spark of hope that I've outgrown my strange affliction has me wondering if perhaps my life could be more than it is . . . more than it's been. Perhaps it *wouldn't* be so terrible to find a man to flirt with, one who might be willing to abscond to a dark corner and press his lips to mine . . . like the lips on the stranger I caught staring.

Get a hold of yourself, Raelyn. One man glances your way and you lose your head. It has to be hormones . . . definitely hormones. I calculate the time of month and laugh to myself, even as I let my gaze wander.

The ballroom is the grandest space in the manor with its polished floors and gleaming pillars. The ceiling reaches to the top of our three-story home, and a dozen crystal chandeliers shine down upon us. Lavender wisteria drips off the ends of them, their potent scent lingering in the space. I'm grateful the doors to the outside terrace are open, allowing fresh air in to combat the competing scents of perfume and sweat from all the dancers twirling about the space.

The new Lady Astoria's decorator ought to be fired. While the front hall reeks of death and pumpkins and is decorated in an array of autumn colors, the ballroom clings to the last vestiges of summer with violet flowers and pastel drapes.

After draining my glass, I set it on the table next to me and cross my arms under my breasts, trying to perk them up a little.

"Looking for someone?" A silky smooth voice caresses the back of my neck as a warm presence steps closer. When I glance to my left, I hold back a gasp and look away. It's him. *What do I do?*

"Wouldn't you like to know?" I quip, feeling oddly flustered.

"I actually would, hence my asking."

I squeeze my eyes shut. *Why am I so bad at this?* "Who are you?" I ask, changing the subject.

"Ah, ah, ah, I asked you a question first, love."

"Excuse me?" I spin to look at him, my mouth gaping. "Are you always so informal with strangers?"

Hurt flickers in his eyes, but he quickly masks it, his lips quirking into a grin. "My mistake. I thought we were acquainted."

I frown. "I think I'd remember you." I try to wrack my brain for who he might possibly be, but once again, I fail at placing him.

A harsh laugh comes out of him. "Nice to know I'm so forgettable. I thought everyone knew me."

I roll my eyes. So conceited. "Who do you think you are, a prince of Rakveren or something?"

"That is precisely who I am."

Well shit.

I step back and drop into a deep curtsy, my eyes glued to the floor as my cheeks heat with mortification. "I apologize, Your Highness. I truly did not recognize you."

His feet step into view, and a hand reaches out, tilting my chin up so I meet his stormy gaze. There's a hint of humor there, and I relax a little, fairly certain I'm not headed for the gallows.

"Please rise. I promise I won't tell anyone you didn't recognize your prince, love." He winks before pulling his hand away.

Rising from my curtsy, I can't keep from saying, "Stop calling me that. It's Lady Raelyn."

"I'm well aware."

Something about his words and the way he looks at me tugs on something in my chest. Before I can respond, he reaches down and pulls my gloved hand up to his mouth, placing a kiss on it, and butterflies erupt in my stomach.

"Dance with me, my lady?"

I hesitate. The prince has me completely flustered and confused, and we've only spoken for a few minutes. Is it really a good idea to subject myself to his company for an entire dance? I've already completely embarrassed myself; Luna forbid I make it worse.

"Don't leave me hanging here. People will talk."

I bite my lip before nodding. "Okay, fine."

A wide grin splits his face. "Delightful."

The prince leads me to the dance floor and sweeps me into a flowing waltz. I stumble for just a moment before I let muscle memory take over. The rise and fall of the music flows through me, and we glide across the floor as if we've done this before. His right hand is like a brand on my shoulder, my awareness of him heightened. I can feel his eyes on me, but I'm too afraid to meet his gaze. There's something about him that has me off-kilter.

"You have freckles," he blurts out.

"What?" I ask, whipping my face up.

"Freckles," he repeats. "I'm aware of your . . . affliction, so I didn't expect freckles. I don't remember—"

So surprised at his observation, I trip on the hem of my gown and almost go sprawling, but he deftly catches me before anyone seems to take notice.

"Thank you," I breathe, my mind still trying to work through what he said. I hate that people at court are aware of my affliction, but I suppose that can't be helped.

"My pleasure." He hums. "I enjoy holding a beautiful woman in my arms."

Something about his words are oddly familiar, but I can't place them. "I think I need some air."

"Let me escort you to the gardens," he replies.

Finding myself unable to deny him, I nod.

He places his hand on the small of my back, and a shudder courses down my spine as he leads me out to the terrace.

"You have such a lovely garden," he says.

Small talk . . . I can attempt small talk, I try to reassure myself. Taking a deep, cleansing breath, I turn to face him, the torchlight casting shadows over the sharp planes of his face.

"Yes, I probably ought to spend more time out here," I admit.

He's not wrong. There are torches all around the terrace emitting warmth and light while the jasmine-and-vanilla scent of the moon-flowers tickles my nose. I spy a couple sneaking off into the hedge maze in the direction of our fountain, and my mind flashes back to thoughts of kissing in dark corners.

The prince opens his mouth as if to speak but then glances around, running a hand through his hair in an almost endearing way.

I allow a small smile to slip through. *Is he just as nervous as I am? Interesting.*

A cool autumn breeze caresses my bare skin, and I wrap my arms around myself. I can't explain the nerves, like I'm a young girl attending her first ball all over again.

"Are you cold? Would you like to go back in?" he asks, breaking the awkward silence.

"No, the cool air feels nice, actually." Before I can lose my nerve, I ask, "Would you like to take a walk?"

"Are you sure?" He raises a brow. "We don't have a chaperone."

"Quite sure," I reply as I start walking down the hedge-lined path. Either he'll follow or he won't.

"You aren't worried about what someone might say about the two of us out here alone?" His voice dips lower.

I laugh. "Trust me, I'm fairly certain my new stepmother would actually be thrilled that I'm talking to a man, and besides, we're not truly alone." I gesture toward the other couples walking the terrace behind us.

"You don't typically talk to men?" He frowns.

"Hardly. I've heard the whispers tonight. I know I'm considered the reclusive Astoria, the daughter my father is unable to get rid of." I can't keep the bitterness out of my voice.

"Forgive me, love, but I don't understand. You're absolutely alluring. You could easily have your pick of eligible men."

My shoulders tense, and I pause. "Perhaps I don't want just any eligible man." I refuse to admit to the prince that no one wants me—no one has wanted me for years.

"Oh? Waiting for a prince to sweep you off your feet?"

Heat flushes my face. "That's not what I meant!"

The laugh that comes out of him is so rich, I wish I could bottle it up and listen to it forever.

"Then what *did* you mean?" he asks, taking a step closer. "Waiting for true love? A soul-bonded mate?"

My throat bobs, and I shake my head. "I don't believe in true love . . . or mates."

He takes another step closer, and I'm backed into the flowered hedge wall. "Who hurt you, love?" the prince asks, his head tilting at a slight angle, eyes glinting darkly in the moonlight.

He's so close, I could pull him in for the kiss I was thinking about, but that is a dangerous road I dare not travel.

"Stop calling me love," I say breathlessly, ignoring his question. "You haven't earned the right. I am nothing to you."

The prince stiffens, backing away from me, and while I feel like I can breathe again, I mourn the loss of his weighty presence. I don't understand the reaction he elicits from me, nor his reaction to my words.

"My apologies. This was a mistake," he says before whirling around and marching back toward the manor.

I want to call after him, apologize for my rude behavior, but something stops me. I'm a fool for allowing myself to even entertain the thought that a prince might be interested in me. Gods, if my sisters had seen, they would have never let me forget it.

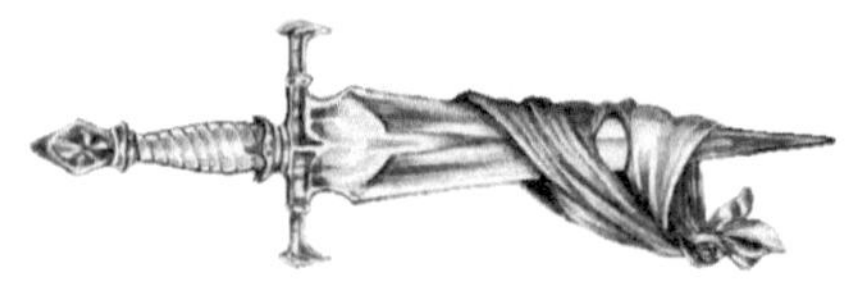

Chapter Nine

KIAN

Those damn eyes haunt my every waking thought. Perhaps I'm the biggest ass for leaving so abruptly yesterday, but standing there, seeing her look at me like I'm a stranger, was too much. I had to get out of there before I said something I'd regret. It's time to focus on what really matters—my quest.

Nothing like a little light reading from the journal I snatched out of Cary's study to distract me.

Cyrus is back. Gods help me, I'm about to call him out for a duel. Doesn't he know Lynette is mine? The moment her jade eyes met mine across the room, I knew who she belonged to. The papers have been drawn up, and our families agree—she is meant to be bound to me by the end of the year. Everything was going perfectly until that blond, woman-thieving man showed up at court, but I'm not truly concerned. Silenius is about to name me as advisor, and then we'll have every-

thing we could ever need.

I re-read the first passage of Cary Astoria's journal, dated some thirty years ago. Cyrus? Who in the realms is Cyrus? I run through all the names of Father's nobles, and Cyrus does not ring a bell. Unfortunately for me, Cary is terrible at journaling, and many pages and dates are missing, but I find another entry from the same year:

In the mother of all plot twists, turns out Cyrus is a god—the sun god Kyros, to be exact. Why he decided to come parade himself as a mortal here in Rakveren makes no sense to me. The gods haven't been seen in centuries. Why now? And why her?

Lynette is completely enamored by him, begging me to let her out of the marriage contract, but why in the hells should I do that? He's a god. She's a fool to think he could ever actually love her. Doesn't she know the stories? Kyros and Luna—the sun and the moon—are forever intertwined. The goddess Luna will never relinquish her hold on Kyros for a mere mortal, and I shudder to think of the wrath she will pour out on Lynette if Kyros doesn't leave her alone. She is mine, and I must protect her.

Hells. Cary *was* mixed up with the sun god. Excitement hums beneath my skin. Perhaps I need to look for more information on Cyrus. Surely, if he spent time at court, others would have been aware of him. Should I ask Father? Except Father always shuts me down when I bring up the sun god. He would rather pretend everything is fine in our realm.

The next few pages are filled with more rants about Cary and Cyrus' rivalry. He never lists Lynette's family name, so I'm not sure which family she came from or what happened to her. Cary's late wife had a different name. The last page of the journal has a short entry and a care-fully folded piece of paper tucked in next to it.

She's gone. My beautiful Lynette is gone, and I alone bear the weight of her secrets. All she left me was a note. I'll never forgive myself for failing to convince her that I'm what she needed . . . She has to be wrong. I don't for one second believe that Kyros has her best interests at heart. I must find a way to make things right, even if it costs everything.

Unfolding the aged piece of parchment, I read:

Dearest Cary,

I'm so sorry to tell you this way, but I feared you'd stop me if I were to speak with you in person. While I will always have a fondness for you, Cyrus has my heart. I know he's a god, but our love is true. He'd burn the realms for me if he had to. I hope you can forgive me for breaking our contract; a priestess will bind Cyrus and me tonight. While I might care for you, I need someone who will fight for me, choose me. Can you understand that? I do believe that you think you love me, but I'm certain you love your status and position more. I deserve to be more than just a trophy. As unusual as it might be, I truly believe I will find happiness with Cyrus, away from court. He swears to protect me from Luna—there is nothing between them anymore. Please don't come looking for me.

Affectionately,
Lynette

Cursing under my breath, I drop the journal onto my desk. I'm nowhere closer to finding out *where* the sun god might have run off to. Cary must have more information, but how do I get it? After examining the journal more closely, it appears that multiple pages have been ripped out of the back, which makes me wonder what else he's hiding. Perhaps I need to pay House Astoria another visit, but he's away, and the last thing I need is to torture myself with another encounter with Lady Raelyn.

A knock at the door has me slamming the journal shut and stuffing it into my desk.

"Enter!"

Alex pokes his head in, a grin plastered on his face. "Fancy going out tonight?"

"Absolutely," I reply, waving him in. "What did you have in mind?"

"Really?" Alex closes the door and looks around. "Are you sure there's no Shadow work to be done?" He plops into the chair across from me. "Because I really want to go out and have some fun."

"The Shadow's work is never done," I joke, "but tonight, he's free to join you. He could use a break."

Alex rubs his hands together, a mischievous look in his eyes. "So, you know tonight is the Havordshire ball."

My lip curls. "And?"

"How about we skip it and go into Elsmont instead?"

"Thank the gods," I breathe. "If you tried to drag me to that ball, I'd have had to decline."

Alex laughs. "I was actually hoping your father wasn't making you go, or if he was, you'd be willing to ditch. I'd much rather do something a little more casual."

"Sounds perfect."

ALEX and I gallop into Elsmont on horseback. While I'm sure Father expects me to be on the hunt for a wife at the Havordshire party, there is no way in hells I'm ever going back there.

This little excursion is the perfect opportunity for me to check in on my people and see if there are other ways I can help, and it will provide a distraction from dwelling on a certain green-eyed beauty. We left all the finery behind, dressed in simple clothes to blend in.

"Have you been to Lou's Tavern?" I ask Alex as we secure our horses to the post.

"Maybe once," he replies. "As long as the ale is cold, I don't care where we drink."

"Thank the gods the colder months are upon us then, eh?"

We push through the doors and enter the dimly lit tavern, assaulted with the scent of ale and vibrant sounds of music. The musician plays a lively tune on a stringed instrument, a crowd of dancers around him kicking up their feet. My boots stick to the floor as we make our way to the bar. This place has seen better days, but spirits are high and the wine and ale flow freely.

Alex leans over the counter, catching the bartender's eye. "Two, please!"

We settle into our seats and clink the foaming glasses together before turning to observe the crowd.

I needed this. A few moments away to distract myself from her. Seeing Lady Raelyn again after so many years was far more painful than I'd expected. Having her not remember me was even more so, but—no, I can't let my focus drift from my main purpose. I have a god to find and people to help.

"Do you come here often?" Alex asks.

"Not as often as I'd like," I admit. "It's been a little while."

"Tell me, do you know who *she* is?" Alex nods toward a blonde beauty dancing unreservedly to the music, her hair shining like spun silk as she twirls around, violet eyes sparkling with joy.

I shake my head. "Sorry, friend. I can't say I do." A word catches my ear from somewhere behind me, and I motion for Alex to be quiet. He frowns and tilts his head but refrains from speaking.

"Do you know how to get word to the Shadow?" a low, gruff voice speaks.

"I wish," another replies. "He shows up sporadically."

"We could really use some help in Marietta," the first man says. "Sickness has swept through our village and our food supply is low. The king takes everything we bring in."

I bristle, my muscles tense. Father leaves nothing for them to survive on. Is he trying to set the stage for a rebellion?

"I'll see if we have anything to spare," the second man replies. "It's the least we can do."

Pride for my people swells in my chest. I need to make a point to deliver supplies to more of the outer villages; they need help just as much as the people of Elsmont. Perhaps I can swing by my healer Margot's place and ask her to check in on the people of Marietta as well.

"Everything okay?" Alex whispers.

I blow out a breath. "Yeah, just eavesdropping on my people." I give him a wry grin. "The Shadow has some work to do."

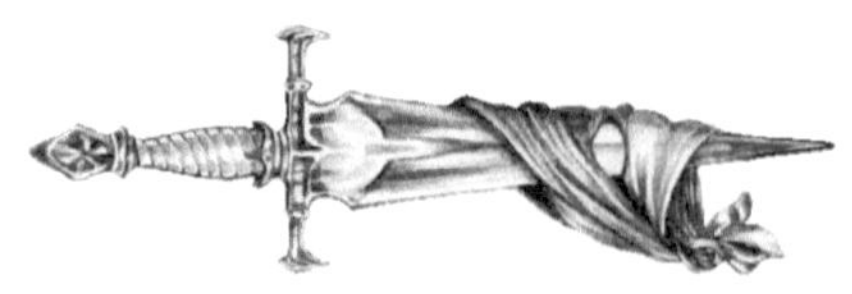

Chapter Ten

KIAN

"What has you looking so glum?" Alex asks.

We continue our brisk walk to the training arena, and I debate how much I want to share. My secrets keep me and others safe, and sharing them with him still feels wrong.

"Shadow stuff."

Alex nudges me with his elbow. "You know you can talk to me, right?"

"Right."

When I stay quiet, Alex grabs my arm and pulls me into a small alcove. "Then talk to me, Ki," he demands.

I lean against the wall, crossing my arms and legs, trying to remain casual. "Has anyone ever told you you're annoying?"

Alex smirks, showing off his straight white teeth, and mirrors my position. "It may have been mentioned before . . . but I'm not going to let this go."

"Fuck it. Fine," I mutter, running a hand through my hair. "I got word from Margot that there was trouble with one of my drops."

Alex arches a brow, tilting his head. "What kind of trouble?"

"I can usually count on the people of Elsmont to distribute the goods after I drop them off. It would appear, however, that someone pilfered the supplies for himself and is now selling them to the highest bidder."

"Shiiiiit," Alex groans. "Let me guess, you need to go steal back the goods you already stole once?"

"Something like that." I sigh.

"Is this the first time this has happened?" Alex asks.

"To this scale, yes. Some have taken more than their fair share, but trying to charge people for it? That's a new low."

"Does the king know?"

"If he did, we would've heard something or there would have been a public execution," I say. "Father is quite put out that he hasn't caught the Shadow yet and would take any opportunity for a win. So, no, I don't believe he's aware of it."

Alex starts to pace, making the small alcove feel even more cramped. "So what's the plan? When do we head out?" he asks.

There is no way in hells Alex is tagging along, but I can't tell him that.

"I'm not sure yet," I lie. "I have some more research to do on Kyros, and that takes precedence right now." *Only a partial lie . . .*

"You're not alone anymore," Alex says. "It's okay to accept help."

"I'm good tonight. I'm overdue for a night off. All the balls these past few weeks have been exhausting."

"Still haven't found your choice of bride?"

Unwittingly, my mind goes back to *her*. It's only been two weeks since the Astoria ball, and I haven't seen her since. Lady Erika and Lady Chessa have been at all the balls I've attended, but not her. Is she all right? Why do I even care? She clearly moved on years ago, and so shall I.

"Not even close." I sigh, straightening. "Come on. I need to punch something."

"As long as it's not me." Alex chuckles, and we continue on our way to the arena.

GODS, I hope Alex will forgive me. Hopefully he won't ask about it and I won't have to lie to him . . . again. I'm a terrible friend. But this is for his own good, and I work better alone.

Margot's note is practically burning a hole in my pocket. I wait until Phantom and I are safely off palace grounds before pulling it out and rereading the information. Antonio's warehouse is on the outskirts of Elsmont, so my ride will be a short one.

He will regret his decisions. Stealing from the innocent to line his pockets sure was a choice.

After securing my mask, Phantom and I gallop off into the night. The wind is biting, and I crouch lower in my saddle. What I wouldn't give for the warmer summer nights I had been complaining about just a few months ago.

All too soon, I spy my target. Phantom and I slow to a walk and I lead him into the nearby forest.

"That's a good boy," I say, rubbing Phantom's muzzle affectionately, making sure his marking is still covered before feeding him an apple I had stashed in my pocket. "Listen for my signal, okay, boy?" He snorts at me, and I move to the saddle bags to grab my supplies.

I glance up to the sky—Luna's moon is brighter than normal, which is not great for my mission. Almost as if she's listening, clouds roll in and cover it. *Thank you, Luna.* I grin; the gods are on my side. Tonight is sure to go perfectly.

On swift, silent feet, I run the short distance to the warehouse. The buildings are more run down out here, and I'm reminded of the crown's negligence. Not that my father would care to spend his coin to help them . . .

When I make it to the building, I hug the wall, doing my best to blend into the shadows. Margot's note says Antonio has a small living space on the upper level. I just need to get in first. I scope out the building, and the only guards present are at the front. Silently making my way to the main entrance, I pause before turning the corner and dip my hand into the pouch of sleep dust I recently acquired. Putting guards to sleep is faster than knocking them out physically, and though admittedly less fun, I'm going for stealth tonight.

My hand full of dust, I casually turn the corner and blow it into their unsuspecting faces.

"What in the h—" one chokes out before slumping to the ground.

The other starts to pull his sword, but before it's all the way out of its sheath, I sweep a foot behind his legs and he falls. I almost chuckle at the loud snore that comes out of his mouth as the sleep dust takes effect. Step one complete.

Feeling around for a key in their pockets, I grimace at the violation. I really don't enjoy this part. Thankfully, I find a key in Sleepy Guard Number Two's pocket and oh-so-quietly fit it into the lock. When the door swings wide into the dark open space, I pause. Is this far too easy? Is this a trap? No. I'm just jittery.

The floor creaks beneath my boot, and I wince, pausing for any kind of reaction, but when none comes, I suck in a deep breath. I almost wish I hadn't when the stench of unwashed bodies, stale ale, and rotting fruit assails my nose. My eyes finally adjust to the darkness, and I take in the open space. Two large unlit wooden chandeliers hang from the ceiling, and barrels and boxes of supplies line the walls, but as far as I can tell, all is quiet and no one lies in wait. I head for the narrow stairs that lead to the upper level.

When I make it to the small landing, I pause as a strange chill creeps down my spine. Glancing down into the mostly empty warehouse space below, I check for movement. Something isn't right . . . Everything in my gut is telling me to turn and run, but I hate running from a fight, and I need to teach Antonio a lesson.

There's a faint glow underneath one door. Before I can overthink it, I pull my sword and barge in.

Antonio rises from his seat at the table, the firelight flickering in his amber eyes. "So, you've come to exact your revenge? I was wondering when you'd show up." He looks far too relaxed in his weaponless state as I stalk closer with my sword.

"You thought you could steal from the very people I aim to protect?"

My sword pokes his chest, but I don't put enough pressure to cut.

He lifts his hands in mock surrender, refusing to back away as a laugh chortles out of him. "You'd kill an unarmed man?"

I flash him a smile. "Would you like to find out? Though you're lucky it's me and not the king who's discovered your treachery. Were it him, you'd already be dead."

Antonio relaxes his stance even further, raising a calculating brow. "Are you so certain, *Shadow*?"

The mockery does not go unnoticed, and his complete lack of fear gives me pause. What am I missing?

His eyes flicker behind me, and the subtle whoosh of a blade has me spinning away, leaping to put Antonio between me and my new opponent.

My blade pressed against his chest, I draw Antonio closer to me. "No sudden moves," I growl at him and his accomplice, who's standing right where I used to be. "Throw down your weapon, unless you'd prefer to see Antonio without a head."

"Do what he says," Antonio grits out.

The burly man throws down his sword with a clang and backs up a step.

"No sudden moves," I remind him.

I pull Antonio with me and skirt around the man, leaving the room and making my way to the railing that overlooks the open warehouse. This is feeling more and more like a trap.

A sudden shout, and guards pour into the warehouse below. A few hold torches that light their faces in a menacing glow.

Shit shit shit.

Antonio chuckles. "Turns out the king cares more about catching you than me earning a little extra coin."

"You're a snake, Antonio," I grit out before I smash the hilt of my blade into his temple and he crumples to the floor. I turn, and Burly Man takes a step toward me, so I point my sword at him. "You want to impale yourself? Be my guest." He must have some brains because he stays put, to my relief; I really don't want to kill anyone tonight.

The thundering of boots on the steps signals I'm almost out of time. With a hop, I'm up on the railing, and before I can think too hard, I sheathe my sword and leap, grabbing onto one of the large wooden chandeliers. My stomach almost jumps up into my throat as I swing across the room toward my exit. The guards freeze, staring at me in shock as I let go and barrel into them and they go down in a heap. My ankle twinges as I land on it wrong, but I keep moving, dashing toward my exit. I pull up short as Burly Man from before blocks my way with his sword. Damn, he got down here fast.

He has me on size alone, but I'm stronger than I look, and equally fast . . . when my ankle isn't twisted. I draw my sword, trying my best not to reveal my weakness as I fend off Burly Man's attacks. Before I know it, I'm back in the center of the room and the guards I knocked down are recovering. As much as I'd love to show off my impressive sword skills, survival is more important. These are my father's men, and for all I know, they have orders to kill me and forgo the questions.

"Hey, big guy," I yell out, hoping to distract him. To my utter shock, his brow crinkles in confusion, and he pauses. "Behind you!"

When he actually looks over his shoulder, I hold back my laugh as I use the time to sprint in the opposite direction. There's got to be a rear exit somewhere. My ankle twinges again, and I almost stumble, but I keep running, the yelling and thudding of boots lighting a fire beneath my feet.

I can't get caught. My people need me . . . my realm needs me. What was I thinking, trying to do this on my own? I should have realized this was a trap the minute I walked in so easily, but I can chide myself later. I still need to make it out of this alive.

Searing pain burns through my side, but I don't have time to look. The clatter of a knife hitting the floor is my first indication, sticky wet blood running down my side is the next. Damn it. I don't have much time.

Thank Luna there's a window two feet away, and without second-guessing, I run into it shoulder first, gratified at the shattering glass as the window gives way. I hit the ground and roll with an "oof." Struggling for breath, a weak whistle leaves my lips before I stumble to my feet and run for the woods. Gods willing, Phantom heard me.

More glass shatters, followed by shouts, and I send up another prayer to Luna for help in my escape. Thundering hooves send a rush of relief through me as Phantom breaks from the trees. I barely manage to pull myself into the saddle, but we're off. An arrow whizzes past my ear, and Phantom and I race back into the woods, hoping the darkness and trees will slow their pursuit. I reach a hand back and press into my wound, grimacing in pain. I need to get this taken care of quickly before I bleed out.

Alex is going to give me so much shit for this.

Chapter Eleven

RAELYN

It's been a month. Thirty days with our new stepmother as lady of the manor. I'm ready to scream and run away. Gods, can I?

Curse Father and his financial woes. He could not have chosen a worse "mother."

I scrub at the tiles, my hands and knees burning. This is absurd. We used to have maids for this until Stepmother dismissed the majority of them only days after the ink on the marriage contract dried. Have they found other employment? I worry for their ability to provide for their own families.

To my dismay, even Sera was let go. The only remaining lady's maid is assigned to Stepmother and the twins while I am left to fend for myself.

I wipe a hand across my sweaty brow. How I long to be curled up in my favorite chair, working on my needlepoint or reading a good book instead of being assigned to seemingly endless chores. I curse under my breath.

Footsteps click down the hall, and I bite my tongue, hoping whoever it is didn't hear me. The last thing I need is more punishment for speaking out of turn about our dearest stepmother.

"Oops!" a feminine voice says right before the bucket hits the floor and a flood of dirty water soaks my knees.

I let out an unladylike screech and jump to my feet, spinning around to glare at Chessa. "Why would you do that?"

She quirks a brow, her lips curling into a smile I want to smack right off her face. "I'm sorry. I must have tripped."

I throw the filthy sponge at her, and she ducks while screaming, "Don't you dare, Raelyn! I will tell Mother about this, and you will pay!"

"You traitorous filth," I hiss at her. "What makes you think you are any more special than I? You should be down here cleaning with me."

Chessa straightens, her nose pointing toward the ceiling. "Clearly, our new stepmother knows what she's doing. You're just a waste of space. You should have been married off by now, but instead, you sit around, lazing away, wasting Papa's money."

My eyes widen. "Is that what you think?" She has another thing coming if she thinks *I* am the waster of our funds. I haven't gotten a new wardrobe in years, while she has new dresses made every week. She is completely delusional.

"It's what I know," she replies. "Besides, I need to make sure I am presentable for all the suitors Mother has set up for me. I dare not break a nail while cleaning the floors." She sniffs haughtily.

"Get out of my sight, Chess, before I pull you onto the floor and make you clean up this mess with your brand-new dress." I clench my fists at my sides, daring her to come at me or say another word.

A flash of fear crosses her face before she turns and runs. I wish I could say that was the last of it, but I have a feeling I'll be hearing about it from Stepmother. That vile woman. I'm not sure what it is she holds against me other than being unmarried, but surely Father wouldn't let her treat me this way if he knew?

He left on a business trip only a week after their ball, and Stepmother immediately implemented her evil plan to destroy me—at least that's how it feels. Father can't get home soon enough.

I retrieve the sponge I flung across the room and get back to work, the spill doubling my cleaning time. My soaked dress clings to my legs, and I shiver with cold. There is nothing I want more than a hot bath and some tea, but there will be hells to pay if I leave the floor in this state.

MY BATH IS NOT NEARLY AS good as I dreamed it would be. By the time I hauled up enough water from the kitchens, it was barely warm anymore. I'm regretful for taking our servants' hard work for granted all of these years.

I lean my head back against the cool edge of the tub and allow tears to slip down my cheeks. A pity party serves no one, but the unfairness of it all makes me want to scream. My fingers are cracked from the harsh soaps I use to clean the floors and scrub the laundry, and they sting as I clean my aching body. After not even a month, calluses have formed, and they're rough against my sensitive skin.

My mind wanders to the needlepoint I started weeks ago that has lain neglected in my sewing basket, the art that has been itching to get out left wanting. Will I even remember what it was I wanted to create? Will my fingers remember the dance of thread and material?

More tears streak down my face as I grieve the loss of my time. Everything I do is to serve another, every task piled on meant to break my spirit, and I fear I'm nearly there.

I'm utterly overwhelmed. As soon as I complete one list of chores, another is handed over. Inundated with all the things I must do, I no longer have time to do any of the things I *want* to do. How long will this be my lot? Will Father put a stop to it when he returns?

Sometimes I wonder what would happen if I left the manor—just started walking, never to return. Would they even miss me? Unlikely. They'd only miss the things I do for them.

For just a moment, I try to dream of a better time. Fencing with Father in the training room, the pride in his eyes when I hit targets with his knives . . . and then, almost unwillingly, my mind drifts back to the ball and the handsome prince whom I managed to offend, and I'm depressed all over again.

When I told Father about my run in the sun, he panicked, insisting I could not take that risk again. No matter how much I told him I felt fine, he was certain it would eventually make me sick . . . and he was right. Despite the prophylactic medicine he gave me, I was violently ill for days after the ball, confined to my bed. By the time I felt well enough to rejoin the family for meals, Father was gone and Stepmother decided I was well enough to clean.

I slip beneath the water, letting out a muffled scream. It's oddly cathartic.

Now that that's out of my system, I use what little energy I have left to wash my hair. The clock chimes, and I'm taken back to the night weeks ago when I almost caught the thief in Father's study. Will he come back? Has he come back? With the endless chores Stepmother assigns me, I can barely keep my eyes open after dinner. Forget staying up late to keep vigil for his return. By the time I fall into bed each night, exhaustion pulls me under before I can read more than a sentence or two in my book. So many stories I want to read, but my mind cannot handle another moment awake. Not only does my body ache, but my mind is also fuzzy and overloaded, incapable of focusing on one more thought. Every night, I'm plagued with dreams: some of a forested island with a large golden lion pacing its shores and others of smoky grey eyes that pierce my soul.

Shaking my head to clear my thoughts, I rise from the tub and grab a towel to dry off before pulling on a simple dress. Stepmother has disinvited me from formal meals, which is fine with me. The less time spent with her the better.

Out of habit, I reach for the chain to call Sera to come fix my hair but then pause and find tears welling up in my eyes all over again. She's gone. Unless a miracle happens, my life will never go back to the way it was. I can only hope Father will right some of these wrongs when he returns.

My stomach rumbles, but I try to ignore it. I'm far too exhausted to make my way to the kitchen this evening. No one will care. No one seems to notice me anymore, except for Chess, who loves to torment me along with Stepmother. Even Erika, whom I thought might be on my side out of everyone, ignores me.

Curling up in my bed, I hug my knees to my chest. I miss Father. I miss my old life. I feel completely helpless, but what else can I possibly do? I was raised to listen to my elders, to respect authority. Do I even have another choice? I hate it here, but I have nowhere else to go.

MY ENTIRE BODY heats in the most delicious way as I awaken to the sun streaming into my room. I stretch my arms overhead before panic sets in. No! Not again. I must have forgotten to close the curtains in my infinite exhaustion last night.

Jumping out of bed, I pull them shut, my heart beating quickly with the sudden exertion. There's no telling what Stepmother will do if I'm out sick again for days. I send up a quick prayer to the gods for mercy. Perhaps it won't be as bad as it was. I'm inside, and it could only have been shining on me for a few minutes, right?

My body feels fine. The aches and pains from yesterday have all but faded, and I'm ready to face the day, even knowing there will be a long list of chores for me.

I slip down the servants' staircase toward the kitchen and peek my head in. Our cook is hard at work on breakfast, and my stomach rumbles, reminding me that I didn't eat the night before.

"Good morning, Fred," I greet him.

He grumbles a response, and I reach out to grab a croissant from the basket, shoving it into my mouth.

"Lady Raelyn! You know you aren't allowed to eat those," Fred says, glaring at me as I polish it off as quickly as possible.

"Oops, I forgot." No, I didn't.

"Lady Astoria would be most displeased if she knew you were in here eating her breakfast."

"I'm a lady too, you know," I huff angrily. "It's not my fault she's lost her damn mind and relegated me to staff."

"Not my problem." Fred sniffs. "I just do what I'm told, and I'm told you are *not* to eat the pastries." He points over to the corner where a giant tureen of unflavored oats sits. "The staff breakfast is over there. Do not test me again." His posture softens as he takes in my defeated appearance, and he gives me a sympathetic look. "I can't lose this job . . ."

I blow out a breath, trying to release my anger as I head over to the . . . slop, and serve myself a small portion. No one respects me anymore. No one treats me like the daughter I once was. I'm just part of the help. I try not to be angry with them—I know how hard they work. Their families would suffer without their jobs and whatever meager payment they are given. My payment is the roof over my head.

"Don't forget your tonic." Fred nods toward the shelf.

"Oh, of course. Thanks for the reminder."

I grab it and put it into my pocket. After my accidental sun exposure, I definitely cannot miss this dose, but my stomach is roiling from the porridge, and the thought of taking the sickly-sweet tonic makes me want to vomit. Gods willing, it will be more palatable after my morning tea.

Filling a stone mug to the brim with the beverage, I take a sip, enjoying the warmth.

"I'll be right back, Fred," I say, slipping back into the hall and making my way toward my old sanctuary. With any luck, I just might get a few moments to myself.

The sitting room remains mostly untouched, and I take a deep breath as I light a few lamps. The familiar scents of parchment from the abundance of literature and of cinnamon from my favorite candles assault my nose. I really need to make it a point to come and relax with a good book soon.

I take another sip of my tea, allowing it to soothe my stomach. My fingers trail along the spines of the many books. I could use a little joy, and perhaps escaping into a story would help me manage the misery of my current situation. My fingers stop on a shimmering, opalescent tome —one of my favorites that is surely due for a reread. I trace the silver embossed title: *The Fall of the Iris.*

My stomach is much more settled, so I set down my mug and pull the tonic out of my pocket. I pop open the stopper and—

"*Raelyn!*"

My name is screeched so loudly, I startle and drop the vial. As if in slow motion, I watch in horror as it bounces off the edge of the bookcase and shatters on the floor, the golden liquid staining the carpet.

Chessa screams my name again, and I groan. So much for my moment of solitude. Father would not have been pleased at the wasted tonic; perhaps it's a good thing he's not home to fret. I'm certain the medicine is expensive to acquire. One missed day can't hurt too badly, right? I send up another prayer to the gods that I'm not making a big mistake. I'll come back and clean this up later.

I almost bump into Chess out in the hall.

"You can stop screaming," I say, unleashing my snark as I march past her toward the kitchen. To my annoyance, she follows me.

"What in the hells do you think you're doing relaxing in the sitting room when you have work to do?" she accuses.

I point at the rich breakfast laid out on the tables. "Breakfast hasn't even been served yet, Chess. You're being unreasonable."

She sniffs. "I'm only doing what Mother commanded—making sure you're doing what you're supposed to do."

"What, you're my keeper now?" I scoff.

"Clearly, you need someone to stay on top of you, you lazy wretch."

I fist my hands at my sides, desperately holding myself back. She's not worth the potential punishment.

Chess holds out a piece of rolled-up parchment, a haughty smirk on her face. "Better get started . . ."

I snatch it out of her hand, and despair hits as the list of tasks overwhelms me before I've even begun. I really hate it here.

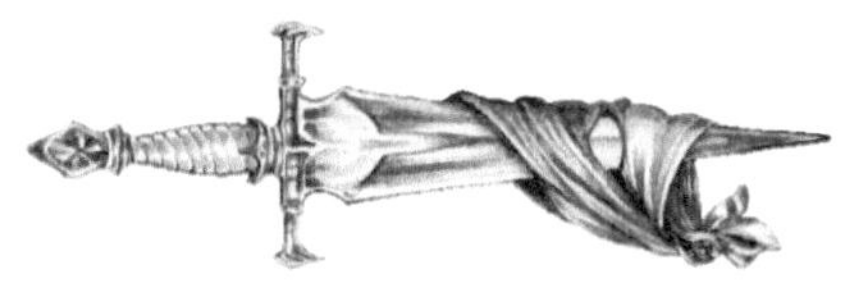

Chapter Twelve

KIAN

TWENTY YEARS AGO

Colin grumbles in annoyance, complaining that he can't ride his brand-new horse as we climb into the royal carriage for the hour-long ride to House Astoria.

"But why do we have to go?" Colin whines again.

Mother shushes him, but Father gives him a stern glare. "Lord Astoria is my oldest friend and one of my closest advisors. Paying our respects to their newest children is the least we can do."

Mother smiles and pats my knee. "Who knows? Perhaps we'll arrange a marriage for you with the family, Kian. They do have three daughters."

I screw my face up in disgust. "Why would you even say such a thing?"

Colin laughs at me, quieting when Mother gives him another look before turning her attention back to me.

"Part of being royal means our marriage bindings are important," *she says softly. "Colin is already betrothed to the princess of Tallinnia to maintain alliances. As heir, that's his responsibility."*

I tilt my head. "I'm not the heir, so why do I need to be betrothed? I'm only nine years old!"

Father smirks from his seat across from me. "Son, there will be quite a few things in life that you won't understand until you get older. You probably don't need an arranged marriage quite yet, but your mother is right. Perhaps we'll marry you off to one of the Astorias. I'm sure Cary would love that. He's been dropping hints for years."

"Gross," I say, and Mother chuckles as she pats my knee again.

"Don't even worry about it, my little love. You won't need to marry for quite some time."

When we finally pull up to the manor, I excitedly jump to my feet, almost tripping over my brother in our race to get out, eager to stretch our legs after being cramped in the carriage.

"Boys!" Father calls out. "You will behave."

"Of course, Father," we say in unison.

Colin straightens the collar on his jacket and gives me a look that makes me wary, reminding me of all the times he's gotten me into trouble.

When we're finally ushered into one of the family's sitting rooms, my gaze is immediately drawn to the young girl seated by the fire, completely focused on some kind of sewing project. She looks a couple of years younger than me, but her prim and proper posture makes it clear she's been raised to be a lady.

We trail behind Father and Mother as he greets Lord and Lady Astoria. Two babies squeal in their mother's arms, one wearing bright pink and the other purple. I always wanted a baby sister, but Mother said Colin and I were all the gods would bless her with.

"Please, have a seat!" Lord Astoria exclaims to my parents while Lady Astoria tries to hush the crying babes. "Boys, I think there are some treats laid out over there."

I look to Mother and she nods, so Colin and I wander over to the table laden with pastries and sweets.

"How long do you think they'll make us stay?" I whisper to Colin.

Colin shrugs as he pops something sugary into his mouth.

I look back at the girl, who is completely in her own little world, ignoring the screeching babies and everyone else in the room. Grabbing a small plate, I put a few treats on it and walk over to her.

"Hi," I say.

"Hello," she replies, keeping her eyes trained on her project.

"I brought you some sweets."

"Thanks," she mumbles.

What do I need to do to get this girl's attention?

"You're being quite rude. Don't you realize I'm a prince?"

That does it. The girl drops her sewing and tilts her head up to look at me, irritation flaring in her green eyes.

"I'm sorry, Your Highness," she says, putting on a fake tone of respect. "Do you need me to get up and curtsy?"

She's feisty, but something about her sparks my interest.

"I could tell my father you're being rude," I say, crossing my arms.

She snorts a laugh. "As if he could hear you over the screaming babies."

"Do they do that a lot?" I ask, crinkling my nose in disgust.

"Unfortunately." She sighs. "Chessa is worse than Erika."

"What's your name?" I ask.

She reaches for one of the pastries I brought over and smiles. "I'm Raelyn. How did you know croissants are my favorite?"

"I didn't."

"Lucky guess then." She grins. I like her smile. "What's your name?" she asks between bites.

"Kian, but my friends call me Ki."

She screws up her nose in the cutest expression. "That doesn't make sense. If your name is pronounced 'key-inn'"—she draws out my name—"then why in the gods' names would they call you something that rhymes with 'sky?'"

I laugh and shrug. "No idea, but you shouldn't swear."

"I can do what I want," she says defensively. "Sort of."

"Ladies aren't supposed to swear," I retort.

"Ladies aren't supposed to do a lot of things." She sighs. "I bet you get

to play outside all the time and climb trees and have adventures like I read about in books."

I frown. "You're not allowed to play outside?"

"Papa says it's not safe."

"Why? Because you're a girl?"

She shrugs. "He's never really explained it. Just says it can make me sick."

"That seems silly."

She nods.

"What if you went outside with an escort? Would that make it safer?"

She shrugs again. "I don't know . . ."

I look around the room, noting that Father and Mother are completely distracted by Lord and Lady Astoria and the babies, who finally stopped crying. Colin is perusing a large bookshelf and appears to be reading the titles. Finally, I spot a glass door that leads out onto some kind of terrace, and an idea pops into my mind.

"How about we find out?" I ask.

Raelyn frowns. "Find out what?"

"If it's safe to go out . . . with me."

She bites her lip and shakes her head. "Father would never allow it."

I shrug. "Our parents look rather busy right now, wouldn't you say? My brother always says it's easier to ask forgiveness than permission."

She hesitates for a moment before a sparkle of mischief lights her eyes. "Okay, maybe just real quick."

A thrill of adrenaline courses through me as I offer my hand and she takes it. We casually walk toward the table of treats, as if we're just getting another snack. I peek over my shoulder and see the adults are still lost in conversation, so we veer off to the side and try the door.

To my excitement, the door is unlocked, and we slip out onto the terrace that's aglow in the late afternoon sun.

"Well?" I ask. "You haven't burst into flames. Are you all right?"

Raelyn giggles and twirls in a circle. "It smells so fresh and clean out here."

I scrunch my nose and sniff. Smells normal to me. "Want to go explore?"

"Sure!" she says excitedly.

I take her hand again, and we run toward the gardens.

Raelyn is like a beam of light. Her face almost glows in the sunlight, and her eyes light up in wonder as we skip through the grass and she stops to admire the wildflowers. I pull her toward the garden maze, and we dart into it.

"Try not to get lost!" I call out as she runs down one path and I try another.

Her giggles ring out, and I find myself chasing after her, enjoying her excitement.

We finally make it to the center of the maze to find a giant fountain. Both of us are panting from exertion, and sweat drips down my back from the heat of the summer sun beating down on us.

"I dare you to jump in," Raelyn crows as she dips a finger into the cold water.

"No way," I protest.

A mischievous look crosses her face before she sends a wave splashing my way.

I sputter in shock before reaching in and splashing her right back.

We're a mess in our soaked clothes when we finally decide to head back to the manor.

Raelyn looks down at her soiled dress and ruined slippers. "Father and Mother will be furious."

"But nothing bad happened!" I try to reassure her. "Maybe they're just being overprotective."

She nods but bites her lip again, looking anxious.

As we round the corner, muffled shouts come from the manor.

"Kian! Raelyn! Father's booming voice mixes with Lord Astoria's.

"Uh-oh," Raelyn says.

We hurry our steps, and when we reach the terrace, we're met with worried and angry glares.

"*What were you thinking, leaving without asking?*" *Father scolds me loudly, and I can't help but feel embarrassed.*

"*We just wanted to explore a little," I try to explain.*

Raelyn's father looks like he's about to explode, his face a mixture of anger and fear. "Get in the house and clean up immediately, young lady," he commands. "Do you have any idea what could happen?"

She shakes her head and mumbles an apology as she runs into the manor.

"*I'm sorry, Cary," Father says. "Kian can be a little impetuous at times."*

Lord Astoria clenches his fists at his sides. "She's quite allergic to the sun. I only hope we can get her some medicine before—" He sputters, then rambles on, "I don't know what your son did to make her take that risk. Gods help him if—"

"*I said I was sorry, Cary, but don't forget who you're speaking to," Father interrupts, using his king voice. Lord Astoria looks immediately contrite.*

"*Apologies, Your Majesty. I just worry for my daughter."*

"*Quite all right. We should probably be leaving anyhow."*

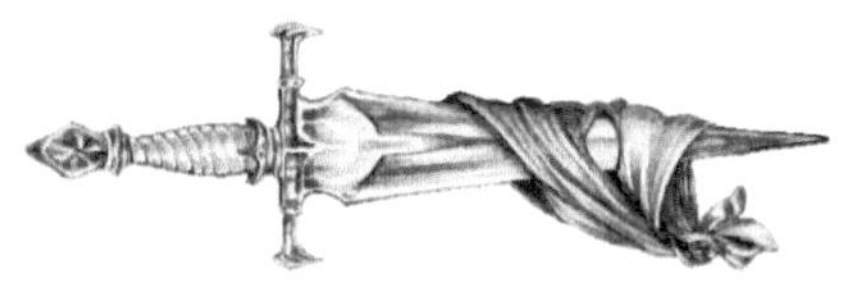

Chapter Thirteen

KIAN

PRESENT

I shake myself from the memory as the front door of House Astoria creaks open and a butler clears his throat. "The master is not in today, but I can tell him you called."

Before he can close the door, I wedge my foot in. "Ah, ah! Not so fast, my good sir. You are aware of who I am?"

The butler frowns and raises a brow. "You don't look familiar, sir."

I repress a groan. The little shit. How would he know who to say had called if he didn't recognize me? Slamming a hand onto the door frame, I try to channel my inner royal. "Prince Kian. Be grateful I'm not making you bow." I shudder inwardly at the asshole prince persona. I never was good at it, unlike my brother. "If the master of the house is not available, I am more than happy to speak to his wife."

This plan has to work. After the disastrous warehouse incident, I've spent all my recovery time pouring into research on Kyros . . . or Cyrus, as I now know he was called. But nothing has turned up any new leads, and I'm feeling desperate. Those missing journal pages have to be somewhere, right? At the very least, I hope I can scope out the study more thoroughly in the daylight so that if I need to return again, I'll know where to look—or where to not waste my time looking. I can't risk being caught again, as delightful as it was having Lady Raelyn on top of me all those weeks ago. I smirk even as I chastise myself for letting her take up space in my mind.

Nothing about the woman makes sense to me. From the way I'm inexplicably drawn to her to the way all of our encounters seem to be erased from her memory. Am I cursed by the gods to fall for a woman who can't remember me, or is she playing some sick and twisted game?

"Apologies, Your Highness. It has been too long since I've been to court," the butler simpers as he takes my hat and coat to the cloakroom.

"I'll let it go this once," I call after him before straightening the lapel on my undercoat, taking a moment to look around the foyer without the overabundance of flowers. The grand staircase gleams in the afternoon light, polished to perfection. They must have quite a few servants to keep the place looking as pristine as it does, which strikes me as odd, considering what I know of Lord Astoria's financial difficulties. Perhaps the new lady of the house had enough to refill his coffers or the debt I thought he was in had been an exaggeration.

The butler returns, his posture stiff as he refuses to meet my gaze. "I'm not quite sure where the lady of the house is, but I'm happy to go look for her if you don't mind waiting."

Perfect. Some time alone is just what I need.

"Surely you wouldn't have me standing here, waiting in the foyer," I say. "Lead me to the lord's study. I'm certain he would be appalled if I wasn't offered a drink while I waited."

The butler pauses, and I can see him turning the request over in his head. I realize it might be a little unorthodox to invite myself into someone's study, but sitting in an empty parlor will not help me accomplish what I came here to do. Gods willing Lord Astoria is as stingy with his liquors as I suspect and stashes them safely there.

Before he can say no, I tip my head and motion. "Well? Lead the way."

To my relief, he acquiesces—perhaps being the prince comes with some perks—and I follow him down the hall toward the study.

A melodic sound filters through the click of our heels on the polished floor, and I catch a flash of auburn as I pass an open doorway.

Wait. I halt and back up a pace, peeking into the room. The melody continues, and the hairs on the back of my neck rise at its haunting simplicity. A maid with reddish-brown hair kneels on the marble floor, polishing away. Ah, so not the Lady Raelyn then. I shake off the flash of disappointment as I hurry to catch up with the butler.

The melody follows me down the hall, and I fight the urge to turn around and go back, but no. I'm here for a purpose.

The butler ushers me into the study and draws back the curtains. With a glance at the overcast sky, he shakes his head and moves to light the lamps while I nonchalantly wander over to the drink cart and pick up a crystal decanter. After giving it a quick sniff, I hum approvingly.

"Yes, this will do nicely."

I pour myself a glass before the butler can reach me, and he sighs in clear exasperation. "I guess I'll leave you to it then. I'll return with Lady Astoria shortly." He glances over his shoulder at the door, as if second-guessing his decision to allow me to remain here unattended.

I give him a lazy smile and knock back a sip of the liquor before settling into one of the leather armchairs. "No rush. I'm happy to enjoy this fine drink while I wait."

He nods before disappearing out the door.

The second he's gone, I set down the drink and get to work. My gaze sweeps the room, looking for anything I might have missed in the dark. I curse under my breath. This will take way longer than I probably have. With any luck, Lady Astoria will be indisposed and unavailable for at least ten minutes. Is that asking too much? Gods, I hope not. Even as I think about them, I can't help but wish they might send a little extra luck my way.

Standing in front of the bookshelves, I start where I left off, randomly tugging on items, wondering if there might be a secret room full of valuable information hidden behind it.

Idiot. That only happens in books, not real life. Perhaps there's a hollowed-out book full of the loose pages I'm looking for? A map? I start to feel dismay as I realize this is not going my way.

Time to check out the desk. Opening a drawer, I carefully look through the documents, trying not to disturb anything. I fumble around for any hidden drawers or locks until the melody that captivated me comes closer. I curse again.

Dashing back over to the chair, I pick up my drink, hoping I look relaxed when the maid enters the room, a large bucket slung over her arm.

Her jade eyes meet mine, and she gasps, quickly taking a step back. The soapy water sloshes over the side and onto the floor, and to my surprise, a filthy curse leaves her mouth.

Wait.

"Lady Raelyn?" I ask, shocked that she's in maid's garb and doing hard labor in her own home.

She sets the bucket onto the floor and grumbles something unintelligible as she drops to her knees and sops up the soapy mess. Overcome with surprise, I completely forget my manners. I'm about to jump up and offer my help, but she turns her eyes back up toward mine and glares. How interesting. Is it too much to hope she hasn't once again forgotten who I am?

"Do you normally wait unusually long amounts of time to answer simple questions?" I blurt out, needing to break the awkward silence.

"You said my name. I didn't hear a question."

"Surely you heard the tone."

"If you say so," she says, tossing her braid over her shoulder and rising. "You shouldn't be in here."

I hold my hands out. "Well, I am."

She scoffs before tucking a stray tendril of hair behind her ear. "Father isn't home. You have no business in his study, prince or not."

So she does remember. What's different this time? I tilt my head.

"Shouldn't you be off having tea or something? Why in the gods' names are you cleaning the floors?"

I don't miss the flash of anger in her eyes before she dons a mask of indifference.

"Lady Astoria likes to keep me busy."

"And what of your sisters? I don't see them cleaning the manor."

Her shoulders stiffen. "I presume they are too busy planning weddings and the like."

My glass clinks as it hits the stone coaster on the table, and her eyes follow the movement. I jump to my feet and prowl toward her. Her brow crinkles, and as I step closer, she takes a step back.

"What are you doing?" she breathes.

I reach out and grab one of her hands, inspecting it, then holding it up to her face. "Your hands are cracked and bleeding. You mean to tell me your father approves of this?"

She tugs her hand away. "It's none of your concern, Your Highness."

The bitterness in her tone gives her away, and I'm inexplicably angry on her behalf. "I think I'll have a word with Lady Astoria about this."

A flash of fear lights up her eyes. "No. Please don't. She would only find a way to take it out on me."

Ah. This *is* the lady's doing. I step back. "If you insist."

"I do." Lady Raelyn straightens again. "Sorry to bother you, Your Highness. I'll get out of your hair and leave you to your drink."

She picks up her bucket and nearly collides with Lady Astoria and the butler in her rush to leave the study.

Gods help me. My time has run out.

"Fool girl," the lady chides. "You almost ruined my gown!"

"Apologies," Lady Raelyn mutters before escaping.

The disdain written all over Lady Astoria's face makes me irrationally angry. Why in the realms would she loathe Cary's daughter this way? Whatever did she do to her?

"Your Highness," she says stiffly. "What a surprise to see you here." She drops into a halfhearted curtsy. "Is there something I can do for you? My husband is out of town, as you are aware."

"I believe the lord has information for me. Would you happen to know where he left it?"

Confusion flares in her eyes. "I'm afraid I have no idea what you're talking about, Your Highness."

"What a shame," I say. "To think I wasted my time coming out here for nothing." I desperately wish to say something biting about her treatment of her stepdaughter, but I also want to respect Lady Raelyn's wishes. I'd hate to make things worse for her.

Lady Astoria huffs in annoyance. "Pardon, Your Highness, but your presence has caused quite an interruption in my day. If there is nothing else I can do for you, I suggest you leave."

Shock at her disrespect sends a surge of anger through me. "Do not forget yourself, my lady. I'd hate to let the king hear of your lack of hospitality."

"Apologies, Your Highness. I was not expecting to entertain today."

Before I say something I regret, I turn up my nose and walk past her.

THE DOOR THUDS behind me as I march down the manor's steps toward my horse. Was it all a fool's errand? Does Cary even have what I need?

He has to. I have no other leads, and I'm desperate.

Father has also been getting on me about not having chosen a wife yet. His threats to arrange a marriage loom over me like a hangman's noose. The absolute last thing I want is to be tied to some simpering lady who only cares about which dresses she can commission for the next ball or party at court.

Of course, perhaps that is exactly the kind of woman I need to keep my vigilante work unnoticed . . . but then wouldn't she expect me to attend said parties with her? I can't win. No matter who I end up with, my marriage will effectively shackle me into a life I don't want. Maybe I just need to get it over with and procure a back-up heir so Father will loosen the reins a little and allow me to go on my quest. Except our people are running out of options. Our land grows more barren with each passing season, and I'm not sure how much time we realistically have left.

I pace in front of my horse, and he gives me what I think is a wry look—if horses can do such a thing. What am I still doing here? I need to be on my way, but something holds me back.

Jade eyes flash in my mind. Is she close to her father? She did seem rather protective of him and his space. Is it possible *she* might know of the information I seek? Not that our latest encounter did me any favors with her. But still . . . what if there's a way to solve both of our problems? She didn't ask for my help, but I hate how she's being treated. Past hurts aside, I'm finding it hard to let go.

Moving on impulse alone, I walk toward the side of the manor. Godly intervention, or restlessness? Not sure, but in this case, I choose to trust my instincts.

Chapter Fourteen

RAELYN

I have never been more humiliated in my entire life. Well, perhaps that's an exaggeration, but running into Prince Kian while cleaning the floors is not what I had in mind for today, or any day, for that matter.

Why do I even care? Perhaps because I still have some pride left despite Stepmother's attempts to break me down. The last time I saw the prince, I still had some status in my own home, and now . . . I sigh. Now I'm the family's primary housemaid.

Once again, water sloshes out of my pail, and I bite back a curse. Dropping to my knees, I sop up the mess, which again reminds me of earlier. I flush when I recall the filthy words that came out of my mouth in the prince's presence—mad that I even care what he thinks. I've heard the rumors about the playboy prince. Though I hadn't officially met him before the ball, my sisters love to share court gossip.

According to them, he has never seriously courted anyone and is rumored to be with a new woman every night. Him choosing to dance with me meant absolutely nothing. I was just the latest in a long line of conquests, not that he conquered me.

I can admit to myself that he holds a certain appeal. His quicksilver eyes drew me in, heating parts of me I thought long dormant. The phantom touch of his hand around my wrist flares as I recall the look in his eyes when he realized how far I've fallen in the month since I saw him last—my dried and cracked hands unable to hide the destruction wrought by harsh soaps and chemicals despite my attempts at healing them with oils every evening. No. I have no interest in the prince. I need to put him out of my thoughts and memories.

Blowing out a frustrated breath, I make my way to the kitchen to empty my bucket of its filthy contents. After ringing out the rags, I deposit them in the laundry basket. That's my next task, and I shudder; my hands will likely be in even worse shape after that. There isn't a hope in my heart that I'll have any energy to spare for my needlework later this evening. I almost miss the occasional finger pricks, which pale in comparison to the abuse my hands suffer now.

An icy breeze blows through the door as one of our cooks enters the kitchen with a basket full of produce, and a sudden longing for fresh air fills me. The laundry can wait another moment. I still feel fine after my accidental sun exposure this morning, and an irrational part of me thinks being sick in bed for a few days might actually be better than cleaning from sunup to sundown.

Like a string pulling me, I'm drawn to the door and step out into the late afternoon sunlight. My breath catches as its rays warm me from the inside out despite the cold. My hands start to tingle ever so slightly, but I continue to breathe deeply as I turn my face to the sun.

"Now that's a sight," a low, familiar voice remarks.

My heart skips a beat as I turn toward the prince. "What are you still doing here?" I demand, annoyed yet somehow thrilled that he's managed to disturb my brief moment of respite.

"You wound me, love. It's almost as if you don't want to see me." He smirks.

I can't help but roll my eyes. "First you were in Father's study, which

I'm sure he wouldn't approve of, and now you're wandering the grounds without an escort?"

"I'm a prince. Why would I need an escort?"

My jaw drops. "Entitled much?"

He laughs brightly, and the sound sends shivers down my spine. Why do I love his laugh so much?

The prince tilts his head. "Cold?" He starts to shrug out of his overcoat, but I hold up a hand to stop him.

"No, thank you. I'm quite all right."

He frowns as he pulls his coat back into place, and the harshness of his features instantly make me long for his laughter again.

"Shouldn't you be back at court doing 'princely' things?" I ask.

He quirks a brow. "Trying to get rid of me again, my lady?"

I scoff and point at my ruined clothes. "Clearly, I am no lady anymore."

He tuts as he takes a step closer. "While some might say clothes make a lord, a lady, or even, daresay, a prince"—he pauses and flashes brilliantly white teeth at me—"it is one's character that defines them."

"That was oddly . . . profound," I reply.

Hurt crosses his features, and he steps away. "What? Is it so hard to believe that the playboy prince has an ounce of profundity to him?"

I open my mouth to respond, but he waves me off. "I'm fully aware of how people speak of me and what my reputation is."

The surge of empathy I feel toward him almost chokes me. Perhaps I've misjudged this prince.

"While my reputation as the reclusive Astoria might not be quite as negative as yours, I do empathize with the pain of not being understood." I offer him a smile, and tension leaves his body, his own lips turning up slightly.

Clearing his throat, he says, "Regardless of what brought me here, perhaps our meeting is of the gods' design. I have an idea I wish to speak with you about."

I frown. What in the realms could he possibly want to discuss with me?

The prince looks up into the sky and then at me, worry creasing his brow. "Is it safe for you to be out here now? With the sun?"

I shrug. "It's complicated, but it's a risk I'm willing to take."

He frowns again. "Okay . . . in that case, would you please walk with me?"

Hesitating, I chew on my lip and look around. I really ought to be starting the laundry before dinner, and I hate to think of the foul mood Stepmother will be in after the prince's unexpected visit.

"I don't know, Your Highness." I tug on the fabric of my skirt. "While clothes might not define a person, I'm still expected to complete the tasks Stepmother has for me, and the day is running out."

"This won't take long, but I really would rather not be overheard," he replies.

My interest piqued, I glance around once more. "Okay, fine. As long as you make it quick."

He dips into a slight bow. "You have my word, my lady."

I take his proffered arm without a second thought. The prince frowns as he stares at my hand. Immediately self-conscious, I try to pull away, but he starts walking toward the gardens, and I quicken my steps to keep up with his long stride.

"So, Your Highness, what is it you wish to discuss?" I ask.

"I'm not sure how far the rumors have spread, but perhaps you might have heard my father intends for me to marry by the end of the season."

My heart skips a beat. It seems to happen quite a bit around him. *Why is he telling me this?* "And this is something you are looking forward to?"

A wry laugh leaves him. "Absolutely not. I have no desire to be bound in marriage."

The odd flicker of disappointment surprises me. Not that I have any reason to care one way or the other. "Forgive me, my prince. I'm not quite sure what any of this has to do with me. I'm sorry you're being forced to wed though. I, for one, think marriage is a waste of time if you have no actual interest in it."

The prince stops and turns to face me. "Perhaps this will work even better than I thought."

"Pardon?"

"Let's get betrothed." The words tumble out of him so quickly, I surely must be hearing wrong.

"What?"

"It's perfect," he declares. "Neither one of us wants to be wed, but on paper, it will make my father happy, and with the status of our betrothal, surely your stepmother will have no choice but to release you from these ridiculous chores she has you doing."

I sputter in shock. I don't even know where to start with this absurd idea and the conflicting feelings overwhelming me.

"Let me get this straight," I say. "You want me to be bound to you in name only just to please your father and to get me out of doing laundry?"

A laugh bursts out of him again, and I hate how my body responds to it.

"Something like that, my lady. You can live your life how you choose, and I can live mine. We can make up some excuse regarding heirs so you won't need to worry about that either for the time being."

Warmth heats my cheeks at the insinuation, and I look down at my feet. What do I even say to that?

"No need to look so scandalized, love," the prince teases. "As I said, this would be on paper only, no need for it to go any further than that, as you've made it clear you're not interested in marriage."

True as that might be now, what if I were interested someday? If I were bound to the prince, that would take away any chance of me ever having a real marriage. Was that something I could live with?

"I . . . uh . . . That's an interesting offer, Your Highness," I finally reply, daring a glance back up at him.

His lips turn down. "I thought for sure you'd jump at the opportunity."

I should. I really should. My home is not my home any longer. I'm miserable and tired, and life has felt so entirely hopeless.

The prince gently turns my face back to his, and I loathe how I respond to the simple touch. "Do you need more time to think it over?"

Staring into his eyes, I wonder if I'm about to make the biggest mistake of my life. My stomach is doing somersaults, but I take a breath before saying, "Okay."

His brow rises. "Okay?"

"Okay as in yes. I'll marry you."

"Perfect. I knew this plan would work." He grins.

Oh gods, I'm in trouble.

"But I have some requests," I add.

"Oh? Already?" He shakes his head before motioning with his hand. "Out with it."

I bite my lip, noticing how his eyes dart toward the movement and linger before he raises them back to mine. "I don't want to be the laughingstock of court."

"Go on."

"If we are to wed in name only, I am sure you will still have *needs* that must be met."

"I do admit, I'm quite curious where you are going with this, love," the prince replies. I can't stop the blush as he takes a step closer. "Are you offering your services to meet my . . . *needs*?"

"Gods no!" I exclaim, even as the flutters in my belly make it hard to breathe.

A wicked grin curls his lips. "I'm still very much intrigued."

I blush even more furiously. "Nothing like that, Your Highness. I just mean to ask . . ." *Gods, why is this so hard?*

"Yes?"

"What I was trying to say is that I'm aware of your reputation, and even if our marriage is on paper only, I do not wish for everyone at court to think I'm unworthy of your affections."

A flicker of understanding lights his eyes. "I see."

"Do you?" I ask, hating that I even need to try to explain myself . . . explain these thoughts.

"You're asking me to stop my 'playboy ways.'"

"Yes—well, no . . ." I stammer. "I realize you have needs. I would just request that you be discreet in the ways that you meet them."

The prince stiffens, and I note the way he clenches his fists at his sides, but he nods. "That's fair."

I heave a sigh of relief but tense up as the prince takes another step toward me.

"And what of *your* needs, love?" The way his voice envelops me sends another rush of heat, only this time, it heads south.

"My . . . needs?" I stammer.

He takes one more step, and our bodies are almost close enough to touch. I have to crane my neck to look him in the eyes. What in the gods' names is his game?

"It's only fair," he continues. "I'll keep my needs met discreetly so long as you do the same."

I swallow, and his gaze drops to my throat. "I can agree to that." My voice comes out all breathy. I hate it.

"Good."

"Good," I repeat. "Oh, and one other thing."

"Yes?"

"Stop calling me love." Our gazes hold, and for a moment, I forget to breathe, but then he winks.

"Now that's too much, love."

He steps back, and the sudden breathing room brings a sense of relief along with the tiniest prick of disappointment.

I take a deep breath. This is probably a huge mistake. "So what now?"

The prince looks thoughtful. "I suppose I need to speak with your father about the marriage contract. Do you happen to know when he'll return?"

I shake my head. "I would like to hope he'll return soon, but I have no way of knowing. He hasn't sent word."

"That will definitely slow our plans," the prince muses.

I have to admit, I'm confused why it matters to him. Surely if he told his father his intentions, that would assuage the king's concerns. The delay only really affects me.

"Perhaps you could come back to the manor later on and inform Stepmother of your intention to court me?" I offer. "Surely she couldn't turn you down."

"I suppose." The prince smirks. "That just means you'll need to suffer my presence once more."

I scoff. "It could be worse. I could be doing laundry."

The prince places his hand on his chest. "Once again, you wound me, lady. I am only better than laundry?"

"Only slightly," I tease, offering him a smirk.

"Fine then. I will inform my father of my intention to court you, and when I return, hopefully the news will improve things for you here at home."

I nod. "I hope so."

"Well, I should be off before someone catches us out here alone. Best not start our relationship off with a scandal."

"How kind of you, Your Highness."

"Kian."

"What?"

He smiles, a softer one than I've seen. "Please call me Kian. If I am to be your husband, we can do away with some of the formalities."

"Kian," I test out. It will take some getting used to. Court formalities have been drilled into me my entire life, but I suppose he is right.

Kian grabs my hand and presses a soft kiss to it. "Until we meet again, my la—"

"Raelyn," I interrupt.

A devilish smirk makes him far too delectable for words, and I can't ignore the butterflies in my stomach as he replies, "Farewell, Raelyn."

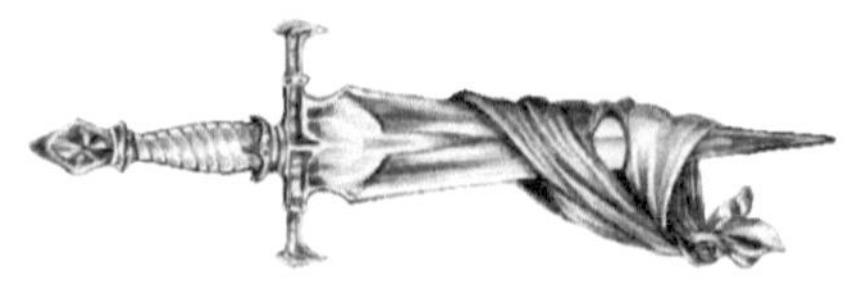

Chapter Fifteen

KIAN

My steps are light as I rush back through the gardens to my horse. While my visit did not quite go to plan, this new development sends a thrill through me. Perhaps I'm a fool to betroth myself to a woman who doesn't actually want to be with me, but I'm no stranger to foolish choices. The arrangement should at least appease my father and improve Lady Raelyn's quality of life.

I look to the sky and curse; the sun has disappeared behind the tree line, indicating that I have dallied far too long. Another shipment is expected this evening, and my alter ego has plans to disrupt it. As much as it pains me, I promised Alex he could come along this time. A trial run to see if he can keep up.

My mind drifts back to Raelyn . . . Gods, I really hope this marriage isn't a mistake. Despite all the unanswered questions, I believe her to be a cunning thing. I will need to be extra careful to not let her get caught up in my work as the Shadow.

Memories of Raelyn holding me at knifepoint in the study that night weeks ago flash before my eyes, putting thoughts in my head I dare not dwell on . . . but those curves pressed up against me? I swear under my breath. That is not what we just agreed to. Besides, being the Shadow is what matters most—saving my people and finding the lost god. Getting distracted by a beautiful woman will not do. Even if she is my wife . . . especially if she is my wife. Better for her to believe the lies about my playboy persona and keep her at a distance.

⊶━

"Welcome back, Your Highness. I realize you just got here, but His Majesty has requested your presence in his wing immediately upon your return."

I hold back a groan as Giles delivers the unwanted missive. Time is already short. The last thing I want is another lecture from my father.

"Can you pretend you didn't see me?" I joke.

Giles looks around uncomfortably. "I'm afraid not, Your Highness."

"Fine then. I'll head there immediately."

Almost as if he doesn't trust me, Giles follows behind as I climb the stairs and veer to the right instead of the left toward my wing. Perhaps if I inform Father of my upcoming betrothal, he'll be too happy to lecture me.

Pushing open the door to his favorite sitting room, I'm surprised to see my brother in deep discussion with Father. With his child due in the next week or two, I thought Colin and his wife, Juliana, would be sequestered on our country estate, far away from the noise of court.

It bothers me that we've grown apart. Once he was bound, his new wife became his entire world and he completely shut me out. That and his seeming lack of care for our people has made me keep my distance. Every once in a while, I find myself wishing things were different, that we could be as close as we'd once been.

"Kian!" my father calls out. "We were just discussing you."

Fantastic. *What did I do this time?*

"Good evening, Father, Colin."

"Have a seat, my boy," Father says jovially. He must be deep in his cups.

I sit on the edge of the settee, nodding when my brother holds up an empty tumbler. Something tells me I'm going to need this drink.

"Where are you coming from?" Father asks.

Better now than later, I guess. "I was at House Astoria."

My brother frowns. "Why in the gods' names were you there?"

"I was hoping to discuss a marriage contract with Lord Astoria. Unfortunately for me, he was not home."

The king laughs. "I could have told you that. His business for me took him quite a distance."

Well shit. This could definitely put a damper on my plans.

"Did you say marriage contract?" my brother asks.

"Yes. Haven't you heard? Father demanded I marry by the end of the season."

"Cooperating with Father's requests? That *is* quite a shock," Colin mutters.

I shoot him a glare before knocking back the burning liquid.

"I suppose it's for the best he wasn't home," the king says, staring at me over the rim of his tumbler. "Your brother has managed to procure a much better match for you than one of the Astorias."

I almost choke on my drink. "He did what?"

"Yes, that's why I needed to see you so urgently," Father replies, his demeanor ironically far from urgent.

"Is that so." I shoot another glare at my brother. "I was unaware Colin was on the lookout for a wife for me."

Colin gives me a wry grin. "It was fully unintentional, I swear. Obviously it couldn't be someone from our court due to your *reputation*."

His words sting, but I try to hide it. It's bad enough Father thinks the worst of me, but to know Colin does as well is a knife to the gut. Even with the distance between us, I thought he knew me, but I guess I was wrong.

"Unintentional as it might have been," Father continues, "the match is advantageous to our kingdom."

"You said I could choose," I grit out. "I chose."

"I'm sure it's nothing that can't be undone," Father replies.

"Damn it, Father. I made a promise and now you want me to back out on my word?" I try to keep myself from shouting.

"Kian, why don't you hear us out before losing your temper," Colin says smoothly. "I'm sure you'll agree to this arrangement."

"Not likely," I mumble.

"Princess Helene is the perfect match for you, son," Father says.

Princess Helene? As in my brother's sister-in-law? I grimace.

"She's at the country estate with Juliana now, and she's dying to have you come and call on her," my brother continues, amusement coloring his tone.

"Forgive me, but how in the gods' names is it advantageous for me to marry into the same damn family Colin is already married into?" I seethe. "Surely your alliance with the kingdom of Tallinnia is already secure."

Father strokes his chin. "You're not wrong, but—"

"But nothing," I interject. "Princess Helene is barely seventeen years of age. I have no desire to be shackled to that infant."

"Come now, brother, she is a beautiful young woman, and with a betrothal in place now, you will have at least one more year to dally as you please before settling down. I thought that would make you happy?" Colin looks perplexed, as if he thought I would thank him for offering his wife's baby sister up to me on a silver platter.

"I refuse."

"Excuse me?" Father glares. "How dare you refuse me? I am your king, and you will do as I wish."

"I *have* done as you wished, Father. I have procured a betrothal to Lady Raelyn and have no need of Princess Helene."

"I had no idea you were even still interested in that family," Father says. "Didn't the girl reject you years ago?"

My face heats in humiliation.

"You can't seriously be considering giving in to his demands," Colin spits out. "I already promised—"

"You promised me without my permission?" I shout at Colin. "What in the ever-loving fuck is your problem?"

"Boys!" Father exclaims. "You will cease with the name-calling and cursing. I didn't raise you to be a bunch of low-class rabble."

I pinch the bridge of my nose, attempting to ward off the inevitable headache.

"As you do not actually have a contract with Lord Astoria in place, let's table this discussion for now," Father declares. "I am willing to compromise . . . a little."

Both Colin and I look at him and then each other, wondering what he has up his sleeve.

"As I do not wish to anger the royal family of Tallinnia, you will take some time to court Princess Helene. If you are still not amenable to the idea by the end of the season, I will allow you to marry the Astoria girl."

"That is unacceptable, Father. I have already promised to court Lady Raelyn."

"Court them both! I don't give a fuck at this point."

Father must be truly well into his cups if he is willing to cuss at us, especially after telling us not to.

My face falls into the palm of my hand, and I hold back a groan. Leave it to Father and Colin to make my life even more complicated than it already is. At this rate, I don't know if I'll make it to the drop point in time. But I need to find a way to prove to Father that Raelyn is of more value to our family than Princess Helene.

A niggling voice in my head wonders why I care so much about keeping my word to Raelyn. She did reject and hurt me, and yet she seems oblivious to that. Would she care if I called it off? It's not like it was going to be a real marriage . . . but just the thought of letting her down has my stomach roiling.

Courting both Raelyn and Princess Helene at the same time is the absolute last thing I have time for. I am truly and completely in over my head.

Chapter Sixteen

RAELYN

Did that really just happen? Did the prince . . . did Kian truly just ask me to marry him? I shiver as the sun dips beneath the horizon and night sweeps across the land. Damn. I'm so behind on my chores.

I desperately want to leave them be. Kian will make his intentions known soon enough, and gods willing, I won't be trapped as our family's primary maid any longer. At least, I hope not.

A part of me wants to squeal with joy at the thought of escaping the home that has become like a prison. I will have the status of a princess of the realm without actually needing to fulfill the role. Could it be any more perfect?

I try to ignore the voice in my head asking me if this is what I really want—asking if I no longer believe in marrying for love someday the way I used to. *No. Hush. That's ridiculous.* Love is a fairytale not meant for me.

But, oh, to be able to laze about for an entire day with nothing to clean and endless books to read . . . it's the best dream. If Kian can give me that, I can willingly shut the door on the possibility of love. While he said I could find lovers of my own, that sounds exhausting. If I truly need a release, there are other ways to go about it.

Hurrying back into the manor, I try to sneak through a side door to grab the wash, but when I turn the corner, it's gone.

"Forget something?" a snarky voice cuts from behind me.

I turn around, and there's Chessa, swathed in a pink silk dress, tapping her foot next to the basket of rags. It's almost comical seeing the juxtaposition of filth and riches, but I know this is merely a ploy meant to cause me misery.

"I could have sworn I saw laundry on your list of chores today, *sister*," she sneers. "You're always so forgetful."

"Are you offering to take care of it for me?" I retort.

Chessa's eyes almost bug out of her face in horror. "Me?" She lays a delicate hand on her small chest. "There is no possible way my nails could withstand that chore."

"Or any chore," I mutter under my breath. "What are you doing here then?"

"Looking for you, of course. You're always with the help." Her pretty face turns ugly with the vitriol she spews toward me.

"Well, you've found me."

"Yes, I have . . . and I have much to report to Mama."

I can't stop the eye roll. The fact that she calls that witch of a stepmother "Mama" is a disgrace to our dead mother, may she rest in Celestia with the gods.

"Well, get on with it then." I wave my hand at her. "I obviously have much work to do."

"Unfortunately," she grits out, "you've been requested at dinner this evening. I was told to make sure you show up presentably."

"Dinner?" Has Kian spoken to my stepmother already? Am I finally going to be free? I'm almost afraid to get my hopes up.

"Yes, that's what I said, wasn't it?" She flips her hair as she turns around. "Dinner is in thirty minutes. Do not make me look bad."

Of course it's always about her in the end, but thirty minutes is not nearly enough time to make myself presentable, especially without Sera's help. Oh, how I miss her biting tongue and stories of other realms.

The laundry will have to wait. I dash up the servants' stairs toward my room and barrel through the door. While I don't have time for a bath, I can at least change my clothes and fix my hair.

I fly into the bathing chamber to take care of my needs, but as I wash my hands, I gasp. They are smooth and soft, the cracks from the harsh soaps nowhere to be seen. What in the gods' names happened? Before I can fixate on my hands too much and find myself late to dinner, I splash water on my face and startle again. The late afternoon sun turned my skin a flushed and healthy-looking pink, so different from my normally pale hue. A few freckles spatter my nose, just like the ones from the day of the ball that disappeared after my stint in bed. Interesting. Today has been full of surprises, that's for sure.

Closing my eyes, I take a moment to really consider how I feel. I'm not sure if the weird flips in my stomach are from the anticipation of my impending betrothal or the beginnings of a reaction to my affliction. I've been so careful for years and years, and now I've risked my health twice in the matter of a month.

I dry off and move to my closet, looking for something acceptable to wear. Unfortunately, it looks as if my sisters have stolen all of the nice dresses I own. An out-of-style day dress is all I have, so I quickly change into it. Gods willing, it won't be the cause of more ire between myself and Stepmother. Perhaps I'll steal my dresses back when my sisters are occupied.

It really is shocking how quickly they turned on me and decided treating me like the help was something I somehow deserved. All because I'm unmarried. I'll show them. Their jealousy will eat them alive when they find out that Kian chose me as his bride.

The ringing of the dinner bell has me cursing as I twist my hair into a coil on the back of my head while I run out the door and down the stairs. Dinner will not wait.

"Ratlyn," Charlie says, sounding surprised as I enter the dining room.

"Good to see you too, brother," I bite out. Gods, I really hate that nickname.

Erika and Chessa are chattering with each other but grow quiet when I find my seat, taking a deep breath to calm my nerves. "No need to stop talking on my account," I grumble.

Giving each other knowing looks, Chess tosses her pin-straight hair over her shoulder and continues their conversation. "I thought *you* might have had a chance with the prince after he danced with you," Chess says to Erika, putting on a fake pout.

"With a princess in the mix? Unlikely," Erika replies morosely.

My ears perk up. A princess?

"What are you two going on about?" I ask as I fiddle with the silverware in front of me.

"Erika just got back from court today," Chessa brags. "I was supposed to join her, but Mama had me in lessons all afternoon."

The ache in my back reminds me of how much time I spent scrubbing on my knees today, and it takes everything in my power to bite my tongue to keep from sniping at her.

"What rumors are floating around court these days?" I direct my question to Erika.

She blushes, refusing to meet my eyes. Perhaps she, out of all my siblings, actually feels a touch of guilt about how I've been treated. "Well, Princess Helene is in town visiting her sister . . ."

I nod. With Princess Juliana so close to giving birth to the long-awaited heir to the Rakveren throne, it makes sense.

"All of court is abuzz with word that an arrangement between Princess Helene and Prince Kian is imminent."

A pit forms in my stomach. Why didn't Kian say something about this earlier? Perhaps Erika is mistaken.

"Interesting," I choke out.

"Raelyn," Stepmother sneers as she enters the dining room. "I see you got the message."

A thank you almost rolls off my tongue, but I stop myself. This woman deserves no thanks for inviting me to dinner in my own damn home.

With Stepmother's appearance, the kitchen staff start placing the first course in front of us, and I say a thank you to them instead. "It smells delicious." I smile.

"Raelyn," Stepmother reprimands, "you will not speak to them."

The maid almost cowers as she hurries back to the kitchen, and I turn to glare at Stepmother.

"Why not? You treat me like one of them, so why wouldn't I speak to them?"

The daggers coming out of her eyes make me want to hide, but I refuse. I can't wait to wipe the smug look off her face when she hears my news, assuming the rumors about Kian's betrothal are false . . .

"If you are not able to show a modicum of decorum at my table, you might as well leave now." She seethes.

I'm ready to throw my napkin onto the table and rise to my feet, but no. I deserve to be here just as much as my siblings. I grit my teeth and plant a fake smile on my face. My sister has to be wrong about the princess. This had better be a swift betrothal, because I am more than ready to get out of the manor.

"To what do I owe the pleasure of this invitation to dinner?" I ask, feigning pleasantness.

Erika chokes on her drink, and I turn my gaze to her. Will it ever stop hurting? That my siblings so callously aligned themselves with Stepmother?

"Ah yes." Stepmother clears her throat. "I just wanted to inform you that you will need to move out of your room by the end of tomorrow."

"Excuse me, but did I hear that correctly?" My eyes dart around the table, and neither one of my sisters nor my brother will meet my eyes.

"Don't play dumb, Raelyn," Stepmother chides. "It's unbecoming."

I flinch. "Surely, I misheard you. Why in the realms must I leave my room?"

"I have need of it," she replies matter-of-factly.

"Where am I supposed to go?" I ask, fighting to stay calm.

"You can make up one of the rooms in the servants' quarters."

"That is utterly absurd," I say, no longer caring about decorum. Rising to my feet, I point a finger at my horrible stepmother. "Father will not stand for this."

"Oh, sweet child, he's not here, is he?" She smirks.

"You have no right!"

"I have every right," she says with a sneer. "I am the lady of this manor, and you will do as I say, or, quite simply, you will leave."

Tears prick my eyes. I glance around the table once more at my traitorous siblings. Still, none of them will look at me. Rage builds inside me, and my hands burn with heat.

"You are dismissed. And Raelyn? I am aware of your laziness and refusal to complete your chores today. The staff have been informed not to feed you tonight as your punishment."

So my invitation to dinner was a complete farce. Got it.

I rush from the room, and as much as I desperately want to fight the injustice, I cannot. How much more can she take from me? I withhold my sobs as I race up the stairs toward my room . . . well, my room for the night.

How did I get here?

Collapsing onto my bed, I let the sobs overtake me. I'm alone. So incredibly alone. My heart is shredded inside my chest.

I have no one. Father, the only one who might have stood up for me, is no longer here. My siblings have abandoned me. For all I know, the prince will abandon me too, his plan forgotten now that a better option has presented itself.

A gnawing sensation eats at me from the inside, and I double over in pain. My jaw aches, perhaps from clenching my teeth, but there is no relief.

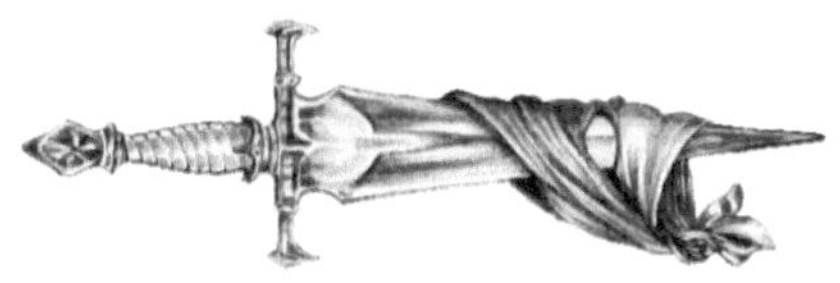

Chapter Seventeen

KIAN

"Well that all went to shit," Alex grumbles as he runs a hand through his muddied hair.

"You're telling me," I agree.

We had hardly any time to prepare for the night's raid after my disastrous meeting with Father and Colin.

Things did not go to plan, and we barely escaped capture. Though if Alex hadn't been with me, I probably wouldn't have made it out at all.

"I fear my father is getting smarter," I say. "There were definitely more guards than usual."

"I can't believe you've been doing this on your own."

I groan as I peel my bloodied leathers off my body. As much as I hate to admit it, we work well together. I hate the extra danger he's putting himself in though.

"Hells, your shoulder is a mess." Alex grimaces at the sight.

"It'll heal." Burly Man, my current nemesis, nearly got the better of me again.

"Going to see Margot?"

"I don't have a choice. A court healer is way too risky. Besides, she's my favorite."

He sighs. "I can't believe you stepped in front of that arrow for me."

I shake my head. "It wasn't even a choice. It was my fault you almost got caught out there with me. The last thing I'd allow is for you to take an arrow meant for me."

Alex pats my opposite shoulder, but I can't hold back the wince as it reverberates through me.

"Oh shit. Sorry, Ki."

"Don't worry about it."

"I'm just glad you actually asked me to come. If you'd been out there on your own . . . there's no telling what would have happened. The guards seemed keen on killing first and asking questions later."

"You're not wrong."

Father's tactics for catching the vigilante are escalating. It's clear he wants him taken out of the picture completely.

Alex follows me into my closet, and I open the secret compartment filled with medical supplies. I toss him a roll of bandages and grab the bottle of antiseptic. After pulling the cork out with my teeth, I spit it out and use my good arm to splash it onto my shoulder, hissing at the sting.

"Have you decided how you're going to handle courting two women?" Alex asks, changing the subject.

As much as I appreciate the distraction, I don't have the answer to that question just yet.

"I'm not sure how I ended up here. I didn't want to marry anyone at the beginning of the season, and now Father and Colin are shoving Princess Helene at me the second I make an agreement with the Astoria girl."

"That's some terrible luck, that's for sure," he agrees as he wraps my shoulder with the bandage.

I groan, partially from the pain, partially from the aggravation of my situation. "What do you think I should do?" I ask.

"Well, the biggest concern is keeping your secret, right?"

"That's definitely up there," I say. "But to be honest, I'm torn. Raelyn might have the access I need to her father's information on the lost god, but on the other hand, a betrothal to Helene would mean I'd have more time to go out and search for him. I'm not sure that would be the case were I bound to Raelyn."

"That does seem like a problem," Alex replies but then waggles his eyebrows. "Who do you think is more attractive?"

I shake my head. "Helene is still practically a child. I don't even want to think about her like that."

"As much as I hate the practice, we both know that betrothals are arranged between royals all the time, regardless of age," Alex says matter-of-factly. "Wasn't your brother betrothed when he was still a child?"

"Yeah . . . but still." I shudder. "No thanks." My mind flashes back to Raelyn, and I groan again as my attraction for her makes itself known in my already tight pants. "Raelyn and I agreed to a marriage on paper only."

Alex's eyes widen. "Why in the hells would you do that, you fool?"

"It's complicated but all the better for me to sneak around and do what I need to do. Acting on feelings would be the worst possible idea."

"What is it with you two?" Alex asks. "You're clearly omitting something. Besides, I saw the way she melted in your arms at the ball last month. You could have her out of her clothes in no time if you desired it."

"You better shut the hells up," I say, but there's no bite in my tone. "It's better this way. I can have my freedom and she can have hers. I still can't believe her stepmother is treating her like a servant." I bristle at the thought and walk back into the sitting room, collapsing into my favorite chair.

"I never liked Lady Carlisle—I mean Astoria," Alex says, going to pour me a drink. "There's something about her I just don't trust. Are you aware that every one of her late husbands died under mysterious circumstances?"

"I had no idea," I muse. "Gods, I hope she didn't do something to

Lord Astoria. I still need his approval if I decide to move forward with my betrothal to Raelyn. The way she treated me today and the way she treats her stepdaughter, I worry she wouldn't allow it."

"If Lady Astoria refused a match between you and Lady Raelyn, she'd have to be barking mad," Alex says.

"It wouldn't surprise me though. I have a hard time believing Lord Astoria would be perfectly fine finding out she treated his daughter like a servant, but then again, I have been wrong before."

"Aw, look at you Ki. That's growth. Admitting you might be wrong sometimes."

I halfheartedly punch him in the shoulder. "Goodnight, Alex."

Chapter Eighteen

RAELYN

I'm almost embarrassed at the amount of tears I shed last night. My eyes are still puffy, but I refuse to cry anymore. With my plans of stealing back my dresses on hold after the disastrous sham of a dinner, I look around my room, trying to decide what is most important to bring to my new quarters.

Grabbing an empty trunk from my closet, I drag it into the middle of the room. A few trinkets I collected over the years go in, along with my favorite books, completed needlework projects, and a few pieces of jewelry. When the trunk is full of the only things I care about, I take one last glance around the room I've spent my entire life in before leaving, lugging the heavy thing behind me.

My stomach rumbles as I pull the trunk down the hallway and almost run into Ingrid, the only remaining kitchen maid.

"Here, let me help you with that, Lady Raelyn."

"Thank you, Ingrid," I say with a smile.

"I can't believe they're kicking you out of your room," she says almost conspiratorially. "Rumor has it that Lady Astoria is just trying to put you in your place."

"As if she hasn't done that enough already," I scoff. "Haven't I done everything she's asked of me?"

"She thinks you are your father's weakness," she whispers. "She hates the fact that you're his favorite."

"What does she think is going to happen when he returns?" I question. "Surely this won't win her any favors with him."

Ingrid looks around nervously. "One of the footmen overheard her discussing his lengthy absence. I don't think he'll return for quite some time."

My heart sinks. Not only do I miss him, but he also needs to be home if there is any hope of arranging a marriage contract between Kian and me. Knowing Stepmother, she'll reject all offers just to spite me.

"I'm sorry, Lady Raelyn. I didn't mean to make you sad," Ingrid says.

"It's okay. I was just really hoping he would return soon."

"Lady Astoria is nearly tyrannical. He can't return soon enough."

We finally arrive in the cramped servants' quarters, and Ingrid stops in front of one of the doors. "This room is available, if you want it."

"Thanks," I say, and she gives me a nod.

The door creaks as it opens on a shoebox of a room. A rickety-looking single bed is pushed up against one wall, and the tiny window barely lets in any of the morning light—probably for the best, though surprisingly, I feel okay despite my venture into the sun yesterday. A small wardrobe takes up the other half of the room. I almost shudder at the dirty bucket that looks like it's been used as a chamber pot.

"Thanks again for your help," I say, and push my trunk to the only remaining wall space next to the bed.

"Let me know if there's anything I can do to help you feel more settled," she replies, turning to leave.

"Do you know what happened to Sera?" I ask, stopping her and suddenly feeling more alone than ever before.

"I'm sorry." She shakes her head. "She was dismissed with the others right after Lord Astoria left."

My shoulders sag. I'd hoped her absence was only temporary.

"You should come down to the kitchen for breakfast, Lady Raelyn," Ingrid says. "You're looking a little weak."

"You're right. And please, just call me Raelyn. I'm fairly certain 'lady' has been stripped from my title by my dearest stepmother."

Ingrid smiles awkwardly. "If you say so."

My stomach grumbles again, reminding me that I haven't eaten since breakfast yesterday. Once we enter the kitchen, our chef looks at me with pity in his eyes. *Oh no.* He points toward the table where my tonic sits. "Your tonic is ready for you, my lady, but you are not allowed any breakfast. Lady Astoria's orders."

Rage washes over me, and I hold back a scream. "Are you kidding me, Fred?"

"I do apologize, but Lady Astoria was very clear. She promised to take it out of my wages if I give you any food." His shoulders curl in on themselves, and I do think he actually feels bad. Pointing to a sheet of paper next to my tonic, he says, "There's a list of your chores for the day."

"I'd sure like to know how Stepmother expects me to get anything done when I'm about to pass out from hunger."

Fred shrugs and turns back to his chopping, as if looking at me for one moment longer would only make him feel guiltier.

Ingrid gives me a pitying look and starts to prep the eggs. I snatch up the tonic and the sheet of paper and march out of the kitchen. The pile of clothes has doubled in size since the night before, and I shove the tonic into my apron pocket along with the list and start pushing the cart toward our washroom.

My anger radiates off me in waves. Best I take it out on the laundry instead of the other servants. They are only taking care of themselves, and Stepmother *is* quite vindictive.

I want someone to choose me. To look out for me. I'm tired of being treated like I don't matter.

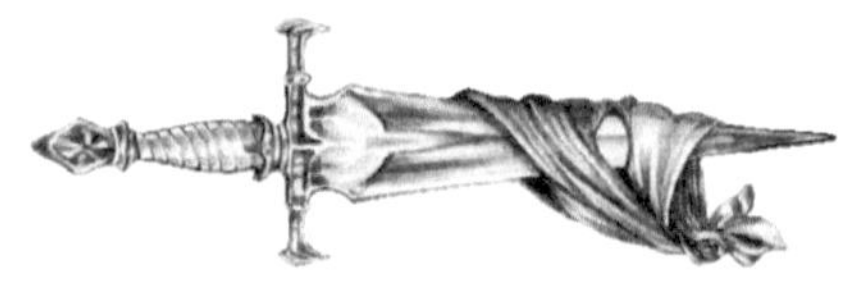

Chapter Nineteen

KIAN

Striding into the dining room for the breakfast I was told to attend, I stop short when I see my heavily pregnant sister-in-law chatting with her baby sister. Of course it's a damn setup. Colin is known to always get his way. He's in deep discussion with Father, but all conversations pause as I take my seat next to him.

"Good morning," I say with false cheer.

"Nice of you to finally show up," Father grouses. "You should have been here forty minutes ago."

"Apologies," I reply. "I had a rather late evening of debauchery."

"Kian!" Colin chastises. "You'd do well to consider your audience."

I turn my gaze to his wife, Princess Juliana, and then to Princess Helene. Giving them a quick nod, I say, "Apologies, ladies."

Princess Helene flushes a bright shade of pink, her blonde ringlets pulled up in a way I assume is meant to make her look older. It's not working. She still looks like a child to me. I have to put a stop to this farce. There is no way I can marry her.

"It's so nice to see you again, Prince Kian," she says shyly. "It's been years."

"Likewise," I reply before turning my attention back to my brother. "I thought you said they were at the country estate," I say under my breath.

"Did I?" he replies. "They arrived yesterday evening. It's Juliana's last chance to be at court before the baby comes."

"Wonderful," I mutter.

"Don't be rude, Kian," my brother says. "Catch up with Princess Helene."

If I could shoot knives out of my eyes, they would pin Colin to the wall, but I paste on a fake smile and turn my attention back toward Juliana and Helene, who are seated across the table.

"You look well," I say to Juliana.

A joyful laugh emerges from her as she puts a hand to her swollen belly. "I don't quite believe you, Kian, but thank you."

I force my gaze to Helene. "Are you enjoying your time at court?"

Another blush stains her cheeks, and she bobs her head excitedly.

All I can think when I look at her is that this child has no business being stuck with me—a potential husband who could very well be tried for treason if caught. Could I really do that to any woman though? My mind flashes to Raelyn, and I feel a pang of guilt.

"I do hope you can take some time to show me around this afternoon," Helene says.

Not happening. The last thing I need is more fodder for the court gossips and busybodies.

"I have quite a busy day today," I say, "but perhaps another time."

Colin kicks me under the table, and I grit my teeth as pain reverberates up through my shoulder. *Asshole.*

"Can't you move some things around?" Colin asks.

"I'm afraid not," I reply, turning to glare at him. "I have some business in town I must see to." My shoulder aches just at the thought of it, but I really need to go so that I'm not found out. Word of the vigilante's injury could have reached my father for all I know, and I need to get to Margot before he notices me favoring it.

"What a shame," Helene says demurely. "We'll be here another day or two before heading back to the country estate. Of course, you are always welcome to come call on me there." She smiles at me, but the whole situation feels wrong. I have to find a way to make Father see that this match is unreasonable. If only I'd had the idea of marrying Raelyn a week earlier, I wouldn't be in this mess.

"That sounds nice," I lie, then rise to my feet. "As lovely as this has been, I really must be headed out. I'm afraid I overslept this morning and am now running behind on my appointments."

My father waves a hand at me dismissively. "Do stop by and see me later, son."

"Yes, sir."

I nod at the ladies and give my brother a glance. His displeasure is written all over his face. I'm sure he'll give me an earful later as well.

PHANTOM NICKERS as I dismount and tie him to the post outside Margot's business in town. The steps creak underfoot as I jog up them. At the sound of the jingling bell, Margot comes out from the back room.

"Your Highness," she greets me, her eyes immediately darting toward my shoulder.

How she always knows, I'm not sure. I don't think I'll ever find out. Must have something to do with the diluted godsblood in her veins. She is said to be directly descended from a demi-god in Galyna's, the goddess of healing's, line. Margot is incredibly sought after in our kingdom, and I am more than lucky she is on my side, not to mention discreet.

"I wish I were here under better circumstances." I grin.

"Hush now, Prince. We both know you'd never visit unless you actually needed me."

I bark out a laugh but wince as my shoulder shakes.

"Come on back before you make that shoulder worse," Margot chides.

I follow her into her workspace and hop up onto the examination table. As I unbutton my shirt, Margot goes to her workbench and starts mixing some herbs into a paste.

"As much as I love to see your handsome face, I've been seeing a little too much of it lately," she remarks.

"I'm not quite sure what you're talking about," I reply. "Though my trainer did get a little too bold yesterday."

She snorts as she unwraps the bandage. "The court healer must have been too busy, huh?"

"You're the only one for me," I tease.

A faint flush heats her weathered cheeks. "You're too kind."

I play along with our usual song and dance. While she's aware of my alter ego's nighttime activities, thanks to an injury that almost took me out, we rarely speak plainly of them, and never face-to-face. As my eyes and ears around town, she finds other ways to send word. One can never be too careful.

"Have you been to Marietta lately?" I ask, treading carefully.

Her gentle fingers prod at the wound, and there's a spark of heat as if it's warming from the inside. The instant relief makes me close my eyes and sigh. The court healers truly have nothing on Margot.

"It's been a few weeks," she replies, "but they seem to have no need for me anymore."

Wishing I could pry for more but not wanting to put her at risk, I choose to take her on her word. She cares about the people of our kingdom just as much as I do, if not more, and I'm grateful for her help.

After covering the wound with her special paste and rewrapping it, I'm feeling almost as good as new.

"You might want to hold off on training that shoulder for a few days," she says.

"Got it. Healer's orders."

She shakes her head and mumbles something under her breath that sounds vaguely like she doesn't know what to do with "foolish bleeding-heart princes."

"Shall I send your usual payment?" I ask. A bob of her head is all I get, and I hop off the table. "Thank you again," I say, pressing a kiss to the top of her head.

"Get out of here before someone sees you," she reprimands. "Oh, wait." She turns back to her workbench and reaches up on the shelf for a small pouch. "Here are your monthly contraceptive herbs."

I utter a thanks and stuff them into my pocket. No use telling her I haven't had much need for them despite the prolific rumors that circulate about me. As much as everyone thinks I'm sleeping my way through our kingdom, I haven't been with a woman in quite some time. All the vigilante shit has kept my evenings full. Yes, I might stop at parties just to show my face, and I may have slipped into some dark corners and exchanged kisses among other things, but no woman has fully captured my attention in quite a while. Until *her*. I should have known from the moment we met that she'd be trouble.

Chapter Twenty

RAELYN

An entire week passes with neither sight nor sound of the prince. Perhaps he truly is going to marry the princess like the rumors say. *It's better this way*, I try to rationalize as I carry out yet another chore. With no word of when Father will return, my betrothal didn't stand a chance of happening anyway.

Chessa wasted no time and commandeered my room the very day I left it. Consider me shocked. At least it wasn't Erika, but her betrayal will always hurt the most. Sometimes I question if she ever liked me at all, or if our pleasant memories are nothing but lies.

I'm also starting to wonder if Stepmother has heard the rumors about me not belonging . . . but that makes no sense to me. Surely Father wouldn't accept and love me the way he does if he wasn't actually my father.

Since it's looking like the prince's plan is not going to come to fruition, I've started dreaming of escape. Perhaps I am delusional, but I don't want to spend the rest of my days waiting on my family and being treated worse than our paid servants.

Only, if I did leave, I'd have nowhere to go and no way to provide for myself unless I stole from my family. My only other hope remains in Father's return. I have to believe he will not be okay with the way Stepmother has been treating me. Perhaps when he returns, he will set things right, or I can beg him to send me to live with our distant relatives in Sillamae.

All I know is that something has to change. It's as if I'm withering away on the inside. I'm becoming no one. No longer allowed to do anything that brings me joy, but forced to work so hard from sunup to sundown that all I have energy for is collapsing into bed every evening.

The rest of the servants have stopped calling me "my lady" these past five weeks, and I'm just Raelyn now. That part doesn't even bother me; I actually prefer it—if I can't belong with my family, I want to belong somewhere.

I'm carrying a basket of sheets when a commotion from the front of the manor pulls my attention. *What in the realms could that be?*

Stepmother's shrill voice echoes down the halls, but it's unclear to me what she's saying. Were we expecting guests today? I didn't notice anything out of the ordinary on my list of tasks. Usually, if Stepmother is entertaining, she makes me clean the parlor twice for good measure. As if the dust could multiply in an hour. I snort in annoyance just thinking about it.

A velvety baritone voice drifts down the hall, and I freeze. I know that voice. Has the prince finally deigned to show up? I'm simultaneously angry and excited—perhaps a little bit scared. Stepmother does not sound pleased at his appearance, which is absurd when I really think about it. A prince is in our home, and she dares to speak to him like that?

I shuffle as silently as possible toward them, hoping to overhear some of their conversation.

"This simply isn't the time for a visit, Your Highness," Stepmother says, sounding miffed.

The prince's unworried, smooth drawl sends a shiver down my

spine. "I apologize for the lack of notice, my lady, but there *simply* wasn't time to send word."

I bite back a laugh at how he throws her words back in her face.

"Lady Raelyn is not available for callers at this time," Stepmother replies.

The bitterness coating her tone makes my stomach ache. The prince is finally here, but she won't even allow him to see me? I debate the merits of "accidentally" waltzing into the foyer. She would be furious, and I hate to think of how she'd take it out on me. Does she realize the prince recognized me the last time he was here? Does she know he's aware of my current status as maid in the household? If I were to come out and embarrass her, there's no telling what she'd do to me.

"Is she ill?" the prince asks.

"Nothing like that, Your Highness," Stepmother replies.

Idiot. He might have actually bought that lie if she'd been smart enough to play along.

"Lady Erika is available if you'd like to call on her," Stepmother continues.

When the prince doesn't reply right away, my heart drops. Would he give up so easily? What should I do? He's perhaps my best chance of escaping this hellscape.

"I really must insist on seeing Lady Raelyn," the prince says firmly. "Considering she herself told me she never leaves the manor unless she's deathly ill, I don't understand why she isn't available."

Darling Stepmother is going to find a way to punish me. I just know it. Should I just make myself known now?

If I'm going to be punished anyway, might as well go all in.

I take one step when Stepmother says, "You are quite forward, Your Highness. I suppose I can check on her and see if she is willing to take a caller. Don't get your hopes up."

I sag against the wall. She's just going to make more excuses for me.

"I'm happy to wait as long as it takes," he replies smoothly.

Gods, I could almost kiss him. Thank Kyros and Luna he is willing to stand up to that witch.

Footsteps come toward me, and I quickly run in the opposite direction. *Shit.* If Stepmother catches me eavesdropping, it will only be worse for me.

I turn the corner just in time and toss the sheets into the never-ending pile of laundry.

"Raelyn!" Stepmother snaps.

I spin and look at her, hoping I don't come across suspiciously. "Yes, Stepmother?"

"A certain prince is here looking for you. Would you happen to know anything about that?"

"Um . . . well, we met formally at the ball last month and he seemed to take a liking to me," I reply, hoping no one saw us together last week.

"He is quite insistent about seeing you, but clearly, you're in no condition to see him." She looks me up and down judgmentally, as if she isn't fully responsible for my current state. It takes everything in me to bite my tongue and keep from retorting back.

"I can go change and send him away?" I offer hesitantly.

Stepmother taps her toe as she holds a perfectly manicured finger to her lips. "You must be delicate about it. I can't have you offending the prince now, can I? If he's not going to marry Princess Helene, I fully intend for him to match with one of your sisters, and I won't have you stand in my way."

"Yes, Stepmother," I say quietly. Why she won't let me have this, perhaps I'll never understand, but just maybe . . . "I can encourage him to call on Erika or Chessa, if that's what you prefer."

"Of course I prefer it, you insolent brat. You can't possibly think *you* deserve a prince, can you?"

I try not to flinch at her tone, at the words that cut even though I don't want them to.

"You are far past your prime, Raelyn. You had your chance to find a husband, and now it's too late. You are nothing but proof of your mother's disgrace." Stepmother stands before me, wagging an accusing finger, and I shrink in on myself. "You don't even deserve to have the name Astoria. Your father is a fool to allow you to remain here. If it were up to me, I'd have exposed you long ago. But I am a gracious woman and allow you to serve in this household. If you do not, you will be cast out. Do I make myself clear?"

Each word is a blow. Does she have proof? The way she can say that without a shadow of doubt makes me want to curl up in a ball and cry.

Unbidden tears prick my eyes as I stare up at her, recognizing the triumph in hers. After weeks of trying, she finally found the words to break me.

"How can you say such hateful things?" I blurt out.

All of her beauty fades as the scorn on her face takes over. "I know your secret, Raelyn. You are not your father's daughter."

"Th-that's not possible," I stutter. "Father would have surely said something to me if that were true."

"He is all the more a fool for not telling you then. Don't you think it odd that you're the only sibling who needs a special tonic to keep your illness at bay?"

I close my eyes, as if it will keep her words from being true.

"I found the doctor's notes. You don't have an ounce of Astoria blood, and if you do not convince the prince to choose a worthier sister to call on, I will expose you for the disgrace that you are."

A pit of despair threatens to overwhelm me. Any joy at seeing Kian today is overshadowed by this new knowledge Stepmother has thrown at me. Is she telling the truth? Perhaps she's just saying this to hurt me.

But deep down, her words ring of truth. I have always felt different. My illness is unique to me, as she said. Perhaps it really is Father who has been lying to me all these years.

I hang my head. The prince won't want to marry a bastard. That much is obvious. I suppose it's time to end things. Stepmother knowing this truth means she can hold it over my father and prevent him from doing anything to change my situation. He wouldn't want that shame to get out to court. All hopes of my father's intervention crash and burn like a star falling from the sky.

"Now hurry and make yourself presentable," Stepmother commands. "Best to get this over with."

I nod and make my escape to my room, tears flooding my eyes. Through blurred vision, I rifle through my limited options and pull out the least offensive dress.

The room-temperature water in my small basin doesn't do much to clear the puffiness of my eyes, but it's the best I can do. I pin up my hair and pinch my cheeks—I look like a mess, but it's not like I'm supposed to impress the prince. I'm supposed to push him toward one of my sisters . . . or half-sisters, I guess.

Rolling my shoulders back, I take a deep breath. I can do this. I can face the prince and turn him away, and then I'll plan my escape. I owe this family nothing.

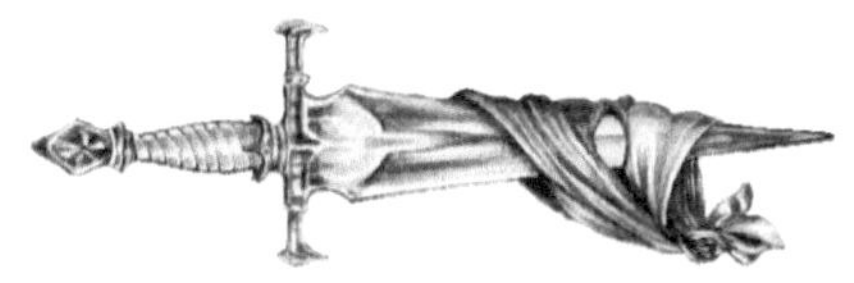

Chapter Twenty-One

KIAN

Lady Astoria sweeps back into the foyer, a self-satisfied look in her eyes, like the cat who's eaten the canary. Or at least won some prize she's been after. My shoulders tense. I don't trust this woman. Not a single bit.

"Lady Raelyn agreed to see you," she says. Her smugness now surprises me. I'm the one who won here, right?

"Wonderful. Now, will you show me to the parlor, or are you inclined to have me stand in the foyer for another hour?" I bite back.

Her lack of regard shocks me after how she fawned over me at the ball. I like to think I'm somewhat of a catch despite my alter ego's nighttime activities. Perhaps even more so because of them. I seem to be the only prince who cares about the welfare of his people, not that anyone other than Alex and Margot know. I also highly doubt Lady Astoria cares much about anyone other than herself.

"Of course," she croons. "My apologies for my rudeness, Your Highness. I have been a little out of sorts trying to manage the manor. My husband has been gone for quite some time now, as you perhaps know."

A little too late to turn on the charm.

"I never knew how challenging it would be to arrange marriages for so many daughters. I only have sons from my previous marriages." She laughs, but it sounds fake to my ears.

"I'm sure that has been difficult for you," I reply, hoping I don't come across as too annoyed. Her audacity in changing her tone with me from one moment to another is astounding.

She leads me to the parlor and urges me to take a seat on the settee facing the windows. The sky is quite overcast today, and I can't help but wish for sun, even if for nothing other than healthy crops. I haven't found any information or word of Kyros since the mention in Cary Astoria's journal from almost thirty years ago. The urgency to find the lost god is even more pressing with the visual reminder.

"I'll have tea sent in for you momentarily," Lady Astoria says with a sickening sweetness. "I can send Lady Erika or Lady Chessa in to keep you company while you wait."

"No, that's quite all right," I reply. "I don't mind the quiet."

"Nonsense," she declares. "I'll send one right in. Lady Raelyn might be a while."

What in Luna's name is going on with Raelyn? Does her stepmother know I saw her cleaning the floors like a servant last time I was here? I palm my face. None of this is going to plan.

I fully intended to call on Raelyn earlier this week, but Colin made it impossible for me to get away. The king also made it very clear that if I did not at least attempt to spend time with Helene, there would be dire consequences. I feel like the worst kind of ass, knowing that, in all likelihood, Raelyn has heard rumors of my courting Helene and probably thinks the worst of me.

Spending time with Helene is what I imagine spending time with a little sister would be like. And as lovely as she might appear, no single part of her is appealing to me as a partner. It doesn't help that she comes across completely vapid. The more time I spend around Helene and Juliana, the sorrier I feel for Colin. What a drag to be married into that family.

When Colin announced they were finally returning to the country estate last night, I wanted to jump for joy. I couldn't wait to get away from court.

Lady Erika sweeps into the room, excitement making her eyes glow. Fantastic. I truly have little desire to entertain Raelyn's sister, but what else can I do?

A maid enters with the tea service and starts bustling around, preparing our drinks.

"Your Highness, such a pleasure to see you again," Lady Erika simpers.

Her voice puts me on edge, but I suppose I can at least be grateful it isn't Lady Chessa. Her reputation of being the most aggravating female to attend court precedes her.

"A pleasure to see you as well," I lie.

Lady Erika adjusts her full skirts as she sits across from me. I don't miss how she tries to perk up her chest to show off her assets, or lack thereof. The women of court are all the same, thinking they can flaunt their bodies and have us men falling all over them. And yet, can I blame her? If one were to listen to all the rumors at court, this is exactly what one would think I look for. Times like this make me wish I didn't have to play a role. I wish I could be myself and fully known. Regardless of who I marry, that will never be possible.

"I have to say, I'm quite surprised to see you here," Lady Erika says, arching a brow. "I understand you've been courting Princess Helene all week."

I force a smile. "Our families have been close since we were children. It was my duty to escort the princess around court during her visit."

"Oh," Lady Erika muses. "Funny. That's not at all what everyone is saying."

"Perhaps you shouldn't put so much stock in what people say."

She flutters her lashes and gives a coy smile. "Don't get me wrong, Your Highness, the prospect of your availability greatly pleases me." She leans forward a bit more, squeezing her breasts together, and I want to roll my eyes at her desperation.

"I am here to court Lady Raelyn, or didn't your stepmother tell you?"

A flash of surprise lights up Lady Erika's eyes. She didn't know. Interesting.

She laughs airily. "We'll see. Raelyn isn't really the marrying type."

I frown before taking a sip of my tea. Raelyn's family is quite possibly worse than mine.

Before I can respond, there is a rustling at the door. *There she is.* My heart skips in my chest at the sight of her. Her hair is haphazardly piled atop her head, and if I'm not mistaken, there is a smudge of dirt on her collarbone. I greedily take her in. So unlike the women of court, so unlike her sisters. There is something about her that takes my breath away, but . . . she looks sad. The urge to take care of her is strong and surprising. *What in the hells is wrong with me?*

I quickly stand. "Lady Raelyn, thank you so much for taking the time to see me."

She bobs her head but doesn't move any closer.

I close the gap between us, reaching a hand out. Hesitantly, she lets me take hers, and I press a kiss onto the back of it, noting the dry roughness of her skin, probably from all the ridiculous chores.

"I apologize for not coming sooner," I say quietly.

"You have nothing to apologize for," Raelyn replies, and I lead her over to the settee.

Lady Erika looks appalled when I seat myself next to Raelyn, but she tries to hide it as she sips from her cup.

"Thank you so much for keeping me company, Lady Erika, but there are some things I would like to discuss with your sister."

The dismissal is clear, and she sets her teacup onto the table with a clatter. "I'm sure we will see each other again soon enough," she replies before sweeping out of the room.

"You may go too," I say to the maid. "Thank you for the tea."

She looks to Raelyn for confirmation, and Raelyn nods, albeit a little nervously.

Once the maid leaves, Raelyn asks, "Is it even proper for us to be in here without a chaperone?"

"You didn't seem so worried about that when we were alone in the garden," I quip.

"That's completely different," she retorts.

Ah, there it is. The spunk I like.

I point toward the doorway. "It's open, and was the butler not stationed outside when you came in?"

She looks out of sorts. "True. But he can't see us. You could be doing something inappropriate in here."

I grin and lean in closer, breathing in her intoxicating scent of citrus and vanilla. "Would you like me to be doing something inappropriate, Raelyn?"

Her skin turns a delicious shade of pink, and without meaning to, I find myself grazing her neck with my nose before I pull back.

Raelyn looks scandalized, but I love the flush in her cheeks and how her sadness has dissipated just a little. I decide right then and there I'm going to enjoy finding ways to make her blush.

"Your Highness," she says breathily.

"Kian."

"Kian," she repeats.

I smile, but when her lip quivers, I straighten. "Did something happen?"

She shakes her head. "No more than usual."

"Then what's wrong?"

She inhales before saying, "I'm sorry, Kian. I can't be bound to you. The arrangement is off."

I frown. I expected her stepmother to push back, but this is surprising.

Raelyn wrings her hands on her lap. "I never should have agreed to it. I'd make a terrible princess."

She isn't making any sense. I tilt her chin up so she looks at me. "That's a lie."

She squirms under my scrutiny. "I just can't," she whispers.

"What did she do?" I demand. "What could have possibly changed in a week?"

"Everything."

"Talk to me, Rae."

She blinks. "No one has called me that in years."

I smile. "It fits you."

She smiles briefly before her face falls again. "I'm sorry, Your Highness, but you'd be better off courting Lady Erika. In fact, I insist you do."

Has this woman lost all sense?

"Raelyn, I don't understand."

She shakes her head sadly. "I'm sorry to ruin your plan, but trust me, you can't marry me. Court my sister or go back to Princess Helene."

"I don't want Princess Helene," I bite out. Is that it? Is she upset I took an entire week to call?

Her eyes well with tears.

"Did you think I forgot you?" I ask. "I could never forget you . . . In fact, you've been all I could think about this past week."

Shit, I probably shouldn't have said that.

Chapter Twenty-Two

RAELYN

This is not going to plan. This proposed marriage of convenience should have been easy to end. He doesn't care about me nor I about him. I merely wanted to get out of this dreadful situation, and I thought he wanted a wife in name only so he could go about as he pleases, but his words give me pause.

"You've been thinking about me?"

He looks abashed. "Trust me, I feel dreadful for making you wait all week. The night I got home after our agreement, my father and brother thrust Princess Helene upon me and insisted I court her despite the fact that I could not see her as a wife, only as a sister."

My lips turn downward. "I'm sorry. That sounds challenging."

"No need to apologize," he insists. "I just feel bad that it took me so long to make it back out here."

I try to wave him off, but he grabs my hand and intertwines our fingers. I want to pull away, embarrassed at the roughness he surely feels, though his hands are far less delicate than I expected. He must train with a sword.

"Raelyn, I might be wrong, but it feels like you're hiding something from me." He gently squeezes my hand.

"You don't understand," I whisper. "There's a scandal—if it were to get out, my family would be ruined."

He tilts his head. "You can trust me. I swear upon Kyros."

A bolt of heat zings through me at his words, and for some reason, I decide to trust him.

"I'm not truly an Astoria," I whisper.

His brows rise. "What do you mean?"

"My stepmother said she has proof. Proof that I am not my father's child, but a bastard."

Kian sits back but does not let go of my hand as he considers my words. To my surprise, an amused laugh bursts out of him. "You are far too kind to be an Astoria; just look at the rest of your family."

A strangled cry leaves my throat, and I reach up to wipe away a stray tear. This is not the response I expected.

"Rae, if you think I give two shits about who your parents are, you're mistaken."

"But surely your father would care, would he not?" I ask. "I can imagine if he had to choose between a pedigreed princess or the bastard child of Lord Astoria's late wife, there would be no question."

He shakes his head. "It truly doesn't matter to me."

"Stepmother will never agree to a match between us, even if the king does approve," I say. "And it sounds like Father won't be home for a good long time."

"If ever . . ." the prince mutters under his breath.

"What did you say?"

The prince winces. "I don't mean to worry you, but there is some concern regarding the death of your stepmother's previous husbands . . . I worry she might be hiding things."

My entire body freezes up. Despite knowing that he most likely is not my true father, he is all I've ever known. The thought that perhaps he won't return at all turns my blood to ice.

"Do you think he's in danger?"

"I'm honestly not sure. I can try to pry some information out of my father about where he went, if you like, but at this point, all I have to offer is speculation."

I shake my head. "Regardless, my stepmother has made it clear that I am to end things with you or she will reveal my secret."

Kian lets go of my hand and rises to his feet, pacing back and forth on the decorative rug. "Do you really think she would?" He ponders. "Perhaps she is merely bluffing. The news would make her look bad too."

I wrap my arms around my middle, my stomach aching with all the surprises and information I've gleaned in the past hour. "Perhaps you're right," I admit. "But you don't understand. She can make my life here a nightmare. She already has."

Kian bristles as he stops in front of me, his hands clenched into fists. "I need to get you out of this house."

I have to ask, even though I'm not sure I want the answer. "Why do you even care, Kian?"

His frame softens, and he kneels before me. My heart starts to thud in my chest at the proximity. "I care about the people of my kingdom," Kian says. "That includes you. I hate seeing how unfairly you've been treated here, and if there's something I can do to help, I want to do it. Besides, this marriage is good for both of us. We both get what we want."

The flicker of hope that perhaps he might have been growing fond of me is quickly doused. He's not doing this out of some unfounded sense of love or loyalty. He's doing it because he's a good person *and* it's beneficial for him. I need to remember that.

I roll my shoulders back and let some sarcasm slip free. "Glad I can be your charity case, then."

Kian blows out an exasperated breath. "Believe what you will, but I do want to help."

Shrugging, my hands open in helplessness. "But how?"

Kian's silver eyes light up before he whispers, "We elope."

"What?" I yelp.

The butler pops his head in the door, an eyebrow raised to ask if I need help. I shake my head, and he disappears again.

A devilish grin brightens Kian's face. "Yes, exactly."

"Have you gone mad?" I whisper.

"If we elope, my father can't force me to marry Princess Helene, and your stepmother won't be able to do anything about it. If she tells your secret, it will only make her look bad for marrying into such a scandalous family."

"Won't an elopement be scandal enough?" I gasp.

"Don't forget, I do have a reputation in court of being somewhat unpredictable."

"Ha," I scoff. "No one will believe you've given up all your conquests for *me*."

Kian frowns. "Stop that, Rae. Do you even realize how beautiful you are? How kind, witty, and intelligent? If anything, all of court will be jealous they didn't get to you first. You'll have no trouble at all finding someone willing to *meet your needs*."

He winks, but his words turn sour in my ears. He doesn't know me, and I can't even begin to grasp the idea of trying to have a secret relationship while married to the prince. I'll just be alone. I'm used to it.

"If I agree to this elopement," I whisper conspiratorially, "how do you propose we make it happen? Stepmother will never allow me to just waltz out the door with you."

"We meet later tonight in the gardens," he says. "When everyone is asleep, we leave. I will find a priestess to marry us at first light."

A flutter of excitement fills me. Is this it? Will I finally make my escape?

"Okay . . ." I say hesitantly.

"Now, there is something I need from you."

I quirk a brow. "What could I possibly have to offer you?"

"Has your Father ever mentioned the lost god Kyros to you?"

The sudden change of subject throws me for a loop. My forehead crinkles as I ponder. "Not directly," I reply.

"What do you mean?" Kian asks.

"Well, one time, there were a few notes on his desk mentioning the gods, and I heard him muttering something once about repercussions when he didn't realize I was around."

Kian leans in, his interest clearly piqued. "Do you happen to know if he kept any of those notes?"

What an odd question. I think back and shake my head. "They were mostly just scribbles on a map, but I never saw them again after that one time. I'm sorry."

Kian deflates. "No worries. I thought he might have information I've been looking for, but it sounds like he doesn't."

"It's a shame he's gone and I can't ask him for you."

"That's all right, Rae. Don't trouble yourself with it."

A memory pops unbidden into my head. The evening I caught the masked man in Father's office weeks ago. *Is* there something of importance hidden there? Something to do with the lost god? I'm about to say something but pause. While I've trusted the prince with the secret of my scandalous parentage, I'm still only getting to know him.

"I'm sorry if that's not the answer you were looking for," I say.

"It's fine," he reiterates. "All right then, as far as tonight, I'll meet you in the garden when the clock strikes twelve. Will that work for you?"

I nod, almost unwilling to believe this is happening. I'm getting out.

As soon as Kian leaves, Stepmother swoops into the parlor and starts interrogating me. I lie through my teeth—what else is there to do?

"Erika made it sound like he wasn't interested in her," she accuses.

"Can you blame him?"

She smacks me in the face with impressive force before I can even blink. "You will hold your tongue, girl."

In complete shock, I back away from her, my hand pressed against my sore cheek.

"You had better get back to work immediately," she screams at me. "You've already wasted enough time today."

Hating myself for cowering, I scurry away as quickly as I can, practically running to the laundry. At least the mindless work will keep me distracted. Just knowing my escape is close will get me through the day —I couldn't hide my smile if I wanted to.

When I finally collapse onto my bed, it's half past eleven. I curse under my breath. There is hardly enough time to gather my things before I need to meet the prince. Filled with a sudden burst of energy, I jump up and start moving. Knowing I can only take what I can carry, I fill a small satchel with a few of my most prized possessions. I'm slightly self-conscious about running off with the prince without bathing first, so I splash some tepid water on my face and try to tame my unruly hair into a low bun. I already ruined my nicest dress doing chores today, so I pull the next least offensive option out of my small wardrobe. I have to admit, this is not how I saw myself getting bound; an elopement was never something I could have imagined. At the very least, I expected to wear a pretty gown and have my father present.

He's not even your father, a small voice whispers, but does that matter? He has always been there for me, and he was very protective. Though, now that I think of it, sometimes, he'd get a sad and faraway look in his eyes when he looked at me.

Blowing out a breath, I return to my chest of belongings and pull out one more item—the blade I stole from the masked man. I'm not completely sure why I've held on to it, but it is a beautiful piece of weaponry, its balance impeccable. I carefully strap it to my thigh underneath my gown, using one of the sheaths I nicked from Father's small armory. I'm as ready as I'll ever be.

The gong of the clock striking midnight chimes distantly through the walls of the manor. I'm running out of time.

With a final glance around the room, I oh-so-quietly open my door, only to be met with the haughty glare of my stepmother.

No. No, no, no.

"Going somewhere?" she sneers.

"I was just going to get some water from the kitchen," I stammer.

She takes an ominous step closer, eyeing my satchel, and I back away, remembering the sting of her slap.

"You're a terrible liar, Raelyn. Did you really think I wouldn't find out? Did you truly think no one was listening to your little plan with the prince?"

My heart sinks in my chest. We'd been foolish to speak so plainly with the door wide open. Trying to find my courage, I puff out my chest. "Well, if you're already aware, then you know there is nothing you can do to stop us."

A hideous laugh leaves her lips. "That's where you're wrong, Raelyn. The prince might not care about your status as a bastard, but the king surely will. He will be more than happy to reward me when I inform him of your little scheme."

"Have you?"

"Have I what?" Stepmother asks.

"Have you already informed the king of our plan?"

Her lips turn up. "Of course not. I play my cards when they are most advantageous to me."

Good, so the prince is likely waiting for me already.

I make a mad dash for the door, hoping to skirt past her, until I'm wrenched back by my hair. A scream erupts out of me as she cackles. "Not so fast, girl."

She's surprisingly strong, her grip on my hair excruciating. I reach back and claw at the hand holding me, digging my nails in as deep as I can. She grunts and throws me to the floor before examining my handiwork. She winces, and I look down at my fingers smeared with blood. At least I got her good.

"You've made a big mistake, Raelyn. I hope you ate a large dinner, because it will be a while before you eat again."

Her eyes glint in the darkness, and she slams my door shut. The clang of a key turning in the lock echoes through the room.

Chapter Twenty-Three

RAELYN

"*No!*" I cry. "No, no, no!"

The heels of Stepmother's shoes click down the hall as she leaves me trapped in my prison. This can't be happening. I was so close to escaping. I want to collapse into self-pity and tears. There's no telling what new forms of torture she will come up with now.

I bring my hands to my face, trying to hold back my sobs. *It's going to be okay.* I'll figure it out. I have to.

The coppery tang of blood hits my nostrils and awakens something in me. Just like that night with the intruder, my jaw starts to ache. Unable to stop myself, I lick the blood from my fingers. I'm simultaneously disgusted but also can't hold back the groan of delight as the taste hits my tongue.

There must be something seriously wrong with me.

I push off the floor and straighten my hair, shoving that abnormality to the back of my mind for now. I will get out of here if it's the last thing I do.

Glaring at the locked door, I slam my fist against it in a fit of frustration, and it splinters.

I look at my hand in shock. I mean, I've gained some strength with all the manual labor I've been doing around the house, but strong enough to splinter a door?

I slam my fist on it again in the same spot, and the wood cracks enough for me to push my hand through. Hopefully Stepmother isn't close enough to have heard. I reach through, fumbling for the door handle, but there is no key. I hold back a scream of frustration.

Okay, Raelyn, think. My mind wanders to the window above my bed. It's small, but I can possibly squeeze through it. I'm four stories up though. If I fall . . .

I shudder. Cross that bridge later. I debate the merits of trying to break down the rest of the door, but the noise will surely have someone coming to investigate. For all I know, someone is already coming after my first attempt. The very last thing I need is for Stepmother to catch me again.

The window it is.

I climb up onto my bed and pull at it. It probably hasn't been opened in years, and the wood has warped.

Some of that supernatural strength would sure come in handy right now.

When the window finally gives way, I almost crow with excitement. I have no idea how much time has passed and whether or not the prince is waiting for me. What if he thinks I changed my mind? No. I have to believe he's waiting. He needs this marriage just as much as I do.

I stand up on my tiptoes to peek out the window, immediately hit with nerves when I'm reminded how high up I am. Is there a ledge or something to land on? I can't see from here. *Damn it.* Will this even work? I grip the edge of the window and hoist myself up and out. I really didn't think this through. As I lean halfway out, I'm relieved to spy a narrow ledge to my right. Perhaps I won't die tonight after all.

When I finally make it to the slanted roof, I stop to catch my breath.

Luna's moon shines mockingly on me, and I worry once again that I'm too late.

I make my way toward the western side of the house and gardens and creep along the edge of the roof, praying to every god I can name that I won't fall and break my neck. I still haven't the faintest clue how I'm going to get down.

Maybe next time, you should think before you act, I chide myself.

When I finally make it to the part of the roof that faces the gardens, I peek over the edge, looking for something, anything to cling to that would help me climb down. I lean just a little too far, and my foot slips. Before I can stop myself, I'm sliding down the side of the roof toward the ledge.

Unable to hold back my shriek, my fingers scramble for purchase, and I claw into the roof, hoping to slow my descent. My feet hit air, but I manage to grasp the edge as my body crashes into the side of the manor. I bite back another scream when pain ricochets through me. My fingers start cramping, barely holding the weight of me and my satchel as I dangle off the roof.

"Rae? Is that you?" a harsh whisper calls up to me.

I could almost cry with relief when I look down at the prince staring up at me in confusion.

"What in Luna's name are you doing?"

My left hand cramps and slips, and I swing toward the manor again. "A little help would be great, Ki," I grit out.

He mutters something under his breath before he disappears into the garden.

Where the hells did he go? I'm barely holding on, and I'm afraid my hand is going to give out at any second.

The pounding of hooves signals his return as Kian pulls up beneath me on a magnificent black stallion. "It's okay. Let yourself fall, Rae. I'll catch you. I promise."

He must be insane. Surely I would crush him from this height. "I can't," I whimper, fear strangling me.

"Trust me. I've got you," he says reassuringly.

What do I have to lose? I take a deep breath and let go, the air leaving my lungs as I fall and fall and fall . . .

"Oof!" Kian grunts as I quite literally land on top of him. The horse snorts, and I take a deep breath.

"I can't believe you caught me."

Kian scoffs. "I can't believe you thought I wouldn't."

"Did I hurt you? Or your horse?"

"No, of course not," Kian replies. "We do tricks all the time."

I shudder as the adrenaline courses through me. "We should go," I say. "Stepmother is on to us. She locked me in my room."

Kian curses.

"If she catches us out here there's no telling what she'll do. She already threatened to go to the king."

"Well then, we'd better get out of here," Kian agrees. "That explains the servant I saw snooping in the gardens. I almost gave myself away."

"What did you do?"

"You do realize it's far past our meeting time, right? He went back in when the clock struck one."

"Oh," I say. *I can't believe he waited this long for me . . .*

Kian settles me in front of him and wraps an arm around my waist, leading us out through the garden and into the woods.

The events of the night finally catch up with me, and I find myself shaking as I come down from the adrenaline.

"Rae, are you all right?" Kian asks, sounding alarmed. He pulls his horse to a stop and turns my face toward his.

"No," I say, my teeth chattering as my entire body starts to convulse uncontrollably.

Kian jumps off and pulls me down. I'm out of control. I don't know what's happening to me, and Kian says something, but I can't even comprehend his words. His firm grip with one arm around my waist keeps me up while his free hand draws soothing circles on my back as he holds me tight.

"Shhh, it's okay, love, I'm here," he repeats over and over.

I'm not sure how long it takes, but slowly, my heart rate comes down and my body starts to feel more like my own.

"I'm sorry," I whisper. "I didn't mean to lose it on you like that."

His soft chuckle rumbles through me as he continues to hold me close. "Damn, Rae, you scared me. I had no idea what to do."

"Well, whatever you did clearly worked," I mumble into his chest. Taking a deep breath, I inhale the scent of leather and spice, allowing it to calm me. I'm completely weak but also feel oddly safe.

"Thank you for catching me," I say.

"No problem, love," Kian replies. The endearment sends a flutter of butterflies dancing in my stomach instead of the usual annoyance.

I pull back and look up at him. "What now?"

Kian sighs and lets go, running a hand through his windswept hair.

"We go somewhere to wait until dawn."

I frown. "Out here?"

He chuckles. "Where else? I can't take you back to the palace until you're my wife."

Wife. Damn, that sounds strange. I'm not sure I'm ready for this.

"Come, let's go. I know a place," he says.

He lifts me back onto his horse and hops up behind me. Now that the shock has worn off, I can't help but notice the way his body envelops mine. He's hard and warm and . . . hard. I blush, grateful he can't see in the dark.

It's only natural. Our bodies are cramped together on this horse and every jolt makes me rub up against him. It's just his body's response.

Thinking it might help, I lean forward a little, but all I manage to do is grind my rear against his hardness. A grunt comes out of him, but he seems too polite to complain. If anything, *my* face turns an even brighter shade of red.

Lovely. What a great start to our elopement.

The silence is awkward, so I break it. "How close are we?"

"It's not too much farther," he grits out.

"I'm sorry, I don't ride much," I admit. "I'm not trying to make you uncomfortable."

He laughs. "It's fine, love. Just try to relax—it will make it a little less bumpy."

I try my best to sink into him, his arm holding me tightly enough that I won't fall.

We finally make it to a clearing in the woods. It must be a common enough place to rest, as there is a firepit in the middle encircled by charred stones. Large logs are set around it, providing seating for weary travelers.

"How do you know about this place?" I ask.

"Believe it or not, this is a popular spot for some of the younger members of court to get away, especially during the spring months when the evenings are warmer. We light fires and dance and drink the night away."

"Sounds fun," I say. Not that I would know. I hardly ever leave the house; I certainly would never attend a court party in the woods.

Kian hops off his horse and reaches up for me. I grab hold of his arms as he takes his time lowering me to the ground. My breasts brush up against his chest, and the tingles that shoot through me are almost embarrassing. Once again, I'm grateful for the dark, my face surely a beacon of redness.

His hands gently squeeze my waist before he steps back and goes to tie up his horse.

I take a seat on one of the logs and look up at the moon and stars. They glitter, almost as if Luna approves of the evening's shenanigans.

Kian comes back with an armful of branches that he throws into the pit, and I jump to my feet. "Do you need help?"

"I've got it, love. Just take a seat and I'll have a fire going in no time."

"Okay," I say meekly. It's kind of nice having someone take care of things—take care of me—again.

Kian returns with another armful of wood, and after depositing it, he cocks his head, likely noticing the way my arms are wrapped around myself and rubbing at the thin material of my dress. In my rush to get away, I forgot to grab a cloak. "Here," he removes his own and drapes it over my shoulders before I can protest. "I'm sorry. I should have offered sooner," he admits.

"I didn't ask."

"You shouldn't have to," he scoffs. "Hells, I'm already doing a bang-up job as a husband, aren't I?"

I can't help the small laugh that comes out of me. "We're not bound yet, Kian."

"We will be." His devilish grin sets something alight in my stomach. Hells. I can't fall for my soon-to-be husband.

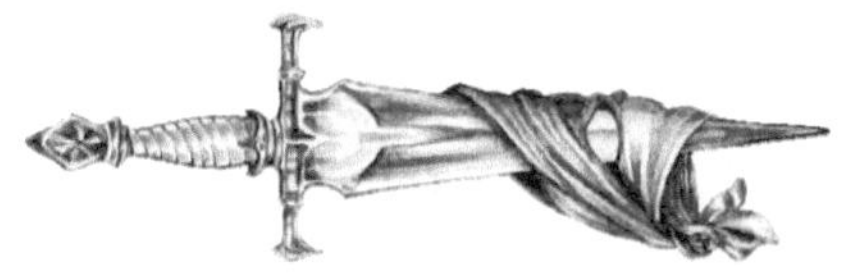

Chapter Twenty-Four

KIAN

After arranging the wood in the pit, I grab a flint from one of the saddlebags and make quick work of lighting the fire. The evening is only growing colder, and we still have quite a few hours until dawn.

I tried to prepare as best I could for this night. Alex was sent to procure a priestess and will meet us at first light just outside the city. The last thing I expected was to find Raelyn hanging off the roof. The way my heart almost stopped in my chest . . . I throw up a quick thanks to the gods that she's all right and that Phantom and I were able to catch her. For a moment there, I thought she'd changed her mind.

With the fire coming to life, I grab the bedroll and the rest of the supplies I brought with me. Raelyn arches a brow as I set the roll down near the fire and begin arranging a picnic for the two of us.

"You brought wine?" she asks, almost in disbelief.

I chuckle. "Of course. We need something to keep us warm out here."

She smiles. "I suppose I didn't quite consider what it would mean to be out all night."

"Are you warm enough?"

She nods, even as she pulls my cloak a little tighter around her.

"Why don't you come and join me?" I ask. "I promise it's warmer, and there's wine and cheese."

"Fine," she says, sounding resigned.

I mockingly put a hand to my heart. "Ouch, that stung."

"What?"

"It's just so clear you want nothing to do with me," I tease.

She snorts as she lowers herself to the bedroll and takes a seat. "Yes, I absolutely loathe your presence. That's exactly why I agreed to marry you."

Her sarcasm makes me laugh again, and I'm secretly pleased that I'm able to bring out this side of her. Especially the smiles.

"Wine?" I ask.

She nods, and I pour her a generous serving.

"Thank you, Kian."

"It's the least I can do, considering we're not having an engagement party or a fancy bonding ceremony."

"It does feel fast," she admits.

"Are you sure you want to go through with this?" I ask. Perhaps I rushed her into it, but I wanted to get her out of that manor as quickly as possible. Once we are priestess-blessed, there will not be a damn thing my father or her stepmother can do . . . at least not if I have anything to say about it.

"Yes, I'm sure," she says before taking a large gulp of wine.

A cloud shifts, the moon casting her glow upon Rae, and I stiffen. I hadn't noticed before in the dark, but her cheek is red and swollen, almost as if . . .

"Who hurt you?" my voice drops as I barely contain the rage welling up inside.

Her eyes widen. "What?"

My hand reaches out and oh-so-gently brushes her cheek.

"Oh," she says, looking down. "Stepmother didn't like what I had to say earlier this evening. It's nothing to worry about."

"Like hells it isn't," I growl. "That she would dare lay a hand on you at all . . ."

Raelyn reaches up and places her hand over mine. "I'm fine, Kian. It doesn't even hurt anymore."

I flinch, realizing I could have caused further pain, even if I hadn't meant to. I pull my hand away. "I'm sorry. I didn't mean to touch you without your permission."

"It's okay. I didn't mind it."

Needing to do something else with my hands, I pick up another log and throw it into the crackling fire. "Ouch!"

"Are you okay?" Raelyn asks.

"Nothing to worry about, just a splinter," I reassure her as I peer at my hand, trying to see if I can pull it out.

"Here, let me," she says and gets up on her knees to move closer.

I hold my hand up for her, and she twists and turns it, trying to find the best angle in the minimal light.

"Ah, there it is. Do you want me to pull it out?"

I chuckle. "If you're offering."

With a swift movement, she pulls the splinter out of my hand and tosses it toward the fire.

"All better," she says. "Oh, wait, you're bleeding."

I look down, and sure enough, a bead of blood exits the tiny wound. "It's nothing."

She stares at the droplet, her jaw clenching. How odd. Raelyn shakes her head and sits back on her heels.

"I'm sorry, love, I'll keep in mind that blood makes you squeamish."

"What? No!" she says, almost sounding alarmed. "Hang on."

Her hand slips into a slit in the side of her dress, and she pulls out a dagger—my dagger. I hold my breath, trying not to react as she slices a small piece of fabric from her gown and ties it around my hand.

The tiny cut probably doesn't need the makeshift bandage, but I'm not about to stop her.

"There. Probably not the most sanitary, but better than nothing. Maybe a healer can check it in the morning?"

"I'm sure it will be fine," I say, watching as she slides the dagger back into her gown, into what I assume is a thigh sheath underneath. Gods, why is the thought of her wearing my blade so damn arousing? How I'd love to drag her skirt up so I could see it with my own eyes. *Fuck*. I'm in dangerous territory.

A yawn escapes her. "Sorry, I'm tired."

I pat the blanket gently. "Why don't you lie down and sleep a little? I'll keep watch."

"Are you sure?" she asks. "I hate to leave you awake on your own."

"No need to worry about me. I don't mind the quiet." Though being alone with my thoughts might prove risky for my heart. "Oh, wait." I jump up and run back to Phantom, who is looking at us with judgmental eyes. I scratch behind his ears and pull a carrot out of the saddlebag, which he chomps gratefully. Grabbing another blanket, I return to the fire. Raelyn has finished her wine and is now lying on her side on the bedroll, her head propped up on her satchel.

I can't help but take in her lovely form and the way her curves slope and dip in that position. My mind goes to the hidden blade, and I curse the direction my thoughts have gone yet again.

"Um, here's a blanket for you."

She yawns once more and offers a sleepy thanks as I drape the blanket over her. I don't mind looking after her . . . this woman who will become my wife in just a few hours.

I shake my head. *On paper only. Don't forget it.*

"Thank you again, Kian," she whispers, and damn, my heart warms at her words.

Her delicate eyelashes kiss her cheeks and her face relaxes as she almost immediately drifts off to sleep.

Oddly enough, I'm wide awake—perhaps it's the thought of being married in a few hours. As I stare at my sleeping betrothed, I can't help but wonder why in Luna's name I proposed this arrangement. She is captivating and strong . . . and I love her sense of humor, but perhaps I haven't thought this all the way through. I fell for her once, and I'm dangerously close to letting her in again. Just the thought of dishonoring our marriage vows and finding other women to warm my bed feels wrong, but I need to keep my distance. I swore to myself I wouldn't let her hurt me again.

FAINT STREAKS of light crack the night sky as dawn makes its arrival. I rise to my feet and stretch, my body sore after sitting on the hard ground for hours. The fire has dulled to embers, and I quickly pack the leftover food and drink into the saddlebags.

Kneeling down next to Raelyn, I nudge her shoulder. "Sorry, love. It's time to wake up."

She startles and blinks sleep-filled eyes at me, her body stretching like a cat's.

"Gods, how long was I out?"

I chuckle. "You crashed pretty hard."

"Did I snore?" She looks almost horrified.

"Absolutely not. You were perfect."

She rolls her eyes, but there's a smile twitching at her lips. "Are you sure it's time? I don't want to get out from under this blanket," she complains.

"Unfortunately, yes." I wink. "But let me make this easier for you." I grab the edge of the blanket and rip it off her.

"Kian!" she shrieks, sitting up with murder in her eyes.

"Hey, it worked. You're up." I grin.

Muttering to herself, she gets to her feet while I fold up the blanket and put it away. When I return, she hands me the neatly folded bedroll.

"Thank you, Rae."

"I'll get you back for that," she threatens with only a little bite.

"I look forward to it."

She scrunches her nose, which makes me want to drop a kiss on it, so I quickly turn away and untie my horse.

Raelyn hands me my wrinkled cloak. "I'm sorry, I should have taken it off before sleeping."

"Aren't you cold? Keep it," I insist.

"Okay . . ." She smiles.

I help her back up onto the horse, and within minutes, we're cantering down the road toward the meeting place. My heart almost skips a beat knowing what's coming, but I try to shake it off.

Raelyn's warm body is doing all sorts of things to me that I'm attempting to ignore. I'm ninety percent certain she felt how hard I was for her on our initial escape from the manor. *Way to get turned on in inappropriate situations, Ki.*

When we finally arrive at our destination, I sigh in relief when I spot Alex's horse attached to a small carriage next to the abandoned temple. He made it.

I slow Phantom to a walk, and we pull up next to it. Knocking on the door, I'm pleased when Alex pops his head out, stifling a yawn.

"Oh good, you're here," he says. "I'm almost certain the priestess thinks I made the whole thing up."

I roll my eyes at him before dismounting and helping Raelyn down.

"Rae, this is Alex, my most obnoxious and loyal friend," I say.

Alex frowns and throws me a glare before turning on the charm and smiling at Raelyn. She holds her hand out, and he presses a kiss to it that oddly has me feeling like I want to rip her away from him.

"Charmed, Lady Raelyn," Alex says.

"Nice to meet you, Alex," she replies with a demure smile. "So *we* are to be married?" She winks at him, and he laughs heartily.

"Is that a proposal, my lady?"

Alex still hasn't let go of her hand, and if he doesn't in the next three seconds, I will remove it for him.

"You're hilarious, Alex," I grit out. "Is the priestess ready?"

"Sort of. Let me wake her again," he says, finally letting go of Rae and walking back to the carriage. "As you can imagine, she wasn't thrilled about the early wake-up call and fell asleep on our drive."

"As long as she performs the ceremony, she'll be well rewarded," I reply before looking at Rae. "Last chance, soon-to-be princess. Are you sure you want to go through with this?"

"I'm here, aren't I?"

It's not the yes I was hoping for, but it will do.

Alex helps the priestess out of the carriage, her golden robes a little wrinkled. Her wizened brow crinkles in disbelief when she sees me standing with Raelyn.

"What is this?" Her voice is harsh.

"A bonding ceremony," I reply matter-of-factly.

She glares at Alex. "This is not what I agreed to, young man. If the king were to find out—"

"I'll handle the king," I interrupt her. "Trust me, you will be greatly compensated for this last-minute affair."

"As I should be," she harrumphs.

"Alex will escort you wherever you need to go after this," I promise, and Alex nods.

My father's wrath knows no bounds. It will be good for the priestess to get out of town for a little while to give the king a chance to calm down.

"Let's get this over with," the priestess demands.

The sky starts to light up as the sun's rays peek up over the horizon, and I lead Raelyn to the small abandoned temple of the sun god. I hurry to get her inside, worried about her potential reaction to the early morning sun, but the beams appear to reach out for her, her skin taking on a faint glow.

Alex shudders as he brushes away cobwebs hanging in the entrance. Nature has started to reclaim the temple—only a few benches remain intact, the roof over the altar is essentially gone, tree branches poke through broken windows, and roots have burst through the stone floor —but it will serve its purpose.

It's dusty and dirty, and I feel somewhat bad that this is the best I could do for my bride, but it is what it is.

The priestess takes her place by the altar, and we stand before her. She binds Raelyn's right hand to my left with a golden ribbon, reciting the sacred words of blessing over us and our union.

I pull out a ring with a giant oval-shaped emerald on top, and Rae's eyes fly to mine in shock as I place it on her right forefinger.

"To you I pledge my undying love and devotion. I will care for you and cherish you until the gods take me home," I vow.

"I-I don't have a ring for you," Raelyn stammers.

"I've got that covered." I wink.

Alex hands her a simple gold band, and she blinks before turning back to face me, slipping it onto my left forefinger.

"To you I pledge my undying love and devotion. I will care for and cherish you until the gods take me home," she repeats.

Despite knowing this isn't real . . . knowing there is no love between us . . . a band of *something* squeezes around my heart.

The priestess continues with the ritual, anointing us with sacred oil. "Now, in honor of the gods' ways, you will unite not just your lives, but your bodies and blood as well."

Shit, I forgot about this part. Raelyn's hand tenses in mine, as if nerves are getting the better of her as well. Real or not, our marriage will be unbreakable, even by the gods, if we complete this part. There's no undoing it.

The priestess pulls out a ceremonial dagger and a golden chalice. Before I can say anything, she pricks my exposed thumb with the sharp blade. She squeezes a few drops of blood into the chalice and repeats the motions with Rae's thumb.

The goblet is swirled, mixing our blood together.

In an almost macabre show, the priestess dips her fingers and paints Raelyn's lips with our blood before turning to paint mine. I'm not sure if I'm just seeing things or if it's the golden chalice, but the blood has an almost shimmering quality to it.

"Now kiss," the priestess declares.

Raelyn looks up at me hesitantly.

I close the gap and take her mouth with my own, the tang of our blood a foreign but not completely unwelcome taste. Her lips are velvety smooth, and she tastes of tart cherries and the richest chocolate. Every part of me wants to deepen the kiss, to devour her like the finest of wines, but Alex clears his throat, and it's as if I'm waking from a spell. I desperately wish to kiss her again and again . . . to taste all of her.

I meet her gaze, and she looks almost as unsettled as I am. Unable to stop myself, I reach over and gently wipe the leftover blood off the side of her mouth, and her jade eyes darken with something I can't quite decipher.

The priestess makes an annoyed sound before we turn back to her, nodding for her to complete the ritual.

She pulls out an official binding scroll from somewhere deep within her robe and has us mark the page with our bloody thumbprints before she pierces her own and signs her name in blood.

The parchment glows as the seal of the gods completes our marriage, and the golden ribbon tying our hands shimmers and sinks into our skin before disappearing. There is no turning back now. Not that I would choose to. For better or worse, Raelyn and I are bound.

"It's done," Rae whispers.

"It's done," I reply.

"Do you feel any different?" she asks almost hesitantly.

I move my wrist where the gold ribbon disappeared and shake my head. "Not really, no."

"Huh," she replies.

"Do you feel different?" I ask.

She pauses, as if afraid to answer, before she shakes her head. "It's nothing. Probably just nerves from the whole thing."

"Are you ready to go to the palace?" I ask.

"As ready as I'll ever be."

The priestess hands us our binding scroll before bustling back out to the carriage, shouting orders at Alex.

He gives me a wry smile before mouthing, "*You owe me,*" and they take off toward the city.

"Let's go start our new lives then."

Chapter Twenty-Five

RAELYN

My rear end is incredibly sore after all the riding we've been doing, and my inner thighs are screaming for relief. I'm so nervous about what's going to happen next. We show up at court, and then what? Will I have time to bathe or rest? I shudder to think about meeting the king in my current state. It's been quite a while since I've been in his presence. This is certainly not how I would have chosen to get reacquainted.

The palace gates are finally in sight, and we thunder toward them. I still can't believe I'm actually married. So much has changed in only a few hours, and I'm struggling to figure out what it all means. My new taste for blood, the most pressing of all.

I recall my first taste that night the intruder came in, when I shook it off as a weird occurrence. Now that I've tasted blood again—twice within hours of each other—I fear there might truly be something wrong with me. When I pulled the splinter out of Kian's hand, it took all my willpower not to draw it to my mouth and suck. Drinking blood is not something humans do except for the rare ritual, but does this mean what I think it does? I shake my head. I'm utterly exhausted and grasping for straws at this point.

The guards at the gate wave Kian through without trouble, and before I know it, he's helping me dismount near the stables.

I peer up at him through the hooded cloak, grateful for the protection from the sun. Two days in a row of clear skies must be a record. "So what now? Please tell me I can take a nap." I give him a wan smile.

"Well, considering your stepmother has probably discovered your disappearance by now, we want to make sure we get to the king first."

I frown as I look down at myself. "Surely you will allow me to clean up before then."

Kian laughs. "Of course, love. My father is probably still asleep, as early as it is. Do you have something to change into?"

My shoulders sag, and I tug at my small satchel. "Does it look like I have court apparel hidden in here?"

"Fair point," he agrees.

"Not to mention, my sisters ransacked my closet and stole all my gowns the moment Stepmother relegated me to service."

"That's incredibly shitty," he says. "Don't worry. I'm sure we can find something for you to wear. I just need to sneak you into my wing for now until we can meet the king."

The palace appears to be waking up as we make our way inside. Maids and footmen scurry about, and the wafting scents of bread and meat fill my nose, causing my stomach to rumble.

"I'll have breakfast brought up to us as soon as we get settled."

"Thank you, Kian."

He's not what I expected. With all the rumors floating about court of his partying and womanizing, his care toward me is a surprise. But then, perhaps his amenable nature is precisely why he is adored by the women of court. Is this how he treats his nightly conquests? I try to shove the feelings deep down before I find myself drowning in them. I just need to keep reminding myself that this isn't real.

When Kian finally escorts me into his wing, my eyes widen as I take in the main living space. The midnight blue and ebony fabrics mixed with walnut wood seem to fit him perfectly. While everything is clean, there's organized clutter on tables and shelves. The room looks lived in. I gaze longingly at the oversized settee by the fire. How I'd love to curl up and take a much-needed nap.

"Would you like to bathe?" Kian asks, startling me from my perusal.

"That would actually be quite lovely," I admit.

Kian rings for his valet, and I take a seat, waiting to be told what to do. I feel so out of place in the palace, everything foreign compared to home.

Within minutes, Kian leads me to his private bathing chamber, the giant tub already filled with piping hot water, a luxury I haven't had in what feels like forever.

"Um, I've asked for clothing to be brought for you, but for now, I'll leave this robe for after your bath," Kian says. He seems almost shy, which is so unlike the prince I've barely begun to get to know.

"Thank you. This is perfect." *And intimate . . . and stirring up all kinds of confusing feelings . . .*

"Well"—he clears his throat—"I guess I'll leave you to it. Shout if you need anything."

"Thanks."

"Of course." His gaze lingers, and I need him to stop looking at me that way.

I wrack my brain for something, anything to distract me, when a thought pops into my head.

"Kian?"

"Yes?"

"I had a lady's maid at the manor who was dismissed a little over a month ago when Stepmother took over . . ."

Kian nods for me to continue.

"Is there any chance I might be able to employ her here?"

"I'll see what I can do." He smiles. "Just give me her name, and I'll see if we can find her."

I feel a little guilty that I'm not sure where she lives—so used to her being at my beck and call in the manor, I hadn't ever considered where she's from. I'm a terrible friend.

"Thank you so much. Her name is Sera Elsterbrock."

Once Kian leaves, I strip off my filthy clothes and sink into the bath. It's so luxurious to be allowed this simple pleasure after days of working morning til night with hardly a break. While this isn't necessarily how I envisioned my life, it's better than the prospect of serving my family for the remainder of it. I'm also starting to doubt Father would have even been able to put a stop to it with Stepmother holding the scandal of my parentage over our heads.

After scrubbing every inch of skin and washing my hair thoroughly, I stand and reach for a towel to dry off. Kian's soaps and oils worked wonders on my rough hands, and I look at them in awe, my mind snagging on a thought, but my exhaustion seems unwilling to allow me to go there.

I towel off and try to ring as much water out of my hair as possible before I put on the black, oversized robe Kian left me. Glancing in the fogged-up mirror, I catch sight of my reflection. Wiping the mirror with the sleeve of my robe, I lean in closer, holding back a gasp.

My cheek looks completely normal, no bruising or swelling in sight, and most surprising of all, tiny flecks of gold that I never noticed before surround the green of my eyes. Is this an effect of the marriage bond? I glance down at my right wrist, and the faintest shimmer of the ribbon glimmers up at me.

I'll have to ask Kian to show me the palace's library. There are some things I desperately want to research . . .

I'm startled by a soft knock on the door.

"Rae? Are you all right in there?" Kian's voice sounds muffled.

"Quite all right. I'll be right out," I call back.

When I make my way back to the main sitting area, Kian is seated at a table piled high with breakfast delicacies.

"Gods, this smells amazing," I say with a happy sigh.

Kian looks up and almost does a double take at me in his robe. His eyes appear to darken as they peruse my form, causing me to shiver at the intensity.

"I have to say, I enjoy seeing you in my clothes," he says.

The forwardness brings a blush to my cheeks, and I hurry to sit so I can hide behind the mountain of food on the table. Kian clears his throat and sits back in his chair, his eyes seeking mine. I'm captured by him—I couldn't look away if I tried.

"Rae, there is something we need to discuss before we meet my father."

A rush of trepidation chills me. "Oh?"

"I apologize for not doing so sooner, but time slipped away from me."

I nod as I serve myself a helping of bacon and eggs. Kian holds out a basket full of croissants, and my eyes widen. "Those are my favorite."

Kian nods. "I remember."

I blink, confused by the statement. I don't recall telling him that, but perhaps I've forgotten.

I take a bite of the flaky pastry and close my eyes, savoring the taste. "Mm-hmm . . . this is amazing . . ." Opening my eyes back up, I meet his gaze again. "Well, what did you have to say? Spit it out. Stop keeping me in suspense and distracting me with pastries, as much as I love them."

He grins but looks a little pained. "We need to convince the king that we are madly in love."

"Excuse me?"

"My father will be furious that I eloped without his permission . . . so I need to give him a reason. The simplest solution is to convince him that we are so madly in love, we couldn't help ourselves."

My jaw drops, and I stammer, "But . . . that's not at all what we agreed upon. You said this marriage was on paper only. If we have to convince him that we're in love . . ."

Kian winces. "Yes, I'm sorry . . . If we'd had more time to court and get permission from your father and had a proper wedding, that would have definitely been the case, but the elopement has changed things."

"You didn't think to mention this *before* we eloped?" My voice has climbed to a higher register, and I hate the shrillness of my tone.

Kian shrugs. "It doesn't really change things. We just need to pretend a little."

"Pretend?"

"Give each other loving glances, perhaps little public displays of affection . . . nothing too over the top."

I shake my head in disbelief. "I'm a terrible liar, Kian. I don't know that I can do this."

"We'll be fine," Kian says, waving a hand dismissively. "It's only when we're out in public or with my father. Most of the time, you won't need to worry about it."

I take a deep breath, considering all that he just shared. It makes sense, but I also have the feeling it's just going to complicate everything between us, even more so than it already is.

"Okay, fine. I'll try . . ."

Kian sighs in relief. "Great. I'll admit, I was quite worried about bringing this up to you."

"As you should have been," I admonish.

"Would it have changed anything?" he asks, looking almost penitent. "If I'd told you before our vows, would you have said no?"

I pause to consider. "Probably not, no . . . I needed to get out. If pretending to love you is the worst thing I have to do, I suppose I consider that fairly lucky."

"I'm sorry." Kian groans. "I didn't mean to screw up our marriage before it's even truly begun."

I reach across the table and place my hand on his, giving it a light squeeze. "It'll be all right. Don't beat yourself up."

His smile looks part grateful and part relieved. "Eat up, Rae. You're going to need your strength to face the king."

I shudder. "He is quite intimidating."

"I'll be with you every step of the way."

"I'll hold you to that," I threaten, but my voice is light.

After we devour the food, a maid shows up with an armful of

dresses for me to choose from. Where they came from, I'm almost afraid to ask. If Kian has a secret room stashed with dresses for his conquests, I'll die of embarrassment.

Having a maid fuss over me and fix my hair is incredible. I missed being taken care of, but even the thought just makes me feel spoiled. I vow to treat people better. Having been forced to look after myself has given me a sense of responsibility that feels good. I can take care of myself if I need to, but I also appreciate that the servants who work for us deserve to earn a living wage for their work.

Feeling refreshed and prepared to face the king—as much as I can be —I pace the prince's sitting room, waiting for him to finish getting ready. I worry that if I sit still for too long, I'll nod off from exhaustion.

Kian finally enters the room, looking completely put together in his tailored pants and matching grey waistcoat. Damn, he really is good-looking. I can't believe he's my husband.

He throws me a smile and offers his arm. "Ready?"

Kian leads me down the long hall. Portraits of his family line the walls, ranging back generations before him. Old-fashioned suits of armor stand guard in the alcoves. The halls are so quiet, I feel like I have to whisper, so I do. "Where are we meeting him?"

Kian looks at me oddly and speaks at a normal volume. "He's in the throne room. Today is the day he listens to petitions from our people. I'm hoping to catch him before he starts."

A fresh wave of nerves crashes over me. Gods, I sure hope this goes better than I'm anticipating.

As we get nearer to the throne room, Kian pulls me a little closer, leaning his head down to whisper in my ear, "Smile, love. We need to sell that we've never been happier."

I really hope I can do this.

"Just take a deep breath. We have the bond seared into our skin. He couldn't stop this if he tried."

Except he can. Death is the only thing that can end a marriage bond, and while the king might not be willing to kill his own son, he has no such loyalty to me.

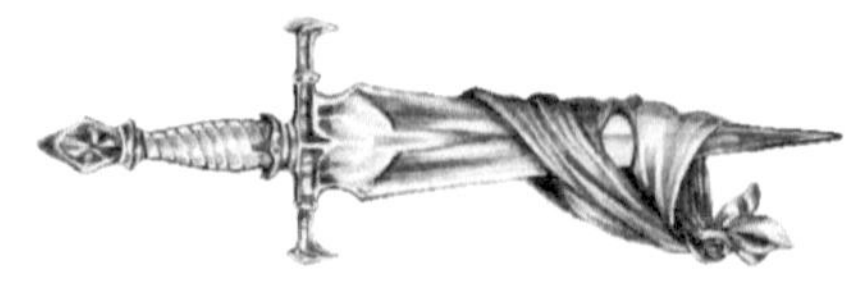

Chapter Twenty-Six

KIAN

I have to be strong for her. Showing my nerves will only make the beautiful woman on my arm even more anxious than she already is, and I really need us to sell this.

We take the side entrance into the throne room, and to my relief, the king isn't yet seeing petitioners. He's seated on his throne, flipping through pages of intelligence. I can only pray to the gods he's in a good mood today.

"Father! I'm so happy I caught you," I call out as we approach. Letting go of Rae's arm, I wrap an arm around her waist, tucking her into my side. To my relief, she rests a hand on my chest, turning in toward me while her other hand slides around my waist. Her curves press into my side, and for a moment, I forget what I'm supposed to say. She fits so perfectly—as if she were made for me.

The king raises a brow and looks down on us with a frown. "Kian, what a surprise." His gaze moves to Raelyn, suspicion high. He probably doesn't recognize her.

Might as well get this over with.

"Father, I'd like to present Lady Raelyn Astoria." I pull her in just a little closer. "My wife."

The king's face turns a sickly shade of purple, and the veins in his temple protrude as he rises to his feet. "What. Is. The. Meaning. Of. This." Each word is punctuated with spittle as he accusingly points a finger in my direction. "Tell me you're joking."

Raelyn flinches, and I squeeze her waist in what I hope is a reassuring way.

I straighten my shoulders as I hold his glare. "Is that any way to treat the brand new princess?"

Fury pours off him in waves, and I feel very bad for whoever walks through that door next.

"You can't be married," he spits out. "Not without a priestess."

I pull the scroll out of my pocket as I let go of Raelyn and step forward. "We were priestess blessed this morning."

Father snatches the scroll out of my hand and opens it, his eyes wide. "Ethan!" he screeches, calling his faithful advisor out from the shadows. He hands him the scroll. "Find this priestess and bring her to me immediately."

I'm thankful Alex is getting her out, even though there's nothing she could have done to undo this.

I try to keep a casual air and not let my father's rage rattle me. "As I said, it's official." I raise my arm, letting him see the shimmer of the marriage bond.

My father seats himself back on his throne, his nostrils flaring. I step in front of Raelyn in an attempt to protect her.

"What makes you think I'll allow this to stand?" my father asks in a sinister tone.

"Because I did what you asked—I married before the end of the season—and most importantly, I love her."

"Love?" my father scoffs. "When did you even have time to get to know the girl?"

I turn back to Rae, noting the nervous smile on her face. My hand cups her cheek, and I stare into her eyes, trying to project to him that she's my world. "I've known her for years, and it's always been clear she was meant to be mine." The half-truth feels oddly hollow in my chest.

Raelyn's body quivers ever so slightly, and there's something akin to longing in her eyes. She's a better actress than she gave herself credit for. Her throat bobs, and my hand slides from her cheek, gently encircling her neck as I lean down and press a soft kiss to her forehead. Her sweet scent envelops me, and my heart catches in my chest.

"Is she with child?" Father blurts out.

Rae jumps back in surprise, her hands flying to her mouth as her cheeks turn bright pink.

"Surely that is the only reason to explain your impetuousness," he continues.

"Father." I bristle. "Do not insult my wife with false allegations."

Raelyn appears to have gathered herself as she steps in front of me, dropping into a deep curtsy before the king. "Your Majesty, Prince Kian is more than I could have ever dreamed of. I promise to love and cherish him for the rest of my gods given life."

My father raises a brow, as if not entirely sure he believes the charade. "Well, Kian, I have to say this news is quite shocking to say the least. I'm not thrilled you went behind my back, but if you're as infatuated with the girl as you claim, I can perhaps understand a little recklessness." He flicks a hand toward Raelyn. "You may rise."

My father is being far too reasonable, what is he trying to play? His switch from anger to this sudden understanding gives me pause. The king's eyes harden to a steely glint—perhaps he isn't fully buying our ruse.

"Kian," he continues, "if I find you have deceived me, there will be consequences. Do you understand?"

I swallow and nod, my father's stern voice taking me back to the child I used to be, always on the receiving end of his anger.

Rae turns to look at me, a glimpse of fear shining in her eyes. I close the gap between us, pulling her back into my side protectively.

"Well, Father, now that we've shared our news, I'd love to take my bride to our rooms. We have a lot of celebrating to do."

Raelyn blushes again, and I grin at her, my hand possessively gripping her waist.

"You're dismissed," the king declares.

We exit through the side door, and I take a deep breath, relieved it didn't go worse. The murmur of petitioners around the corner fills the air, and I start to lead Raelyn back toward my wing when a disturbance causes her to stiffen and stop in her tracks.

"You'll let me through to the front of the line immediately," a shrill female voice commands.

That almost sounds like . . .

"I have urgent news for the king!"

"Stepmother," Rae whispers.

Kyros help us.

"She could ruin everything!" Raelyn sounds panicked. "You heard what your father said. If she reveals our plan or exposes my questionable parentage, he could have me put to death!"

I close my eyes. What in the hells was I thinking. There is no way I will be responsible for her death. I won't allow it.

"Let me handle it, love. Head back to my wing, and I'll see you soon."

Rae bites her lip, wringing her hands, but nods.

I march back into the throne room right as Lady Astoria is led in before the king. She reminds me of a peacock, the way her teal silk dress floats about her and a giant feather adorns her golden hair.

"Your Majesty," she croons before dipping into the most exaggerated curtsy I've ever seen. "I have urgent news I must share with you."

The king looks up from his papers, boredom seeping from his pores, and he hasn't even started yet. "Please do share."

"I'm afraid the prince has run off with my stepdaughter, Lady Raelyn Astoria."

The king snorts. "Old news. Is there anything else?"

Lady Astoria's haughty sneer turns to disbelief, and she seems at a loss for words when I step into sight.

"Are you here to congratulate me?" I ask. "I suppose we are family now."

Her eyes drop to the shimmering bond on my wrist, and she stiffens before a calculating look lights her eyes. How far will she take this? Would revealing Raelyn's parentage harm or benefit her?

"Oh my, I see . . . Your Majesty, I hope you can understand. I'm most concerned that we were unable to draw up official betrothal papers. And her father is away, so the matter of her dowry . . ." She trails off. "Clearly you can see this is unacceptable."

The king sits forward on his throne, looking down his nose at her. Will he pretend to be as outraged as she is or will he be afraid of that making him look bad?

"Do you think I'm unaware of what happens in my own kingdom?"

Ah. His pride wins out. I sigh a breath of relief.

Lady Astoria looks flummoxed and starts to stammer. "I'm sorry . . . Your . . . Your Majesty, I thought—"

"You thought what?" the king demands. "You thought I wouldn't be aware of my son's priestess-blessed marriage before it happened?"

"I can see I was mistaken, Your Majesty." She sinks to the floor, keeping her eyes downcast.

"As far as the papers, trust they will be handled between me and Lord Astoria when he returns."

"Thank you, Your Majesty," Lady Astoria simpers. "I look forward to celebrating the union of our families soon."

I roll my eyes. Of course she would try to get some kind of party or notoriety out of the match.

"Dismissed," the king's voice booms out.

Before she's led away by one of the servants, she catches my eye—the cold look of cunning sends a shiver down my spine. My relief is short-lived. This isn't over.

"Kian, a word."

I close my eyes. *Shit. What now?*

I make my way to the dais. "I thought you were off to celebrate with your *wife*," he says suspiciously.

"Yes, I was, but I—"

"I will not be made a fool of, Kian!" the king interjects. "I might have saved face with Lady Astoria, but clearly there is something going on that you wish to hide. Now, I'd like to believe that your infatuation caused you to behave like an imbecile as you claim, but if word gets out that you deceived me, I meant what I said, and you won't be the one to pay the price for your mistakes."

"Yes, sir," I reply.

"Now out of my sight before I change my mind. Lord Astoria is a loyal subject whom I once considered a close friend, and he is the only reason your lovely wife still has her head."

I bite my tongue as I nod and hurry out of the throne room. The king cannot find out about her parentage. He'd have no trouble at all getting rid of a bastard princess.

By the time I make it back to my wing, I find my new wife curled up on the settee, fast asleep. Why isn't she in bed? Surely that can't be comfortable. With half a thought, I turn down the sheets before returning to carry her to my room, laying her gently on the black silk sheets. She murmurs something unintelligible before falling silent, her slow, deep breaths telling me she's still asleep. I gently brush her hair off her face before tucking the blanket around her.

Failing to hold back a yawn, my own exhaustion hits me like a ton of bricks. The bed is quite large, and sleeping somewhere else would surely raise suspicion. After shrugging out of my coat and kicking off my shoes, I slide in, taking care to keep my distance from Raelyn. I don't want her to be frightened when she wakes up next to her husband.

Chapter Twenty-Seven

RAELYN

"Come out and play, sissy!" Erika calls from the terrace. The yellow ribbons in her hair fly out behind her as she dances around, waving a wand made of pink and purple silk streamers. I desperately want to play outside with her, but Papa told me to stay indoors. It's not safe outside under the sun. I can't remember, but he's told me many times how sick I get if I don't obey. But Papa isn't home.

Chessa whines for no discernible reason, and I roll my eyes as the governess attempts to distract her.

I try to focus on the puzzle in front of me, but my attention keeps getting pulled back to Erika dancing on the terrace with the wind in her hair, her skin aglow from the sun. It's not fair.

"Why don't you play outside with Erika?" the governess asks Chess.

"I'm bored. Take me to my dolls. Now," Chess demands.

Gods, five-year-old Chess is almost more insufferable than four-year-old Chess,

but maybe this will work in my favor.

The governess mutters something under her breath as she leads Chessa toward her room. "Keep an eye on your sister," she calls out to me.

As soon as she disappears, I rush to the door and poke my head out. A tiny part of me worries what will happen if I break Papa's rule, but then again, the governess told me to watch Erika. I'm the big sister—it's my responsibility.

I stick my slippered foot out the door, waiting for something bad to happen, but when all I feel is a pleasant warmth from the sun, I jump out onto the terrace.

"Sissy!" Erika cries and flings her arms around me. "Do you want to dance with me? I'm pretending to be at one of Mama and Papa's grand balls. I'm the new princess!" She twirls around and around, and I can't help but laugh and join her. After the king stopped by with Prince Kian earlier today, she's been convinced she's going to be a princess someday.

She gives me a turn with the ribbon wand, and as I twirl it around me, it almost appears as if light is dancing off the ribbons. Prismatic rainbows reflect off the windows and the glass lanterns hanging around the terrace, and Erika oohs and ahhs at the light display.

"My turn!" she cries out and grabs the wand from me, but when she dances, the sun is no longer shooting out the beams of light.

She pouts. "What did you do? Did you break it?"

At a loss, I shrug and continue dancing around the courtyard, enjoying the warmth of the sun on my skin. How can this be bad when it's so warm and comforting?

"Raelyn!" my mother's voice shrieks from the manor. "Get inside this instant!"

"Sorry, Erika," I say as I run back.

My very pregnant, very angry mother stands next to my puzzle, her hands on her hips and her eyes alight with fire. "Have you lost your mind?" she yells. "You know the rules! If your father were to find out what his child had done, he'd send you away."

In a fit of rage, she sweeps the puzzle I'd been working on for days onto the floor, and I cry out in frustration. All my hard work is gone. I crash to my knees and attempt to salvage any pieces that remain locked in place.

"Go to your room," Mother commands.

"But can't—"

"Now!" she screams.

Tears stream down my face, and I try to brush them away as I rush toward the stairs. Mother never has a kind word for me. Sometimes I think she wishes I'd never been born. I've seen the way she dotes on the twins and the way she warmly rubs her belly. What I wouldn't give for her to hold me and explain why there are different rules for me. Why does the sun make me sick? I look down at my skin, and other than being a little pink from the heat of dancing around, it looks normal.

SOMETHING warm and hard is around my waist. My eyes fly open, and I'm immediately disoriented, both from the strange dream that felt like a memory and my new location. Wasn't I by the fire? My stockinged feet curl and flex as my body wakes up.

The extremely muscled arm banded around me and the silk pillow under my head tell me that I've been relocated to a bed—a very comfortable and luxurious one at that. One would think I'd panic at the fact that a man's arm is around me, but instinctively, I know it's Kian.

Why in Luna's name he's in bed with me is a question I will have to ask when he awakens. For now, his soft, even breaths tickle the back of my neck, and I'm afraid to move for fear it will disturb him—and shockingly, I'm really enjoying this. It'll never happen again, but still, it's not altogether unpleasant.

A low growl comes out of Kian, and I stiffen. Did I move too much? He pulls me closer, and . . . yes, that's an erection pressing against my backside. A flush of warmth heats my cheeks, but no. That's completely normal for men, right? I try to think back to the stories Sera told me about her conquests, recalling how much they'd made me blush and also feel a tiny bit jealous.

Kian moves again, and I think I feel lips on the back of my neck. He moves his arm, and then there's a hand pressed against my stomach. I'm a bundle of nerves and butterflies as his hand dips lower.

Okay! That's enough. I grab his hand, fling it away from me, and promptly roll away from my husband.

"Rae?" a sleep-addled voice says. "Oh shit, did I do something wrong?"

I sit up and look down at my dazed and confused husband. "No, everything's fine. I just need to get up to use the privy."

Kian smiles sleepily and stretches his arms overhead. "I'm sorry for moving you without asking. I thought you'd be more comfortable here."

I blush, pushing a strand of hair behind my ear. "It was very comfortable, thank you." A yawn overtakes me, and I cover my mouth with my hand. "What time do you think it is?"

Kian glances at the window. "I'd guess it's late afternoon by now."

I laugh. "We must have been tired."

"Well, it was an eventful night to say the least."

"I'll be right back," I say and hop out of bed, running to the bathing room to take care of my needs.

My face is completely flushed when I look into the mirror. I feel lazy for sleeping the entire day away, but my body clearly needed it.

Oh hells. I palm my face. I completely forgot to take my tonic. I'll need to see about procuring more, but I have to admit, I'm not completely sure what's in it. I accidentally skipped a few doses here and there in the last month, and it didn't seem to negatively affect me or make me feel all that different, which begs the question—why does my father insist on me taking it?

"Kian?" I call out as I re-enter his room. "Do you know where my satchel is?"

Kian responds from the sitting room, "It's in here, love."

I pad into the sitting area to find Kian lounging in a leather armchair, a drink in hand. "Would you like some?"

"No thanks." I shake my head and glance around the room, finally spotting my satchel. After digging around, I pull out the single vial of tonic.

"What's that?" Kian asks.

"My tonic."

Kian chuckles. "A contraceptive tonic?"

My eyes flash to his, cheeks heating with embarrassment. "No! I mean, I don't know?"

Kian frowns. "What do you mean you don't know? You're about to take a tonic and you're not even sure what it does?" The incredulity in his voice makes me feel rather foolish.

I shrug, almost helplessly. "My father has been making me take it for as long as I can remember. He says if I don't, it will make me sick . . . I've only missed it a few times and so far nothing bad has happened . . . but I'm not sure if I should risk it."

Kian sets his glass of amber liquid down and strides over to me. "May I?"

I nod, and he holds the golden tonic up to the light.

"Perhaps one of our alchemists can determine what it's for and replicate it if necessary. Who prepared it at home?"

"Our chef always had it for me, but I'm not actually sure where he got it from. I never thought to ask."

"Ah, sweet Rae, so trusting now, aren't we?"

Trying not to feel defensive, I roll my shoulders back and feign confidence I don't really have. "Why would my father give me something I don't actually need?"

Kian flicks my nose. "I'm just teasing, love. No need to get riled up."

The truth is, after the lies Stepmother exposed, a part of me wonders what other falsehoods my father has told and if there are other surprises awaiting me.

My mind flashes back to my unexpected taste for blood, and with sudden clarity, I realize that all the strange experiences I've been having center on me either forgetting to take my tonic, tasting blood, or being out in the sun. Is it all connected somehow? I'm almost afraid to think the words. It's utterly ludicrous. There's no possible way.

"Where did you go?" Kian asks. "You slipped away."

I shake my head. "I'm sorry . . . I'm just dealing with all of these changes, and it's quite overwhelming. I'm also not really used to being with someone else this much. I was mostly left alone at home."

"Already sick of me?" Kian winks. "Should I leave you alone?"

"Oh gods, no." I blush. "I'm sorry, I didn't mean to make you feel unwelcome in your own rooms."

He laughs. "It's quite all right."

"Speaking of rooms . . . where might mine be? Are the maids preparing one nearby?"

"About that . . ." Kian winces, and I go on alert.

"What?" I hold my breath.

"I think we need to hold off on separate rooms for the time being. My father is quite suspicious of us, and if he finds I've stuck you in another wing of the palace already, our entire plan falls apart."

"But I can't seriously share a bed with you!"

"We already did. Was it so bad?" Kian asks.

"We were fully clothed and it was during the day!"

"So?"

"So . . . that's completely different," I stammer. He might be used to waking up next to women, but it was a whole new experience for me having him pressed up against me . . . his touch causing my pulse to race and invoking all sorts of other feelings we can't act on.

Kian folds his arms and leans against his chair. "I'd love to hear your reasoning on this."

"We're not actually 'together,'" I whisper-shout. "Marriage on paper only, remember?"

Kian frowns. "I'm trying to protect you from my father, Rae. It might be a little uncomfortable right now, but it won't be forever. Soon enough, he'll forget about us."

I scoff. "Sure."

He runs a hand through his hair. "I'll keep my hands off, I promise."

"Like you did today?" I throw back at him.

His eyes widen. "What did I do? Surely if I touched you, I'd remember."

I roll my eyes. "You were asleep."

"Well, that's disappointing. I'm jealous of myself."

I shake my head. "You're ridiculous. My point is, how do I know you're not going to keep doing that."

"I didn't realize my touch would be so unpalatable to you."

I blush but try to cover it up. "That's not what I said, and you know it. I just don't want to confuse things between us. We made an agreement, and we should honor it. If you need to be close to me in public, that's fine, but when we're alone, hands off."

Kian blows out a breath. "You're a difficult woman."

"Thank you."

"That wasn't a compliment."

"It was to me," I say.

His lips quirk into a half smile. "Well, we need to make an appearance at dinner tonight, so be prepared to be touched."

"Why does that sound like a threat?"

Kian shrugs. "Take it as you will." He downs the remainder of his drink, then nods at the door. "I'll bring your tonic to the alchemist and see about making more for you if that's all right."

"Fine with me."

He swipes it off the table and saunters past. I hate that my eyes are drawn to his incredible backside as he walks out the door.

I'm in trouble.

AN HOUR OR SO LATER, there's a knock at the door, and a familiar face peeks in.

"Sera?" I practically squeal.

"Raelyn!" she cries out and runs in, tackling me in an embrace.

"Gods, I thought I'd never see you again." Emotion clogs my throat as I choke out the words.

"I almost didn't believe it when the messenger came!" Sera exclaims. "This job is a dream come true, Raelyn, thank you so much. You have no idea how much of a difference this will make for my family." Her eyes are filled with tears, which makes mine tear up, and suddenly, we're both crying, blubbering messes, trying to catch up on the time we've missed.

"Thank you so much for coming, Sera. It's already more like home having you here."

"Are you kidding me? I wouldn't have said no for anything. Working in the palace? This is insane. I can't believe you actually married the prince!"

"Yes, it's quite shocking to say the least. I'm just relieved to finally be away from Stepmother. And also, can I just profusely apologize for any time I took you for granted? Your work is so incredibly challenging."

Sera smiles, wiping a tear off my cheek with her thumb. "You were always loving and kind to me. You're family, even if you need me to take care of you."

I let out a weak laugh and pull her back in for another hug.

"Okay now, enough crying. I need to get you ready for dinner, right?"

I shrug. "I suppose so."

"Well, let's make you look like the princess you now are."

My face blanches. "I forgot about that part. Will I have to wear a tiara?"

Sera laughs. "Don't you worry about a thing, my lady. I've got you."

"You know you're my only friend, right?"

Sera sighs and pats my cheek. "I know, but I wish I weren't. You deserve to have other people in your life who love and accept you for who you are. I think this change will be good for you."

"I sure hope so."

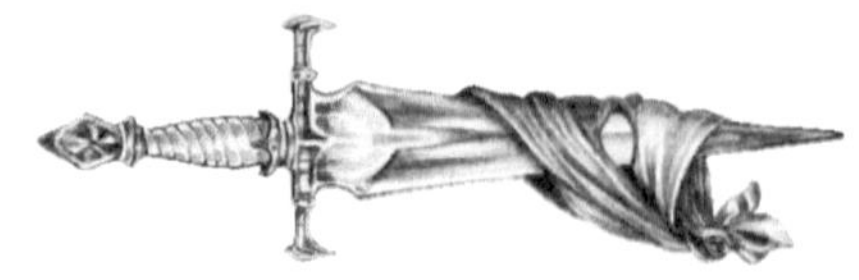

Chapter Twenty-Eight

KIAN

My wife is a vision. I almost need to pause to catch my breath as I take in the goddess before me. Her hair is artfully piled atop her head and glittering with gemstones. Soft curls frame her face, and I wonder how she'd respond if I tugged on one. Raelyn looks bridal in a dress the softest of pinks, it almost looks white, and it drapes her body in the most delicious of ways. Her unblemished shoulders and back are on display, and I wonder if her skin is as soft as it looks.

I clear my throat, gripping the back of a chair in our sitting room. "You look lovely."

Her cheeks, already tinged a pretty shade of pink, deepen at my words, which pleases me. I love that I can get reactions out of her. I let go of the chair and take her proffered hand, sweeping it up to my lips.

"Thank you, Kian. You don't look so bad yourself."

"This old thing?" I scoff. "No one will be looking at me when they have you to feast their eyes upon."

She shrinks in a little, her shoulders curling. *Did I say the wrong thing?*

"I don't much enjoy being the center of attention, to be honest," she mumbles, her eyes downcast.

I take a step closer and tip her chin so she looks in my eyes. "I'm so sorry if this is uncomfortable for you, but trust that you're not alone—I'm with you. You are beautiful. Don't be afraid to own it."

She gives me a quick bob of the head and purses her lips in determination.

We proceed to one of the grand dining halls in companionable silence, and the room goes quiet as we enter. Rumors have already spread about our elopement, and from the looks of it, nearly every courtier in the kingdom had begged for an invitation to tonight's dinner.

Raelyn is stiff beside me, her nerves radiating off her in waves. I lean in and brush my lips on her neck and whisper, "Relax, love. I'm with you." I press a kiss to her pulse point, and tiny goosebumps pepper her skin from my touch. "Try to play along," I whisper in her ear before placing another kiss on the side of her head.

"Their Royal Highnesses, Prince Kian and Princess Raelyn D'Amaris of Rakveren," the herald announces before we move to take our seats near the king. I'm happy to see that Colin actually left for the country estate, as the last thing I need are his judgmental stares. He's probably spitting mad that I ruined his plans for me and Princess Helene.

"Am I actually a princess now?" Raelyn asks under her breath.

"You're married to me, aren't you?" I tease.

She elbows me lightly, and I smile as she lightens up just a little.

"All rise for His Majesty, King Silenius D'Amaris of Rakveren," the herald announces, and we stand, heads bowed in deference as the king marches into the room in all his finery.

"You may be seated," the king says with a wave of his hand. "Thank you for joining us this evening for the celebration of our new princess."

Conversations resume and murmurs fill the air as all eyes are on us.

"Thank you, Father, for being so gracious."

"Don't mention it," the king replies. "How are you liking the palace, Princess?"

"It's so lovely," she replies, and I squeeze her hand under the table.

"You two must be quite taken with each other to have rushed into sacred marriage bonds so quickly," the king says.

Raelyn looks at me instead of Father, and I smile as she says, "What can I say? Kian swept me off my feet."

I'm tempted to kiss her right here and now, but while we want people to think we're in love, Father wouldn't stand for such a public display. Perhaps I only want to kiss her because I won't be able to in private, but after that brief kiss we shared during our binding, I can't help but ache for more.

"I'm sure there is plenty of disappointment among the court ladies that you're no longer available, Kian," the king says.

"They'll manage just fine, Father," I reply, trying to keep my ire at bay. Did he really need to say that in front of my *wife*?

"Let's eat," the king commands.

Raelyn is stiff as a board again, and I lean in to whisper in her ear, "The hard part is over, I promise."

She turns to face me, and we're so close, our noses graze.

Gods, I *really* want to close the distance and kiss her.

"Sorry." Her breath ghosts over my lips.

"You have nothing to be sorry for, love. You're perfect," I whisper before I pull away to stop myself from doing something I'll regret . . . not that I could ever regret kissing her.

She scrunches her nose in an adorable way, and I'm about to speak again when—

"Well, aren't you two the most adorable couple ever. It's almost sickening."

Raelyn freezes, and I turn to look behind us. *Great.*

"What are you doing here?" Raelyn asks her sister Erika.

"Oh, just wanted to pay my respects to the happily bound couple," she says with fake niceness.

"Well, you've done it. Move along now," I say dryly, turning back to my plate.

She sputters in disbelief before gritting out, "He's a delight. Congratulations." The rustle of her skirts announces her departure, and I blow out a breath.

Good riddance.

I slide my hand across Rae's bare shoulders, enjoying how her skin pebbles beneath my touch. "Please tell me Chessa isn't here as well."

"Gods, I hope not. But that dismissal was incredible," she breathes, her lips curving into a smile.

"Anything to put a smile on your face, love."

She blushes, but her body has finally relaxed. If only I didn't need my hands to eat, I'd find every excuse to keep touching her.

To my relief, the dinner moves forward without complication or other unwanted guests. Course after course is brought out, and Raelyn grows more at ease as the dinner progresses. The courtiers have asked her a few questions here and there, but overall, they are focused entirely on their own conquests and achievements. I can't wait for the dinner to be over; if I hear one more lord brag about his lands, I will shove some land back at him.

It always infuriates me how no one seems concerned about the lack of food being produced. As long as their bellies are full, they couldn't care less about the rest of our people—many who suffer because the lords continue to take more than their fair share. If it weren't for the Shadow, our people would be in much worse shape. Father should be thanking him instead of putting a bounty on him. The king is creating the perfect circumstances for an uprising with his lack of action.

Any time I bring up trying to seek out the lost sun god in hopes he'll save our land, Father claims I'm acting foolishly and that it's a complete waste of time. *"If the god wished to be found, he would be."*

I can't quite put my finger on it, but I know in my heart he's wrong. *Something* is wrong. Us sitting around doing nothing is not going to save us. And what happens when the land stops producing completely? No. I can't allow that to happen.

AFTER DROPPING Raelyn off in our wing, I head back to the alchemist's chambers. I would have brought Rae, but she looked dead on her feet despite our long nap earlier today.

"Your Highness, I have the information you requested," the palace's primary alchemist, Hennig, says.

I prop my elbows on the high counter, intrigued to find out what he discovered. The room has an odd medicinal smell that is not completely unpleasant, but it isn't somewhere I'd want to spend all of my time. The multitude of colored glass bottles and containers lining the shelves behind him refract light into the space, giving it an almost ethereal glow. Hells, I'd get way too distracted working in here.

"What have you got, Hennig?"

"It's the strangest thing," he says, scratching his chin as he holds the small vial up to the light. "The ingredients aren't altogether uncommon, but they surely aren't for any ailment I've ever heard of."

"What do you mean?" My interest is highly piqued, and concern for Rae filters in.

"The ingredients are typically used to suppress and weaken."

My eyebrows fly up. "Suppress what, exactly?"

Hennig shakes his head. "I'm honestly not one hundred percent sure. One of the ingredients is what I'd use to help an alcoholic manage cravings, but it's hard for me to imagine a young girl dealing with that issue. Have you noticed anything strange about her?"

I'm completely baffled. Is Rae withholding some deep secret from me? Or is this her father's doing? She seemed uncertain of what exactly the tonic did as well.

"I'm honestly not sure how to answer that, Hennig."

He frowns. "Well, if she insists on continuing to take this tonic, I have reverse engineered it and can provide it for her. However, I am not so certain it's helping as much as it's harming. Though I'm concerned that, if she's been taking it for years, it could be dangerous for her to stop without weaning off it."

"My guess is that she will want to come speak with you herself," I muse. "I'll bring her the information and let her decide how she wants to proceed."

Hennig raises a brow. "How magnanimous of you, sire. I can't imagine the king would have done the same for your mother. He was most controlling."

"Tell me about it." I sigh. "My gut is telling me she needs to wean off this shit, but I think she should be allowed to decide for herself."

"Very good, sire."

He hands me back the vial before making a careful note in his ledger. "I'm available for Princess Raelyn any time she'd like to speak, but for now, if she decides to wean herself off, I would recommend taking half of a dose today and half tomorrow and then continue to decrease the amounts. I can prepare more and have it delivered to you."

"Thank you so much."

WHEN I GET to my wing, an unfamiliar blonde maid is leaving the bedroom.

"Are you Sera?" I ask.

She dips into a curtsy and nods. "Thank you so much for the employment, Your Highness."

When she lifts her head and meets my gaze, I'm taken aback by the intense violet hue of her eyes; they're almost otherworldly.

"I'd do anything for Rae." I smile.

"I'm very happy for her, Your Highness." She straightens and appears to take an interest in what I'm holding. "Is that my lady's tonic?"

"Yes, it is. I need to speak with her. Is she awake?"

Sera shakes her head. "I'm sorry, Your Highness. She passed out pretty quickly upon her return. Would you like me to hold on to that for you?" She shifts on her feet, no longer meeting my gaze. "I can give it to her in the morning."

I purse my lips. Hennig said she might want to take some tonight, but I hate to wake her. "Thank you, Sera, but I've got it. I won't disturb her until the morning, and I will give it to her then."

"If you're certain. It's no trouble," she says.

"I'm certain. Thank you."

"Yes, Your Highness." She scurries off, and I lean against the door and sigh.

Something about Sera's response to the tonic gives me pause . . . Does she know something? I can't quite put my finger on it, but things are not adding up—from the tonic, the gold flecks in Rae's eyes, the almost shimmering quality of her blood, the unnaturally quick healing of her cracked fingers . . . Hells. There's no way . . . She can't be, can she?

Pocketing the tonic, I make my way toward Alex's rooms. Rae didn't seem too keen on sharing a bed, and I really don't want to make her uncomfortable. Gods willing he's back. Though with each step away from my sleeping wife, my heart aches and my mind whirs with possibilities.

Chapter Twenty-Nine

RAELYN

Shock. Utter and complete shock is the only way to describe how I'm feeling after Kian explains the alchemist's findings. I was betrayed and lied to by the person I thought had been protecting and caring for me all my life.

"What in the realms? I don't understand . . . How could he?"

Kian lays a hand on my shoulder and squeezes. "I'm sorry you had to find so many things out this way . . ."

I palm my face and take a breath to calm myself before I start crying or screaming. "What do you think I should do?" I ask.

"I think you should wean off the tonic unless something serious happens when you get off it."

I bite my lip. "I agree . . . but I can't help but wonder *what* it's suppressing and how that could alter my life even more."

"Hennig is one of the best in our realm, and I trust his skill. I'm sure he will help you with whatever comes up."

"I sure hope so." I fling my hands in the air. "I just wish I had some clue of when Father will be back. I have so many damn questions for him to answer. If he's not my actual father, who is? What has he been hiding by forcing this tonic down my throat?"

The worrisome suspicion in the back of my mind wants to crawl out and scream, but I'm scared Kian will think I'm a lunatic. Until I have definitive proof, I'm keeping my suspicions to myself.

"Thank you for looking into this for me . . . I guess I should take my half portion of tonic now . . ."

Kian grimaces but hands me the vial, and I swig down half of it.

"Hennig said he would make you more and send a weaning schedule for you."

"I'll try to make note of any changes or weird symptoms," I say.

"Would you like to go for a walk in the gardens?" Kian asks. "It would probably be good for us to be seen together. I believe it's an overcast day if you're worried about the sun . . . though you haven't seemed any worse for wear after the last few instances."

"True," I muse. "But doesn't it make our case if we stay locked up in our room all day?" I joke.

Kian smirks. "What a compliment that you believe I have such stamina."

I flush beet red. "Um, that's not—"

Kian holds up a finger to stop my sputtering before leaning in and whispering in my ear, "Trust me, love, I can more than hold my own. And I'm willing to prove it if you ever want to find out."

Heat floods my core, and I bite my tongue to keep from reacting and goading him further.

"A walk sounds fine."

He chuckles and rolls his eyes. "Let's go then."

We make our way through the halls toward the entrance to the gardens. To our surprise, the sun is out in full force, and as soon as I step out into it, I hiss as it beats down painfully on me.

"Rae? Are you all right?" Kian looks concerned and pulls me into the shade. "What happened?"

I look around, confused. "I . . . I don't know what that was," I admit.

Kian places a hand on my forehead. "Are you ill? You feel a bit warm."

"I think I need to go lie down," I say. "I'm sorry."

"Of course, I'll escort you back."

"No, I'll be fine. Go for your walk. I insist."

He looks around uneasily. "Are you sure?"

I give him a wan smile but nod. "Of course I'm sure. Please. I want you to enjoy the beautiful weather . . . and I kind of want to be alone right now."

Kian's jaw tightens and he looks like he's going to fight me on it, but he concedes. "I'll see you at dinner."

I nod and he walks off, shoulders drooping. While I regret sending him away, I really need a moment to myself.

This doesn't make any sense. The last time I was sick had been hours after my sun exposure following the wedding ball. But maybe that was because I'd taken my tonic earlier in the day and it had worn off some? When Kian proposed out in my garden, my tonic had broken in my sitting room, so I'd skipped it and had no reaction to the sun . . . Is my tonic responsible for my reactions? Does it somehow cause my affliction? And if that is the case, why in the realms would Father want me allergic to the sun?

A pit of rage forms in my gut at all the deception. I march through the halls, feeling instantly better in the protection of the palace. Perhaps it's time to dig into the research I've been avoiding for fear of what I might discover.

The library smells of parchment and ancient texts, and I couldn't be happier. Cozy alcoves with lighting bright enough to read but not so bright to make one squint look perfect for my research. I glance around for a librarian or someone to help me navigate the seemingly endless, sprawling space, but there is no one to be found.

I wander down one of the towering aisles of floor-to-ceiling bookshelves, my fingers grazing along the books, and I hope something will jump out at me, something that will tell me if I'm in the right spot or not. Most of the tomes are organized by century, and there are plenty of textbooks on the history of our realm. Wandering down another aisle, I take in the colorful spines that look like delightful stories to get lost in. I make a note to return to find some fresh reading material for later, but so far, nothing seems to hold the information I seek.

I turn the corner and stumble upon a librarian in aubergine robes.

"Oh, hello." I smile. "Do you have a minute to help me find something?"

"Of course, my dear," she says, looking pleased. "What is it you're looking for?"

"Are there any texts on the gods and their offspring?" I ask almost hesitantly.

The librarian frowns and looks around. "We don't have many . . . but I think I might have something along those lines. Do you mind if I ask why?"

I shrug. "Just curious. Since the gods left our realm, they weren't really taught in my studies."

"Fair enough," she replies. "Follow me."

We walk down more aisles, and a few turns later, she points me toward a small section of ancient-looking texts.

"Now, you might be aware, the gods haven't been seen in almost a century. Rumors of offspring even longer than that."

"Is that so?" I ask.

"Rakveren's royal line comes from the offspring of the moon goddess, Luna, but that was at least two centuries past. Their bloodline would be almost completely diluted by now."

"Fascinating," I say. "Now, being directly descended from a god, wouldn't that have given their offspring some form of immortality?"

"Yes, to a degree, but unless the gods deigned to grant full immortality, even their offspring could perish. They might have been a little bit stronger and lived a little longer than the average human, but that was the extent of it."

I take in all her words with rapt attention. So much information that has never been taught in all my years of study at home under the tutelage of governesses.

"I know some healers are said to be descendants of the goddess Galyna's line."

The librarian looks pleased to have my attention. "That's correct, though only one comes to mind who might actually carry some of her blood. The king employs a few truth-sayers descended from the god of truth—Veritius. Again, their bloodlines are so diluted, I'm not sure how much power they truly carry."

"Was there anything else unusual about the offspring?" I'm almost afraid to ask.

The librarian taps her chin. "Let me think . . . oh, yes, actually. Demi-gods—how the texts refer to the gods' offspring—were said to be able to replenish strength by either drinking blood or drawing from the element they were tied to. Say one were descended from Luna, they would find their power strongest at night."

An icy chill trickles down my spine. "That's interesting . . ."

"Yes, well, as I said, it's been centuries since our realm has had any demi-gods. Apparently, the gods, when they left, decided we were no longer worthy to bear their children, or perhaps they worried that their power would be abused."

"Why did the gods disappear?" I ask.

"That is the age-old question. Some believe they grew tired of this realm and left it to slowly wither away."

"But they can't abandon us like that, can they?" I ask.

"My dear, the gods will do as they may. Perhaps we angered them somehow. But our realm is most definitely paying the price."

"What do you mean?"

She looks around, almost as if she shouldn't utter her next words. Her voice drops to a hushed whisper. "The lords and ladies are doing just fine, and the palace is obviously not seeing any lack, but the people in our city and surrounding towns and villages . . . they are suffering. If it weren't for the Shadow, I'm afraid they would be much worse off."

"The Shadow?" I gasp. "What? Who's that?"

"My dear, how sheltered are you?" The librarian tsks, then frowns a little. "Are you even supposed to be here?"

"I'm sorry . . . I'm Lady—I mean Princess Raelyn. I was bound to the prince yesterday. I hardly ever left my manor before now."

The librarian looks me up and down. "Interesting."

I shrug awkwardly, not sure how to respond to that.

"Anyway, as I was saying, if it weren't for the"—she mouths the word "*vigilante*"—"our people would be suffering even more. I fear for our world if something doesn't change or if the gods decide to truly abandon us."

I stand in shock, my mouth agape. I had no idea things were so dire in our world. Though when I consider the state of our lands and Father's declining crops . . . I suppose I should have put things together. Was the masked man in my home this "Shadow" she spoke of? Does my father have something to do with this? Once again, I'm frustrated by all the questions I have no answers to.

"Thank you for sharing the information with me. You've opened my eyes," I say softly.

"Not a problem. Please let me know if there is anything else I can assist you with."

I nod, and she walks away, leaving me to my conflicting thoughts. I move toward the shelf she pointed out and pull a few of the tomes. Unfortunately, I fear I already have the answer I'm seeking, though it doesn't fully make sense to me.

If I take all the information I've been given thus far, it would indicate that I'm descended from a god . . . but surely there's no way, is there?

Finding an empty alcove, I open the first text. My finger skims through the list of gods and their gifts and where they gain their strength. I have a sneaking suspicion, but I want to make sure I cover all my bases.

When I get to the entry for the sun god, Kyros, I stop. According to the text, he was strongest under the rays of the sun, and descendants of the god noted that being in the sun sped up the healing of wounds and ailments. Immediately, I'm reminded of the afternoon outside with Kian, when my hands healed from their cracked state far more quickly than what would be considered normal. I recall the time I sprinted through the gardens, feeling completely rejuvenated by the sun's rays.

Am I descended from Kyros? If that's true, why did the sun burn me only an hour or so ago? Is it the tonic? Was my father knowingly poisoning me so that I wouldn't gain strength?

I'm going to be sick. This can't be possible. But that would explain why blood is suddenly appealing to me. Does the tonic suppress that desire as well? All this information makes me want to purge the tonic from my system as quickly as possible. Will it harm me if I just stop taking it altogether? I know he suggested I wean slowly, but perhaps I need to discuss it with the alchemist.

THE SAVORY SMELLS of meat and vegetables make my mouth water as Kian and I sit down for dinner in his wing. The food here in the palace is incredible.

Guilt trickles in as I pile an abundance of delicacies onto my plate, my mind going back to what the librarian said earlier.

I set down the roll I just took a giant bite out of, and after I swallow, I look across the table at Kian.

"Are there really people out there who are starving while I gorge myself on more food than I could possibly need?"

Kian tilts his head and sets down his fork. "That's an interesting question coming from a noblewoman."

"I'm serious, Kian. Please don't lie to me."

"I wouldn't dream of it," he says before taking a large sip of wine from his goblet. "The truth is, ever since the gods disappeared, our land has been slowly dying."

I nod for him to continue. Somehow, hearing the words from him, confirming what the librarian said, only makes it feel all the more real.

"I wish I could say people aren't starving while we live here with excess, but that would be a lie." He frowns. "I've begged Father to do something, anything, to aid our people, but he's just too selfish and caught up in his own desires to help anyone else."

Loathing toward the king trickles into my body, but then I stare across the table at Kian, a prince with power.

"Why are you looking at me like that?" Kian asks. "Why the sudden disgust in your eyes?"

I push away from the table. "What are *you* doing to help our people, Kian? Begging your father to do something means nothing if people are still dying. And now that I have this knowledge, if I sit back and do nothing, I will be just as culpable."

Kian looks like he's about to explode, his fingers gripping the table tightly in front of him.

"Rae, I'm doing what I can. I can't explain it all to you, but please trust me when I say that I haven't given up on trying to help."

"And yet here you sit, letting some self-appointed avenger take care of your people. At least the Shadow is doing something," I say, crossing my arms in front of my chest. "I heard if it weren't for him, people would be way worse off." The disappointment I feel toward my husband hurts . . . or is it just guilt that *I've* been so naive about our world?

Kian leans forward. "Ah, so you're a fan of the vigilante, huh?"

"I'm not sure what I think, but it sounds like he is doing some good."

"Well, I wouldn't risk bringing him up at court. My father isn't too fond of him, and there's a price on his head."

Have I misjudged the prince? His reaction doesn't make sense.

"Fine."

"Good."

We stare at each other across the table, and I wonder how our evening ended up so horribly wrong. As much as I wanted to share my revelations with him, something holds me back. I still barely know the man. What if I can't trust him? In some ways, I wish I could have remained in my innocent little bubble instead of feeling like I now have to carry the weight of our realm on my shoulders.

Kian rises from his seat, throwing his napkin onto the table. "I've got to go. I'll see you tomorrow."

An ache burns in my chest. Where is he going? Who is he going to be spending time with? Do I even have a right to ask?

"Okay," I respond meekly. I don't have it in me to ask for more. It will only hurt.

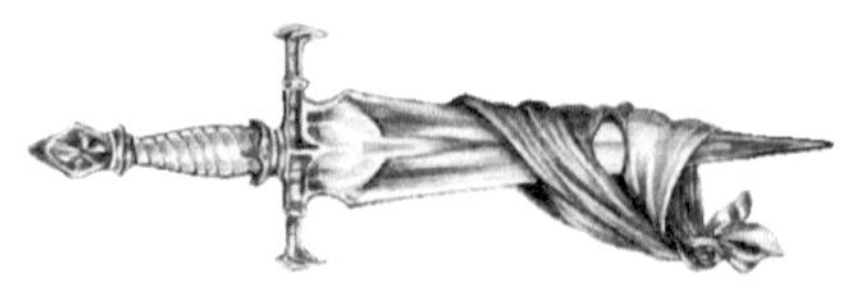

Chapter Thirty

KIAN

I crash onto the settee in Alex's rooms, groaning loudly. The Shadow was sloppy tonight, my argument with Raelyn from days ago still ruminating, distracting me.

Alex throws a damp towel at me. "The least you can do is wipe the blood off before you ruin my settee permanently."

"Shit. Sorry, Alex." I sit up and clean my face before rubbing the towel along my arms and hands, trying to get all the dirt and blood off.

"Don't you think we've done enough for a few days?" he asks as he pours me a drink and brings it over. He collapses onto the leather chair next to me, knocking back a drink of his own. "You've been running us both ragged. I don't think I've had a decent night's sleep since before you got married."

I take a sip of the amber liquid and relish the burn as it slides down my throat. "Sorry for continuing to drag you into this. I just—I need to do something, and sleeping in my wing is obviously not an option."

Alex snorts. "Says you. I see the way she looks at you. I bet she'd happily invite you back to her bed."

I don't know what I'd do if I found myself waking up with her in my arms again, not that she'd welcome me. Well, that, and I couldn't very well show up battered and bloodied in the middle of the night after one of my escapades.

"That wasn't our agreement, and clearly, she thinks I'm just as much a waste of space as my father does."

"So instead of figuring things out with your wife, you're staying out all hours of the night, getting beat up by the extra guards your father has put on every single caravan and shipment coming our way? Sounds rational."

I shake my head and drain my glass. "Never said it was rational. At this rate, she probably thinks I have an entire group of women I'm spending all my time with instead of her."

"Why don't you just tell her about your work as the Shadow?" Alex asks. "Surely she would keep your secret, especially with you keeping hers about her questionable parentage. It's mutually assured destruction —beneficial to you both not to share."

"As if I would share her secret with my father."

Alex shrugs. "I just think she's cleverer than you think. Better you come clean before she finds out for herself how you actually spend your evenings."

"But once again, Alex, need I remind you that her knowing also puts her in danger? It's bad enough that you know what's going on. I'm just hoping you're a good enough liar if I ever do get caught."

"You care about her," Alex says matter-of-factly.

Maybe I do. Maybe I always have.

"Did I ever tell you that I knew her before this season?" I say miserably. "And for some reason, she doesn't remember."

"What are you talking about?" Alex frowns as he pours me another drink.

"I have met her many times over the years, and every time, she forgets me."

Alex laughs. "How is that even possible?"

I shrug. "I wish I knew. There's something about her . . . I can't quite put my finger on it, but I know there are things she's not telling me."

"Have you asked her?"

"No."

"Of course you haven't. Don't you know that communication is an important skill in relationships?"

I laugh bitterly. "Not when you have secrets. Secrets that can get you and everyone you care about killed."

"Tell me about her," Alex prods.

"Fine." I blow out a breath and recount the story of the first time I met Raelyn. "I always thought it strange that it took so long for me to see her again. I remember asking Father when we could go back, and he just went on a rant about how overprotective Lord Astoria is. My stunt taking her out to the garden was not appreciated."

"You didn't know about her sun allergy," Alex says. "You were just a kid."

"I don't believe she even has one," I grumble. "Rae's father is clearly hiding something, especially with that so-called tonic he was making her drink."

"Is she doing any better?" Alex asks.

I shrug. "I've been avoiding her, as you know, other than the few court appearances we've made at luncheons with Father and some of the lords and ladies. We haven't tried to go outside again, but I believe she is weaning herself off her tonic."

Alex pours me another drink. "I know you're not hung up over the girl because of one encounter when you were nine."

I snort a laugh. "True. But each time I saw her after that, I only liked her more."

11 YEARS AGO

"I can hardly believe you're getting married today," I tease Colin as his valet fusses over his cravat.

"Just doing my duty, little brother," he says, but there's a pleased glint in his eyes.

"We haven't seen Princess Juliana in at least five years," I muse.

"At least I got to meet her once before our binding ceremony," Colin says, then he glares at me from where I lounge haphazardly on a brown leather chair. "Get off your ass, Kian. You're wrinkling your jacket."

I groan. "Fine." I walk over to the fancy liquor cart in Colin's room and sniff at all the bottles. "Do you want something?"

"Pour me a finger of the golden one," he says.

I don't completely get what he likes about the stuff, but he keeps telling me I'll like it eventually too. I'd much rather work on my sword skills, and the fancy liquors just seem to make me tired and lazy, so I usually don't drink.

After pouring some in a glass for him and deciding to try some myself, I walk over with the tumblers.

"Here's to your binding," I say, clinking my glass with his.

"To binding," he repeats.

I down the liquor and wince at the burn of it. "Damn, Colin. How do you drink this shit?"

Colin winks. "Slowly."

"Are you feeling nervous?" I ask, even as the soft buzz of alcohol starts to work its way through my system.

"Nah," he says. "I always knew this was coming. I've been betrothed for so long, the idea of wanting something different never even crossed my mind."

I shake my head, not quite believing him. "I don't like being told what to do."

"No shit, Ki. Just be glad Father never arranged one for you. You have time to just live . . . to experiment. See what life is like outside of court."

There it is. The not-so-hidden longing in his voice. I might have a little more freedom than he does, but so many aspects of our lives were decided for us before we could even speak.

"I think, after losing Mother . . ." I choke. I hate that it still hurts as much as it does. It's only been two years, but it feels like a lifetime.

Colin places a hand on my shoulder and squeezes gently. "I miss her too. Father hasn't been the same."

I nod. Yes, Father has been lost to his grief, but it also derailed all his plans for arranging a marriage for me. He's held it as a threat over my head for as long as I can remember, but now he just doesn't care. As long as Colin is married and secures an heir, everything is fine. My life and subsequent marriage don't matter. Besides, I'm only seventeen. I'm in no rush to settle down.

"You'll have your pick of girls at court when you're eligible to marry in a few months," Colin winks.

"Fuck, don't remind me."

He laughs. "Mother would kill you for that language."

"As if you're any better."

He shakes his head, ignoring my comment, his brows drawn together in what I recognize as anxiety. "I suppose it's time to go."

The herald announces the two of us, and we march down the velvet-draped aisle littered with golden rose petals. My gaze snags on Lord Astoria seated halfway down the aisle. Seated next to him is her . . . the girl who has been almost an obsession of mine despite my not seeing her for four long years. She must be about sixteen now. Her younger siblings are seated next to her, all with the darkest of hair, making her auburn locks stand out like fire.

I almost trip, and Colin grabs my arm to steady me. "Eyes up front, Ki. This is not the time to get distracted."

The ceremony passes in a blur of speeches and vows. When the room erupts into cheers as Colin and Juliana hold their arms high, showing off their new binding marks, I sigh with relief. With the gods' blessing, surely it means prosperity for our realm.

The sun dips below the windows, and the room dims to its candle-lit glow. Now, it's time to feast . . . and with a little luck, I can reacquaint myself with Lady Raelyn. Does she ever think of our afternoon adventure nine years ago, or the one time Father finally allowed me to visit after that?

The king leads the procession to the grand dining hall and ballrooms, and the hallways are already filled to the brim with all the lords and ladies who were unable to fit in the temple, waving golden ribbons and shouting their well-wishes as we make our way to the rest of the celebration.

"Congratulations, brother." I clink my glass of bubbly wine with his as the feast commences.

"Thank you, Kian," he replies, knocking back his entire drink in one sip. "For a moment there, I wasn't sure if the gods were going to bless us," he admits.

I glance at the shimmering band around his arm and shudder. "Seems funny to imagine the gods even care about our marriages at all."

He chuckles and nods at his brand-new sister-in-law seated next to her mother. "Maybe Father will arrange a marriage with Princess Helene and you can stay unmarried for at least the next decade before worrying about your binding ceremony."

My nose wrinkles in disgust. "She's a child, Colin. What is wrong with you?"

He shrugs. "I was betrothed when I was a child."

I shake my head and roll my eyes. "You better not put any ideas in Father's head. I mean it."

Colin raises his hands in mock surrender. "Fine, fine, but at some point, you will need to find a wife and settle down. It's part of being royal."

I take a sip of my sparkling wine and hum my acknowledgment, all while my eyes eagerly search the rows of tables, looking for the fiery hair and jade eyes of the girl I can't stop thinking about, especially now that I know she's here.

I think I spot her and go to rise, but Colin clamps a hand down on my arm. "Where do you think you're going?"

"I thought I spotted someone," I reply.

"Dinner is being served. You can wait."

I sigh. "Fine."

Being responsible all the time must be exhausting. I'm also not entirely sure why he is paying such close attention to me when he should be focusing on his new wife. I glance over at Princess Juliana, and she appears sad. Huh.

I shake it off and dive into the feast in front of me.

When we are finally dismissed for dancing and socializing, I go hunt for her. My brother is dancing with Juliana, and most of the crowd is watching them glide across the floor. I start to regret not approaching Lady Raelyn at dinner when I don't see her anywhere. The children have all been dismissed at this point in the evening, and I can't help but worry that she left with them. But Colin was right, if I got up and made a scene in the middle of dinner, Father would have never let me hear the end of it.

"Kian!" Dylan Havordshire, a lord's son, calls out, pulling me aside before I crash into a waiter holding a tray filled with bubbly drinks. "Watch where you're going, friend."

"Shit. Thanks, Dylan." I wipe my hand across my brow. "I think I might have had a little too much to drink tonight."

Dylan rolls his eyes and laughs. "I thought you couldn't stand the shite."

"I was trying to be there for my brother," I say. "We had shots before the ceremony."

"That explains it." He laughs, then frowns. "But wasn't that hours ago?"

"He made me take shots at dinner too . . ."

Dylan chokes on another laugh. "You poor sucker."

"Have you seen the Astorias?" I ask suddenly.

"Who?"

"You know, the Astorias. Remember that girl I told you about four years ago?"

"You really must be wasted if you think I'd remember a girl from four years ago," Dylan teases.

"Just forget it," I say and shove off from him, back on my hunt.

"Hey, sorry, Ki. I didn't mean to offend . . ."

"It's fine. She's never at court, so it makes sense you wouldn't know who I was talking about."

"Sorry, but if I hear of her, I'll let you know."

"Thanks."

Within minutes, Dylan is distracted by another pretty girl and leaves me to continue my search alone. I try to remember the color of Lady Raelyn's dress, but all I can think about is her eyes.

The ballroom is split down the middle by tall tanks of water, filled with colorful fish. I think I heard someone say it was in honor of the bride's coastal kingdom of Tallinnia and their love of the sea.

Lady Raelyn is not on this side of the ballroom as far as I can tell. I wander the length of the tank, peeking through the glass to the other side when I catch a flash of auburn hair and pale skin out of the corner of my eye. Is it her? It's hard to see through the fish and floating flora.

I duck to look beneath a cluster of fish, and my eyes meet vibrant green ones through the glass. A smile curls her lips, and I give her a wave. Now that I finally see her, my breath catches in my chest, and I'm frozen to the spot. I lift my hand to the glass and press into it, almost as if I could touch her if I pushed hard enough. She tilts her head and starts to walk toward the opening, and I follow, my steps quickening the closer we get to each other.

When we finally meet face-to-face, she drops into the deepest curtsy. "Your Highness!"

I grab her hand and pull her up. "Hi there, I've been looking for you," I say almost breathlessly. My eyes drink her in. She's no longer the child I chased through the garden maze or the girl I argued with over puzzles, but a beautiful young woman whose eyes are filled with . . . confusion? Does she not remember who I am again? I mean, she obviously knows who I am . . . but does she remember me?

"Why were you looking for me?"

I smile, trying not to let my disappointment cloud my face. Clearly, I didn't make the same impression on her that she did on me. "I just wanted to catch up with an old friend," I say.

She frowns, looking as if she's trying to figure out what I'm saying. "Have we met?"

I sigh but give her a smile. "Yes, we met when we were children," I try to explain. "The twins had just been born, and then we met again a few years later..."

Her brow furrows, and she puts a hand to her forehead, almost as if it pains her, and shakes her head. "I'm so sorry, Your Highness. I do not recall that, but I really was quite ill as a child."

I want to scream at her, No, you weren't. You were fine. We played together! *But I am starting to doubt my own memories. Do I somehow remember it differently than it was?*

"I didn't mean to upset you, Your Highness," she says quickly, her eyes taking on a worried gleam. "I don't remember a lot about my childhood. Perhaps I've just forgotten."

I nod. "It's quite all right, Lady Raelyn. It's a pleasure to make your acquaintance now." I give her a broad smile, hoping I haven't completely ruined things between us.

She flushes a pretty shade of pink and looks around hesitantly. "Nice to meet you too, Prince Ki."

I freeze. Maybe she does remember? Not many people call me that anymore, except my brother.

"Would you like to dance?" I ask, holding my hand out to her.

Her blush deepens. "I don't know . . . I think Father wants me to retire with my siblings."

"Just one dance?" I ask again, taking a step closer to her.

She glances around, as if looking for someone to tell her no, but when she doesn't see anyone, she finally agrees. "Just one dance."

I lead her to my side of the ballroom, and we sway to the music. She fits perfectly in my arms, and I can't quite explain the rush of feelings flowing through me. There's a connection between us despite the fact that I hardly know her . . . I want to know her . . . and it's not just because she's exquisite. My eyes drop to her lush pink lips, and I think about kissing her . . . I'm in trouble.

"Did you enjoy the binding ceremony?" I ask.

"It was fascinating," she admits. "I always thought the disappearing ribbon was just a fanciful story."

"*Don't you believe in the gods?*" *I ask, raising a brow.*

"*To a point . . .*" *she says.* "*They haven't been seen or heard from in centuries or something, right?*"

"*That's correct,*" *I admit.*

"*Is it not valid for me to wonder how much of what we're taught is accurate or even still holds true anymore? What if the gods have moved on from our realm and no longer want to be involved?*"

She might have a point there. "*But doesn't the binding ceremony prove there is still magic in our realm?*" *I prod.* "*If there's still magic, the gods aren't completely gone, right?*"

She smiles, and my heart flips in my chest . . . She's magic.

"*Fine, I'll give you that.*" *She grins.* "*I do like the idea of there being some magic, even if the gods are gone.*"

I shake my head. "*You're very opinionated, aren't you.*"

"*That didn't sound like a question.*"

"*It wasn't.*"

She smiles again, and it lights up the entire room. "*It is true. I've been told so many times.*"

"*Why don't you ever come to court?*" *I ask breathlessly before spinning her out, then bringing her back in.*

"*I'm not old enough, silly,*" *she replies.*

Hells. I almost forgot. An ache forms in my chest at the thought of not seeing her again for . . . years.

"*In fact,*" *she continues,* "*it would probably be frowned upon that I'm out here dancing with you when I'm not of age yet . . .*"

"*I'm not of age either. Let them talk,*" *I whisper in her ear as I pull her in closer. Gods, I really want to kiss her.*

"*Ki! It doesn't work like that, especially not for me,*" *she exclaims before whirling out of my reach. She looks apologetic and mouths the words* "*I'm sorry!*" *before disappearing into the crowd. I realize my hand is still outstretched, as if reaching for her.*

What can I do? Take chase? Find her?

My hand drifts down to my side. No. She's right. Being the center of gossip would only harm her reputation before she's even old enough to have one. I'll wait. It's only a few more years. I only hope she'll remember me next time.

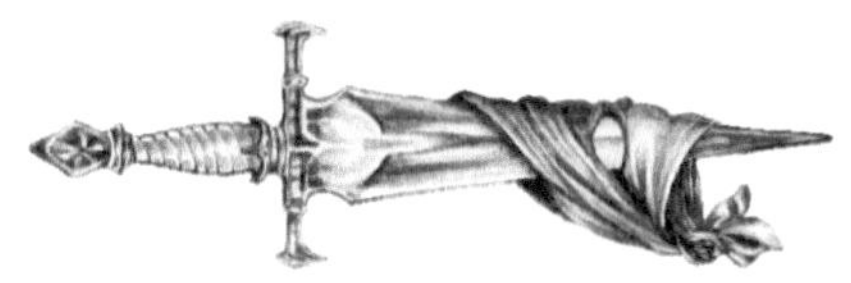

Chapter Thirty-One

KIAN

Slamming my book shut, I nod at Alex. "Are you up for some sparring in an hour?"

Alex groans, stretching his arms overhead. "Why do you have that look in your eye?"

"What look?"

"The look that says you're planning something I wouldn't approve of."

He's not wrong. There is a mystery I've been longing to solve, and I have an idea I'm dying to try. If I asked him, Alex would tell me I'm being dumb and that I should just talk to Raelyn, but I can't help wondering if she would even tell me the truth . . . Or if she even *knows* the truth? My idea will definitely make solving this mystery more fun.

"Don't worry your pretty little head about it," I retort. "Maybe Sera will tag along."

Alex's ears perk up. "Who?"

I roll my eyes. "Meet me in an hour."

Alex blows out a breath. "Fine."

As I walk back to my wing, my mind drifts to this dumb plan I've concocted, running over the signs I've picked up on.

What if Raelyn is the key to everything I've been searching for? A direct connection to the lost god. Does she have godsblood running through her veins like I suspect?

What if the tonic was used to suppress her godlike qualities? What would she think if I told her my suspicions? I'm inclined to believe that she's unaware—that her father kept this information from her. But why did he feel the need to? I haven't the faintest idea, but I'm determined to find out.

Can I tempt that part of her out somehow? Coax whatever godlike qualities she might carry to the surface to prove to her my suspicions?

Entering our wing, I'm happy I don't have to hunt her down.

"Raelyn, love, would you like to come out to the sparring ring with me?"

She looks up from her seat by the fire, pausing her current needlework project. "Sparring?" She frowns. "Why in the realms would I want to join you for sparring?" Her nose crinkles adorably as she looks from her needlepoint to me standing casually by the fireplace.

"Well . . . we haven't gotten out much together, and the sparring ring is indoors if you're worried about the sun."

"What about me screams 'wants to spar' currently?" she says, raising an eyebrow.

Is she still mad? I hate how awkward things have been, and what better way to make things right than by spending time together?

"Nothing, which is precisely why I think it would be a good time," I tease, hoping for a smile. She might pretend not to be interested, but I remember how easily she had me on my back all those weeks ago. I'd bet my finest liquor she has experience sparring. Why she's pretending not to has me curious.

She shakes her head and puts her attention back on her needlework. "You're ridiculous."

"Come on. It will be fun. I bet you've never handled a sword before." *Please, Rae. Take the bait.*

The faintest flush tinges her cheeks pink. "Not that you know of."

Success.

I plop down on the settee next to her, slinging my arm along the back. My fingers trail down her shoulder, and she shivers. "Come on, love. Exercise is good for you. You shouldn't spend your days locked up in here."

She shoots me a fiery glare. "What if I *like* being locked up in here?"

I sigh in exasperation. "Okay, fine. I won't force you. But it *would* be good for us to be seen together."

A low blow, but I'm not beyond fighting dirty at this point.

She sets her needlework down on her lap somewhat forcefully. "You are relentless."

I lean in closer, and her eyes widen. "You're not wrong, love. I always get what I want."

"Well that was the wrong thing to say," she quips. "Now I absolutely won't go with you."

I let out a hearty laugh. "Okay, how about this. You come and watch Alex and me spar. Sera can come too if she wants."

She squirms beneath my scrutiny, but I know I've won when her shoulders slacken. "Fine. But it'll just be me. Sera is visiting her family."

"Perfect. Be ready in an hour."

I move to get up when I notice the needlepoint. A large lion with golden eyes is at the forefront. What an interesting choice.

"What are you working on?" I ask.

She spreads the piece out on her lap to reveal an outline of an island and a deep, thick jungle.

"I've made this before, but all my old projects are back at the manor . . . For whatever reason, this vision of the lion keeps coming to me. It follows me in my dreams, and the only thing that makes it stop is when I create this art."

"Your needlework is exquisite," I compliment her. "So very detailed."

"Thank you." She smiles. "I probably spend way too much time on these projects."

"And you dream about this? The lion and this island?" I ask, tracing my fingers lightly along the pattern.

I catch her nod from the corner of my eye.

"You know . . . the stories say that the gods could shapeshift into animals."

Her body stiffens next to mine. "Oh, really?"

"Yes," I reply, turning to look at her more closely. Does she know something after all? "If the stories are to be believed, the sun god had a preference for his lion form."

Raelyn swallows, her eyes trained on the needlework. "I had no idea."

"Maybe the gods are speaking to you," I muse.

"Wouldn't that be something," she says with a forced laugh.

I'm more determined than ever to find out what she might be hiding, if anything.

AN HOUR LATER, I'm in my training clothes, waiting for Raelyn to come out of the closet. I told her to find something comfortable to wear, even if she was only planning to watch.

Raelyn finally walks out wearing fitted leather pants with a long, flowy purple tunic. "Are you sure this is appropriate?" She frowns, spinning around for me.

"Completely appropriate. I only wish the tunic were shorter," I tease. Her shapely legs are a sight, but I can only imagine how her round backside looks beneath.

She flushes red, as usual, and I offer her my arm as we walk out of our wing.

Ignoring my statement, she asks, "Is Alex meeting us there?"

"Yep," I reply.

"Is he your closest friend?" she asks.

"The very best. I wouldn't survive court without him." I look over, noting her downcast expression. "What's wrong?"

"I guess I just wish I had more friends."

"Have you gotten to know any of the ladies here at court?"

She shakes her head. "No. I should try to get out more. It's just . . . making friends doesn't come very easily to me."

My heart aches for her. I wish she'd let me pull her into my arms and hold her, but boundaries . . . though I'm fairly certain I'm about to cross some.

Chapter Thirty-Two

Kian absolutely has something up his sleeve, and I'm intrigued enough to risk finding out what. He's right; I can't stay locked up in our wing forever, and while I don't want to admit it to him, sparring actually sounds incredible. I *am* feeling a little stir-crazy. Other than venturing back to the library to read up more on the gods, I've hardly done anything in the palace other than dine with the court; there is always a worry in the back of my mind that I'll run into the king on my own, or that someone will call me out on this sham of a marriage.

Despite Kian insisting we need to share a bedroom so that people won't wonder about us, he hasn't slept in our room, much less in our wing. It's honestly kind of a relief when I consider how uncomfortable I was waking up from my nap with his body curled around me that first day. Or maybe I was just uncomfortable with how much I liked it.

Perhaps he found some other woman to share a bed with . . . maybe someone from before who wouldn't let him go. I try not to dwell on that, as I'm worried I'll just get depressed. While, rationally, I know it's what we agreed upon, that doesn't mean I like it. As long as no rumors spread around court about my husband cheating on me, I suppose I can deal. Despite the gods "blessing" our marriage, they don't care about faithfulness. Odd, when a marriage bond is supposed to be forever.

Sneaking a glance at Kian, I can't help but admire how handsome he looks in his training clothes, the supple leather pants hugging his legs like a second skin. He tucks a stray lock of hair behind his ear, and his strong, stubbled jaw draws my eyes. What would that feel like beneath my fingers? Not that I'll ever find out. Despite the tension between us, it's never gone beyond teasing.

I was almost relieved when he asked me to spend time with him today. After our disastrous conversation a few nights ago, I realized I might have been too harsh. I don't actually know what Kian does for the kingdom. Perhaps I should have asked first instead of judging so harshly.

I blow out a breath while tugging at the hem of my tunic. Even though it covers my rear, I feel almost naked with these formfitting pants on. It's not as if a stray breeze will fly through the corridor and reveal my figure to anyone in proximity, but I'm still uncomfortable. These are nothing like the loose-fitting clothes I train in at home, but it was the best I could come up with.

My mind wanders back to what Kian said earlier about the lion and the sun god—the deity I might have some relation to. Is he right? Is a god—or even Kyros himself—trying to send me some kind of message? Maybe I should pay closer attention to my dreams . . . but just thinking that will probably make my dreams float away on a breeze and never return.

Kian leads me into the large training arena. The ground consists of softly packed dirt, and the walls are covered in colorful targets of all shapes and sizes. One section of the arena has a ring with mats for hand-to-hand combat. The wall of weapons is the most breathtaking of all: so many shiny swords and knives and beautiful wooden bow staffs.

Alex is doing some kind of warm-up with one such staff. He's wearing loose-fitted pants but has removed his shirt. While he isn't quite as defined as Kian, there is definitely muscle underneath some of the softness, and he's quite pleasant to look at.

"Kian! Raelyn! Nice of you to finally show up," he calls out cheekily. His gaze darts behind me, as if looking for someone.

I haven't seen him since our bonding ceremony, but his warm welcome exudes a sense of familiarity that I don't hate—as if we're already friends.

"Hi." I wave shyly.

"Did you have to take your shirt off, Alex?" Kian groans in mock annoyance. "I don't need my wife ogling another man."

Alex laughs, flexing one of his biceps. "Trust me, once your shirt is off, she won't be looking at me."

Kian shakes his head as he climbs into the training ring, kicking off his shoes. "Looks like you've been keeping up with your training there. Good job."

I watch them with amusement. I can't even begin to imagine the amount of exercise needed to achieve their muscle mass.

Sure enough, once Kian removes his shirt, my eyes are drawn to his impressive physique. When my gaze dips to the V leading beneath his pants, I quickly look away, embarrassed at my staring. Alex was right though. He's a fine specimen of a man. It really *is* too bad there's no chance I'll get to enjoy it.

At the thought of an eternally loveless marriage, my heart sinks. I was a fool for agreeing to this. But he also saved me from a horrible situation, and I wouldn't want to return to that ever.

Alex sets down his staff, and he and Kian go through some warm-up stretches together. I'm fascinated at their movements and itch to join in, but I'm also stubborn and unsure. I haven't sparred in months, and while all the cleaning around the manor kept me somewhat in shape, it's not the same.

"Swords?" Kian asks.

Alex groans. "Okay, fine. But you're gonna kick my ass."

"As usual." Kian winks.

I laugh at their antics and watch in fascination as their swords meet with each strike and parry, their moves fluid like dancing. Longing fills me at thoughts of the training yard back home and all the sessions with my father. I miss my rapier.

At one point, I think Alex just might get the better of Kian until Kian completes a stunning move of agility and flips out of the way just in the nick of time. Within seconds, he has his sword at Alex's throat, and Alex drops his own in surrender.

I break into applause, and they both turn to gawk at me. I stop clapping and shrug. "Am I not supposed to do that?"

Alex lets out a hearty laugh. "I like her, Ki. You picked a good one."

I flush at the praise, and Kian gives me a grin. "I hope it hasn't been too painfully boring for you to stand and watch."

"It's actually quite riveting," I reply.

"Are you sure you don't want to give it a go?"

"I don't think I could handle such a large sword."

Alex almost chokes on a laugh as Kian rolls his eyes. "Better watch out, Rae. Alex is just as bad with innuendo as I am."

"I sort of walked right into that," I admit with a grin.

"I reiterate, I like this one," Alex repeats. "But come on, Rae. You don't have to start with a broadsword. How about daggers?"

"Perfect," I agree. "Target practice? Probably better I not start with sparring. I'd likely fall on my rear like you did."

"That's how you learn, love." Kian winks.

"Target practice," I repeat. As much as I'm itching to take him on, I'm out of practice and he's clearly a better swordsman than my father . . . not that I'd tell Father that.

"Fine, you win," Kian agrees.

Alex retrieves some small daggers, and we head over to the targets. Kian makes a show of how to properly throw them, and I try not to roll my eyes. To be fair, I haven't actually admitted to them that I know what I'm doing. All the more fun for me to surprise them.

"Try not to cut yourself," Kian says, and before he can utter another word, I let two of the daggers fly in rapid succession.

The satisfying thunk of the blades sinking into the wood makes me glow with pride. I haven't lost my skill. I turn to look at the men, whose jaws are slack.

"She's better at this than you are." Alex laughs, punching Kian in the shoulder. Kian grunts, rubbing at a fresh scar. What could have caused that? I walk to the target to retrieve the blades, and while I didn't hit a perfect bullseye, my throws aren't half bad.

"I love a woman who knows how to handle a blade," Kian purrs in my ear, and I almost jump.

"You should know better than to frighten a woman holding sharp objects."

His answering laugh sends a thrill through me.

Kian, Alex, and I spend the next hour throwing blades from different angles and positions, all trying to best each other while attitudes remain light. It's such a change from practice with my father, who easily got frustrated when I bested him. Not all men are equal.

"Now that you're warmed up, how about a little knife sparring on the mat?" Kian asks before taking a long drink of water.

"I don't know . . . I haven't really done that before."

"It's one thing to throw knives at targets, but if you ever really needed to defend yourself, it would be helpful to actually practice with another person. Don't worry, we'll use dull practice knives."

My mouth goes dry, and I swallow. "Is self-defense something I need to be worried about living in the palace?"

"Trust me, love, I hope you're never in a position where you need to worry about that, but with a vigilante running around, you never know what might happen," Kian says.

Alex chokes on his water, and I frown. "Are you okay?"

"Yep." He coughs. "Fine."

"If nothing else, it's good exercise." Kian grins.

Both men take turns walking me through some of the basic moves: simple thrusts, hooks, horizontal and vertical slashes. They guide me through them slowly, and I feel powerful and strong. It's almost like dancing. Kian's hand wraps gently around mine as he demonstrates the best places to attack if I were ever in a compromised position. The air crackles and hums with energy, drawing us together like magnets.

At some point, Alex makes his farewells and leaves the two of us alone.

"You're doing wonderfully," Kian says with a smile. He pulls his hair back and knots it on the back of his head, and my eyes are immediately drawn to his strong, beautiful neck, to his throat . . . where his pulse hammers. Hells. *Stop looking*, I chastise myself.

Ever since the librarian told me about demi-gods using blood to strengthen and revive themselves, I can't stop thinking about it. Why this craving is stronger in Kian's presence specifically is beyond me. Is it because I tasted it during the binding ceremony? My further research suggested the urge to drink faded with each generation, but that can't be right. Surely the bloodline was diluted enough by the time it got to me.

I chew on the inside of my cheek, trying to focus.

Kian looks at me strangely, motioning for me to attack. I swipe at him with my right hand, but he easily twists out of the way, coming up behind me, holding my arms out of reach.

"You're getting there. You just need to be a little quicker," he taunts.

I twist around, thrusting up with my left hand, and he blocks the strike. I grunt in frustration. It would be nice to land at least one hit.

Kian twists me around and plants a kiss on my cheek. "Try again, love."

I back away, following his every move. He looks like a cat ready to pounce. Hoping to catch him off guard, I rush him, going straight for his chest. As if he expected it, he braces himself for impact, but I swerve at the last moment and try the move I saw him use on Alex, sweeping my leg out to knock him off-balance. The look of shock on his face as he hits the ground is so incredibly satisfying, I crow in celebration as I pin him with my knees. It reminds me of the night I knelt over the vigilante. When I hold one of my blades to his throat, the deja vu is so strong, it almost shocks me out of the moment.

"Got you," I say as I lean down and stare directly into his beautiful smoky eyes.

The grin on his face is contagious, and I can't stop the answering one on mine. "That you did, love."

In a split second, he pushes himself up to a seated position, and my eyes widen in horror as the dull blade I held to his throat slices into him.

"Kian!" I shriek, immediately dropping the knife and fumbling to put a hand on his throat to stop the bleeding. What if I nicked his carotid? *Oh shit, oh shit, oh shit.* If I accidentally murder the prince, the king will surely have me killed.

Kian winces but tries to shush me. "Don't panic, love. It's just a small slice. Trust me, I've had way worse."

I pull my hand away, and sure enough, there's no blood gushing out of his throat, merely a small trickle. Relief and anger well up inside me.

"*Kian!*" I scream at him again. "What in the ever-loving hells is wrong with you? I could have really hurt you!"

"But you didn't. I'm fine." He smiles reassuringly, but there's a flash of something like disappointment in his eyes that I was not expecting to see.

I take a deep breath, and my nose is assaulted by the scent of his blood. *Damn it.* I realize I'm practically on Kian's lap, but as I go to pull away, needing to put distance between the tantalizing smell and me, Kian's eyes darken, and he leans in toward me.

What is he doing?

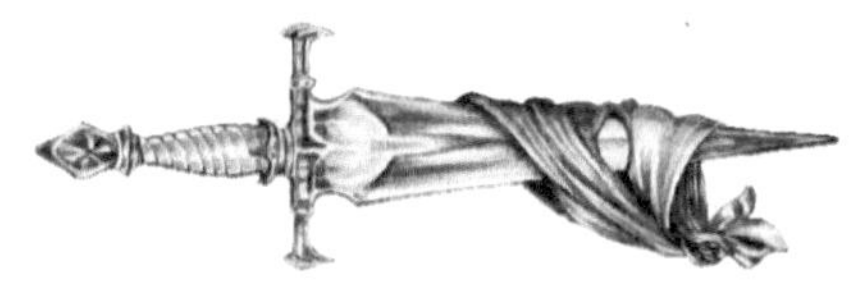

Chapter Thirty-Three

KIAN

This isn't going to plan. If she is directly descended from the gods like I suspect, why isn't she lunging for my blood? Have I completely miscalculated?

Suddenly, I realize just how close we've gotten and how all her soft parts are lined up just right. An unquenchable hunger for her lurches in my chest, and all I want is to capture her mouth with mine and taste her again. I can almost remember the softness of those pillowy lips if I try hard enough. But here she is, my strong, beautiful wife, looking at me in a way I can't quite decipher, her mouth so temptingly close to mine.

"Rae . . ." A strained whisper leaves me as I lean in closer.

She scurries away from me, landing on her ass on the training mat. A soft "oof" leaves her as she hits the ground. I will not touch her against her will, as much as I want to chase after her in this moment.

The fear in her eyes instantly makes me feel regret. I didn't mean to scare her. I'd only hoped to awaken the little goddess inside of her.

"Rae," I say again, a little louder. "Are you all right, love?"

She shakes her head as if coming out of a daze. "I'm fine. Sorry, I just . . ."

"You don't have to explain," I reassure her.

I stand and go to her, offering a hand to help her to her feet. Thankfully, she takes it, and I pull her up and into me, steadying her while also enjoying the soft feel of her body against mine.

"Are you sure you're okay?" she asks. Her concern for me makes me feel like the worst man.

"I told you, it's just a scratch." I put my hand up to my throat and wipe the blood away with my thumb. "It's probably closed up already, right?"

She looks up at me and sighs. "You're right."

I might be mistaken, but I think I detect a hint of need in her eyes as she stares at the spot where my blood was flowing.

She reaches for her jaw and massages it. *Interesting.*

Perhaps I need to be more direct.

I hold up my thumb with the smear of blood. "Would you like a taste, love? I see that hunger in your eyes."

Shock and maybe revulsion flash across her face but they're quickly replaced with that hunger again.

She swallows and takes a step back. "Don't be ridiculous, Kian. Why would I want a taste?"

I shrug and give her a devilish grin, taking another step toward her. "It's not like you haven't tasted it before."

"That was for a ceremony," she retorts.

"But you liked it."

"So what if I did?" she blurts out.

Ah. Sweet victory.

"There's absolutely nothing wrong with that, little goddess."

Her eyes light up with surprise. "What did you just call me?"

"Little goddess?"

"You don't know what you're talking about."

"Don't I?" I ask, closing in. "It all adds up . . . the tonic, the blood, everything. Do you even know what you are?"

Her shoulders droop, and she looks at the ground. "No, Kian, I truly don't. I have suspicions, but no evidence."

I gently grip her shoulders, and she looks up at me, her eyes filled with sadness, longing, but also betrayal. "Let me help."

Her body shakes with anger as she pushes away from me. "Is this all that stunt was? Were you hoping I'd slip up and attack you for your blood?"

I run a hand through the messy hair that came loose during training. "It wasn't my best plan, I'll admit."

"You're completely unbelievable. Why didn't you just ask me?"

"Would you have told me? It's not like you said anything to me about this before now."

She laughs bitterly. "I've only just started coming to terms with it myself. Not to mention, in this last week alone, I've found out that so many parts of my life—of who I am—is a lie. That would be a lot for one person to manage, don't you think? I barely know you. Why would I trust you with this?"

We stare at each other, her pain clearly etched on her features. She's right not to trust me . . . it's not as if I've shared all of my secrets either.

"You're right, Rae. I shouldn't have gone about things this way. I just thought that if I told you my suspicions without proof, you'd think I'd lost my mind. I thought if I could show you . . ."

"I think I *have* lost my mind," she says wearily.

I step closer to her again, and this time, she doesn't back away. Reaching up, I brush loose strands of her hair behind her ear and tilt her chin up so she has to face me. "I'll say it again: let me help you."

"How?" she asks, the hope and longing in her gaze nearly doing me in.

I unsheathe a sharp blade from my side and hold it up to my throat. "Taste me, little goddess. Drink and see what happens."

She shakes her head. "I'm afraid, Kian. I'm afraid of what it means and of everything changing again. What if we're wrong about all of this?"

"What if we're right?" I dare her.

She squeezes her eyes shut, the war within her finally coming to a head. At her barest nod, I breathe a sigh of relief that she's trusting me, and before I can second-guess myself, I reopen the shallow wound on my neck with a flick of my wrist.

"Drink, Rae."

She opens her eyes, and I'm almost shocked at how ravenously she attaches her mouth to my throat. The softness of her tongue lapping at my neck almost does me in. I would have never thought something like this would turn me on, but oh gods, am I in for it.

The featherlight flutter of her tongue, her soft lips on my skin, and the quiet moan of hers that thrums through me make me want to throw her onto the ground and take her right here and now. I grow uncomfortably hard as she presses closer and closer to me. When her teeth scrape against my neck, I can't stop the guttural sound that comes from my throat, and I pull her even closer, seeking some relief from the fire she's ignited in me.

As if the roll of my hips shocked her, Raelyn gasps and pulls away, her hand going up to her mouth.

I blink, and everything is a little clearer, the lust-ridden fog moving from my mind as the space between our bodies grows. What in Luna's name was I thinking? I had no idea it would be like this.

"Did I hurt you?" Raelyn gasps. Of course she's not thinking about herself. Damn selfless woman . . . or goddess?

"I'm fine, love," I rasp out, closing my eyes as I catch my breath from the raging flood of emotions and lust that roiled through me. "Give me a second." I turn away from her, trying to adjust myself in my pants and let my body calm down.

When I turn to look at her, she's frozen in place, her hand still at her mouth, as if she's just as shocked.

"Are *you* all right?" I tilt my head. "Do you feel any different?"

She finally meets my gaze, and I gasp. The gold flecks in her green eyes have multiplied and almost glow ethereally.

"What?" she questions. "Did something happen to my face?"

I chuckle and walk toward her. "Your eyes, love. They've changed."

"Hells," she says. "I thought—"

"Thought what?"

"After our binding, I noticed some small flecks of gold in my eyes and thought it was strange . . ."

I nod in agreement. "I tried to convince myself that I just hadn't noticed them before, or that it had never been bright enough when I'd seen you."

"Is it bad?" she asks.

I shake my head and smile. "It's actually quite beautiful. Right now, there's almost a glow to them."

"Well, that's going to be hard to hide," she laments.

I shrug. "This is completely new territory. I don't even know where to start . . . but you never answered my question. Do you feel any different?"

She pauses and appears to take inventory of her body. "I feel . . . I think I feel stronger? There's an energy buzzing through me," she admits.

"I wonder if you have any powers," I say softly.

"Powers?" she squeaks.

I suspect you're descended from the—"

"Sun god," we say in tandem.

My eyebrows fly up. "You know?"

"I suspect . . . I don't have any way to know for sure." She shrugs.

"Damn," I say quietly. "Have you noticed anything else?"

"Well, I think my hands healed in the sun," she admits. "I think the tonic makes me want to avoid the sun because it would give me strength."

"I think you're right. Brilliant girl."

She blushes at the praise, and I take note.

"Are you sure I didn't hurt you?" she asks again, raising a hand to touch my throat.

"I'm perfectly fine."

"I didn't take too much?" She bites her lip.

I shake my head. "Absolutely not."

"I'm suddenly quite ravenous for food," she admits.

"Well, you did put in quite a workout before this."

She smiles. "I'm glad the blood isn't fulfilling that requirement. Food tastes too good to give up."

I chuckle before picking up Raelyn's fallen daggers, putting them away, and then pulling on my discarded shoes and shirt. "Let's get cleaned up, and I'll have food brought to our wing."

"Sounds perfect," she says.

I put an arm around her and pull her in close to my side, feeling oddly protective of her as we walk. She keeps her eyes trained on the ground, worried, I guess, of someone noticing the change in them.

When we get back to our rooms, she dashes into the bathroom to look for herself.

"Gods," she calls out. "You weren't kidding."

"I hardly think anyone will notice," I call back before pulling the bell to ring for a servant.

"Liar," she grumbles under her breath before the sound of running water hits my ears.

After requesting dinner be sent up for us, I meander over to my room and pull off my soiled shirt. Some of my blood got on it, and I want to bathe regardless.

The bathroom door is still cracked open, so I assume she's decent as I knock. "Rae, are you nearly finish—"

My jaw drops as I step in and spy my naked wife rinsing soap out of her long auburn tresses in the tub. The streams of water gleam on her unblemished skin, caressing her as they slide down her back.

"Um, I'm sorry. I didn't realize—" I stammer as I back away and grip the doorframe to combat the need to go to her.

Raelyn looks over her shoulder and shrieks, her hands flying up to cover her breasts, even though I can't see them from this angle. Shame. I'm sure they're lovely.

"Kian! What are you doing in here?"

I point toward the door. "It was open."

She flushes deeply. "That's my fault."

I grin. "It's all good. I'm enjoying the view."

"Get out!" she cries.

"Of course! Sorry." I back out of the bathroom and lean against the wall. Shit. We could really use more rooms, especially of the bathing variety. The fresh longing and desire for her overwhelm me.

Water sloshes, followed by the sound of Raelyn leaving the tub. I feel bad for cutting her bath short.

"You don't have to rush on my account, love," I call out.

"It's fine, Kian," she replies. "I'm starving, remember?"

I turn to the door as she exits, her body wrapped in a fluffy towel. Her shapely legs make me think about how much I'd enjoy having them wrapped around me. *Damn it. Stop, Ki. You're better than this. She's not interested.*

I can't help but watch a droplet of water trail down her leg until a squeak comes out of her as she trips and goes sprawling toward the floor.

I swoop in and catch her right before she hits the ground, one arm banded around her chest and one around her waist. The now-familiar scent of vanilla and citrus assails my senses, and I long to unravel the towel and take my time exploring . . . but our damned agreement.

Once I help her to her feet, to my shock her towel comes undone and slides to the floor, as if the gods are mocking my own thoughts. She gasps, and this time my face flushes red, as I don't know where to look or what to do with my hands. I chuckle awkwardly, spinning on my heel, but I've seen enough. Enough to fuel my fantasies for days and nights to come.

"I might as well just die now," Rae moans. "How many times do I need to flash you in one day before you kick me out of your rooms?"

She thinks I can't stand this? That is the furthest thing from the truth.

Keeping my back to her, not wanting to make her even more uncomfortable, I try to make light of the situation. "Walk around naked for all I care, love. It's just a body."

She lets out an awkward laugh as she maneuvers around me, heading toward the closet. "I'll try to watch my step this time."

I palm my face. I'm in such deep shit. Cold bath it is.

Chapter Thirty-Four

RAELYN

This evening has gone absolutely *nothing* like I expected. My body is pleasantly sore from the training, and my skin is still flushed from the embarrassment of Kian walking in on me in the bath *and* me flashing him moments ago. What in the hells is wrong with me? Did I forget how to walk?

Kian's words replay in my head. *"It's just a body."* Did he mean to imply there's nothing special about *my* body?

I mean, I think he finds me attractive. I can recall multiple occasions now when I've clearly felt his attraction due to our proximity.

Sinking onto the floor of the closet, I put my head in my hands. My body is buzzing with energy from Kian's blood and everything that happened. All I know is that I've never been so turned on in my entire life than when I tasted it . . . him. Was that purely the blood, or was it Kian?

I think back to the strength that surged through my body when I had a drop of Stepmother's blood and how I almost broke through the door with my fist. I wasn't turned on then . . . and yet . . . the night I tasted the vigilante's blood, I experienced a similar feeling, only, not quite as strong.

My mind also can't even begin to wrap around the fact that we quite possibly confirmed I'm part of the sun god's lineage. Mind blowing. Life altering. What in the ever-loving hells am I to do with this information?

The tonic still hasn't completely left my system. Hennig told me I should probably take a few small doses over the next week to avoid any terrible withdrawal symptoms. I can't wait to test out more of my theories . . . see what being out in the sun can do for me. Already, I feel so much stronger.

Just to experiment, I unwrap the thick, fluffy towel from my body and try ripping it in half. To my surprise, or perhaps not, it rips cleanly with little to no effort. I grin. This could be interesting.

I'm desperate to do more research on what this all means, but for now, I pull on a long, comfy tunic and soft pants. Once I get some food in me, I plan on passing out from exhaustion.

Feeling slightly bad about ruining the towel, I decide to sew it back together. I carry both halves into the sitting area and hang them up after using one half to thoroughly dry my hair.

The cozy spot by the fire calls my name, and I sink onto the settee. My heart rate is still elevated from all of the excitement, so I pick up my needlepoint project to work on while I wait for the food to arrive. Ever since Kian said the lion was the sun god's preferred shifted form, I keep wondering if that's who I've been dreaming of, who I unintentionally created a likeness of. Was he a long-lost ancestor? My gut feeling says that he isn't too far back in the family line despite the information that says the gods haven't procreated in hundreds of years. What if Kyros had done so secretly? I can't help but wonder once again who my true father is. The longing to know who I am and where I came from is overwhelming.

What would the king make of this information? Surely, the gods-blood would be my saving grace in society, even if I'm not a true Astoria.

"You look deep in thought." Kian's baritone voice surrounds me, making goosebumps break out on my skin. I can't stop thinking about how good he felt and how much I enjoyed having his arms around me.

"I was just thinking that perhaps we could stop lying to the king."

He sits down next to me, raising a brow. "How do you figure?"

"Well"—I gesture at myself awkwardly—"would he dare to execute one of the only potential demi-gods in centuries?"

Kian stiffens and leans back. "To be honest, it could go one of two ways . . ." He ticks off one finger. "Either he will be overjoyed at the prospect of adding more godsblood into our family line through you and demand we produce an heir immediately." He ticks off another finger. "Or he will see you as a threat to his rule, since the kingdom was established by a child of the gods. If your blood is purer than ours—which, let's face it, it clearly is—he would eliminate you out of fear that you would lay claim to the throne."

My eyes widen. "But I have no desire to take over the kingdom!"

"You might say that now, but my father holds tightly to his rule. Not just him, but my brother—his heir—will likely see you as a threat to his position as well. I can't imagine Colin murdering my wife, but I wouldn't put it past Father."

"Hells. Another secret," I moan.

Kian puts an arm around my shoulders and squeezes in what he must think is a reassuring way, but it really isn't. I'm terrified of what this newfound information means, what my heritage could imply for our kingdom.

"Rae, look at me," Kian says softly.

I turn my gaze to him, trying to hold back the fear and the tears that threaten to spill.

"I won't let anything happen to you. I've got you. I promise."

I try to nod, but my lip quivers and the tears slip free anyway.

"Oh love," Kian says, using a thumb to swipe them away before pulling me into his arms. My body stiffens at the contact, but when he rubs my back, I melt into him, accepting the comfort. I close my eyes and take in his scent of leather and spice. I'm starting to love the smell of him. I can almost taste him on my tongue, the memory still vivid.

As heat floods my core, I push away and sit up, not wanting to put myself in another compromising position with him.

"Thank you," I say, needing him to know I'm grateful for the comfort.

"I want to be here for you, however you need me," Kian replies.

"*However* I need you?" I ask, and I'm shocked at the sultriness of my voice and the fact that I even said that to begin with. Damn hormones and blood.

Kian's eyes darken, and he leans in toward me, a glint of something in his expression I can't quite decipher. "Did you have something specific in mind, little goddess?"

"What if I need . . . release?" My face immediately flushes. *Who the hells are you, and what have you done with Raelyn?* I ask myself furiously.

"Are you asking for my assistance?" Kian's voice is a low purr, wreaking havoc on my insides.

I freeze, unable to react or respond. What did I do? How do I get out of this? I don't really want this, do I?

Kian reaches a hand to my cheek, his thumb gently running along my lower lip before tilting my head back. He moves just a bit closer and trails his hand down so it rests lightly around my throat. "Tell me what you want, love. Just say it, and it's yours."

My body is alight from his touch. It's too much. It's not enough. I don't know if this is what I want. I take a breath to say something—what, I'm not entirely sure—when the door opens and a maid brings in a tray of food.

The spell broken, I pull away and get up, marching toward the table and thanking the maid. Turning back to Kian I say, "I feel like I could eat a horse."

Kian chuckles. "Don't let Phantom hear that."

"I wouldn't dream of it." I laugh as I start piling food onto my plate.

I'M PURPOSELY AVOIDING my husband. Again. If I close my eyes, I can see his smoldering gaze staring me down across the table last night during dinner. Would something have happened if we hadn't been interrupted? I lay awake for hours, wondering if he would slip into our bed. All I had to comfort, or perhaps torture, myself with were images of his shirtless body gleaming with sweat, muscles bunching as he lunged for me, disarmed me . . . and my fingers, wishing they were his.

I pick up a book and fan myself with it. *This is not why you're here. Focus, Rae!*

The hidden library alcove I'm seated in is cozy. I brought a warm blanket from our rooms so I could hole up here all day. It's pouring rain and completely overcast, so I'm not able to go experiment in the sun anyway, as much as I want to test and see just how strong the godsblood is within me. Being alone with my books is my comfort zone, and I don't want to be disturbed. I'm trying to read anything I can get my hands on about the gods and their offspring.

Flipping a page, I yelp when the sharp edge slices into my finger. I look around for a handkerchief or something to staunch the flow but stop when the drop of blood on my finger catches the light. I'm almost mesmerized at the shimmer. It's so faint, it's hardly noticeable. I try to recall if I've ever noticed that before, but nothing comes to mind, or perhaps I've just never thought to look. Why would I have ever suspected this about myself? Absolutely no reason. Because my family has lied to me my entire life. *Not bitter at all, huh, Rae?*

I suck the blood off my fingertip after not finding anything to bind it, and to my surprise, the cut has already sealed. That's new . . . but the books do say advanced healing is a part of being a demi-god. Perhaps my blood intake from Kian boosted my abilities despite the lack of sunshine. Plus, it was only a papercut, not exactly a mortal wound. Fascinating though.

Anger and betrayal cut me like a knife every time I think about how my father spent my entire life trying to keep me weak. What a fool I'd been to trust him . . . but he was the only father I knew.

I let out a muffled groan of frustration at all the conflicting feelings running through me. I'm exhausted.

Chapter Thirty-Five

RAELYN

"You have a visitor, my lady," Kian's valet says, scaring the hells out of me. I didn't hear him come in and was just finishing my breakfast alone.

"Giles, I didn't see you there." I hold a hand to my heart, willing it to calm. "Do you know who it is?"

"I believe it's your father, Lord Astoria."

My heart starts racing again and my palms dampen at the mention of his name. On one hand, I'm excited to see him—it's been almost two months. On the other, he lied to me, drugged me . . . I'm scared to face him, but oh, I have so many questions.

I clear my throat and rise, gripping the table to steady myself. "I'll see him."

"Where would you like to host him?" Giles asks.

I shrug, looking at him helplessly. Even after weeks, this place still doesn't quite feel like home.

"Might I suggest the sitting room across the hall?"

"Sure, that sounds perfect. Thank you, Giles. I'll be over in a few minutes."

He nods and slips out of the room.

I pace back and forth, surely wearing the ornate rug thin beneath my feet. I can do this. I can face him. Do I pretend not to know anything? Do I wait for him to say something? Gods, I don't know.

Smoothing my hair back, I take a few deep, calming breaths before crossing the hall to the sitting room. I'm glad Giles suggested it; it juts out toward the gardens, and the floor-to-ceiling windows let in copious amounts of light.

Memories of Father asking our servants to draw the curtains in the middle of the day fills me with a renewed sense of anger. I'll let that little bit of rage fuel me for the conversation ahead. I can do this.

Sweeping into the sitting room, I plaster a smile onto my face. "Father! How lovely to see you."

"Raelyn, my darling." He smiles broadly, but sweat dots his brow . . . Is it just me, or has my vision significantly improved? Another effect of the godsblood running through my veins, if I had to guess. He looks older . . . tired.

Meeting me halfway, he pulls me into his arms. I blink, my entire body stiff as tears choke my throat. I honestly can't remember the last time he's done so . . . I swallow them down, trying to keep my wits about me. The last thing I need is for him to manipulate me. I need answers.

I can do this, I remind myself once more.

I pull away and blink back the tears before they escape. "You look well," I lie.

"So do you, my darling." He takes me in from head to toe, wiping at his brow with a handkerchief until he stops and focuses on my gold-flecked eyes. "Are you actually well? Have you been taking your tonic? When I arrived at the manor and you were gone, you have no idea how terrified I was. I've missed you so much and had to come as soon as I could to make sure you were actually all right."

"Father, please. I'm fine, as you can see. Have a seat." I motion toward the sitting area that is currently flooded with rare sunlight. Has the sun been shining more frequently as of late? I need to discuss this with Kian. Before my thoughts run away with me, I turn my focus back to Father and the way he's fidgeting in a manner so unlike him. I must really have him rattled.

"Raelyn, dear, should we have the servants draw the curtains? You know the sun makes you ill."

"Does it now?" I respond dryly.

Father continues to dab at his sweating brow. "Raelyn—"

"No, Father. No more lies," I say firmly and take a seat. "Are *you* ill?"

He waves me off as he sits down. "I'm fine."

Seconds that feel like hours tick by as he silently peruses me, waiting for me to reveal my hand first or perhaps waiting for me to answer his questions. My hands grip my skirts, and I stare him down in defiance.

"Eloped, Raelyn?" he spits out. "That damned prince. After everything I did—"

"What did you do?" I interrupt, hoping for some truth, but he just keeps going.

"And now my firstborn—"

"But am I?" I demand, finally getting him to stop. "Stepmother told me without any hesitation that I'm a bastard."

Father flinches. "That was not her secret to tell."

"So it is true."

His silence is deafening. To finally hear it from him hurts in a way I can't explain.

"Were you ever going to tell me?" I ask, unable to hold back the tears welling up in my eyes all over again. "Do you have any idea how many questions I have?"

He looks at the floor, squeezing his handkerchief in his hands. Before he says another word, a maid comes in with a tea service and pours refreshments for us.

"Thank you," I murmur, and she escapes the awkward silence as quickly as possible. I don't blame her.

"Raelyn, regardless of your birth, I have always considered you my daughter," Father says calmly.

I look up into his dark eyes, searching for truth . . . searching for lies. I'm not sure what to believe.

"Was Mama my mother?" I ask. If he's lied about everything else, I have to know what's real . . . if anything.

He picks up his teacup and sips from the steaming beverage, his hesitancy making my heart drop.

"Well?"

"I didn't come here to talk about that," he deflects. "I came here because my eldest child ran off and got married without even discussing it with me. After everything I have done for you, all I have sacrificed, how could you betray me like that? How could you steal such an important moment from me?"

"You sound like Chessa," I mutter under my breath.

"Excuse me?"

Ignoring him, I repeat, "Was she my mother? I need to know!" My voice starts to rise, and I'm a child all over again, fighting with my father. When he refuses to answer, I switch tactics. "Do you have any idea how Stepmother treated me when you left?"

He frowns. "Whatever do you mean?"

My eyes widen. Does he really not know? "Father, she let go of most of our staff and replaced them with *me*."

His jaw goes slack, and he struggles for words. I want to believe he's actually shocked. I really do.

"That's preposterous!" He shakes his head.

"It's true. Ask anyone at home and they'll tell you, unless she managed to threaten them somehow."

"But your brother and sisters—"

"They were treated the same as always. Stepmother hates me. Gods only know why."

"Raelyn, please believe me when I say I would have never allowed that. That never should have happened." His body shakes with rage, each word clipped as it comes out. "That was unacceptable on her part. I shouldn't have left you. How can I make this right?"

I laugh bitterly. "What's the point? I'm here now. A princess of the realm. Look at that."

Father stares up at the ceiling, defeated. "I'm sorry I couldn't protect you. That's all I've ever wanted . . . to keep you safe."

"By poisoning me?" I accuse.

His eyes flash back to mine. "I *was* protecting you."

"So you keep saying," I grit out. "By what? Lying to me? Suppressing the godsblood in my veins and keeping me from my source of power?"

Father sits back in his seat. The fear flickering in his eyes looks real.

"Do you know something? About the lost god?" I ask.

When he continues to sit in silence, I let out a frustrated scream. "Why won't you answer any of my questions?" I jump to my feet and pace the room.

"Raelyn." My father's voice cuts through the noise in my head.

I whirl and glare at him.

"I can't expect you to understand until you're a parent, but you have to trust that everything I did was for your protection."

"That's not good enough," I bite out, my hands on my hips. "Besides, you're not my father, are you?"

He cracks an odd smile. "You're feistier than when I left."

I want to crumple to the floor and cry. He has no idea how broken I am. This is a mask. That's all. I'm not strong—I'm weak.

Father gets to his feet and stalks toward me, surprising me when he once again throws his arms around me and crushes me into a hug.

I stiffen, hating how comforting his arms feel.

My body slowly loosens, and I hug him back, silent tears streaking down my face.

When he pulls away, the fear in his eyes is almost disconcerting. "I worry for you, daughter."

"Bu—"

"Regardless of whether or not you are my blood, you are still my daughter."

"What *can* you tell me?" I ask. "There has to be something . . ." I leave my words hanging, my desperation clear.

Father sighs, rubbing his hand across his face in an unfamiliar manner. So different from the father he'd been for so many years, as if now that the mask is stripped off, this is all that remains.

"As you've discovered, you do have godsblood," he admits. "I fear that since you've awakened your gifts, he'll come after you."

"Who?" I frown. "What do you mean *come after me*? The lost god? Wouldn't that be a good thing? We need him to heal our land."

"There are some things you won't be able to understand, daughter, things I cannot tell you, but trust me, it would be better for you to go back to the way things were. You don't want him to find you."

"'Him' who?" I ask again, desperate for an answer, any kind of answer.

"Your true father."

I still. "But why wouldn't I want that?"

"He's not who you think he is," Father says cryptically.

I frown, confusion making it hard for me to even grasp this conversation, let alone the circles he's running me in.

"Is he a demi-god? Where has he been hiding?" I ask. "Everyone thinks the gods have ignored us for centuries . . . Is that a lie too?"

"Tell me, have you had dreams yet?" he asks almost frantically, ignoring my questions.

"Doesn't everyone dream?" I say, not hiding my snark at his continued withholding.

He shakes his head in aggravation. "No, child, I mean a dream that doesn't feel quite like another. Has anyone spoken to you?"

"I've been having dreams for years, Father . . ." I admit. "Dreams that are different."

He palms his face again. "Perhaps all of it was in vain . . ."

"You're not making sense."

He fists his palms, and I can sense the tension radiating off him. "Please, Raelyn, get back on the tonic. I need you to trust me on this."

I back up a few steps. "I like being able to experience the sun. I like the strength it gives me."

He blinks, as if realizing his battle is lost. "Heed my words, child. Stay here in Elsmont. Do not go looking for him."

I laugh. "Where would I even go?"

He grimaces. "You may never forgive me for my lies or half-truths, but try to remember it was only done out of love."

"Until you are ready to tell me actual truths, Father, I don't want to see you anymore. Tell Stepmother and my siblings they are not welcome here at court either."

He steps away as if I slapped him. A part of me feels awful for my words, but I need to set some boundaries. This is one of them.

"Please leave," I clarify. "Do not return unless you have actual information for me." I step aside so he can walk past.

He gives me a final look, one I can't read, and walks to the door. "Stay here, where you're safe."

I shake my head, unwilling to look him in the eye again. When I don't respond, he leaves, and I collapse onto the floor, shaking, allowing myself to break one last time.

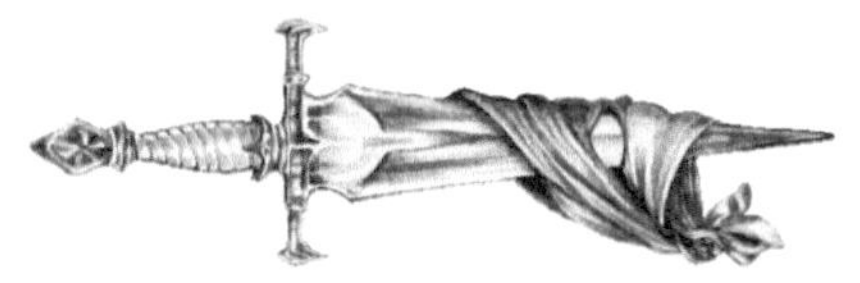

Chapter Thirty-Six

KIAN

7 YEARS AGO

What is this feeling? Giddiness? Why am I giddy at the thought of seeing her again? At least, I assume I'll see her again . . . It's been four long years. Four years of wondering what she's been up to, what she enjoys now . . . Will there still be that spark between us, or have I built her up in my mind in a way she could never live up to? With her strange supposed affliction to the sun, I don't expect her at any of the daytime events, but perhaps tonight she'll be at the first ball of the season hosted by Lord and Lady Havordshire.

Dylan elbows me in the ribs, and I blow out a breath of air.

"Why'd you do that?" I grumble and barely duck out of the way before he comes at me with his sword.

"You're not paying attention, Ki," he teases. "Are we getting our workout in or not?"

I spin and swipe at his lower legs, and he jumps just in time.

"You're getting better at this. Have you been training with Master Waylen?" I ask.

"Someone's gotta keep you on your toes."

I laugh. "We all know I can kick your ass if I want to."

Dylan pouts. "Hey, let me have this one, okay?"

I shrug. "Sure." Before he can react, I kick his long legs out from underneath him, and he lands on the training mat with a resounding thud.

"Damn, Ki. You really are an ass."

"And yet we're still friends."

"Maybe I should rethink that," Dylan groans.

I reach down and help him to his feet, patting his back. "You're definitely improving. I will give you that."

"Are you coming to our ball tonight?" Dylan asks, changing the subject.

I shrug halfheartedly. The last thing I want is for Dylan to rib me for pining over a girl for the last decade. "I might show up."

Dylan gives me a knowing look. "That's right! I almost forgot. The Astoria girl might be there?"

"Shut up."

A stupid grin lights up his face, and he gets in my space. "Do you think she'll remember you this time?"

I push him away and frown. "Gods only know . . . I guess I'll have to see how memorable I am."

Dylan takes a playful swing at me that I easily bat off. "What if I gave you a black eye? Surely that would make you more memorable," he jokes.

"And Father would probably beat me for allowing it to happen." I grimace.

"What has you so hung up on her anyhow?"

Blowing out a breath, I stare at my feet. "I'm not sure how to explain it, but I've always been drawn to her. She's pretty, yes, but every time I've seen her, I've learned something new. She's daring, intelligent, curious, and there's a kindness to her. She treats everyone with respect, even the people serving in her home. I like that she's easy to talk to."

"Clearly, you're smitten," Dylan says with a grin. "Even if she has forgotten you though, I'm sure we can get into some trouble tonight. There will be plenty of fresh young women for you to practice on."

I shake my head but can't stop the smile from stretching my face. He's right. Even if she isn't there, or Luna forbid, wants nothing to do with me, there is sure to be someone who would want the attention of a prince, right?

I'm no saint. Dylan and I have developed somewhat of a reputation these past years. But every girl I've held in my arms has only made me think of one I've never had . . . might never have.

THE ROYAL CARRIAGE pulls up to the large country manor, and I hop out, excitement running through my veins. A vibrant symphony is carried in on the breeze, and I make my way toward the party that is already in full swing. I'm fashionably late as usual. Wanting to avoid the herald, I sneak around to a side entrance and jump in with another crowd of attendees, who are all dressed to impress.

Damn, I forgot this was a masquerade. Everywhere I look, masks are on display.

I stick to the dimly lit corridors and finally spot a discarded black one on a table next to a brightly feathered one. The smack of flesh hitting flesh has me raising a brow. Swiping the black mask off the table, I don't really feel bad. I'm fairly certain they won't miss it.

I stride into the ballroom, the music so loud, I can hardly hear myself think. My eyes scan the crowd, hoping for a glimpse of her. If it weren't for these damn masks, it might be easier. With every glimpse of reddish-brown hair, my heart skips in my chest, but it's never her. She's nowhere to be found.

Needing some fresh air and quiet, I grab a drink off a tray and make my way to the gardens. Fairy lights are strung up all over the courtyard, giving it an ethereal feel. A few couples walk around, quietly chatting and flirting as if there's no tomorrow.

My eyes are drawn to the fireflies lighting up the night sky near the pond, and I stroll over to get a better look.

A dark-haired female in a shimmering gold dress stands with her back to me, and I try to make noise with my feet so as to not startle the poor girl with my approach.

"A beautiful evening, is it not?" I remark.

Despite my attempts, the girl jumps and turns to look at me. This time, I think my heart does stop as I'm met with beautiful green eyes behind a mask of gold.

I can't stop the smile from overtaking my face as I give her a small bow and reach out for her hand. "Lady Raelyn, how lovely to see you again."

She allows me to take her hand, and I press a soft kiss to it, feeling her pulse quicken beneath my fingers.

"I apologize," she says, "have we met?"

My heart sinks in my chest. Again? What in Luna's name is going on with this girl? Am I truly that forgettable?

I let go of her hand and straighten. "Prince Kian."

A slight flush stains her cheeks. "I'm so sorry, Your Highness. I should have recognized you."

Should have because I'm the prince or should have because she remembers me from four years ago or the many years before that?

"That's quite all right," I try to placate her. "It is quite dark out here."

"I apologize, Your Highness. I don't leave my manor very often. I can't even recall the last time I was at court with my family."

I frown. How could she have forgotten a royal wedding? Even if she'd forgotten me, surely a wedding would have been memorable.

"Please, don't worry about it," I say. "Isn't your father close to the king?"

She nods demurely. "Yes, but he doesn't ever bring me with him when he visits."

"What a shame," I say. "You're quite lovely."

Idiot. Why did I say that?

She looks around as if she wants to escape, and I squeeze my eyes shut. "I'm sorry, I didn't mean to come on so strong."

Wringing her hands, she lets out an awkward chuckle.

Trying to ease her back into more comfortable conversation, I ask, "What brings you out to the gardens? Was the music too loud?"

She shakes her head. "I don't get out much, as I mentioned . . . but the gardens here are very soothing. It's a nice change from home."

The scent of roses blows by on a gentle breeze, and she closes her eyes, inhaling deeply.

"The Havordshire family does have such a beautiful garden," I reply.

She smiles at me, and I think my heart stops.

I clear my throat. "So, um, if you don't get out much, what do you like to do for fun?"

She bites her lip and takes a step back, lost in thought. "Well, I spend a lot of time in my library," she admits. "I'm quite good at puzzles and needlepoint."

"Sounds riveting."

She scoffs. "You don't have to lie."

"I'm not," I say sincerely. "If it's something you enjoy, what could be boring about it?"

She rolls her eyes but smiles at me, clutching her skirts in a nervous manner. "I wish I could do more things outdoors, but it's difficult for me. I have quite the reaction to the sun."

"That sounds horrible," I say. "So you only come out at night?"

She nods. "Even then, Father doesn't like for me to be out much. He worries it could worsen my affliction."

"You seem to be doing just fine," I reply.

She shrugs. "He couldn't forbid me from coming to the first ball of the season." She twirls with an almost childlike quality. "How else am I to find a husband?"

At those words, a pang of jealousy runs through me, which is silly. I have no desire to get married any time soon, but for her? Maybe I would . . . The idea of being shackled to someone for a lifetime is overwhelming.

"And have you found any prospects?" My voice deepens unintentionally.

She pulls out her fan and waves it in front of her face in a coy manner. "I've danced with a few young lords, but only one has really caught my attention."

Does she mean me? I'm almost afraid to hope.

"Would you like to dance with me?" I ask, holding my breath for her answer.

She laughs. "Out here?"

"Out here would be perfect," I reply.

I empty my drink, put my glass down in the grass, and approach. Her eyes shimmer in the moonlight, and my mind can't help but drift to the last time we danced and how she left me alone on the dance floor. Shaking the memory away, I gently grasp her hand and pull her closer.

The lyrical strains of music barely reach us, but I lead her in the simple one-two-three steps of the waltz. Her hand barely reaches my shoulder, and I relish the feel of her in my arms as we dance around the small pond, the fireflies lighting up all around us.

She radiates delight as we dance, and moonlight bounces off her pale cheeks when she lifts her face to gaze at the endless stars that light up the night sky. My eyes catch on her full red lips, and I wonder not for the first time what it would be like to taste her.

"You dance beautifully." I speak in her ear.

"You're not so bad yourself."

"Well, I have trained for this my entire life," I joke.

Her laughter lights up the night. I could never grow tired of it.

"How would you feel if I wanted to call on you this season?" I ask, almost afraid of her answer.

Her eyes dart up to mine. "Really? You'd want to call on me?"

I look around playfully. "What, do you see someone else?"

She gently swats at my shoulder. "I just find it hard to believe that a prince would have any interest in courting me."

I frown. "But why? I'm greatly enjoying your company."

"Surely you could find someone better to call on, someone who doesn't need to spend her days locked up inside."

"What if that doesn't bother me?" I ask.

She hesitates, as if she doesn't quite believe me. "I don't know . . . It might be too much."

"It would be an honor, Lady Raelyn."

"I suppose I can't say no to a prince."

I grin broadly. "Well, then consider me one of your prospects."

She flushes oh-so-prettily, and it takes all my self-control not to draw her even closer to me.

"Father will be thrilled that I have not one but two potential callers."

Two?

"Raelyn, darling, I've been looking all over for you." A familiar voice makes my blood run cold.

Raelyn's face lights up, and she breaks away from my hold. "Dylan!" she cries. "I was waiting for you. What took you so long to find me?"

I squeeze my eyes shut as betrayal burns like acid through my veins.

"Are you friends with Prince Kian?" she asks him, her tone full of excitement and innocence.

Finally turning around to face them, Dylan smirks at me as he places a heavy hand on my shoulder. "Oh we go way back."

I want to punch that smarmy grin right off his face. He knew. He. Knew. How could he?

Lady Raelyn grips his arm comfortably as she looks up at him. "Lord Havordshire has business dealings with my father, and I've seen him quite a few times this year."

"How lovely," I grit out. "Dylan never mentioned you."

A frown creases her forehead as she looks from me to him, but then she shakes it off. "I hope this won't be any trouble . . . if both of you come calling."

"May the best man win," Dylan says, putting a possessive arm around Raelyn.

Chapter Thirty-Seven

RAELYN

I'm on an island. Wind whips through my hair, tangling my skirts around my legs. The briny air makes my eyes sting, and sand squishes beneath my feet. *How did I get here?*

A low growl has the hair on my neck standing at attention, and I spin around, spying the largest lion I could possibly imagine prowling toward me.

This is just a dream. This has to be a dream. Why does it feel so real?

I take a step back, wanting to flee but somehow knowing it's completely useless. This beast would catch me before I made it two feet.

I stop, daring to stare into the lion's golden eyes. I vaguely remember my father asking me about dreams . . .

The lion continues prowling menacingly toward me, and I sink to my knees in the sand, bowing before, who I hope, is the sun god—my ancestor?

Warm breath blows across my head, sending more chills skittering down my spine. A soft nudge, and I look up, my heart nearly stopping at the massive creature before me. While I am terrified, a part of me feels safe, which might be completely insane on my part . . . *and yet*, I remind myself again, *this is only a dream*. Can he hurt me in a dream?

The lion chuffs, almost as if he can hear the thoughts racing through my head. Wait, *can he?* If he's controlling my dream, then of course he can. He's in my head.

I think the lion snorts in amusement, and I reach out a hand, hesitating before petting his head. He nuzzles my hand, and a feeling of warmth encompasses me.

"Hi," I murmur. "Can you understand me?"

The lion chuffs again.

"Why am I here?" I ask, wishing he could somehow speak.

The lion nudges me again and motions his head toward the jungle.

"Do you want me to come with you?"

The lion grunts once, and I slowly rise, brushing the sand off my skirts. The visceral nature of the dream is almost shocking; it feels far too real for my comfort.

The lion turns and prowls toward the tree line, and I follow.

Our path is lit by the soft moonlight and twinkling stars, and I mark their position in the sky. I can't help but wonder where I am and whether or not it's a real place.

When we finally make it into the jungle, the darkness fills me with a sense of unease.

"Where are you taking me?" I ask, though why I'm talking to a lion who can't talk back is beyond me.

The lion chuffs what sounds like a laugh again, and I shake my head as he leads me deeper into the woods.

The moonlight barely reaches in through the trees, and my eyes are having trouble adjusting to the dark. The lion comes up alongside me, and I put my hand on his silky back, allowing him to guide me, trying not to trip over roots or get smacked in the face by the low-hanging branches. The trickling sound of water gets louder and louder until we finally reach the roar of a waterfall. The lion stops, pointing his nose toward it, and I shiver. The howls of a man in pain reach my ears, and my heart collapses in on itself. The pain is overwhelming, all-consuming.

"Is this where you are? Are you trapped?" I gasp.

A growl comes from the lion, but when I look down, he's gone. I'm stranded alone on this island, the spray of the waterfall chilling me to my core. The howling cries awaken a deep terror within me, and then *I'm* screaming.

"Raelyn!" A rough voice breaks through the haze of my dream turned nightmare. My arms thrash as I feel hands on me. *Why can't I wake up?*

Light sparks, and I blink furiously as I sit up in bed. Concerned stormy eyes peer into mine.

"Raelyn," Kian repeats, cupping my cheek with his rough hand. "Are you all right? You were screaming."

I take a deep, shuddering breath and shake my head. "Water," I rasp. "Please . . ."

Kian drops his hand and rushes out of the room, quickly returning with a glass of water, holding it up to my mouth for me to drink.

I shakily clasp my hands around the glass, and the tepid liquid slides down my throat, bringing with it a little more clarity.

"What happened?" Kian asks. "Was it a nightmare?"

"I dreamed of the lion," I say with a shudder. "I think you were right . . . It's him, the sun god."

Kian blinks in surprise, and all of a sudden, I *really* see him. He is clad head-to-toe in black leather, and there is blood seeping out of a gash on his forehead. My mouth immediately salivates at the sight and scent of it, but I chastise myself. *This is not the time, Rae.*

"You're hurt," I state.

Kian blinks again, his hand going to his forehead, and he shakes his head. "Just a scratch, love. Nothing for you to worry about."

"Where were you?" I demand, sitting up taller in bed. "Why are you dressed like that?"

Kian avoids my gaze and heads toward the washroom, ignoring my questions.

Jumping out of bed, I follow him, anger at yet another man in my life withholding information pulsing through me.

"Are you going to answer me or not?" I demand.

"I need to get cleaned up, love, so unless you *want* to see me naked, I'd advise leaving the washroom." He starts peeling his leathers off, and my face immediately flushes in embarrassment . . . yet my curiosity is high.

I whirl around before I can see something I shouldn't, but I stay in the room, listening to the sound of clothes hitting the floor and the thud of boots being thrown into the corner. "I . . . uhh . . . I expect an answer out of you, *husband*."

Kian snorts a laugh. "So now I'm your husband, eh?"

I hold up my bare arm, flashing the mark at him, even though I don't know if he's looking. "That's what this says!"

There's a splash as water starts to fill the tub, and I tap my foot impatiently. Kian hasn't lit any lamps, so the only illumination in the room comes from the moonlight faintly streaming in from the small window overhead.

I chance a glance over my shoulder, and my mouth waters for an entirely different reason. Kian's back is to me, and the firm globes of his ass are on display. My eyes take in the muscled masterpiece, and I swallow audibly.

Kian looks over his shoulder, his eyes meeting mine for a brief second before I immediately turn away, embarrassed at being caught staring.

"Like what you see, love?" Kian's voice is a caress down my skin, and I remember I'm only wearing a light shift that doesn't leave much to the imagination.

Another splash of water alerts me to the fact that he is now in the tub, followed by a soft groan and hiss.

I cross my arms over my chest, hoping to hide the hardened peaks of my nipples as I turn back to look at him. "Now, are you going to tell me where that 'scratch' came from?" I ask, daring to take a few steps closer.

Kian turns his head, observing my cautious approach, a sly smirk crossing his face. "I'm touched you're so concerned for me."

I shake my head in annoyance. "If you're just going to make jokes, I'll leave and call for the healer."

"Wait, stop," Kian says, his tone changing.

I tap my foot again impatiently. "You have no idea how much I hate when people lie to me or withhold truths, even when I directly ask. If you won't tell me what's going on, I—"

"What do you mean?" Kian interjects. "Did something happen?"

I blow out a frustrated breath. "My father showed up."

Kian uses a cloth to carefully clean himself, and I draw a little closer, realizing he's covered in bruises.

"Shit, Kian. What have you been doing? Brawling?" I stop before I get any closer, not wanting to tempt myself to look any further. Besides, this is completely inappropriate, me getting turned on by an injured man.

Kian winces again, and I throw up my hands before grabbing the cloth from him, pulling a small stool over, and gently cleaning the area on his back he was unable to reach. I'm behind him, so I can't see . . . much.

"Thanks," he mutters. "I'm not used to someone taking care of me."

I shrug, but then remember his back is to me. "It's the least I can do. I *am* your wife after all."

He chuckles.

I grab a pitcher and dunk it into the water, gently tilting his head back and soaking his dark locks.

"That feels nice," he groans, and it sends a bolt of heat straight to my core.

I pour some soap into my hands and gently massage his scalp, careful not to get anywhere near the cut on his forehead.

Another quiet moan from Kian has me clenching my thighs together.

"Thank you, love."

"You're welcome." My voice comes out all breathy. Shit. What is happening?

"So, your father was here?" Kian asks.

I continue rubbing the soap through his hair, wondering how much I want to share, and grateful for the distraction. "I tried to ask him questions about . . . everything . . . He just kept deflecting." I frown. "Kind of like what you've been doing."

"I'm sorry, Rae," Kian rasps. "I just don't want to say anything that will put you in danger."

I turn the pitcher of water over onto his head with no warning, and he starts spluttering, trying to wipe his hair out of his face.

"Hells! What was that for?"

"I'm so sick and tired of men telling me they're lying to me for *my* benefit!" I rise, knocking the small stool over, the clatter rattling through the space.

Kian stands from the bath, turning to glare at me, and my eyes drink in the magnificent sight of him, completely naked. I grab a towel and thrust it at him, needing him to be covered up because I can't think— can't breathe—with him in front of me like that.

"Why are *you* mad?" I spit out.

Kian huffs a dark laugh as he wraps the towel around his hips and grabs another to dry his hair. "I don't get you, Rae. What do you want from me? As far as we're concerned, this isn't a real marriage. I don't owe you anything."

I take a breath. He's right.

"I'm sorry . . . I just . . . I really wanted answers from my father, and he gave me practically nothing." I shrug, even as the feelings from earlier flood back through me. "He just kept saying he was doing it all to protect me but wouldn't explain more than that . . . And now you show up in the middle of the night, bleeding and hurt . . . refusing to tell me where you've been because you want to protect me?"

Kian squeezes his eyes shut for a second before taking a cautious step toward me. "I'm sorry, Rae. I didn't mean to hurt you."

I laugh almost hysterically. "You didn't hurt me, not really."

He steps closer, tilting my chin up to look at him. "Rae, I—I really want to be able to share with you, but it could mean your death."

I freeze, taking in the seriousness in Kian's eyes—his smoky, grey eyes—and the black leather . . . The puzzle pieces click into place, and I gasp, taking a step away from him in shock. How did I not see it? How could I have been so blind, so dumb?

"It's you . . ." I whisper.

Kian stiffens, his hand dropping back to his side.

I back out of the room, my hand going to my throat.

"Don't say it, Rae. You can't unsay it if you do," Kian almost growls. His eyes beg me to stop before I change everything.

"You're *him*."

I almost laugh again. What is my life? I'm married to a prince who is also enemy number one to the king, the vigilante known as the Shadow, who has been stealing goods for his people, doling out punishment to the king's lords . . . the same vigilante who tried stealing from my father all those weeks ago. It has always been him.

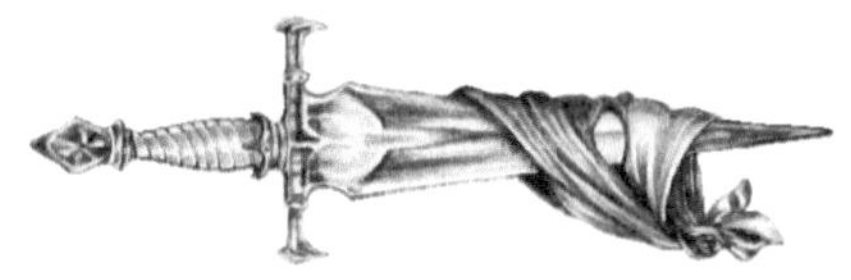

Chapter Thirty-Eight

KIAN

She knows. It's written all over her face. I never should have stopped by tonight, but I hadn't seen her all day, and something had drawn me here. When I found her screaming in bed, I had to do something. I couldn't leave her like that, even though I was still in my dark leathers with blood leaking out of my head.

"Rae," I say again, taking a step toward her as she backs away.

Is she scared of me or just in shock?

"Hells, I'm so stupid. How did I not realize before?" she whispers, her voice trembling.

"You weren't meant to know, love."

Her eyes fill with tears, and my heart aches. Of course I wanted to tell her, but it went against everything inside of me, screaming that my secrets kept her safe. It's bad enough that Alex is in on it.

When she looked at me with disdain for my lack of action in saving our people, I almost wanted to spit it out right then and there. There is nothing I want more than for her to look at me with some semblance of respect and not think I'm a worthless waste of space the way my father does. I want her to know me . . . but I also want to keep her safe. She is mine to protect.

Rae shakes her head, continuing to back away. "What are you going to do?" she rasps.

I pause, tilting my head. "I'm not going to *do* anything."

"You're not?" she asks, stopping when her backside hits the bed.

"Love, I'd never do anything to hurt you on purpose."

She closes her eyes, and it's a knife to the chest that she would even consider me someone to fear. I wish I could tell her how much I care . . . how *long* I've cared . . . how long I've wanted her, but for some reason, she keeps forgetting. Everything we've experienced throughout the years has somehow been wiped from her memory. Is that something else to blame her father for?

I finish drying my hair and throw the smaller towel toward the bathing room.

She opens her eyes at the wet slop of it hitting the floor and wrinkles her nose adorably. "You're so messy."

I chuckle. Her entire body tenses as I approach, and I can't help but notice how her white shift is almost see-through. My cock hardens immediately, but this is not the time.

"I'm sorry, does that bother you?" I inquire as I place one hand on either side of her body on the bed and lean in. I can't stay away from her. It's pure torture knowing she's mine and yet might not ever truly be.

She blows out a breath and, oh gods, I want to taste her so badly.

"I would have thought you'd be tidier based on the usual state of your rooms." She motions around, seemingly unbothered by my proximity with just a towel around my waist.

I smirk. "Giles would disagree with you."

Rae scrunches her nose again. "Ah, so you take advantage of your poor valet, huh?"

I inch just a bit closer, the sweet scent of her skin making me think all sorts of naughty thoughts. "You're right, I could definitely be less messy. I'll have to apologize to Giles."

She smiles. "As you should."

"Thank you for washing my hair," I whisper in her ear, enjoying the way her skin pebbles. Perhaps I affect her just as much as she does me. These rules we gave ourselves are ridiculous. We should banish them immediately.

"You're welcome," she replies before placing a hand on my chest and gently pushing. Her expression hardens, and a door slams shut, closing me out.

As disappointed as I am, I acquiesce and back off.

"I really should try to sleep," she says, a bitter edge to her voice.

"I'll pray the nightmares stay away," I reply, watching as she slides under the covers and turns her back to me.

I turn off the lamp and head to my dressing room to find something to sleep in, carefully putting my towel with the soiled laundry and pulling on a pair of loose-fitted trousers.

The thought of traipsing back to Alex's rooms sounds unappealing. Before I change my mind, I go back to my room and slip into bed beside Raelyn. She's already fast asleep, her breathing deep and even. It's torture being here, but I can't stay away . . . and I worry that she might have another nightmare after the stress of the day. We didn't discuss her dream of the sun god, but that will most definitely be revisited in the morning. For now, I will try to sleep . . . and hope she can forgive me for the secrets.

I inhale, and my nose is filled with her citrus-and-vanilla scent. She's imprinted herself in my bed and my sheets. My pillow smells of her soap. I hold back a groan, not wanting to wake her. To be so close and not have her is a sweet sort of torture.

"Sleep well, love," I whisper under my breath before flipping onto my back, cradling my head with my hands to keep them from finding their way to her.

I awaken to a warm body nuzzled into mine. It takes a moment for me to orient myself despite being in a familiar bed with the morning light streaming in through my window. I look down at the head full of auburn hair nestled into my side and smile. I could get used to this—a heaven I never thought I'd get to experience.

I have no idea how she'll feel about this, so I do my best to extricate myself from the bed without waking her.

Loath as I am to admit it, it was some of the best sleep of my life. Though if I dared to make this a permanent arrangement, things would inevitably get too . . . hard. Fuck. I need a cold bath. I've never needed so many in my entire life since she moved in.

My body is quite sore from the raid last night, but nothing is injured enough to require a healer. I perform a few quick stretches and decide that a run might be exactly what I need.

As much as I want to wake Alex and make him come with me, I decide against it. He's been suffering enough with my nightly shenanigans. He could use the rest.

I throw on a light tunic and lace up my shoes before making my way to the gardens to work off some of the pent-up energy from sleeping next to my tempting wife.

Chapter Thirty-Nine

RAELYN

The sun is calling to me. Bright light fills our wing, and I'm delighted at the idea of a stroll in the gardens. After days of overcast weather, it's about time the sun shows itself.

As I struggle to fight the tangles in my hair, I regret telling Sera to take the morning off. Oh well, I'll manage.

Unbidden, my thoughts drift to Kian and his secret. *He* is the one protecting and trying to help his people. Anger at being left in the dark by another man in my life threatens to overwhelm the pride I also feel for him. As dangerous as it is, proven by the injuries and multitude of scars, he's making a difference. *He* should be next in line for the throne. With his father and brother doing nothing, he's the only hope our kingdom has.

Though . . . that would mean I'd be queen. I shudder. No. I have no desire for that, but unfortunately, I'm stuck with him until death parts us, and I only have myself to blame for that one.

Am I willing to forgive the lies? The secrets? I really want to . . . but my heart aches painfully at the betrayal. One step at a time. One day at a

259

time. Our agreement never said I had to love him . . . but then why does it hurt so much?

I dress and grab a pastry from the table before heading out. The tonic has fully left my system, and my morning walks have given me a fresh take on life. I've never felt this strong or healthy, and it makes me angry all over again that my father kept this from me out of some misguided notion of protection. What else did he do?

I come alive the minute I step into the sunlight, its warmth caressing me from my head to my toes. While it's only been a few days, when I look down at my skin, it's no longer pale; there are freckles dotting my arms, and I know there are some on my cheeks and nose.

My eyes close, and I tilt my head toward the sun as I take a few steps on the path, until I collide with a solid figure.

"Oh, shit!" a male voice exclaims.

My eyes fly open, and I step back, trying to right myself, only to be steadied by the tall man in front of me. "Thank you," I breathe.

"Gods, you shouldn't be thanking me," the man jokes. "I'm the one who nearly took you out!"

"Well, to be fair, I was walking with my eyes closed." I crinkle my nose and frown.

The man laughs, and it's almost familiar. I take in his tall, lanky stature and friendly smile. His blue eyes shine with mirth as he brushes a dark curl away from his face. "As much as I appreciate you taking some of the blame, it was I who walked into you."

I smile and tilt my head. "Have we met?" I ask. "I almost feel as if I should know you."

"My father has business with yours; I've probably seen you around your manor. Regardless, Lord Havordshire, at your service, but my friends call me Dylan."

"My friends call me Raelyn," I reply with a smile.

His eyes light up, and he holds out an arm. "Would you like to stroll with me, Raelyn?"

I pause. Is this appropriate? I'm a married woman. What would happen if I were seen walking with a man who wasn't my husband?

He notes my hesitation, and his eyes immediately fall on the extravagant ring on my right finger and the faint bonding mark on my arm. "My apologies, lady. I didn't realize you were bound. Who's the lucky lord?"

"Prince Kian, actually," I say with a blush.

"Princess!" Dylan's brows arch up in surprise, and he gives a stiff bow. "Once again, I am so sorry."

I force a laugh, looking around the garden. "I'm afraid I'm not used to this yet . . . Please don't get all formal on me now."

Dylan's shoulders relax, and he runs a hand through his hair. "I do apologize. I feel as if I've entirely mucked up this encounter. I just got back to court after an extended absence. The prince's bonding was one of the first things I heard about, but I hadn't heard your name. Please forgive me for being so forward."

I wrap my arms around myself, a slight prickle of unease telling me to be cautious. "I'm fairly new here at court too." I offer him a shy smile. "I hardly ever left my manor, and being here is a bit overwhelming."

Dylan nods. "I believe that. I'm surprised the prince isn't out here escorting you around the gardens himself."

I shrug. "He's very busy."

"I'm sorry to hear that. You shouldn't have to find your way alone here."

The double meaning of his words is clear, and while a part of me wants to stand up for Kian's absence, I can't deny that said absence doesn't look good for the "madly in love" story we told his father. Will people think he's already grown tired of me and moved on to someone new? That he's found some mistress to spend his time with? While I know that isn't the case, or at least I really want to believe that isn't the case, a persistent feeling of doubt crowds in. We agreed to have our separate dalliances; it isn't fair to expect him to stay alone as long as I. Perhaps this Dylan could become a new friend . . .

"Let's walk, Lord Havordshire," I say. "We can keep a respectable distance so no one talks."

Seeming surprised, he laughs and motions toward the path. "I'm happy to accompany you, princess."

"Please, call me Raelyn."

"Only if you call me Dylan."

I nod, and we walk side-by-side. "So where are you coming from, Dylan?"

"I just got back from Sillamae," he says smoothly. "My father is the trade minister, and we have been trying to find some alternate suppliers."

"Oh, really?"

"Yes." He frowns. "The vigilante has been wreaking havoc on our supply chain, and the king is demanding we find a way to make up the difference."

"You don't sound so fond of the Shadow," I posit.

"You could say that." He smiles, but it's strained. "My father has put an immense amount of pressure on me with these new deals, as he is no longer able to travel and hopes that I will take over his position in the kingdom."

"That does sound stressful. Do you also help supply the people in our towns and villages?"

He rubs his chin. "In a manner of speaking, I suppose. The king is the one who doles out any leftover rations. But for the most part, the people need to fend for themselves."

I try not to bristle. I've come to respect what the vigilante—the prince—does. Perhaps this Dylan is not the best acquaintance to make.

"Raelyn." A deep, moody voice surprises me from behind. I spin around and come face-to-face with my husband—my very sweaty and angry-looking husband.

"Kian," I say almost breathlessly, taking him in. He must have been out for a run, because there's a fine sheen of sweat on him, making him almost glisten in the sunlight.

"Your Highness." Dylan nods. "How nice to see you."

"What are you doing out here, alone, with my wife?" Kian growls.

Dylan backs up a step, his hands raised in surrender. "We were just talking. She was all alone, and I was merely keeping an eye on her for you."

"I'm sure you were," Kian retorts, his eyes shooting daggers at Dylan.

"Well, you're here now, Kian," I say, trying to break up the tension. Did something happen between the two of them? I've never seen him act this way. Moving toward him, I lay a hand on Kian's arm, hoping he will let it go and walk away with me. "It was lovely meeting you, Dylan."

"Dylan," Kian repeats, almost sarcastically.

"Lovely spending time with you, Raelyn," Dylan replies and gives me a slight bow before turning on his heel and making a quick exit.

Kian's arm is as stiff as a board, his muscles tense beneath my fingers. "On a first-name basis already?" he grits out.

I gently squeeze his arm. "Relax, Kian. We were just walking together. Nothing inappropriate happened, I promise."

Not that he should care if it did.

Kian turns his glare on me, and I step back at the fury in his gaze.

"What?" I demand. "I can't make friends here?"

"He has no interest in being your friend, I can assure you of that."

I let go of him and cross my arms. If Kian's itching for a fight, I'm happy to deliver. I'm angry with him too. "What else am I supposed to do?" I bite out in a harsh whisper. "You've been avoiding me for days now, not to mention lying to me, and you made it clear from the start that I'd need to find someone else to fulfill my needs."

Kian's nostrils flare, and he lowers his face toward mine. "What needs of yours haven't been met?" The dare in his tone sends a flutter of butterflies through my stomach. He takes a step toward me, and I find myself oh-so-slowly backing away, but he matches me step for step.

When rough, cool stone hits my back, I stop, but Kian cages me in with his arms, his hands on either side of my head.

"You're fed. Clothed. You have more fabric and thread than you could use in a lifetime, plenty of books, and—"

"What about companionship, Kian?" I interrupt. "What if I find myself lonely?"

He blinks, as if not expecting that response. "But you said you were always alone . . . Don't you prefer it that way?"

I swallow, my eyes not leaving his. "What if that's not enough for me now?"

Kian looks away, but his hands still cage me in, his proximity sending flutters through me despite my anger. He struggles for words, and the muscles in his forearms clench before he pushes away, turning his head back to face me.

"If companionship is what you need, I'll find a way to be okay with that. Just not out here. Not where people can see. And for the love of the gods, *anyone* but him."

Is he . . . jealous? Or is he just worried about his father finding out our love is a ruse?

"You idiot," I mutter.

He glares at me. "What, Raelyn? Is that not what you want?"

"No!" I spit out. Because despite everything, despite his secrets, something inside me is drawn to this man in front of me, and I don't want to lose him.

He moves in closer again, and my pulse picks up speed. "Tell me, love, what is it you want then?"

"I want you."

Kian's eyes widen in shock before they darken a shade or two and he pulls me into his arms, his mouth laying claim to mine.

I'm in shock; I almost don't respond. But then I come to my senses, and my hands fly up around his neck, pulling him closer, my mouth opening for his needy tongue as he aims to devour me.

I'm soaring—weeks of pent-up emotion and desire overwhelming my senses. Every fear, every doubt I have floats away on the wind. This moment is *everything*. I let out a moan as he kisses me into the wall and grinds himself against me. Hells, there are too many layers between us. His knee goes between my legs, and I shamelessly try to find friction. Firm hands squeeze my waist, and I'm aching, aching for him to touch me. He kisses my jaw and moves down my neck, leaving a trail of fire in his wake. I wantonly moan as he squeezes a breast in his powerful hand before sliding it back down to my waist.

"Whose hands will you allow to touch you?" he breathes.

"Yours . . . only yours."

"That's right," he whispers, causing molten heat to pool in my center.

He grips my chin, tilting it up so that our lips are only a breath apart. His other hand slides down my stomach, temptingly close to where I really want him, but then he hooks his hand around my thigh, pulling me even nearer.

A shudder goes through me, and everything is too tight. My breasts brush up against his chest with each inhale as he corners me closer to the wall. His grip around me tightens, and I can't stop the moan that comes from my lips as he thrusts his hips against me.

"Do you like that, love?" He dips his head and moves his lips to my ear. "Imagine the sounds I could wring from you if there were nothing between us."

I whimper. "Show me."

His teeth close around my ear, and tingles shoot through my entire body. "You'd like that, wouldn't you?" His voice rumbles through me, and all I can think is how I want him to take and claim me. Ruin me.

I'm just about to climb him like a tree when someone loudly clears their throat, and I gasp, my eyes darting past Kian to the king standing on the path. The look in his eyes is a cross between disgust and lust, and I'm practically doused by a flood of icy water.

Chapter Forty

RAELYN

Kian stiffens at my lack of response, and I gently push him off me. He looks over his shoulder and groans. "Father, what are you doing out here so bright and early?"

The king raises a brow. "What do you think *you're* doing out here in broad daylight where anyone could see?"

Kian laughs darkly. "She's my wife. I can do with her what I like."

I fight the urge to snap at him for that comment, reminding myself it's surely an act for the king's benefit.

The king frowns. "I'm not sure if this is just part of whatever ploy you have going on, but either way, I thought I raised you better than that. Do whatever you like to her in your rooms, Kian. Keep it out of sight."

Kian wilts at his father's harsh tone.

I attempt to discreetly fix my dress and hair as the king speaks, mortified at my actions despite the fact that I was caught kissing my husband and not some random stable boy.

"You are expected to act with the decorum befitting your role as prince. You have responsibilities to our land, and dallying like this only makes you look like a spoiled child. You have been a waste of space and resources long enough, and I'm tired of putting up with your bullshit. Yes, you may have finally settled down, but it appears your behavior has not changed. I've heard talk of you and Alex coming and going from the palace all hours of the night. Back to partying again so soon after your marriage? I am so disappointed in you."

The king's words are clearly meant to hurt, and they hit their mark with precision. Kian curls in on himself as each barbed insult digs deeper.

"Perhaps I should send you away from court for a time. Don't think you're off the hook for your lies and deception, but lucky for your wife, our people seem to approve of your choice. You two can go work on some heirs in case your brother's unborn child dies like the last three."

I try to hold back a gasp at that revelation. I always wondered why no royal heirs had been announced over the last decade. I had no idea. My heart instantly breaks for Princess Juliana and the pain she must have gone through losing children.

"Father, please don't be so crass," Kian begs.

"If you can't behave like a prince, it's not beyond me to strip away your title," the king threatens, completely ignoring his request.

As Kian tries to placate his father, my mind drifts away, still muddled from the breath-stealing kiss we shared. But suddenly, it feels wrong. It feels forced. Did he know his father was coming? Did he kiss me to try to prove a point?

Rationally, I know Kian hasn't been at parties, and I should be glad the king isn't suspicious of his actual activities, but a tiny part of me worries that it's not the entire truth. I want to trust that he won't dally where people can see him—he promised to be discreet. It doesn't change the fact that I've been pining after my own husband all these weeks, wondering why he hasn't been spending time with me.

I can't even comprehend what the king and Kian are saying at this point. I need a moment to think, to breathe.

I'm struggling not to think the worst as I push off the wall and murmur, "Please excuse me," to the king, dropping into a quick curtsy before running off, praying to the gods I didn't just commit an unforgivable sin by leaving without being dismissed.

I race into the palace, but I'm not sure where to run. Our rooms aren't safe—Kian will find me there—so I keep running and running, not knowing where I can possibly go in this large palace I have yet to fully explore.

"Raelyn!" a voice calls out, and I stop short. I'm not sure if I should be happy to see Dylan again or worried that we've bumped into each other twice in the same day. "Are you all right?"

I nod frantically, trying to calm my racing heart. "I just need a quiet place to be alone, and I still don't know the palace well," I try to explain.

Dylan nods. "Follow me. I can help."

Unsure of what else to do, I decide to go with him, even though something within me tells me it's a terrible idea.

Dylan leads me up a few flights of stairs and down some unfamiliar corridors before bringing me to a secluded sitting room that looks like it hasn't been used in quite some time. Sheets are draped over furniture, and the curtains are drawn. It's almost shocking to have found a room in the palace that's been neglected by servants; every other room I've passed during my stay here has always been immaculately dusted and ready for guests at a moment's notice.

"What is this place?" I ask, blinking when Dylan pulls the curtains open and dust motes become visible in the beams of light.

"It's a guest wing that hasn't been used in quite some time," Dylan says matter-of-factly.

"I can tell." I sniff before letting out a sneeze as the dust tickles my nose.

"Galyna bless you," Dylan offers, and I give him a weak smile.

"I'm not sure if this is quite what I had in mind."

"You look parched. Can I get you something to drink?"

"From where?" I laugh awkwardly.

"I like to come up here to get away from people, so I keep a stash," he explains as he rummages around, producing two relatively clean glass tumblers and pouring an amethyst-looking liquid into them.

I give the tumblers a suspicious glance but accept the one he hands me. "How long has this been up here?" I question.

"Oh, not long," he says reassuringly. "It's harmless. Just grape juice. I left the liquor out, as it's not very thirst-quenching."

I sniff at it cautiously and don't smell any alcohol, so I take a sip. The sweet juice has an oddly bitter aftertaste that's familiar, but I am rather thirsty, so I drink it down.

It's quiet up here. The usual bustle of servants and people moving around is absent, and all of a sudden, I'm acutely aware of the fact that I'm alone in a secluded part of the palace with a man I do not know well.

After setting the glass down, I wring my hands as I walk around the room.

Dylan pulls a sheet off a small settee and drapes it over another piece of furniture. He sits down and pats the spot next to him.

"Have a seat, Raelyn. I insist."

I glance around the room and shake my head. "I'm quite fine standing, thank you."

Dylan gives me an annoyed look. "I'm perfectly harmless. Please come and sit. I'd love to get to know you better." He holds his glass casually but doesn't drink from it, which sets off warning bells.

"To be honest, I'm not comfortable being up here alone with you," I say, hoping he'll be respectful and listen.

Dylan scoffs, "What, did our prince say something about me?"

I frown and shake my head. "Should he have?"

"Of course not," Dylan retorts.

I start to back away toward the door. Coming here was a mistake.

"Where do you think you're going, Raelyn?" Dylan tsks. "I can't let you leave just yet."

"What in Luna's name are you talking about?" I ask as I continue backing toward the door.

Dylan stands and stalks forward, grabbing my arm roughly and dragging me farther into the room. "I said you can't leave just yet."

"Stop! You're hurting me," I cry out.

Dylan blows out a breath and continues dragging me toward the settee, setting me down with force. "Now, will you stay put or do I need to restrain you?"

Fear skitters down my spine. What in Luna's name is happening? If I call out, will anyone hear?

Stepmother swoops into the room, looking completely smug and self-satisfied.

"You . . ." My jaw drops, but somehow, I'm not really shocked. If anything, I'm surprised she didn't show her face sooner. "If you wanted to call, you could have done so like a normal person," I spit out.

If she had a mustache, she'd be twirling it, ever the villainous persona oozing out of her in the most cliche of ways.

"Raelyn, darling." Her voice drips with sugary sweetness that makes me want to vomit. "I would have been rotting in a grave before you ever deemed to meet with me."

She's not wrong.

Trying to gain the upper hand, I sit a little taller, looking down my nose at her. "Well, you're here now. What do you want?"

"Thank you for arranging this, Dylan," Stepmother says dismissively. "You can go now."

Dylan appears tense as he looks between us. "Are you su—"

"Leave us!" Stepmother demands as she sits on the edge of the chair across from me.

Dylan gives us a final look before disappearing out the door. One would think I'd feel a little safer with him out of the room, but the way Stepmother is looking at me has me wondering which one of them I really ought to be afraid of.

"Who is he to you?" I ask, wondering if she'll answer any of my questions or just deflect the way my father did.

Stepmother raises a delicate brow as she pats at her immaculately coiffed hair. "Truly none of your concern, dear."

I blow out a breath and glare at her. She's in my home, and I'm no longer beholden to her.

As if reading my thoughts, her smile turns wicked. "You've made quite the mess of things, Raelyn. You really ought to have done what you were told from the start."

"You'll have to be clearer. I've done quite a few things recently."

She purses her lips before saying, "I'm trying to figure out what to do with you. You were never supposed to find out."

I tilt my head. "Find out what?"

"Oh, don't play coy with me, Raelyn. You know exactly what I'm talking about. I know all about your godly heritage. Once I discovered your father's secret, it was easy enough to draw the rest out of him. His shame makes him oh-so-easy to control."

I try not to wince. My father's love had never been a question until I discovered all the lies . . . and still, it hurts to think it was all an act to protect his reputation.

Rolling my shoulders back, I feign confidence. "Why do you care? I'm no longer your concern. You have no control over me anymore."

I spot the subtle flinch before she smoothes her features. "You see, if I were to tell the king about your—let's call it breeding—he very well could take it one of two ways."

"Yes, I'm fully aware of that." I sigh.

"My bet is he will make sure you produce a godly heir before disposing of you." Stepmother sneers.

I shudder. "Kian would never allow that."

"Wouldn't he?" she says, her voice sickly-sweet again. "We both know your marriage is nothing more than a farce. There is no love between you."

While I know she's telling the truth, it doesn't stop the hurt from aching in my chest.

"What do you want, Stepmother?" I spit out, my loathing for her growing with every moment that passes.

"What any stepmother wants." She smiles sinisterly. "A place at court near my darling stepdaughter."

"Never going to happen," I bite back.

"Well, the choice is yours, dear. You either make a place for us, or I inform the king of who you really are."

"And if I accept that risk?"

She leans forward in her seat, her eyes boring into mine. "You'll find, Raelyn, I get what I want without fail. If you refuse me, there are always other ways."

My brows furrow. What could she possibly be up to?

"Dylan!" she calls out, and he appears in the doorway. "My darling stepdaughter needs a little more incentive."

A pit of dread forms in my stomach, and a wave of weakness rushes through me. What is happening to me? My limbs are heavy, and my eyelids start to droop.

I shoot an accusatory glare at Dylan. "What did you give me?"

He throws me an almost apologetic look before he picks me up off the settee, cradling me in his arms. It feels wrong, repulsive, but I can barely lift my head.

Stepmother struts over, pulling at my hair and clothes.

"Please, stop," I manage to get out.

She looks up at Dylan. "Make it look good and do what you will with her. I'll make sure someone sees to back up my story."

"What?" I ask, trying desperately to call on my strength, but it's as if everything within me has gone dormant. The buzz of energy I felt in my veins is gone, like I lost access to that part of me.

"And if she tells the prince?" Dylan asks as he carries me out into the hall and down the corridor.

Stepmother laughs. "She won't remember a thing."

No . . . no . . . this can't be happening. I want to scream, but I can't open my mouth. I want to claw at the man carrying me, but I can barely lift a finger.

Dylan kicks open the door to a bedroom and drops me onto the bed callously. I lie frozen, my heart beating sluggishly in my chest, and I keep blinking, trying to force myself to stay awake. The sound of curtains being drawn grinds against my ears, and tears leak down my face. Hells.

What is he going to do to me in this vulnerable state? Why did I go with him against my better judgment? I'm such a fool.

Dylan returns to the bed and leans over me, rolling up his shirtsleeves, a look of malice on his face.

"What did I . . . ever do to you?" I rasp out with difficulty.

Dylan only smirks as he slowly hikes up my skirts, looking greedily at the length of my legs.

I'm going to be sick. This can't be happening.

"What did you do to me? Where to even start?" Dylan bites out.

I squeeze my eyes shut. This isn't happening.

A grunt and a thud have me forcing my eyes back open, and I look in shock as Dylan falls to the floor, but I can't see who . . .

My world turns black.

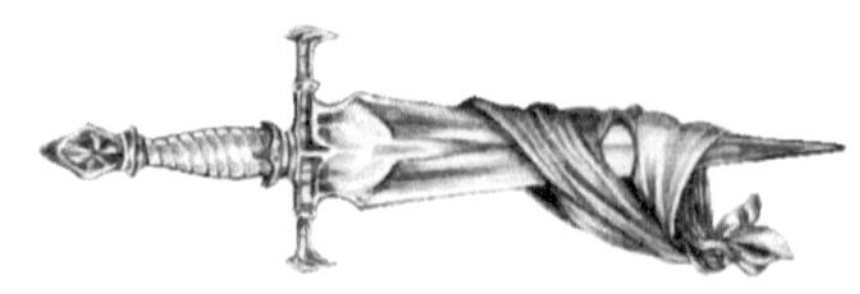

Chapter Forty-One

KIAN

Catching Raelyn with Dylan made me see red. That pompous prick. I still haven't forgiven him for trying to steal her away from me. I trusted him. I thought he was my friend, and he found a way to ruin everything. On top of our history, his father keeps trying to undermine my work as the Shadow, but so far, I've stayed two steps ahead.

Dylan should have stayed in Sillamae. I'll make him regret looking at my wife the way he did and for even trying to lay a finger on her. My only consolation is that she seems to have forgotten him as well.

Once my father finishes shredding me the way he does best, I return to my wing, looking for Raelyn. We obviously need to talk . . . That kiss. I harden at the thought of it. We absolutely need to pick up where we left off. The sooner the better.

Our rooms are completely empty, and a prickle of fear runs down my spine. Something isn't right. Where in the hells did she go?

I decide to check the library when Sera comes frantically rushing into the wing. "Your Highness!" she yelps. "You need to come quickly. It's Princess Raelyn."

Fuck.

"Take me now," I command, and she runs back out the door.

I follow her up to an unused wing of the palace, growing more anxious with each step. Why would Raelyn be up here?

"Is she okay?" I ask as we race down the hall. Sera is impressively fast.

"I'm not sure, Your Highness. I can't get her to wake up."

Fear sluices down my back, and I pick up my pace. I need to get to her. I need to save her.

Sera leads me into a dusty old bedroom, and my heart nearly stops. Raelyn is on the bed, skirts hiked about around her hips, head lolled to the side, and lips parted.

Rage overtakes me when I spy Dylan crumpled on the floor, an old paperweight next to him. If he isn't dead, he's about to be. How dare he lay a hand on my wife.

Sera is trying to wake Raelyn, but she's completely unresponsive. I kick Dylan, and he grunts. Not dead yet.

"I've got her," I say, cradling Raelyn in my arms. Her unresponsive state makes me think she's been drugged, which only fuels my anger, but what was she doing here to begin with?

"Go find a palace healer, Sera. Better yet, have them send for Margot," I command as I rush Raelyn out of the room. I'll deal with the asshole later.

Sera runs off ahead of me, and I carry Raelyn back to our room, laying her gently on our bed.

"Please wake up, love," I say, carefully tucking her hair back and trying to fix her clothes. I feel completely helpless. I should have been with her. I should never have let her leave the gardens without me, but my father . . . I curse under my breath.

Her breathing is shallow, and her skin looks extra pale. She's slowly gained color since going out in the sun, but now she looks almost sickly. What was done to her? I continue squeezing her hand and praying to the gods, to anyone who will listen, that she will wake up.

I vaguely hear the door slam open before Sera and a healer enter the room.

"Please move out of the way, Your Highness," the healer says, waving me away as she gets close to Raelyn, smelling her breath and listening to her heart.

"Someone was sent to fetch Margot," Sera says.

I breathe a sigh of relief. There's no one I trust more.

Trying to stay out of the healer's way, I pull the bell to ring for Giles.

"There's some discoloration around her mouth," the healer muses. "Do we know what she ate or drank before this?"

I helplessly shake my head, looking to Sera. "Did you notice anything out of the ordinary?"

"I'm sorry, Your Highness. I did not."

"What were you even doing up there? How did you know she needed help?" My words come out in a rush, and she looks almost frightened. "I promise, you're not in any trouble, but anything you can tell us would be helpful."

Sera looks around the room hesitantly. "Can you guarantee my family's safety?"

"Of course." I don't even hesitate to reply.

"I saw Lady Astoria wandering about the palace, and she looked up to no good."

I frown. Rae's stepmother?

"I followed her up to the abandoned wing but tried to stay out of sight, so I didn't hear much, and then Lord Havordshire came out into the hall, and I ducked behind some curtains."

I nod for her to continue.

"At some point, they came back out into the hall, and I heard the lady say that Raelyn wouldn't remember anything before Lord Havordshire took her to the bedroom."

Was someone messing with her memory . . . again?

"I had to wait for Lady Astoria to leave, and then I followed him into the room. I had to do something. Things were clearly amiss."

"Thank you for intervening," I say. "Gods only know what he would have done if he'd had more time.

Sera visibly shudders. "I d-don't think . . . he was able to . . ."

"It's okay. Take a deep breath." I try to be reassuring, even as my rage boils beneath the surface. "Do you think you can take Giles and my guards up to the room you first saw them enter? Maybe there is something there that can give us a clue as to what they poisoned her with."

Sera nods emphatically. Just then, Giles comes in, brows furrowed. "Is everything all right, Your Highness?"

"Please get at least two guards and accompany Sera upstairs. Dylan Havordshire should be unconscious, and I want him taken to the dungeon immediately. Someone needs to assist Sera and search for clues. I'll let her explain."

"Yes, sire," Giles says immediately. "And if he's not there?"

"Find him."

I turn my attention back to my wife, who lies completely still on the bed. "Can you tell me anything?" I ask the healer.

She takes her hands off Raelyn and turns to look at me. "Until we know for sure what drugged her, I am hesitant to treat her. Her heart sounds weak but is not faltering, and she is breathing well. The best thing we can do for her is find out what she drank and mix up an antidote."

I run a hand through my hair, wondering if I should tell the healer of her heritage, if that will help anything, but then her secret would be out. Luna help me, what should I do?

"Thank you," I say. "Is there anything we can do for her now?"

"Just try to keep her comfortable," the healer says. "I'll go fetch some fresh water and be back soon."

I nod and return to Rae's side, picking up her hand. Suddenly, it comes to me. My blood. Would that help her? Or should I carry her out to the sun? But if Lady Astoria had anything to do with this and there's a chance she's aware of her true heritage, it's quite possible she did something to stifle her powers. The last thing I want is to cause Raelyn more pain, so bringing her to the sun is out, but perhaps my blood could save her.

I pull a dagger from my boot and slice into my thumb, sliding it between Raelyn's lips.

"Come on. Drink, love," I say under my breath.

She swallows, and I sigh a breath of relief, hoping my blood will do something, anything to help her. Maybe it's wishful thinking, but her skin appears to flush just a little. I pull away my thumb and find that it's already sealed. Strange. I'm about to cut into it again when Margot comes in with a large pitcher of water.

"Thank the gods you're here," I say.

"Anything for you, sire. The other healer filled me in with what she could. Any changes?" she asks as she pours a small glass.

"I don't think so."

"Here, hold her up a little," Margot commands, and I gently lift Raelyn's head and shoulders off the pillow.

Margot brings the glass up to her lips and slowly tips it back. Water runs out of Raelyn's mouth, but she swallows again, and the healer nods for me to put her back down. She feels for her pulse, and a pleased look crosses her face. "Her heart rate is regular, so perhaps she can clear this on her own."

I take a deep breath and blow it out slowly. Whether my blood helped, I'm not sure, but I'm not about to risk doing anything more in front of Margot, regardless of how much I trust her.

I'm not sure how much time has passed, but Sera and Giles come back, holding a short tumbler with an amethyst liquid inside.

"We found this in one of the rooms," Giles explains.

Margot gives it a quick sniff. "Please take it to the alchemists immediately. Hopefully they can tell us what it is and how to treat it."

Giles nods and disappears again with the glass, and I look to Sera. "Was Dylan still there?"

She fidgets uneasily and nods. "The guards carried him down to the dungeon, I believe."

"Good. Can you stay with her?" I ask. "I want to see if I can get some answers out of him."

"Of course, Your Highness," she replies. "I won't let her out of my sight."

"Thank you."

No one touches my wife and gets away with it. Certainly not Dylan Havordshire, regardless of who his father is.

MAKING my way down to our dungeon, I let my anger rise up within me. There will be a reckoning, and one way or another I will get my answers. If I had my way, Rae's stepmother would be down here as well, but I'll have to go about this carefully. She's married to one of Father's oldest friends, and he would not take kindly to what I want to do to that woman.

"Is he awake?" I question the guards as I roll up my sleeves.

"I think I heard him moving around," one guard replies.

"Fantastic. Is he chained?"

"No. Would you like one of us to go in with you?"

"I'm not worried about him."

When the door swings open, I step into the room and wait for it to clang shut behind me. The key turns in the lock, and I allow myself a grin.

Dylan is sprawled against the stone wall, his cheek cupped in one hand. He blinks at me in the dim light as I step forward and crouch in front of him.

"I have some questions for you, Dylan," I sneer. "Please tell me you won't cooperate so I can make this a little more fun."

"Fuck you," Dylan groans.

"What's that?" I growl. "You tried to fuck my wife?"

Fear contorts his features at my words, and he shakes his head. "It wasn't what it looked like! Come on, man."

I scoff. "So you're telling me you did not drug and assault a princess of the realm?"

Dylan straightens, somehow managing to look down his nose at me from his position on the floor. "She wanted to be there. She came to *me*, trying to get away from *you*. She's always wanted to be with me."

Without warning, I throw a punch into his cheek, bone crunching beneath my fist.

Dylan screams pathetically. "You broke my jaw!" His voice comes out garbled.

"You know what we do to rapists here?"

"I barely touched her," he cries out.

I yank him up by the collar of his shirt and throw another punch into his gut. He spits blood, and I pull his head back by his hair. "What did you give her?"

"Hells if I know," he whines, bracing himself for another hit.

"Where did you get it?"

"She'll kill me," he rasps.

I laugh darkly. "Not if I kill you first." For Dylan, I might be willing to make an exception to my moral code.

His eyes flash with fear as he stumbles over his words. "You . . . you can't. The king would never allow it."

"Watch me," I threaten. "Where. Did. You. Get. It?"

He puts his hands over his face, cowering into the wall. Hurting him isn't even satisfying.

Pulling my dagger out, I tip his chin back with the blade. "If you won't speak, perhaps you don't need your tongue." I press the blade in and drag it up his cheek, drawing a thin line of blood. "Or perhaps I should cut out your eyes for daring to look upon my wife?"

There's a frenzied panic in his eyes, and the scent of urine fills the air. Pathetic.

"Lady Astoria," he spits out with more blood. His confirmation is enough to have her brought in for questioning, but I will still need to play my cards right.

Unable to stop myself, I throw another punch to Dylan's gut, and he doubles over, falling to the piss-soaked floor. It takes all my self-control not to use my dagger and carve him to pieces, but as much as I hate it, he is owed a fair trial.

"I'm sorry, Your Highness. It was a mistake," he cries. "She made me do it. I didn't have a choice."

I stomp on one of his hands, and he screams again. The satisfying crunch of bone should disturb me, but I'm angry. "You disgust me. You'll be lucky if you're sentenced to a quick death for attacking the princess, for daring to touch what is mine."

Dylan lies in a puddle of his own blood and piss and whimpers pathetically as he cradles his broken hand.

"You'd better hope she wakes up from this unharmed, or I'll be back, and I won't be so nice."

I knock on the cell door, and the key clicks in the lock.

"Call for a healer in a few hours," I order the guards. "He needs some time to think about what he's done."

"Yes, sire," the guard replies, locking the door back up.

I hoped it would make me feel better, but all I feel is fury and fear as I march back up to my wing. Raelyn has to be okay. I'll accept nothing less.

"Kian!" my father's angry voice rings out, stopping me in my tracks.

Hasn't he yelled enough today?

"What's this I hear about Lord Havordshire's son being in our dungeon?" he spits out as he gets into my face.

"He assaulted and poisoned my wife!" I retort.

The king frowns. "I'm sure it was a misunderstanding. Your wife was looking a little peaked earlier in the garden. Perhaps she is ill."

I can't believe the words I'm hearing.

"He was found on top of her in a bedroom." I seethe.

Father crosses his arms. "Who's to say she wasn't there by choice? Perhaps *she* should be in the dungeon for forsaking her vows."

"You've got to be joking right now."

My father's eyes burn with ire. "Watch your tongue, son."

I point toward my wing. "She is unconscious in our bed! The

alchemists are trying to figure out what she was drugged with. How dare you accuse her of misconduct?"

My father raises a brow, not even fazed by my words. "I was told she was seen with Dylan Havordshire alone in the garden and willingly followed him up the stairs toward the north wing."

"That doesn't make her guilty of anything."

He tilts his head, a menacing smile on his face. "It does not prove her innocence either."

"I'm sure she will make things clear when she awakens."

Father tuts. "You'd better hope so."

"Why not use your truthsayers to question Dylan?" I ask. "I'm sure they can confirm his guilt."

"Lord Havordshire is to be released immediately. I have no intention of interrogating him at this time. If I find you go against my wishes or lay another finger on him, there will be consequences."

I bite down on my tongue to keep from saying something I'll regret. Of course Father would be on Dylan's side. I just have to hope Raelyn can explain when she wakes up, but Lady Astoria's words that Sera overheard haunt me: *She won't remember a thing.*

I STALK down the hall toward the alchemist's chambers.

"Please tell me you have something," I say as I barge in without knocking.

Hennig looks up from his instruments and sighs. "I don't have good news for you, I'm afraid."

"Spit it out."

"The drink appears to contain an overpowered version of the suppression tonic that Raelyn brought when she first arrived at the palace."

Shit. Her stepmother must know. But why in the hells would her father have told that conniving bitch?

"Is that what knocked her out?" I ask.

Hennig shakes his head. "There's also a sedative and paralytic in it."

"Can you counteract it? Wake her up?" I ask, holding my breath.

"I can try," he says, but I can tell he's holding back.

"What aren't you telling me?"

"There are also memory-altering herbs present. I have no idea how much they will affect her—how much she will have forgotten."

Hells.

"And there's nothing you can do to counteract *that*?" My voice rises in pitch.

The alchemist shoves his spectacles up his nose. "I'm afraid not. Now, if you can wait a few minutes, I'll put together what I know I can safely give her."

"Of course."

"Is there anything else about the princess that I should be aware of?" Hennig raises a brow, and I wonder what he suspects, but I need to protect her, and at this point, I don't trust anyone in the palace.

"Not that I can think of."

The look he gives me holds so much judgment, I almost cave, but I stand my ground and choose to pace back and forth instead as he puts together his concoction.

"Okay, give her half now and half tomorrow morning."

I nod, carefully tucking the vial into my pocket.

"If she doesn't wake tomorrow, come back and I'll make more. Whatever they gave her was potent."

My heart aches painfully as I hurry back to my wing. I'm not sure what I'll do if she's forgotten me again. We were so close . . . I thought we were finally getting our chance after all these years, and now? This is my fault. She was mine to protect, and I failed her.

Chapter Forty-Two

RAELYN

Golden eyes and frightful roars haunt me—chills snake up and down my spine. I'm running. Running away from or toward something? The air is filled with smoke, and my vision is blurred. I'm drowning in the dark, and I can't tell which way is up. I've been here before. I hate it here.

With a gasp, I awake and sit bolt upright in bed. *Where in the hells am I?* Nothing looks familiar.

"Raelyn!" A familiar voice breaks through the fog.

"Sera?" I rasp. My throat is on fire, and the strange taste in my mouth makes me want to vomit.

"I'm here, Raelyn. What do you need?"

"Water," I croak.

A large glass is thrust into my hand, and I look up at Sera's relieved face. She looks the same . . . but her clothing is all wrong. I gulp down the water greedily and hand her back the empty glass.

"Thank you," I manage to get out, grateful my voice sounds more normal to my ears. "What in the hells happened? Where am I?"

"What's the last thing you remember?" Sera asks, squeezing her hands in her skirts.

"Sera, you're scaring me."

"I'm sorry, that's the last thing I meant to do."

"What's going on?"

"You were drugged . . . and attacked." She winces, as if hating to be the bearer of such bad news.

My eyes widen, and fear clamps down like a vise in my chest; it's heavy, and I'm panicking, my breathing quickening as I hyperventilate.

"Why can't I remember . . . Why can't I remember?"

Tears prick my eyes, and Sera throws her arms around me, rubbing soothing circles on my back. "You're okay. You're all right. I promise."

"But am I?" I squeak out.

She pulls back, smoothing my hair out of my face in an almost maternal way. "Raelyn, you are safe. I stopped him before he was able to truly harm you."

I heave a shuddering breath. To lose my memory is one thing, but the unknown of what happened or could have happened haunts me, and I try to continue breathing deeply to calm myself. Sera pulls me back into her arms, and I wrap mine around her neck, letting the comforting familiarity bring me back to myself . . . What *can* I last remember?

A glint of gold catches my eye, and I look at my forearm. What in the realms? Is that a—no, it can't be.

I shriek, causing a heart-stoppingly handsome man to burst in through the door. "Raelyn! You're awake!"

Awareness hits me that I'm in a light sleeping shift, so I scramble backward to hide under the covers from this man who acts like he knows me.

He freezes, a look of heartbreak in his eyes. "Sera?" he asks, turning toward her.

She shakes her head. "I'll give you two a moment."

When she turns to leave, I call out, "No, wait. Please don't leave me alone in here."

Her eyes look pained as she hesitates, her gaze flying between me and the handsome and somehow familiar stranger. "I promise you're safe with him. I'll be back in a moment."

"Okay," I say meekly, pulling the covers up to my chin, hating that she is leaving me alone.

The dark-haired man comes and sits on the edge of the bed, and my heart starts thundering in my chest. "I won't hurt you," he says, like he's trying to reassure a skittish animal.

"Who are you?" I blurt out.

He swallows, almost as if he's debating what to tell me, which makes me feel even worse. "I'm Kian—your husband."

He holds up his left forearm, and there's a matching band of gold woven around it. Shit. I'm bound and I don't even remember it. I want to curl up into a ball and cry.

"I don't understand," I whisper. "How much time have I lost?"

"You've been asleep for almost a week. We've been so worried." He runs a hand through his unkempt hair, and I note the dark circles beneath his eyes. "What is the last thing you remember?" he asks cautiously.

When I try to dig through my memories, everything feels like a dense fog. I'm completely lost, and I have no idea what to do.

"I don't know . . . Everything is so murky. I know my name . . . I recognize Sera . . . but—" I throw my hands up, dropping the blanket. "I just don't know. It's all a blur."

Kian pinches his brow and sighs. "I'm so sorry, Rae. This never should have happened."

"We're really bound?" I ask, my eyes dropping to the matching band around my right forearm and the sparkling ring on my forefinger.

Kian scoots closer on the bed. "May I?" he asks, his hand hovering near mine.

I hesitate but nod, and he grasps my hand, a zing of energy racing through me at the contact.

"You know . . . this isn't the first time you've forgotten me," he says, his thumb gently rubbing my hand.

"What?"

He laughs, almost bitterly. "I'm starting to think the gods don't want us together."

I twist my arm, and the golden bond glimmers in the light. "Wouldn't this suggest the opposite?" I ask.

"So *that* you remember?" He smirks, and his smile makes something flutter in my stomach.

I suppose if I have to be bound, at least he's not bad to look at.

I scrunch my nose and try to think. "I don't know how to explain it. Certain facts just make sense to me, but when I try to think about events or what happened to me . . . it's like wading through mud."

His thumb continues to rub circles on my hand, and I take a deep breath. "I can't even begin to imagine," he says softly, and his voice does something to me.

I look up from our hands and meet his gaze, his smoky grey eyes drawing me in. "You feel . . . familiar," I whisper. "I desperately wish I could remember."

He leans in just a bit closer, placing my hand over his chest, where I can feel his heart racing. "Rae, I—" His gaze drops to my lips, and I find myself tilting my head up to meet him. My eyes flutter shut, but the bang of the door startles me, and I pull away.

"I'm sorry," Sera looks between us and flushes bright red. "I didn't mean to interrupt."

Kian clears his throat, dropping my hand and backing off. "No, it's okay. Raelyn needs to finish the tonic the alchemist has been making for her. I nearly forgot."

My heart is pounding, and I'm so confused. I don't really know what to do with myself.

Sera holds up a vial and nods. "Yes, that's why I'm here."

"Perfect," Kian says and rises from the bed but avoids my gaze. "I'll check in on you later."

"Okay."

Sera comes back to my side and holds the vial up for me. I uncork it and sniff, the smell reminding me of the foul taste in my mouth when I woke up. "Do I have to?"

"Unfortunately, yes," Sera says.

"Bottoms up," I reply before downing the disgusting substance. "Ugh, this is almost as bad as the tonic Father makes me take every day."

Sera makes a face before handing me a glass of water to wash it down, which I accept gratefully.

"Sera . . . ?"

"Yes, Raelyn?"

"I'm really struggling to piece things together. Can you please tell me what you know? I'm hoping it might spark something . . . a memory maybe?"

Sera takes a deep breath and sits on the edge of my bed. "If you think that would help, of course I will."

I lean back against the headboard and listen to her recount what little she knows of the last few months.

My eyes bug out of my face when she mentions the palace.

"Wait a damn minute," I exclaim.

"Language!" Sera frowns.

I smile sheepishly. "Kian is the prince."

Sera looks at me as if I've lost my damn mind. "You're telling me you didn't put that together yet?"

"It's not like he said, 'Hi, I'm Prince Kian, your husband,' when he introduced himself," I sass her.

She giggles. "True . . . but you know *some* things. I thought you'd remember the name of the prince of our realm!"

I frown, trying to think through my fuzzy brain . . . It's as if the royal family is hidden in there somewhere, and while I'm aware of them, I can't put faces and names to them. "It is odd," I admit. "But gods, I can't believe I'm a princess. What in the realms?"

Sera smiles broadly. "You asking the prince to hire me brought us back together after your evil stepmother fired me."

"I still can't believe Father is remarried . . . and she really fired most of the staff?"

Sera nods, wide-eyed. "Perhaps it's good you don't remember her treating you like a servant in your own home."

"I'm not sure how to explain it, but when you tell me these things, they don't feel like they could possibly be my life. It's like you are telling stories about someone else's."

"That must be really scary," Sera says.

"Sera . . . you've been with me, what, most of my life?"

"Just about," she agrees. "I became your lady's maid when you were sixteen. Before that, I helped in the kitchens."

"Is this the first time I've lost my memory?" I'm almost afraid to ask, but I have to know. Kian said as much, but I need to hear it from someone else.

Sera's eyes drop to the floor. "I—" She winces. "I can't say."

I frown. "I don't understand."

Sera looks at me, her violet eyes pleading. "I *can't* say."

"What do you mean?"

She shakes her head. She's hiding something from me, but for some reason, she can't tell me.

"I don't understand," I reply, tears welling up in my eyes. The feelings of betrayal and the loss of who I was—who I am—are so incredibly strong. Something was stolen from me, and I don't know if I'll ever get it back.

"I'm so sorry, Raelyn. I didn't mean to upset you."

"No, it's okay. I asked . . . I just can't help but wonder how many times. How many times has someone messed with my memories? How many things have been stolen from me?"

Sera frowns. "I wish I could tell you . . . You were quite sick as a child though. I would overhear the cook talking about it."

My heart is crushed in my chest. So much of my life is a blur, and now I wonder if something worse might be wrong with me because I don't remember feeling this way before . . . but then how would I even know if my memories had been stolen?

"Hells, Sera. I don't know what to do," I cry. "How do I get my life back?"

Sera gives me a sad smile. "I'd give anything to have an answer for you, but perhaps you should try to rest. Maybe things will come back to you slowly."

I slide down into the bed, curling my legs up into a ball. Sera comes and gently strokes my hair.

"I'll be here if you need anything."

Sleep comes hard and fast, and I'm alone with only my nightmares to haunt me.

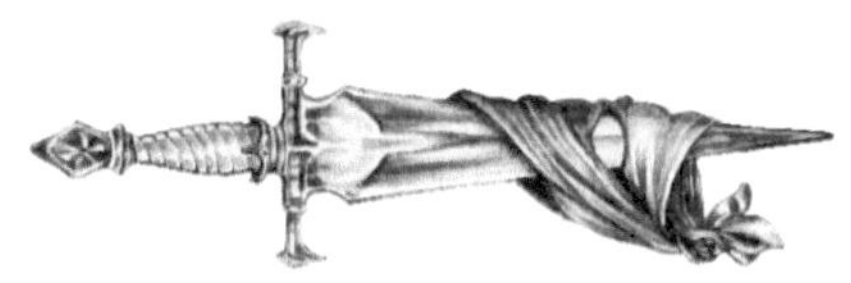

Chapter Forty-Three

KIAN

Sera slips out of my room, and I look to her anxiously.

"Does she remember anything?"

She shakes her head. "It's as if the last few months have been completely erased."

No. I'd hoped it was temporary confusion and she would remember more.

"How many times has this happened to her?" I grit out, my hands squeezing into fists at my side.

Sera won't meet my gaze, her eyes glued to the floor.

"Sera," I growl. "What aren't you telling me?"

Her violet eyes finally meet mine, and she shakes her head, a hand going to her throat. "I can't say . . ."

Her back is ramrod straight, and while I want to push her on it, something tells me I won't be getting the answers I seek. While it might not make sense, I do think she cares for Raelyn and if she could offer help, she would.

"Raelyn has forgotten me every single time I have met her," I say.

"We met as children a few times, and when I saw her again at sixteen, she didn't remember me . . . and the same again at her first season's ball."

I catch a glimpse of sadness mixed with anger and perhaps a hint of fear on Sera's face. "I'm sorry, Your Highness."

"Please send word to Lord Astoria," I tell her. "I need to meet with him."

Sera nods and starts to leave before she pauses at the door and turns back. "Your Highness?"

"Yes?"

"Be gentle with her . . . She's quite lost right now."

My heart softens, and I give her a reassuring nod. "Of course. I'm so glad she has you looking out for her."

I catch myself in a yawn and realize I've barely slept in days. My worry for Raelyn has made it impossible, on top of the latest raid. I'm running ragged. I peek into my room, and Raelyn is tossing about in bed, her hair sticking to her face while whimpers come out of her.

Rushing to her side, I debate if I should wake her. Helplessness creeps in once more. What can I do?

Before I can second-guess myself, I slide into bed and pull her into my arms. Her body goes still, and her heart rate slows. Perhaps, if only in sleep, she will allow me to be her comfort. I sigh a breath of relief and loosen my hold until a soft whimper from her lips has me instantly holding her close again.

The need to be near her, to comfort her, is strong, and I only wish I could do more. I just hope she won't be angry if she awakens with me here, but I've been apart from her for far too long, and that has only made me realize all the more how much I need her . . . how much I want her. She might have forgotten everything, but I haven't. What started as childhood infatuation has grown into something deeper, more lasting, despite all the times I thought to fight it. She's not only beautiful on the outside, but also has strength of character, kindness, and wit that continue to make me fall for her more.

Gods willing, I can get her to trust me again when she's awake. Once more, I want to kick myself for allowing her out of my sight last week . . .

We were so close to opening up to each other fully for the first time. After Raelyn left the garden, Father made it clear in no uncertain terms that he expected an heir from us as quickly as possible, but now, my wife can't even remember we're married.

SOMETHING STIRS NEAR ME, and I blink. I'm met with the startling green-and-gold of my wife's eyes.

"Good morning," I whisper, hoping she's not going to be angry.

"What are you doing here?" she whispers back.

I can't help but smirk. "This is my bed, is it not?"

Her face flushes the brightest shade of red, and she stutters, "Umm . . . yes, I suppose it is . . . I just wasn't expecting you to . . ."

I'm suddenly aware of how entangled we are; one of her smooth legs is fitted comfortably between mine, and a delicate hand rests on my chest. I clear my throat and try to scoot back a little before she discovers just how attracted to her I am.

With my movement, she pushes away from me, as if she too just realized how close we were.

"I'm sorry, Rae. It sounded like you were having a nightmare when I came to check on you last night. My presence seemed to soothe you, so I stayed . . ."

Her brow furrows, and the twitch of her lip betrays the smile she's holding back. "That was very kind of you, Your Highness."

"Please don't call me that." I clench my fist at my side to avoid touching her. I so badly want to touch her. "It's Kian . . ."

"Sorry, Kian. I just—"

"It's okay. I wish I could help you remember."

She sucks in a breath, her eyes widening as she gestures between us. "Were we . . . uh . . ." She flushes and tries to start over. "Sera said our marriage was quite sudden, but, um . . ."

Should I put her out of her misery or let her continue to fish for answers? I clear my throat. *Do I tell her we kissed right before this all happened? Do I tell her how much I desire her?* Fighting against all my instincts, I say, "We were still getting to know one another."

Her brow furrows even deeper, if possible. "But Sera said we were madly in love."

I blow out a breath and chuckle. "That's what we told my father, and by extension, the rest of court. We decided to marry out of convenience for both of us. My father demanded I marry by the end of the season, and I was trying to help you get away from your stepmother."

"Oh," she says, then gestures between us again. "So we never?"

"Unfortunately, no, love. That wasn't part of the agreement." I roll onto my back and stare up at the ceiling, unable to continue looking at her. "Regardless of what rumors might float around court, I would never take a woman to bed who did not wish it."

The subtle scoff has me tilting my head toward her, and I note that she's rolled onto her back as well. I study her profile as she says, "You'll only get into bed with one without permission."

Some of her fire is coming back, and that makes my heart happy. The heavy sadness has been hard to bear, especially when there's nothing I can do to fix it.

My gaze is drawn to her pert nipples, visible through the thin fabric of her sleep shift, tempting me to draw them into my mouth. Does she realize the blanket slid down? I squeeze my eyes shut and retort, "Well, this isn't the first time we've shared a bed."

"What?" she squeaks and turns her head to face me.

"We were trying to make our love convincing."

"Oh." She flushes a pretty shade of red yet again.

Fuck. It's pure torture lying next to her, wanting her . . . knowing she's forgotten everything, again. Perhaps it's for the best. This way, she no longer remembers my role as the Shadow. My mind flashes back to the betrayal on her face when she discovered my secret. Nearly every person in her life has either lied to or betrayed her. I can't do it again. I will come clean to her, but now . . . now, I need to get out of this bed before I do something I regret.

I take a deep breath and sit up, planting my feet on the floor. "There is something we need to discuss, I'm afraid."

The sheets rustle and the bed moves as Raelyn sits up. "That sounds serious."

"If you'd like to join me for breakfast, we can discuss it then."

AFTER WE'VE both bathed and dressed, Raelyn finally joins me in our common area. Giles has procured an incredible spread of food, and my mouth waters at the smell.

"Please, have a seat." I motion toward her usual spot. I hate how new things feel again.

"Thank you," she says, reaching for her favorite pastry.

I fill my plate with eggs and potatoes, sprinkling a healthy dose of cheese on top that melts beautifully.

"Well, I guess I'll just get to it," I say between bites.

She pauses, the croissant halfway to her mouth before she sets it back down. "You're making me nervous, Kian."

"I'm sorry, love. I wish I had better news . . . but this memory thing has put us in quite a bit of a predicament."

"How so?" she frowns.

"Well, my father expects you to testify as to what happened with Lord Havordshire, the man who . . ."

She pales. "But how? I don't remember."

I grimace as I set down my fork. "Sera saw him attacking you, but she didn't see much, and there's no proof that you weren't there willingly with him."

She picks at the croissant on her plate, her face a shade of green I've never seen before.

"Hells, I'm sorry, Rae. I wish I didn't have to tell you."

"So, what?" She blinks back the beginning of tears. "He gets away with what he did, with poisoning me, stealing my memories, and I get accused of infidelity and possibly hanged?"

"Never!" I spit out vehemently. "I won't allow it."

Her body shudders, and I so badly want to pull her into my arms and give her comfort. But she hasn't asked for it, and I already crossed the line sharing her bed.

"What do I do?" she asks, the brokenness in her voice killing me.

"I'll do my best to talk the king down, but in the meantime, I've sent for your father. Perhaps if he can tell us what exactly you were dosed with, we can find a cure for your memories."

"I still can't believe he would have had anything to do with the attack," she says. "Do you think there's a chance he knows what could help?"

A pit fills my stomach. Devastating her all over again with news of his betrayal is the last thing I want to do. "I don't know, love. The alchemist was able to recognize the herbs but was unable to figure out the exact recipe. You have my word, Rae, even if there's no hope left, I will continue fighting for you."

She looks down at her plate, a soft thank you coming from her lips before she makes a valiant effort to eat. It's clear to me, however, that she's hardly eaten a thing and merely rearranged the food on her plate a dozen times over.

"He will pay," I vow.

"What?" She looks up.

"I promise, Lord Havordshire will pay for what he did to you."

She gives me a solemn nod, and we spend the rest of the meal in deafening silence.

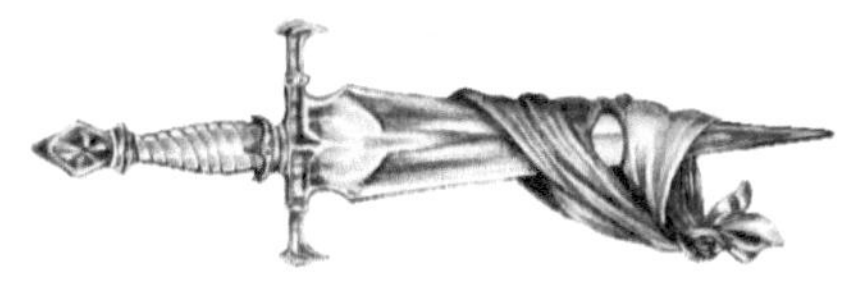

Chapter Forty-Four

KIAN

When the king's summons comes, dread sluices through my body. I loathe the man more each and every passing day. From his selfish rule of our kingdom to his accusations toward my wife. How like him to take the side of his lord instead of the woman who clearly couldn't defend herself.

Father will have to wait though.

Giles ushers a harried and distraught-looking Lord Astoria into my private study. Feigning an air of nonchalance, I sit behind my desk with my feet propped up in an irreverent manner.

"Nice of you to show up," I spit out without preamble.

Lord Astoria gives the barest of bows before dropping into the seat across from me, a sneer on his face. "Don't forget, princeling, I knew you before you could even walk. A little respect goes a long way."

I shake my head. Forget niceties. I mean to get straight to business. "Why have you been poisoning your eldest and stealing her memories?" I demand.

The affronted look gives me pause. He's a good liar.

"That is preposterous," he retorts. "I have poisoned no daughter of mine."

"That might actually be true," I muse, "considering we both know Raelyn isn't your daughter."

His face blanches, and he reaches for the liquor I poured before his arrival. His hand shakes as he brings the glass to his mouth. "I'm not sure what she's told you, but that simply isn't true. Raelyn *is* my daughter. I raised her."

I scoff. "Some father you pretend to be, stealing her memories and withholding the truth. I know you spoke with her a few days ago and spewed only more half-truths to her."

I hold my breath, hoping he'll slip up. I don't know for sure that he's altered her memories, but it's my best guess with how many times she's forgotten me over the years. Lady Astoria must have found out somehow and decided to use it for her own gain.

Lord Astoria bristles. "You don't know what you're messing with, princeling. This is far beyond your understanding."

"Try me," I grit out. "I know about her godsblood."

Lord Astoria throws his hands up in frustration. "You have been a bane to me for years now."

I frown. "I don't quite understand what you mean."

"Every time you and Raelyn meet, her godsblood activates."

"What in the ever-loving hells are you talking about?"

This, I had not expected.

"I don't understand it myself," he mutters. "But without fail, despite the tonic I gave her, you'd show up, and she'd start exhibiting symptoms—they'd break through. The first time was when you visited when she was only seven, but I didn't make the connection until it kept happening with each meeting."

"Why is that so terrible? It's who she is!" I argue. "What harm is there in admitting her blood is a little more golden than the rest of ours?"

Lord Astoria shakes with rage, and I sit back in my seat at the sudden fury.

"She never figured it out, did she?"

"Never figured out what?"

"She is the *daughter* of a god, princeling," Lord Astoria sneers. "Her blood is more gold than anyone else's in our kingdom."

My palms start to sweat, and I wipe them on my pants. Shit.

Lord Astoria laughs bitterly. "I see you understand. By our kingdom's law, she is the rightful ruler. If your father were to find out, he would dispose of her without a second thought."

I palm my face, hating that he's right.

"I did what I had to do to keep her safe," he spits venomously. "And without fail, every few years, you'd come back into her life and ruin everything."

"No one can know," I reply, my voice low and menacing.

"You don't think I'm aware of that?"

"Please explain, then, why you allowed your bitch of a wife to come into my home and risk everything out of, what? Some petty ploy to bribe her way into a more powerful position at court?" I lean forward and yell in his face, "You were okay with her having your daughter assaulted?"

"Do you actually think I wanted that?" he yells back, wiping spit out of his eyes. "That never should have happened!"

"You're a foolish man, Lord Astoria."

He scoffs.

"If I find out you had anything to do with the attack on my wife, I will hang you myself," I growl menacingly, then hold my marriage bond up to his face. "I will not leave her. This is binding."

Lord Astoria sighs, slouching back into his seat. "It does pose quite a problem."

"Can you undo it? The memory poison?"

His eyes glitter with something I can't quite identify. "I cannot undo anything."

"But is there a way for her to get her memories back?" I demand.

Lord Astoria shrugs. "Not that I know of."

I slump in defeat. He's given me nothing of real value, and I'm even more confused about how to move forward. "Something I haven't been able to figure out is why you didn't erase her memories after your wedding ball. I saw her then, and she remembered me when I returned."

Lord Astoria grimaces. "Perhaps that was a mistake on my part, but I had to leave, and the last thing I wanted was for her to wake up and not remember I'd been bound to a new woman. I told Olivia to keep you away from her, but clearly, that didn't work out. The tonic would have kept her symptoms at bay if you'd done as you were told."

"Do you even care about what you've stolen from her all these years?" I ask, remembering the pain in Raelyn's eyes at having lost so much time.

"I don't expect you to understand the choices I've made." He picks a piece of lint off his coat. "Now, if I were you, Your Highness," he says, voice dripping with sarcasm, "I'd find a way to get you and your lovely wife exiled far from here so that your father never finds out the truth. I don't think it's possible to suppress her godhood much longer, but you should still put her back on the tonic to prolong it. I fear the truth will come out if you stay here."

My heart sinks. As much as I'd love to steal Raelyn away and never return, I can't abandon my people. Things are only getting worse, and if I leave without finding a solution to our missing god problem, they are doomed. Despite his fears, there is no way I am going to keep this from her or poison her without her knowledge.

"I'd take this unfortunate event as a blessing in disguise," Lord Astoria continues. "Have you told her about her heritage yet?"

I frown. "With all the shit she's had to deal with? I haven't gotten to that reveal yet."

"It's probably for the best." Lord Astoria's lips form a thin line. "But you should still get her out of here."

"How do *you* know what she is?" I can't help but ask. "How did you, of all people, end up with custody of the daughter of a god?"

Before he answers, my research about the lost god comes back to me. I'm an idiot. I should have seen this sooner.

An almost wistful look crosses his face. "Not that it's any of your business . . . but her mother. I loved her."

"Your late wife?" I ask, confused. The name didn't match the journal, but I wasn't about to admit to him that I'd stolen it.

"No, but she was supposed to be." His eyes shutter. "We're better off with the gods gone. Mark my words."

"You can't possibly be serious," I retort. "Our realm is dying!"

Lord Astoria raises a brow. "Is it now? I hadn't noticed."

"Your sarcasm is delightful," I quip.

Lord Astoria pushes away from the desk and stands. "I've had about enough of your attitude, princeling. You can consider yourself damned lucky I want to protect my daughter, or I'd be headed straight for your father."

A wry laugh leaves my mouth. "I'm not afraid of you, Cary."

He turns on his heel, and when he gets to the door, he pauses, looking over his shoulder. "Perhaps you should be." Then he's gone.

Well, that didn't go as planned. I wearily massage my temples, a headache pulsing behind my eyes. I guess I should make my way to my father before he sends someone after me.

To my surprise, Colin is seated across from Father when I enter. The room is already filled with the earthy scent of cigars.

"Are congratulations in order?" I ask as I plop down in the seat next to Colin.

The broadest grin stretches his face. "Juliana delivered a perfect baby girl last night."

I genuinely smile, slapping Colin's shoulder. "That's wonderful news, brother!"

Father grunts. "Too bad it's not a boy."

I take a deep breath to keep from lashing out. What an ass. As if a woman couldn't rule. My mind flashes to Raelyn . . . perhaps the only true heir among us. Even if she doesn't want to rule, I know she could.

Colin's smile is so big, he ignores Father's misogyny and says, "The new princess would love to meet her uncle."

"Raelyn and I would love to come visit," I reply.

Colin flinches. "Um, you may want to leave your wife home. Helene is quite put out that you went off and got married out of nowhere." His eyes drop accusingly to my binding mark.

"I'm bound, Colin. You'll have to get over it eventually. Sorry it wasn't to your first choice."

He scoffs. "That's not it. I'm rather hurt that you left me out of such an important day of your life."

I reach over and squeeze his shoulder. "Sorry, brother, but when it's love, you just can't help yourself."

Father clears his throat, and I turn my attention back to him. "Speaking of your *wife*, has she lost her memory as the rumor has it?"

I tense up. "It looks that way, Father."

"So she cannot back up either story."

"I'm afraid not."

"You owe Lord Havordshire an apology for how you treated him. The healers have had quite the challenge mending him, and he likely will never regain full use of his left hand."

I blink, and my voice drops low. "He attacked my wife."

"Did you see him attack her? Does she claim he attacked her?" My father smiles cruelly.

"You know the answer to that."

"Then *you* know that you owe Lord Havordshire an apology. I am well within my rights to imprison your wife for her part in this."

My brother places a hand on my thigh and squeezes in warning, as if he knows I want to launch myself across the desk and attack our father. I glare at the king, trying to measure my breaths.

"The absolute last thing this court needs is a scandal," Colin chimes in diplomatically. "With news of my daughter's birth, this whole fiasco should blow over before the day is out."

Father sits back in his chair, his fingers tapping idly on his desk. "A royal execution would definitely put a damper on things," he admits.

I try not to show my relief. "I'll apologize to Lord Havordshire," I grit out.

"See that you do."

"Is there anything else you require of me, Father?"

"That's it for now. But don't forget our discussion from before. If your wife doesn't make herself useful soon, I might punish her after all."

I nod stiffly, pat my brother on the back once more, and flee Father's study.

Everything is going to shit. Raelyn has forgotten me once again and doesn't realize what she is. There are so many answers to search for, but I'm not sure where to start.

I head for the infirmary to make my official apology to Dylan, hating every step in his direction. I'll apologize, but I will also make it exceedingly clear that if he steps one foot near my wife again, he will find himself without his favorite body part. Hells, perhaps the Shadow might pay him a visit.

Chapter Forty-Five

RAELYN

Kian shows up in our wing looking rather worse for wear. I can't fight the draw to him, which I suppose makes sense, considering I did know him before he was taken from me . . . but is it wrong that I enjoyed waking with his arms around me? Is it wrong that I want him to hold and kiss me?

I blow out a breath, continuing to flip through the pages of a book I found in our room. He must be really interested in the gods. Every single book I pick up is filled with stories and fables . . . genealogies of demi-gods.

"How are you feeling?" Kian asks, dropping onto the settee next to me.

"Confused? But much the same as before." I fiddle with the pages of the book. "Are you really into the gods or something?"

Kian chuckles. "Yes, but those are books *you've* been reading, actually."

My brows rise. "That doesn't sound like me at all."

"Well, there are some things I've been meaning to tell you . . ."

I gulp. What new revelation is headed for me now? I pull my robe a little tighter, as if it could protect me. "Please just spit it out, Kian. I'm trying not to panic."

"You were researching the gods because we discovered you have godsblood."

"You've got to be joking."

Kian reaches over, tugging on a tendril of hair that's come out of my bun. "I'm not . . . and unfortunately, it is something we need to keep to ourselves."

I frown, trying to put the pieces together. "Is it a crime to have godsblood? Doesn't your family have it?"

Kian moves his hand to cradle my cheek, and I want to melt into him. He feels so good . . . so right, and it takes all of my self-control not to climb into his lap.

"Perhaps if it were severely diluted like ours, it wouldn't be as big a deal . . ."

"Mine is not?"

"I spoke with your father today . . . and he confessed that he's been drugging you to keep you from discovering your heritage."

"Drugging me? What? How?" I sputter.

"Your daily tonic."

"You're kidding. I've been looking all over our suite for the damned tonic, and Sera got all dodgy when I asked her about it." I shake my head, trying to wrap my mind around it, and the betrayal makes me want to vomit.

"I'm sorry, love. I wish I were kidding."

"So what does this mean? If he's not my father, who is?"

"Apparently, your actual father is a god . . . Kyros, the sun god, based on what Cary told me."

"What in the world?" I gasp. I'm crushed with the hurt that something so vital has been kept from me for almost my entire life. That the man I knew as my father lied to me, poisoned me. I shake my head again. "How is that even possible? Haven't the gods been gone?"

Kian shrugs, his hand moving from my cheek and down my

throat before gently resting on my collarbone. "As far as I know, Cary loved your mother, your real mother, and he raised you to protect you."

"So my mother wasn't my mother either?" I ask, unable to hold back the shiver from Kian's gentle touch. I'm tired of hurting. I'm tired of the emotional devastation. Is it selfish of me to enjoy this simple touch and escape from the life-altering revelations?

"Not according to Cary," he says softly as his thumb rubs along my collarbone.

I can't think, I almost can't breathe, but I find myself leaning in.

"Do you want me to stop?" His voice comes out in a low rumble, sending even more chills down my arms and neck.

"I don't think I can concentrate with you touching me," I whisper. *But please don't stop.* I wish I could say the words aloud, but something holds me back.

Kian lets go, and the sudden rush of cold air replacing the heat makes me want to cry.

"I'm sorry, Rae. I wasn't trying to make you uncomfortable."

"It's okay," I whisper, trying to shake myself out of the spell he captured me in. "So . . . my father is a god," I repeat.

"Yes."

"And that makes me . . ."

"A demi-god."

"Fuck."

Kian's lips curl into a smile. "Such a foul word from such a pretty mouth."

My hand darts to touch my lips, embarrassment creeping in, when I have a revelation. "So I'm not allergic to the sun?"

"No, love."

I wrinkle my nose at my next question. "Does that mean I need to drink blood?"

Kian chuckles. "I don't think it's a requirement, but it can strengthen you. You seem to like it."

"Beg your pardon?" He can't be serious. I've consumed blood?

He scoots a little closer on the settee, offering his throat to me. "You've tasted me before. Would you like to again?"

I swallow, my mouth watering at the thought, which simultaneously thrills and disgusts me. "I . . . I don't know . . ."

"Maybe it would help?" Kian says, his eyes sparkling with mischief. Or is that lust?

I tilt my head. "Do you really think so?"

He shrugs and goes to undo the top buttons of his shirt.

I'm hot and cold all over, my pulse racing in anticipation.

"What can it hurt, Rae? You wouldn't have even thought to try it before . . ."

I take a breath and nod. "Perhaps you're right. What can it hurt?" I touch my jaw. "I don't think my teeth are sharp enough."

Kian laughs. "Don't you worry. I've got that covered." He draws a dagger from his boot and holds it up to his throat.

A bolt of fear rushes through me at seeing him in such a vulnerable position, and I yelp, dragging the blade away. "What are you doing?"

Kian frowns. "Just a shallow cut, love. How else will I bleed for you?"

"I don't know . . . Maybe this is a terrible idea."

Kian tsks. "I am full of terrible ideas, but I'm certain this isn't one. Now let go."

I reluctantly release his hand, and he makes a small cut on his throat with his blade.

"Have at it, little goddess." He smiles.

I'm completely and utterly out of my depth, but the scent from the slow trickle of blood has my mouth watering. "I . . . I don't know how to start," I admit shyly.

"Come here." He beckons me closer, then pulls me to straddle his lap.

I gasp at the sudden contact, my hands landing on his shoulders. My gaze darts to the small stream of blood, and I lunge forward, closing my mouth along the spot. His blood bursts to life in my mouth, and I can't contain the moan that comes out of me. It's as if I'm tasting the finest wine, and this tiny taste is not enough to quench my thirst. I latch on deeper, sucking harder, and Kian lets out a low rumble from his chest that vibrates through me.

Gods. I need more of him. I sink down onto him, immediately greeted by his hard length, which only causes me to moan again as it presses against my core. Kian's hands grip my waist, pulling me impossibly closer, and I grind myself onto him as I continue to suck on his neck.

"Rae, love . . . You have no idea what you do to me."

A whimper escapes my lips as my insides coil tighter and tighter. I rock against him, and he encourages it, one of his hands reaching around and gently squeezing my rear. My thin robe isn't much of a barrier, but there is still too much between us.

A wave of pleasure builds and builds, and finally, I let go, crying out as my release hits, my entire body a quivering mess of pleasure. With a final swipe of my tongue, I pull away from Kian's throat and lean into him, resting my head on his chest while his heartbeat thunders beneath me. Before I can even say a word or have a moment to feel mortified about essentially dry humping my husband, images start to flash before my eyes.

I stiffen, and while I can faintly hear Kian calling my name, I'm whisked away into memories. Memories of a dark-haired boy with a joyous smile . . . memories of splashing in a fountain. The feeling of warmth, sunshine on my skin . . . A royal wedding and meeting those smoky grey eyes across the room. Familiar yet foreign. An ache grows in my chest as I realize what these are . . . stolen memories . . . memories of falling in love and forgetting. Memories of discovery being ripped away. Then there's that kiss . . . all-consuming, all-encompassing . . . a kiss that rearranged my life, re-centered me in a way I can't explain.

A sudden trepidation fills me, fear at what memory is coming. I'm helpless, staring up at Dylan, a monster who wants to take from me, steal from me, and I scream. I keep screaming, my body thrashing.

Distantly, I hear my name being called again, and I sob. I'm stuck in a memory I can't get out of. *Help*! I want to scream, but it's as if my vocal cords are frozen in an unending shriek.

"Rae! Come back to me." Kian's voice cuts through the haze, and I reach for it, I reach for him.

I blink.

Terrified eyes bore into mine.

I blink.

Hands cup my face.

I blink again.

He's closer, pulling *me* closer, and then his mouth is on mine, silencing the scream, flooding me with peace and comfort.

Belonging.

Safety.

I gasp, and he kisses me deeper, claiming me, owning me, restoring me.

When he finally pulls away, I whisper, "Kian."

"You scared the shit out of me," he says, his arms shuddering around me.

Taking in my surroundings, I realize we are on the soft rug in front of the fireplace and Kian is cradling me in his lap.

"I . . . I remember," I whisper. "I remember everything. The fountain, dancing with you and the fireflies . . . *everything*."

Kian stills. "Everything?"

"Yes, Ki."

He swallows, and tears glisten in his eyes. "Catching me in your father's study? Our bonding?"

I nod, a smile splitting my face as my own eyes well up. "*Everything*."

He squeezes his eyes shut, taking a deep breath before looking back at me, tears spilling over. "That's amazing, Rae." He smoothes a tendril of my hair back, his touch light, almost reverent. "Better than I could have ever hoped for."

I smile up at him. He looks different somehow . . . Perhaps it's the knowing . . . remembering the small moments we shared, the ones that were stolen from me.

"Why were you screaming?" He frowns, looking almost frightened to ask.

I shudder. "My last memory wasn't exactly a pleasant one . . . Dylan—"

Kian's gaze turns ruthless, and his body tenses. "I will see him hanged for this after I beat the ever-loving shit out of him again."

"Kian, I'm okay," I try to reassure him, reaching up and turning his face back to mine. "Stay with me. Vengeance later."

He shudders, the tension melting out of him as he rests his head atop mine. "I'm sorry. I didn't mean to scare you, but that scream . . ."

"It's okay . . . I'm okay. He barely touched me."

"Doesn't mean I won't remove his hands from his body."

I shake my head. "I'm here, Kian. I'm safe."

He takes a deep breath and finally relaxes just a little more before pulling back to look at me.

"Why did you go with him?" he asks. "That's the part I don't understand."

The hurt in his eyes takes me back to that moment, and as much as I'd rather forget it, I realize keeping it inside will only harm us . . . if there's actually any chance at there being an *us* moving forward.

"When your father showed up in the garden . . . the way you reacted to him scared me. I started to worry that perhaps our kiss had been purely for show because you knew he was coming."

Something fractures in Kian's gaze, and I rein in the rest of my words.

"Rae . . . it breaks my heart that my actions would have ever caused you to feel that way. I am so sorry I wasn't clear about my feelings for you. None of that was for show, I promise you."

A weight falls off my chest, and I breathe deeply. "I'm so sorry I didn't wait for you. I shouldn't have run off the way I did."

"Love, please promise me that you won't blame yourself for Dylan's and your stepmother's actions, okay?" Kian brushes another stray hair behind my ear. "And promise me you'll talk to me if you're ever unsure about something?"

"Okay," I agree. "Only if you do the same. No more secrets."

"No more secrets," he promises.

I look up at the ceiling when a realization hits me. "This whole time . . . you knew . . . You remembered it all, our history. Why didn't you say something?"

He averts his eyes, staring at what must be a very important speck of dust on the floor. "I don't know . . . I guess I just thought I was extremely forgettable."

I scoff. "Surely you don't mean that."

He shrugs, meeting my gaze again. "I tried once to bring it up, but you looked painfully confused, and I didn't want to hurt you. I didn't understand why."

"And you somehow thought it was a brilliant idea to marry me and live as, what? Friends? Acquaintances?" My brow furrows in confusion. "Why would you do that?"

"I tried to convince myself that it would be enough . . . just having you around. And maybe, if the gods were feeling generous, you wouldn't forget me. Maybe, if I were lucky enough, over time, I could win your heart."

My heart breaks at the words . . . but there's a glimmer of amusement too. "You thought that if I saw you every day, I couldn't possibly forget you again?"

He cracks a smile. "Well, it seemed to be working."

"You're ridiculous."

"Can you blame me? I couldn't let you go. Every time I met you again, I fell a little harder."

My entire body heats under the intensity of his gaze. Memories of moments spent with him flicker in and out of my mind. I think I could easily love this man.

Kian helps me stand, and I lean into him; my legs are wobbly after the maelstrom of memories.

"I'm afraid I need to leave, Rae," Kian says, his hand cupping my cheek. "I've got vigilante shit to do."

I can't deny the disappointment, especially when I remember what we did on the settee *before* the memories came back.

Kian's eyes darken, like he's somehow reading my mind. "Oh, love, if you look at me like that, I don't know if I'll be able to go."

My cheeks heat, but I wrap my arms around him and squeeze. "Be safe," I whisper. "Come back to me."

"Always."

Chapter Forty-Six

RAELYN

"What do you want to do about Dylan?" Kian asks me as we head to the library. "With your memory back, we can tell your side of the story."

I grimace. "As much as I wouldn't mind seeing him punished . . . I also don't want to be dragged through a trial."

Kian's jaw clenches, and I reach for his hand, noting fresh bruises. Perhaps the vigilante has already meted out justice of his own.

"I hope that's not disappointing to you. But we should keep an eye on him, and if he tries to hurt anyone else, all bets are off," I say.

"Fine," Kian says, blowing out a breath. "I just promised you he'd pay, and I don't think he's suffered enough."

"Mm-hmm," I reply, glancing back at his bruised hand.

I drag him through the library until we reach the section I'm looking for. Maps of all shapes and sizes line the shelves.

"You don't think this is a wild goose chase?" Kian says, scratching the back of his head. "You really think you would recognize something from one of these?" He gestures at the endless books and scrolls full of maps.

"I have this feeling," I admit. I've had more dreams of the island, and I just know in my soul I'd recognize it if I saw it.

Kian sighs. "Well, considering that all my other leads have completely run dry, I guess this is the best chance at finding the lost god . . . finding your father."

I crinkle my nose. "It's still weird thinking of him that way."

"I can't even imagine," Kian says as he rummages through the maps. "What am I looking for exactly?"

"Maps of the southern isles," I say as I pour through another stack. "The types of trees and the constellations that were visible narrowed it down that much at least."

"I'm still not sure how you expect us to find one island out of the many," Kian grumbles.

I laugh. "Oh, you of little faith."

After picking out a handful of books and scrolls, I bring them over to one of the study areas. Kian joins me, and we spend all afternoon looking at maps and trying to find references to other books that might have images of what I'm searching for. It's tedious work, and Kian looks like he is about to claw his eyes out, but the research gives me life. I'm just grateful he's willing to help, even though I'm sure he'd rather be sparring with Alex or literally doing anything else.

"Aha!" I shout excitedly.

Kian looks up, bleary-eyed, from where he was reading about different vegetation found on the isles. "Please tell me you found something good," he says.

"I found something good." Relief and excitement course through me, knowing we're one step closer.

"Brilliant." He grins. "I'd say that's cause to celebrate."

"Definitely," I agree. "But don't you want to know what it is first?"

There's a ravenous look in his eyes as he picks me up and sets me on the edge of the table. "I'm rather hungry, love. I think I need a snack."

I clench my thighs together, a wicked thrill going through me at the thought. The tension between us is thicker than ever, but we have yet to take that final step. I sigh and shake my head. "As much as I'd love to be your snack . . ."

Kian pouts.

"Anyone could walk by at any moment, and I need to show you what I've found!"

"Fine. But you owe me."

I wink at him, my stomach flipping in anticipation. "I'll make sure to pay up."

I scoot off the table and grab the book. "This might sound completely crazy, but I recognize this place," I say, pointing at the picture. "It looks exactly the same as in my dream."

"Well, that's definitely a start," Kian says, adjusting his pants.

"But here's the other reason I think I'm on to something." I pull out a larger map of the continent and isles. "I know this map."

"Well you *have* been staring at it all day," Kian jokes.

"Seriously, though," I insist. "My father—Cary—has a map just like this in his study, and I remember him having it open to this isle. I think there were markings on it too. There are vague memories of me asking him about it, but he'd always deflect or distract me with something else."

Kian's posture perks up, and he studies the map more seriously. "And you think that because he knew your real father, he might know where he is?"

"Exactly," I say.

"Why don't we just ask him?" Kian asks.

"I tried, but he was so close-lipped, constantly saying he was just trying to protect me. I don't think he would willingly give up the location." I bite my lip. "I can't explain it really, but I just know in my gut that this is where we should look."

"We?" Kian raises a brow.

"What, you think I wouldn't be going?" I scoff. "I'm the one having the dreams."

"It could be dangerous though." Kian frowns. "I wouldn't forgive myself if something happened to you."

"I'm a demi-god, remember?" I smile. "I don't think I'm that easy to kill."

"Easy enough to poison," he grumbles.

Oof. "Yeah, I should have known better than to accept strange drinks from people I hardly know."

Kian bristles. "I still have half a mind to throw him back into the dungeon."

"And risk enraging your father?" I remind him.

Kian closes the book and stands. "I'll talk to Alex and see about arranging a small party to travel south. We can tell Father we're going away to make an heir or something."

I giggle. "Or something. But what will he say about Alex joining us?"

"I don't need to share all the details with him."

WITHIN A FEW DAYS, we've gotten everything together for our journey. Alex is joining us as planned, and I asked if Sera could come. I finally came clean to her about the demi-god thing, and while she acted surprised, I wasn't completely convinced it was a shock to her. There is a mystery to Sera I want to unravel, but for now, I'm glad she'll be with me. My gut tells me I can trust her.

"We're taking horses?" Sera grimaces.

"What else would we take?" Alex laughs.

"A carriage?" Sera glares at him. She has *What are you, an imbecile?* written all over her face.

Alex raises his hands in mock surrender. "Apologies, my lady. I didn't realize a horse was beneath you."

"I'm no lady," Sera retorts.

"You sure as hells act like one," Alex throws back.

I sidle up next to Kian, who is fixing his horse's bridle. "I'm starting to think we should leave them here."

Kian chokes on a laugh. "It's good for Alex. She'll keep him on his toes."

I roll my eyes. "And annoy the hells out of us."

"We have built-in entertainment for the road."

I shake my head. "You're impossible."

"I do my best."

Kian's gaze drops to my lips, and my skin flushes with heat. Other than the brief moment in the library, he hasn't tried kissing me since my memories returned, and tiny bothersome doubts have me wondering if he no longer wants to . . . but then he looks at me like this . . . as if he could devour me. I take a step closer to him, but before I can say anything, Phantom lets out a loud snort, and the moment is gone.

Kian helps me up, his hand catching on the dagger strapped to my thigh.

"What's this, love?" His hand lingers, sending a fresh bolt of heat through me.

My cheeks flush as I draw the blade from its sheath and meet his molten gaze, remembering the night I held it to his throat with not a clue of who he was and how he managed to elicit reactions out of me even then. "I believe this belongs to you. You can have it back if you like."

"Keep it," Kian replies, placing his hand on mine and sliding it back in. "I love seeing my blade on you." His voice is low and decadent, making me wish we were alone in our rooms. Hells. It's going to be an interesting journey.

Kian mounts up behind me, and the mood is once again broken, but this time, it's because of Alex and Sera.

"Well, are you coming?" Alex asks as he reaches a hand down to her.

Sera stands with her hands on her hips. "I did not agree to this."

"Would you like your own horse then?" Alex quips.

"Have you gone mad? I don't know how to ride."

"So then you ride with me," he says matter-of-factly.

Sera lets out a frustrated sound and allows Alex to pull her up into the saddle.

"Last chance to leave them behind," I mutter.

Kian only laughs and leads us out of the gate. "We'll be happy for their company before the week is out, I assure you."

"If you say so."

TRAVEL IS NOT as fun as I'd hoped. There is nothing glamorous about setting up tents and sleeping on the hard ground. We have one horse carrying our limited supplies, but comfort is at a bare minimum.

"Maybe we *should* have taken a carriage," I moan as I stretch my sore muscles. Alex and Kian are setting up camp for the night in a small clearing off the main road.

Sera snorts. "I could have told you that."

"You hanging in there?" I ask. The look of complete loathing that crosses her face makes me choke back a laugh. "That good, huh?"

"I swear, he rides on the bumpiest terrain on purpose," Sera growls.

I can't hold back my laugh, and she eventually cracks a smile.

"The only reason I haven't murdered him in his sleep yet is that he's not bad to look at," she admits.

Alex rounds a tree with an armful of logs. "Oh, so you think I'm handsome." He grins cheekily.

"I wasn't talking about you," Sera retorts.

"Suuuure." He winks.

Sera looks like she's about to murder him right here and now, so I grab her sleeve and pull her away. "Kian mentioned a lake nearby. Let's bathe," I say, swinging a satchel with supplies onto my shoulder.

"Fine," she grumbles but continues to send death glares at Alex.

The birds chirp in the trees and broken branches crunch underfoot as we pick our way through the dense forest. "He's really not so bad when you get to know him," I say.

"Don't even think about starting with me," Sera says. "I'm only here because you need me. I'd much rather be cleaning chamber pots back at the palace."

"You must be joking."

"You'd think."

I gasp as an enormous lake comes into view. It would take hours to swim from one side to the other, or at least I assume so; I don't actually know how to swim. The waning sunlight bounces off the water, making it sparkle like diamonds.

"Wow," Sera says. "It's almost pretty enough to make me less angry at Alex."

I laugh again as I strip out of my travel clothes. "Come, let's clean up before the sun sets and it gets too cold."

Sera shivers at the thought and quickly undresses. "What I wouldn't give for an actual bath," she complains.

I race into the lake, screeching as the cold water nips at my skin.

"Keep your voice down, Rae!" Sera yells. "Unless you want the men to come running, thinking someone is dying."

"Good point." I grin. Not that I would mind Kian coming out for a swim with me, but certainly not in the presence of anyone else. The thought of his naked body . . . This time, my shiver is not from cold.

Not the time, Rae.

Sera swears loudly when she finally gets into the water.

"I didn't realize you had such a dirty mouth," I tease her.

She blushes. "I'm sorry . . . I think leaving the palace behind has made me a little too comfortable. I'd lose my position in a heartbeat if other servants heard me talking so familiarly with the prince."

"Oh, so Alex doesn't count?"

Sera splashes me, which is answer enough.

"Don't you worry. Your job is safe as long as I have anything to say about it."

She grins, but her teeth chatter. "Let's hurry this up before my tits freeze off."

My toes have gone completely numb, but the water is refreshing. I welcome the final rays of sunlight, enjoying how they sink into my skin, making me feel almost warm despite the icy water. After a quick rinse of my hair and a brief scrub in the waist-deep water, I wade back toward shore.

Just as I reach the sandy bank, a piercing scream freezes my blood to ice. I spin around and witness Sera being dragged beneath the water, a look of pure terror on her face.

Chapter Forty-Seven

RAELYN

I'm frozen to the spot. Surely I'm no match for whatever is down there, but I can't abandon my friend. The water goes still, and my heart sinks like a stone.

"*Kian!*" I scream before I rush back into the waist-deep water and duck beneath the surface, trying to look through the murky depths for something, anything.

What am I doing? I can't swim. I can't save her.

A wild scream erupts out of me under the water. In desperation, I stretch my hands out, shocked when light shoots from my fingers, illuminating the waters.

Almost too surprised to react, I continue soundlessly screaming as light pours out of me. *There!* I blink and spy Sera floating lifelessly twenty feet away as a dark shadow darts away from her. Whatever it is seems to be avoiding the beams lighting up the water's fathomless depths.

I'm wrenched out of the water and start coughing. Kian's entire body is rife with tension as he holds my back to his chest, his arms tight around my middle. "Are you okay? What in the hells is going on, Rae?"

"Sera!" I gasp as I point in the direction I last saw her. "She's not moving," I choke out. "There's something in there."

A splash is the only indication, and we turn and barely catch Alex disappearing beneath the surface of the lake.

"Let go of me, Ki. I can help!" I cry.

With no hesitation, he drops his arms, and I duck back under the water, trying to recall the sensation I felt before the light poured out of me.

Come on, Rae. You can do this.

I close my eyes in concentration, feel for the buzzing in my veins, and will it to leave my body through my fingers. It's different from the ribbons of light from my childhood memories with Erika. It's deeper . . . more powerful. A zap of warmth courses down my arms, and I open my eyes in awe as the light pours out of me again, making a clear path for Alex to find Sera. I hold my breath as he reaches her, then quickly kicks to the surface. Worried about whatever beast might be lying in wait, I continue shooting out beams of light until Alex swims past, and then I burst out of the water, sucking in a deep breath. Alex rushes Sera to shore, and gods, I hope she's okay.

"We should probably get out of here," I say as my teeth chatter with cold. The sun has sunk below the horizon, and darkness is swiftly falling. "Whatever is down there didn't like my light, but I don't think I have anything left."

My body is weak and drained. I could sleep for a week if left alone.

Wordlessly, Kian picks me up and carries me out of the water. He's clenching his jaw so hard, I'm worried he'll break a tooth.

Kian puts me down, and my fear for Sera sends a rush of energy through me as I hurry to her side. Alex laid her on the sandy beach and is doing quick compressions on her chest, stopping only to blow a few quick breaths into her mouth before starting compressions again.

My heart clenches, and I pray silently to any god who might listen. I can't lose my friend.

"Here, love," Kian says, handing me a clean, dry tunic from my bag, and I pull it over my head. Perhaps the embarrassment of Alex seeing me completely naked will hit later, but I'm not entirely sure he paid me a lick of attention, he is so focused on Sera.

I reach out and squeeze her unmoving hand. "Come on, Sera. Breathe," I plead.

It was only moments, but it feels like a lifetime until she finally turns her head and coughs up a lungful of water. A slew of foreign-sounding words bubble out of her, and she grabs at her head.

"Sera!" I cry, tears rolling down my cheeks.

Alex rubs and pats her back. "It's okay. Let it out, Spitfire."

Sera's eyes flutter open, and I sag in relief against Kian. "Thank the gods."

Sera looks around, spies Alex's worried gaze, and snaps at him, "What in the hells are you looking at? Get me some clothes."

Alex snorts and shakes his head, standing to search for her clothing. "Clearly, she's fine."

"There should be something in my satchel," I instruct, and Kian throws him the bag.

Sera wraps her arms around herself and gives Alex a stiff nod as he hands her a fresh tunic. "Thank you," she mumbles under her breath.

"What was that?" Alex asks, quirking a brow.

"You heard me," Sera growls.

"There's the spitfire I know," he quips.

I shake my head . . . These two just won't quit.

"How are you feeling?" I ask Sera.

"My chest aches," she admits. "And my leg hurts something fierce."

I scan her body, looking for injuries, and note the giant welts and bruising on her calf. "What in the hells was down there?" I wonder aloud.

Kian squats next to us, looking at Sera's leg, and frowns. "Some beast I have no desire to tangle with." He shudders.

"How deep is that lake?" Alex asks.

"Surprisingly deep," I reply.

Alex turns and pins his eyes on me. "Care to explain the light show, Rae? Kian never mentioned you having any powers."

I flush. "Well . . . uhh . . . I got mad, and it kind of shot out of me and scared off whatever was down there. I had no idea I could do that."

"Thank the gods for it," Sera says, laying her head on her knees.

"Maybe we should get back to camp," Kian suggests.

I groan as I rise, feeling a little weak in the knees.

Kian immediately steadies me. "Can you walk, love?"

"I think so."

He helps me gather up the discarded clothes, and we stuff them into my satchel.

"Do you need help, Sera?" Alex asks with no bite in his tone.

Sera tries to put weight on her leg and winces. "I might . . ."

"That had to be hard for her to admit," Kian whispers in my ear, and I swat him away.

"Shhh."

Alex offers Sera a hand up, and before she can protest, he swoops her into his arms and stomps back toward camp. Shockingly, Sera doesn't complain.

When they're out of earshot, I look up at Kian. "Do you think . . ."

"One hundred percent. I'd be willing to wager on it."

I chuckle. "I'm not taking that bet."

"Yes, because you'd lose." Kian flicks my nose gently, then his face turns serious. "Hells, Rae. When you screamed earlier and I got here and you were gone, I didn't know what to think."

I put my hand on his cheek, drawing his gaze to mine. "I'm okay, love. I promise."

"Hey, that's your name." He turns his head to press a kiss to my palm. My eyes meet his, and they shimmer with so many unspoken words.

"Thank you for coming for me . . . for us."

"You called."

Gods, I want to kiss him. Ever since I got my memories back, I've had flashes of our brief times together . . . the longest being when he first courted me seven years ago. I understand the warmth I feel toward him, the connection that is deeper than I want to admit. I take in a breath, forcing down the brief surge of anger at what was stolen from us, hoping it's not too late to reclaim it.

Threading my hand in his, we make our slow trek back to the campsite.

"Are we going to talk about your powers?" Kian asks.

"I'm not sure where to start," I admit, holding my hand up. It's almost completely dark now, and I search for that hidden spark within me. A ribbon of light dances around my fingers.

"Incredible," Kian breathes. "Just as beautiful as you."

The light sputters out, and we're plunged back into darkness.

In a breath, Kian swoops me up into his arms and takes me off the path, farther into the forest. My heart thunders in my chest as my mind tries to conjure all sorts of thoughts of what he might be up to. Before I can utter a word, his mouth is on mine. He's pushing me back into a tree, hooking my leg around his hip, and consuming me with a soul-stealing kiss. My hands fly up to his hair, and I dig my fingers in, pulling him even closer.

"I really thought I might have lost you," Kian rasps as he kisses down my neck.

"I'm truly fine, I promise." I let out a low moan as his hand dips under the tunic and I remember how bare I am. His hand trails up the side of my thigh, and oh gods, I need him to stop teasing me.

"Touch me, Ki," I whimper, knowing somehow that he needs to hear me say it.

"I thought you'd never ask."

I reach for him, but he pulls back, retrieving a dagger from his boot.

"How attached are you to this tunic?" he asks.

My breath picks up. "Not very."

"Good," he purrs as he slices through it, exposing my naked body in the dim light of the stars.

I take a breath, and he devours me with his eyes. "Beautiful. Exquisite."

I shiver as the air tightens my nipples to hard peaks. The hunger in his gaze makes me burn, and I reach for him once again, pulling him to me. His mouth captures mine in another rapturous kiss, setting me on fire. One hand makes a slow exploration of my body, starting with my breast, and I cry out as he gently pinches my nipple between his fingers before roaming farther down my side, his hand skimming my waist and finally, finally, sliding between my legs.

"Fuck, you're so wet for me, love."

I shudder again as he kisses down my throat while his fingers gently explore and circle my most sensitive part. I start to throb with want. It's so much, it's too much, it's not enough.

"Ki, I need you."

His mouth closes around my other breast, and he sucks, wringing another cry from my lips. "I need to taste you first," Kian replies as he continues kissing down my chest and stomach, all while his fingers tease and torture me, bringing me almost to the edge. He drops to his knees in front of me, hooking a leg over his shoulder. "May I?"

"Please," I whimper and then cry out as his tongue hits my center and he tastes me like a man desperate for sustenance. Rocking against him, I writhe as he plunges first one finger, then two deep inside me, working me from without and within. Every fear, every doubt washes away as he worships at my feet. He keeps me on the edge of bliss, teasing me relentlessly.

"Ki, I need to come," I beg as everything winds up inside of me.

"I've got you, love." His voice rumbles through my body, and I'm strung tight like a bowstring. My legs quiver, and I explode, biting down on my lip to keep from screaming. My climax roars through me, and my body shakes almost uncontrollably as he works me through the release.

"Rae, you're incredible. You taste like sunshine," Kian murmurs as he gets to his feet, placing my shaky leg back on the ground. "Do you have any idea how beautiful you are when you come undone for me?"

I sag into the tree, truly not knowing if I can stand with how he's brought me to bliss.

"Do you have any idea how many years I've ached for you? How much I've yearned to make you mine?" he whispers, pulling me into his arms. "I love you, Rae. I've loved you for as long as I can remember. Every time we met over the past twenty years, I learned more of who you are, and I still can't get enough."

My heart melts into the ground, and everything within me cries out *Yes* as I pull his face to mine. He kisses me deeply, stealing the air from my lungs.

"Thank the gods," I say. "I thought there had to be something wrong with me for how much I've wanted you. I think perhaps I've loved you all this time and merely didn't understand it because I couldn't remember . . ."

Kian gently pushes a tendril of hair behind my ear before cupping my cheek, a grin quirking his lips. "You could have said something sooner."

I laugh, pulling him in for another kiss. "Make love to me, Ki," I demand, desperate for him to fill me and make me completely his.

"I thought you'd never ask," he moans into my mouth. I can taste myself on his tongue, and it shoots another pang of desire through me. He loosens his pants, then presses me into the tree, lifting me so I can hook my legs around his waist. He lets out a guttural groan as he slides in inch by inch, allowing me to adjust and stretch, the brief pinch of pain quickly forgotten as he kisses my throat. He starts to thrust into me, and I'm soaring. His body fills mine so perfectly.

"Harder," I breathe, wanting him to know he can let go with me. He doesn't need to hold back.

He picks up his pace, and I moan into his mouth, loving the sensation of him so deep inside me. We're no longer two but one.

"You take me so well, love," he praises. He's not gentle as he pounds his cock into me in desperation, like he needs to prove to himself that I'm all right. One hand grasps my breast, and when he pinches my nipple, I gasp as my release barrels through me out of nowhere.

"You're amazing, Ki."

I can feel his grin against my cheek as he gives one final thrust and finds his own release. "*You're* amazing, Rae," he says breathlessly before kissing me softly.

"So much for my lake bath," I joke.

"You'll smell like me," he purrs. "No one will doubt who you belong to."

"You and your filthy mouth," I retort.

He reaches behind me and squeezes my rear. "I can't help myself. You make me wild for you."

My heart soars with joy and contentment, finally feeling like I truly belong. We're no longer bound only by words and blood, but by body and soul as well.

"I think you were always supposed to be mine," I whisper.

Kian cups my cheek again, his gaze boring into my soul. "I know you don't believe in soul-bonded mates, but if there is such a thing, I know with certainty you are mine. I belong to you just as you belong to me."

My breath catches, and tears prick my eyes, my soul screaming *Yes* louder than I could ever express with words. Kian kisses me softly, gently, and I completely surrender to him.

We kiss long and languidly, learning each other by touch and taste, discovering what the other likes, until Kian stills. I can't quite see him in the dark, but I can feel him.

"What is it?" I ask, trying not to be frightened. "Please don't tell me there's another monster out here."

"No, nothing like that," he says. "I was just wondering if you needed some blood after expending so much energy."

I pause. He makes a good point, as I'm not used to this . . . Obviously, the way my light sputtered out signaled weakness. I'll have to learn how to control this gift so I don't lose it when I need it most.

"That might be a good idea . . . but are you sure?"

"I'm sure," he says. "But knowing my experience with you and blood . . . we might want to do it out here so we don't put on a show for Alex and Sera."

I flush, though I doubt he can see it. "Good point, husband. Do you think they're wondering where we are?"

"I think they know exactly what we're doing and are glad it's not at camp," Kian teases. He grabs the dagger out of his boot and holds it up. "Where would you like to drink, my love?"

Almost impossibly, a fresh wave of lust rolls through me. Round two it is.

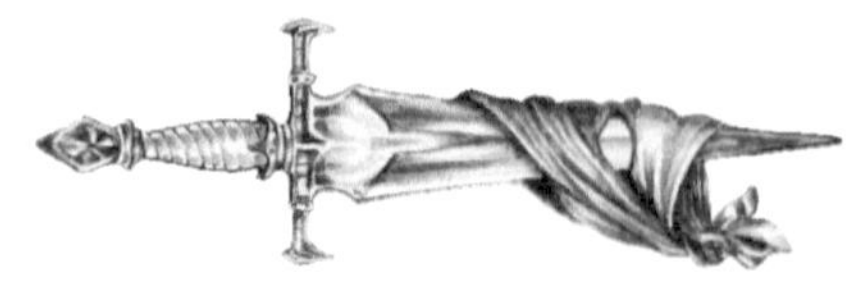

Chapter Forty-Eight

KIAN

When Raelyn and I finally made it back to camp, Sera and Alex were already retired to their tent. I smirk when I recall Sera giving Alex the most glaring of expressions when he told her they were sharing. Rae nearly jumped in to say she could share with Sera, but there was no way in hells I would be sleeping apart from her ever again if I could help it. Besides, the tents aren't that small. It's not like Sera and Alex have to cuddle.

Alex might not admit it, but I have the feeling he's in deep shit. I saw the terror on his face when we heard the girls scream. I've never seen him run so fast in his entire life. Gods only know if they'll ever admit it to themselves, but there is something there, hidden beneath the jibes and loathing. My friend is falling, and he's falling fast.

I look down at my incredible wife, cuddled up into my side, right where she belongs.

"Why did we wait so long to do that?" She smiles sleepily.

I shake my head and laugh. "It wasn't part of the arrangement."

She pouts, and I press another kiss to her lips.

When she stiffens, I pull back. "Is everything all right?"

"I . . . uh . . . I just realized we could have maybe made an heir?" Her voice is a little panicked.

"I'm sorry, I should have said something earlier," I apologize. "I've been taking contraceptive herbs since we were bound. There was no risk."

She shifts in the dark, and I wish I could see her face. "That's good to know, but why only since we were bound? I thought you had a reputation . . ."

I sigh, pulling her just a bit closer. "While I can't claim to have been celibate all these years, I allowed my reputation to become what it is so I'd be able to do what I needed to do in the dark. Margot kept me well-supplied, though I had little need of them."

A tiny ball of light flickers to life, and Rae places a hand on my cheek, understanding in her eyes. "Even if they were true, I wouldn't fault you for finding pleasure amidst the darkness."

The acceptance warms my insides, and I relish the kiss she pulls me in for. It's soft, sweet, and a promise for so much more.

"Do you need to stop taking the contraceptive herbs?" she asks softly. "I know your father is expecting an heir . . ."

"Love, I just want to enjoy you and figure out this god stuff. Children can come later, if ever."

"Sounds good to me," she says.

The thought of bringing a child into all this chaos seems like a terrible idea. Not that I dislike children, but there is far too much else to worry about. I heave a sigh of relief.

"Are we going to stay in Narvae tonight?" Rae asks. "Or are we going straight to the isle?"

"That depends on how hard it is to find a boat," I admit. We should be arriving at the small fishing town soon.

"What if we get there and don't find anything? What if no one lets us borrow a boat?" Sera asks morosely. She's been rather subdued since almost dying last night, and I don't blame her. Every time I look at Rae, I thank the gods she's okay.

"We can't think like that," Rae says. "We need to have faith."

My arm gently squeezes Rae's waist, and I press a kiss to the top of her hair. "Have I told you how much I love you?"

"Only about a dozen times this morning," she replies cheekily.

Now that the words have been spoken between us, a floodgate has opened. I don't want to waste another moment of her not knowing how much I love her . . . how she is my everything.

"Ugh, you two are sickening." Alex groans and picks up their horse's pace, moving out of earshot.

Raelyn giggles, and I'll never tire of that sound. "They just need to kiss already and maybe they'll stop being so grumpy."

THE BRINY SCENT of the sea is our first indication that we've finally made it to Narvae. Raelyn stretches her arms overhead and lets a few ribbons of light dance around her fingers as the sun shines down on us. The childlike joy she has at discovering her powers has been wondrous to watch.

"Perhaps you should take a break before we draw too much attention," I drawl in her ear.

Her shoulders droop. "But it's so fun. I wonder if I can do anything else with it? Or is it just a pretty light show?"

I hop off Phantom and help Rae dismount, purposely dragging her down the front of my body and giving her ass a little squeeze.

"Ki!" she squeaks. "As if *that* won't draw attention."

"I don't mind everyone here knowing who you belong to."

The pretty flush of her cheeks makes me want to pull her into my arms and devour her mouth, but if public displays of affection are not her thing, I'm not going to push it.

"As far as your powers . . ." I consider. "If we find Kyros, perhaps you can ask him about them."

Her eyes brighten at the idea, but the way she chews on her lip makes me realize she's as nervous about this final trek as I am.

"I hope we find him. He keeps haunting my dreams in his lion form. It's a little disconcerting."

I pull her into my side and enjoy the simple comfort I'm able to provide as she relaxes into me. "We'll have answers soon," I reassure her. "Now, let's find a boat!"

Alex and I decide to split up while Rae and Sera scope out lodging for the night if needed. Best to be prepared.

I take one side of the docks and approach a fisherman, enjoying the soothing sound of water lapping against the wooden structure.

"Good afternoon, sir," I start amicably.

"What do you want?" he grumbles as he fixes one of his nets.

"I was hoping I might be able to purchase passage to one of the isles," I reply, not so subtly jingling my coin purse, hoping it will be enough to tempt him.

He looks up at me, as if trying to figure out who I am. "Which isle are ya lookin' to visit?" he asks.

I pull a rolled map from my pocket and show him. "A few friends and I would like to visit Liial. Is it far?"

The man blanches, pushing the map out of his face rather aggressively. "No one goes there. The isle is cursed," he says with a shudder.

"What do you mean, cursed?" I frown.

"Exactly what I said—cursed. You won't find a boat in this village willing to take you there," he spits out.

I tilt my head, looking at his vessel, wondering if Alex and I could handle it on our own. "Would you be open to selling your boat?" I inquire.

"This is my living," he replies. "Nothing you could possibly offer would be worth that."

I roll my eyes. Clearly he doesn't realize I'm a prince of the realm. Surely a small fortune to build a new one and provide for his family in the meantime would be enough.

I'm just about to offer before he shoos me away. "Be gone with ye. I want nothing to do with this," he barks out.

Well, shit.

I'm shut down by each and every fisherman I approach.

"That was a waste of my time," Alex groans as we meet back in the town square.

"Ah, I see it went about as well for you as it did me."

"What do you think they're so afraid of?"

"I'm not sure, but it only makes me think we are actually on the right track."

"I agree," Alex says. "So . . . I guess we're stealing a boat?"

THE THIRD TAVERN we search is filled with clamorous noise and laughter and, thank the gods, Raelyn and Sera. Rickety tables and mismatched chairs fill the space, and spirits are high.

Rae spots us and holds up a large tankard of ale in greeting, a grin stretching from ear to ear. "You made it!"

"Hello, love," I say, planting a kiss on her lips. "Gods, you taste good."

"It's just the ale," she says, her skin flushed pink.

"I'd argue with you, but I'd rather just sit and have a drink of my own."

"Pull up a seat," Sera grumbles, glaring at Alex. "Stop standing there staring."

Ah, we're back to the hostilities.

"How did it go?" Rae asks with a slight hiccup.

"How much have you had to drink?" I tilt my head.

She looks at her hand, ticking off fingers. "Three? No. Four?"

"By the gods, Rae. Slow down a little maybe?" I tease.

"I was soooo thirsty," she slurs.

Sera throws up her hands. "I don't know what to tell you. She doesn't drink much, so it went straight to her head."

"Obviously," Alex retorts.

Sera gives him a death glare that I would never want turned on me, and I quickly motion for a server. The tired-looking female hurries over. "What can I get ya?" she asks.

"The largest glass of water you have and two more ales. Can we also get whatever you've prepared for dinner, please?"

"You got it," she says before scurrying off.

I snag Raelyn's tankard and take a sip.

"Hey! That's mine." She giggles.

"I'm parched too."

"Fine, I think I had more than enough anyway," she says before her eyes brighten and she asks, "Did you find a boat?"

Alex and I make eye contact across the table, and he gives a subtle shake of the head. Probably best not to discuss it out here, where anyone could hear us.

"We've got it figured out, love. Don't you worry about it."

"Perfect." She grins. Loopy drunk Rae is my current favorite.

"Do they have rooms available?" Alex asks.

Sera pins him with a look. "Yep."

"Fantastic," he replies.

"We searched what felt like countless taverns on our way to find you both. Why did you end up choosing this one?" I inquire, noting the rundown appearance compared to some of the others.

"It's the only one with three rooms available." Rae hiccups.

Not wanting to start anything with Sera, I let it go and merely nod. If she wants her own room, I'm not going to stop her. All I can hope is that our lodgings aren't infested with fleas or something equally horrible.

The server delivers the food to our table, and it looks mouthwatering. Perhaps this place isn't so terrible after all.

Rae digs into the fresh fish and moans happily. It really is too bad she'll likely pass out as soon as we get to our room; those moans make my cock twitch way too happily.

The lemony fish pairs perfectly with the cold ale, and we stuff ourselves. A nice break after the meager rations on the trail.

"I think we should retire early tonight," I say once we're all fully sated. "We'll be getting up fairly early tomorrow."

"Ugh, do we have to?" Raelyn complains.

"Yes, love."

"But there's going to be music! The tavern owner told me there'll be dancing later."

"As fun as that sounds, I think we could all use a good rest tonight."

"Fine," she says, sounding resigned.

The girls show us to our rooms, and before we retire, we pile into the largest one to debrief.

Raelyn looks oddly sober as she frowns. "That's the only option?"

"I'm afraid so," Alex replies. "The fishermen are incredibly superstitious, and no one wants their vessels anywhere near that isle."

Sera shudders. "And you're sure we should even go there with those glowing recommendations?"

"Unfortunately, I think it only confirms what we suspect. There is something off about the isle, and an imprisoned god might be exactly what we're looking for."

"Fuck," Sera says.

"Fuck indeed," Alex agrees.

Chapter Forty-Nine

RAELYN

"Gods, I drank too much," I whimper in the dim lamplight of our room. The sun has yet to rise, but we need to make it down to the docks before the fishermen do.

"I'm sorry, love," Kian says, and I cover my ears with my hands.

"Must you yell?"

He chuckles. "Definitely not yelling. Let me see if I have any pain powder leftover, though I'm pretty sure I used up most of it on Sera's leg."

Her leg was killing her all day yesterday after the attack at the lake. I hope it's at least a little bit better. I fall back on the pillow and groan.

"Ah! Found some!" he exclaims.

"Too loud," I moan again.

He sits on the edge of the bed with a handful of the powder, then grabs a glass of water off the bedside table, mixing it in.

"Thank you for taking such good care of me, Ki."

"I've always got you, Rae."

My heart melts. I'm not sure how I ended up with such a wonderful man. Thank the gods.

"I wish my godly powers healed hangovers," I say as I sit up and swallow down the mixture. The taste isn't pleasant, but I've definitely had worse. "Do I remember something about stealing a boat?" I ask, rubbing at my temple.

"Unfortunately, yes," he replies. "But don't worry, we intend to more than compensate the fisherman for his vessel and also return it to him when we're through."

"What if he thinks his vessel is cursed after we sail it to the isle?"

"Well, either way, we'll leave him enough to buy or build a new one if that's the case. I steal from my father because I want to help my people, not because I actually like stealing. I'd never leave someone high and dry out here, even if they don't realize who I am."

I nod with an appreciative smile. I respect him and all that he does, even if it puts him in danger.

We tiptoe down the hall and stairs, thankful it's early enough that the tavern is completely empty and silent. The door creaks as Alex opens it, and we all freeze, worried we'll get caught, even though we technically aren't doing anything wrong. Yet.

A thrill courses through me at this new adventure and the thought that I might soon meet Kyros, the sun god . . . my real father, though I'm not sure I'll ever really wrap my mind around that. It's altogether terrifying and exciting. I only hope he will answer all my questions, unlike my adoptive father, who won't even tell me about my mother, whom he supposedly loved.

Keeping to the darkest shadows, we follow Alex as he leads us to the boat he thinks will best serve us.

As we walk, I can't help but wonder what binds Kyros to the isle. Surely, as a god, his power could free him? Something must have been done to him. Echoes of the screams I heard in my dreams make me shudder. The salty air has a crisp quality to it, and I pull my cloak tighter around myself.

"Here we are," Alex whispers, directing our attention to a modest fishing boat. It's not too large for him and Kian to handle, but also big enough to carry another traveler if needed.

"Remind me again why we need to be here at the crack of dawn?" Sera grumbles.

"Fishermen start their days early," Alex explains as he works to untie the small vessel. "The last thing we need is for a horde of them to come after us."

"I hope you know what you're doing," she says.

"Trust me, Spitfire. I'll get us where we need to go."

She huffs and walks closer to me, her arms crossed in front of her. "I don't have a good feeling about this, Rae," she admits.

"It's going to be okay. Kian will pay the fisherman far more than it's worth."

"That's not what I meant," she says, looking off into the distance. "Something is off."

I rub her shoulder in an attempt to be reassuring. "I trust Kian and Alex. They'll get us out of there safely."

"I hope so."

ALMOST SURPRISINGLY, we sail out of the bay without a hitch. Everything goes smoothly, and I thank the gods for small mercies.

The sun starts to rise, but we're far enough away that we don't see another soul.

I can't help but admire the way Kian draws the sails taut, adjusting them to catch the wind just right. His muscles strain and swell with effort, and I long to run my fingers over them, to memorize the hard cuts and edges. Watching him work is putting all sorts of naughty thoughts in my head, and I squeeze my thighs together.

"Stop eye screwing your husband," Sera teases from where we sit at the stern.

I giggle. "What? I can't help it."

"Sure, you can't."

I nod in Alex's direction, where he's steering at the helm. "Alex is pretty nice to look at too."

She gives me a murderous glare before sighing. "He might be pretty, but he's an ass."

"An ass who saved your life," I retort.

"True," she admits. "I don't know what it is about him, but he drives me to insanity."

I shake my head. I know why, but I'm not going to force it on her. She'll either discover it when she's ready, or she'll move on. It will be her choice.

We sail for hours, the sun beating down on us, and I bask in its warmth, playing with the sunlight as it spins in ribbons from my fingers.

"That's so beautiful," Sera says with awe. "I don't think I ever really thanked you for saving me out there. It wasn't just Alex, you know."

"It was nothing," I say, trying to brush her off. "I had to do something. I'm just glad my power revealed itself when it did."

Sera looks down, chagrined. "I'd probably have run out of the lake and never turned back."

"I don't believe that for one second," I retort.

"I've never been so scared in my life," she admits. "Drowning is—" She shudders "I just . . . I thought I was a goner and my family would starve without me. Father hasn't been well since his accident, and Mother can only do so much. I worry for my little sister."

My brow scrunches. "Your family will always be provided for as long as I'm living. I promise you that."

Tears well up in her eyes. "Thank you, Rae. That means everything to me."

Unable to stop myself, I pull her into a hug. "I was scared too."

She laughs, wiping away her tears. "I don't think I'll ever be able to get into a lake again."

"What do you think it was?"

"Gods, I have no idea. Something slithered around my leg and pulled me under. I didn't get a look at it."

I shudder. "I didn't see it either, just a large, dark shadow that tried to get away from my light as quickly as possible."

"Hey!" Alex shouts. "I think that's it up ahead!"

Sera and I both look in the direction he's pointing, and a thrill of excitement courses through me. We're so close.

Despite the sunlight shining down on us, the island is cloaked in shadows.

"That doesn't look ominous at all," Sera drawls.

"Oh hush," I reply. "Everything is going to be fine."

"Famous last words," Sera mutters, and I roll my eyes at her.

"Can we try to think happy thoughts?"

While I don't want to admit it, a big part of me is terrified at what we'll find . . . or perhaps what we won't find. What if I got this all wrong and am leading us into danger? Cary's worried face flashes in my mind along with his warning to stay in Elsmont. Is this a mistake?

Sera blows out a breath. "Fine." The grin she pastes on her face is so fake, I burst out laughing, which finally makes her smile for real and loosens something in my chest.

"Raise the centerboard and rudder," Alex calls out to Kian as we get closer to shore and the water grows choppier.

"Are we going to get wet?" Sera asks.

Alex opens his mouth to speak, but Kian shoots him a glare. "Don't you dare."

Alex shrugs innocently. "What, you don't want the ladies to realize how filthy our minds are?"

"I'm no lady," Sera says under her breath, and Alex's smile grows impossibly brighter.

I flip my hair nonchalantly. "I'm a princess now, not a lady."

"Semantics, love," Kian teases as the small sailboat runs aground.

After the boat is secured, Kian helps Sera and me onto the beach. I glance around, half expecting a lion to pop out at any moment. *That's just a dream . . . he's not actually in lion form,* I tell myself, even though I honestly don't know.

The beach is surprisingly cool as the clouds overhead cast a darkness over us and a shiver courses down my spine.

"It is a little eerie here," Alex says, handing Kian his pack. "I hope we're not making a mistake."

"Have a little faith," Kian says.

I glance around the beach, looking for something familiar.

"Is this the right beach?" Kian asks.

I frown. "I'm not really sure . . . It looks different than in my dream. Maybe we should start walking? Hopefully something will spark a memory."

Ignoring the looks Sera and Alex shoot each other, I blow out a breath. So what if they don't believe my dreams? My gut tells me we are on the right isle, but the last thing I want to do is spend days searching it or find ourselves stranded here.

Alex adjusts the pack on his back. "Lead the way, princess."

I roll my eyes but start in the direction that *feels* right.

WE'VE BEEN WALKING for maybe an hour, but it's hard to tell. I miss the presence of the sun. Although it's cool, the isle feels sticky, the humidity causing my hair to adhere to my neck and my clothes to cling to my skin in a less than comfortable manner.

A roar rends the air, and we freeze.

"Um, Rae, I thought the lion was just an imagination thing," Alex says quietly, as if being too loud will summon the beast to us.

I shrug. "I mean, it's his animal form, but if he's trapped, as we suspect, he shouldn't be able to roam free, and this isn't exactly the typical climate for lions."

"Perhaps it's not an actual lion but the god summoning us," Kian says.

"Let's go with that option," Sera chimes in.

I give an awkward laugh, trying to ease the tension that's been increasing with each step. While I'm not completely certain, every dream has been the same—the lion leading me to the waterfall and the pained screams coming from somewhere behind it. My gut tells me he is trapped somewhere, and only his spirit could roam free as the lion.

We continue walking, and no oversized lions pop out and scare us, so I consider that a win. But once we round a bend, I'm struck with an extreme case of deja vu. This is it. This is where I was in my dream. I'm certain of it.

Perhaps even more terrifying are the footprints that lead up toward the dense jungle. Footprints the size of my feet with giant pawprints next to them.

What in the hells is going on?

"Can you see those prints?" I ask hesitantly, wondering if I'm hallucinating.

Sera's eyes meet mine, terror filling them. "So there is a lion."

"I don't understand," I stammer. "These look like my footprints, from my dream . . . but how in the gods' names would that even be possible?"

Kian's skin has lightened a shade, and Alex isn't making quips, so I know things are serious.

"I don't think the ways of the gods can be explained, as much as I wish they could," Kian says.

"I never realized how devout you are," Alex replies. "But I guess I shouldn't be surprised. You've been obsessed with finding him for years."

"I think we need to follow the tracks," I say. "This is the path."

Kian's smile is tight. "Ready whenever you are."

"Into the woods then," Alex says with a fake sense of cheer.

We trace the footprints into the jungle, the thick foliage blotting out a majority of the light. It's shockingly cool, and the sweaty clothes make my skin even more clammy and uncomfortable. The scent of rot assaults my nose and coats my tongue.

"What is that foul smell?" Alex complains.

"I don't think I want to know," Sera replies.

For the most part, a hush has fallen over our group. Now that we're following a path, everything is so much more real. I look behind myself and suck in a breath. The footprints we've been following have disappeared behind us, as if they truly are some kind of magic. Gods, I hope we can find our way back out.

As the foliage gets denser, Kian pulls out his sword and swings at the branches, clearing a wider path for us. That will only be in our favor on the way out.

The faint rush of water greets my ears, and I pick up my steps. "We're getting close!" I shout. "There's a waterfall just a little farther."

A sense of urgency overtakes me, and I push forward. Passing Kian, I start running through the woods. My feet are light as air as I speed ahead.

"Rae! Wait up!" Kian calls out, but I can't stop. I'm so close, I can taste it. The roar of the waterfall increases in volume as I race toward it, to what feels like my destiny.

Someone is crashing through the underbrush behind me, and shouts from my party try to reach me, but all I can think about is my destination.

Out of nowhere, the density of the trees breaks, and I almost go flying off a cliff. Despite my improved reflexes, my arms pinwheel as I catch my balance and barely stop myself from going over.

"Hells, woman," Kian growls, pulling me away from the edge so quickly, I fall back into him and we tumble to the ground. "Would you mind saying something before you go racing off through an unknown jungle?" He sucks in a breath and lays his head back on the ground.

"My body took over. I don't know what came over me," I breathe, feeling oddly rejuvenated. "It's like something is pulling me."

Alex and Sera break through the trees, and she collapses to her knees, panting heavily. "What the hells, Rae?" she cries out.

"Damn, I didn't know you could run that fast," Alex gasps as he leans forward, his hands on his thighs.

I sit up, smiling. "Oops."

Kian drags me onto his lap, holding me close. "You need to stop scaring me like that, love."

A bone-chilling growl breaks through the rushing roar of the waterfall, and we fall silent. For a moment, I was almost distracted from my goal. I can't allow that to happen again, not when we are so close.

"It's time," I say, not meaning for the words to sound nearly as ominous as they do.

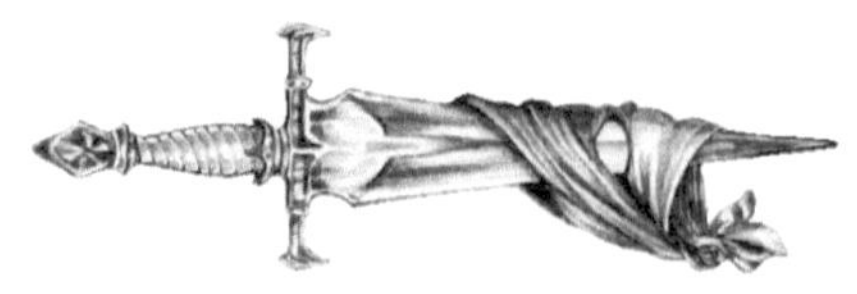

Chapter Fifty

KIAN

Rae chews on her lip as she looks at the waterfall. A pit of dread forms in my stomach, but giving up is not in my nature, and this is the culmination of years of searching. Nervous anticipation buzzes through my veins.

We follow Rae as she skirts the edge of the cliff, traversing a nearly invisible path that leads down to the waterfall. I remember her telling me about the screaming she heard in her dream, and I'm grateful that the occasional menacing roar is all we have to accompany us.

"I think there's something behind the waterfall. The lion led me here over and over; he's got to be here," Rae explains as we approach the thundering water. The pool below looks surprisingly peaceful.

Sera stares at the depths and shudders. I don't blame her. For all we know, there could be more dangerous creatures lying in wait beneath the surface.

Rae looks back at us, the furrow of her brow giving me pause. "I think I need to do this next part alone," she says.

"Like hells you will." I almost explode before reeling it back in. "I'm sorry, love. I just can't bear the thought of something happening to you."

Rae places her hands on her hips defiantly. "You can't tell me how to do this."

I palm my face, holding back a groan. "I know that." I try to soften my voice. "I just really don't think you should go alone."

Her shoulders go up to her ears as she takes me in. Her gaze is calculating, considering her options. She blows out a breath, her shoulders lowering in acceptance. "Fine, but just you."

I'll take it. Even though I wish she actually wanted me with her.

"We'll wait out here then," Alex says. "Call if you need us."

Gods willing we won't. I give Alex a look that I hope he interprets as *keep an eye on Sera* and trail Raelyn toward the waterfall.

The water is so loud, there's no use trying to talk. I'm surprised she was able to hear anything in her dream, but then I suppose it was a magical dream after all.

Misty spray from the falls is refreshing as the path down brings us closer. I grab her waist when she slips on the wet rocks, and she looks back at me, mouthing a thank you. We slow our pace, and the slim path that leads behind the thunderous falls comes into view.

The falls' roar dims as we enter the cave, and faint light shimmers through the wall of rushing water. The cavern is damp and reeks of mold. I just hope we don't have to go far—enclosed spaces make my skin crawl.

Rae lights up the space with a ball of sunlight, and pride swells in my chest. She's a natural. I can't wait to see all she'll be able to do as she grows into her power.

A pained growl echoes throughout the cavern, and Rae pauses, looking around as if to determine which way to go. "I don't know what's worse," she says, "the lack of screaming or what the lack of screaming implies."

I pull her into my arms. "Whatever we find, we'll face it together."

She nods but doesn't respond. I don't even think I can begin to fathom all the things she's feeling right now.

I want to feel hope—hope that we'll find the answer to our realm's struggle. Hope that we'll be able to free the god, even though he's been unable to free himself all these years. If Rae's suspicions are correct and Kyros is trapped somewhere in this dank cave, I worry at the potential state of him. The thought of being locked in here for nearly thirty years would drive a mortal man mad. How would a god feel? Especially one who is meant for the sun?

Raelyn moves away from me, but I grasp her hand. I need to hold on to some small part of her, even if our safety is likely an illusion.

I'm thankful for Rae's ball of light as we walk down, down, down. The sloped path curves and winds around, and bones of long-decayed animals and remnants of torches litter the narrow path. Does that mean humans had something to do with his imprisonment? I frown as I file that information away to unpack later. The thought that any man would dare to imprison a god is terrifying to say the least. I can only hope we're spared from said god's wrath. Having his daughter here might be our only saving grace.

The narrow path opens up to a hollow cavern with what I estimate to be a six-foot hole in the center. Old markings that look like runes are painted around it.

A low, weak growl comes again.

Rae looks at me nervously. She squeezes my hand tightly as we approach the hole and look down into the deep pit.

An emaciated lion lies at the bottom, its golden eyes flinching at the light from Raelyn's orb overhead.

"Hello?" Raelyn calls out.

"It's a lion," I whisper. "I don't think he can talk back. He didn't in your dream."

She shrugs, the look in her eyes screaming helplessness. "I'm here," she says. "I came. What do I do? How do I help you?"

A low growl reverberates up the walls of the pit.

Rae takes a deep breath, stepping away and pacing back and forth. "Gods, Ki. What do we do? How do we help him? Should you lower me down with the rope from your pack?"

"Let's think this through," I reply, trying to remain calm for her, even though I feel just as helpless.

"He looks so weak," Rae replies, wringing her hands, the orb of light above her flickering uneasily in her distress. "Hells! I'm a fool." She stops pacing. "He probably needs blood!" she exclaims. "He's been starved down here for decades."

Shit shit shit. The god would probably need to drain many men to regain his strength. We are ill-prepared.

"It's fine. I can fix this," she says, drawing my dagger from her thigh sheath.

"Rae, I don't know. Maybe we need to think about this," I say hesitantly. "He's going to need a lot of blood. You're only starting to regain your strength."

Angry darts shoot out of her eyes as she faces me. "If that lion down there is truly my . . . f-father," she stumbles over the words. "If that's Kyros, who has been kept from me my entire life, I would never forgive myself for leaving him. I have to do something."

I understand where she's coming from, but something doesn't feel right.

"Fine, we'll give him some of *my* blood," I concede. "You will need your strength for the walk back to the boat."

She scoffs, "I'm a demi-god, Ki. I'm stronger than I look."

"Yes, you are, but your powers have been suppressed for almost your entire life. I'm just trying to protect you."

She shakes her head. "Don't you get it? People have been 'trying to protect me' my entire life. Let me make my own damn choices."

I raise my hands in surrender. "I hear you, Rae. I'm sorry. But please allow me to try some of my blood first?"

She takes a breath. "We can try that, but you need your strength too."

I nod. "How do you think we do this? Cut my hand and drip blood down into the hole and hope he catches it in his mouth?"

She shrugs. "Unless you have a better idea, that's what I was going to do."

"As far as I know, lions can't open water pouches, and I'm loath to empty mine out anyway," I say. Not to mention, there is no way I could fill an entire pouch with my blood without needing some serious recovery time.

She reluctantly hands me my dagger, and I slice into the palm of my hand, holding back a wince at the sharp burst of pain.

Rae looks at me, almost embarrassed. "I don't know what to call him."

I shake my head, but I get her point. She leans back over the edge, and I bite my tongue to keep from reminding her to be careful. She is a grown-ass woman, and she's made it clear she's done with overprotective men telling her what to do.

"Um . . . hello, again, my lord," she calls down. "We're going to try to drip some blood down for you if you could maybe open your mouth?"

I join her at the side of the pit and wait for the lion to open his enormous maw. Gods, I really hope this doesn't backfire.

Holding my hand over the pit, I squeeze tightly. Blood starts to drip down out of my fist and, miraculously, the lion catches it on its tongue.

"How much do I give?" I ask Rae.

She shrugs again. "Whatever you think you reasonably can?"

I stand there another minute, letting the blood drip, when a flash of light surprises me and I step away from the pit, covering my eyes.

A gasp out of Rae has me hurrying back to her side. "What is it?"

She merely points down into the pit, where an emaciated blond male now crouches. His clothes, if you can call them that, are tattered rags hanging off him.

"My lord," Rae whispers in reverence and drops to her knees on the rocky ground.

Damn, that's gotta hurt.

I, too, kneel on the ground, placing my bloodied hand over my chest in a sign of respect. "Lord Kyros . . ." I whisper.

A raspy voice echoes in the cavern, sending a chill through me. "Your offering is appreciated, son of Silenius."

Rae's eyes widen in surprise, hope lighting them from within. She peeks over the edge again.

"Hi . . . I'm Raelyn," she says softly . . . almost timidly.

"I know who you are, daughter," the god replies. "Thank you for answering my call."

Tears fill her eyes, and she holds back a sob. "I can't believe you're real. That all of this is real," she says.

The god's eyes gleam in Rae's orb of sunlight. "I have tried reaching you for many years but was always blocked somehow," he growls, but it's clear his frustration is not with her.

"How do we get you out?" she cries. "What's keeping you down there?"

"Dark magic," the god grits out.

"Do you need more blood?" Raelyn asks.

A low chuckle comes out of Kyros that sends a rush of fear over me. There is something deeply menacing about that laugh, but Raelyn doesn't seem to feel the same.

"I am starved, daughter. Of course I need more blood. Far more than you could give me without draining your life forces."

As I suspected. At least he isn't begging her to sacrifice her life for his. Gods can be fickle, and even though she is his daughter, I don't know how paternal he's feeling.

"Are you alone? Is Cary here? Or is he too much of a coward to show his face?" he demands.

"My fath—uh, you mean Lord Astoria?" Raelyn blanches. "What does he have to do with this?"

"Who do you think put me down here, Raelyn?"

A sob erupts out of her at the confirmation. The questions we hadn't wanted to voice: how much he'd known . . . how much he'd been involved in this.

"He's not here," I answer the god. "He raised Raelyn as his own, and she only recently found out the truth. He suppressed her powers for years, and any time she would come close to figuring things out, he would erase her memories."

The sun god lets out a growl that would terrify the largest predator in our realm . . . but perhaps I'm *looking* at the apex predator of our realm . . . of many realms.

"I will tear him limb from limb," he roars.

Large tears track down Raelyn's face, and I so badly want to pull her into my arms, but something makes me pause.

"How do we get you out?" she repeats.

The god leans weakly against the side of the pit. "You're the key, daughter," he admits.

"Good! Just tell me what to do," she says.

"We can't use our rope to haul you out of there?" I ask.

The god shakes his head. "As I said, dark magic."

"What can Rae do?" I ask.

The god ignores me and looks directly at her. "Daughter, I need you to come down here. I have need of your blood."

A flicker of fear lights in her eyes. "Can't I just drip some down to you like Kian did?"

Kyros' growly chuckle is disturbing. "I'm afraid not. There is a ritual we must complete, and we must both spill blood together."

I look to Rae, shaking my head. "I don't know . . . Something feels off."

"Nonsense," she insists. "You can lower me down with the rope, and gods willing, haul me back up when we're through. Then I can help you haul up my father."

My heart rate picks up, and something is screaming *Don't do this!* in my head, but it's clear Raelyn's mind is made up.

"Should we maybe get Sera and Alex first? We might need their help," I ask, hoping to delay the inevitable.

Rae shakes her head. "No, we need to do this now."

Kyros lets out another weak laugh. "Don't worry, son of Silenius. I can barely hurt a fly in my state."

I secure the rope around Rae in a harness-like fashion and explain how to rappel down the wall of the pit.

Rae bites her lip again, and before she can stop me, I drag her in for a kiss. "I love you, Rae," I whisper.

She smiles at me, the crease between her brows wrinkling. "I'm going to be fine, Ki, but I love you too."

Taking a deep breath, she drops her legs over the edge of the pit, and I pull the rope taut, then allow her the slack she needs to slowly make her way down. Damn, I should have brought gloves. My hands are burning as the rope slides through them, making the wound tear even further.

"Can I get a little more slack, please?" Rae calls out, and I loosen the rope as she kneels down next to the sun god.

Chapter Fifty-One

RAELYN

This can't be real. I can't possibly be looking at the sun god—my father. For a moment, we just stare at each other, both taking the other in. Long, blond hair hangs limply around his shoulders, his skin so pale, it rivals what mine once was. His golden eyes sink into his emaciated face, and his jaw is so pronounced, it could cut glass. His face is foreign to me, but there's a hint of familiarity in his presence. I think we have the same mouth. A shocking warmth radiates from him, even in this dank pit.

The ball of light followed me down, and when I look up toward Kian, there's barely an outline of him. I will the light to lift a little higher, and to my surprise and relief, it responds.

"You look just like her," the god says, his voice choked.

"Who?" I ask, though my heart already knows the answer.

"My Lynette," he rasps. "Your mother."

"What happened to her?" I'm almost afraid to ask, but I have to know.

"That son of a bitch Cary killed her," he spits out, the cold rage coming from him terrifying to behold. His golden eyes are alight with a fire that would scare the bravest mortal.

"No," I say, my hand flying to my mouth, even though it rings true. As angry as I am at my father, I still care for him, but to know he's responsible for my real mother's death and my real father's imprisonment breaks something in me. Something I'm not sure can ever be repaired.

"Do you want to see her?" he asks.

I frown. "What do you mean?"

"I can show you some of my memories."

I hesitate. I want to see who my mother was, but I'm also afraid of how much more it will hurt knowing she is gone. No. I'm being ridiculous. Why wouldn't I want this gift?

"Yes, I want to see her."

The sun god takes a step toward me, and I try not to flinch as his hands come up and he places them around my head. There's a burning sensation in my mind, and then I'm no longer in the cave. I'm in his head but not. It's as if I'm hovering above, observing but not quite present in the moment.

Memories of Kyros courting an auburn-haired beauty with vibrant green eyes takes my breath away. She gazes at him adoringly, and the looks he gives her scream of love, or is that obsession? More memories fly by, and I see my mother swollen with child—with me. The way she speaks about me and her hopes and dreams for my future fill me with a sense of being wanted. A pang goes through me. The mother I'd known, Cary's wife, had never spoken to me in that way . . . never really had a kind word for me. Anger toward Cary burns within me, but I'm not even sure if it's my anger or if it's radiating from Kyros. It's more potent somehow . . .

Another flash, and there I am. A tiny babe with eyes to match my mother's . . . and somehow, despite all the memories that were stolen from me, I never forgot those eyes. Filled with love. Affection. Belonging. A blink, and everything changes. Instead of a flash of memories, I'm pulled into one.

Lightning cracks through the sky, illuminating two dark figures fighting with swords on a mountaintop.

"You've always wanted what was not yours to want," Cary calls out.

The heavens open, rain falling in torrents, and suddenly, I'm seeing this memory from Kyros' eyes, feeling his emotions and hearing his thoughts.

"Ah, that's where you're wrong. She has always been mine," Kyros says.

A piercing wail rends the night, followed by the rumble of thunder as lightning splits the sky once more.

Kyros turns and shouts at Lynette, who is hiding behind a boulder, "Get her out of here! Now!"

It would be his undoing. She'd always been his weakness, and now she'd be his ruin.

A blade pierces Kyros' chest, and he gasps as he falls to his knees.

"Kyros!"

No. No! She needs to leave. She can't be here.

Another flash of light, and jade eyes meet his.

"You need to go," the words gurgle out of Kyros.

"I can't leave you. You're my everything," she cries.

"Think of her. You need to go."

A cackle of laughter rings in Kyros' ears as rain sluices down his face.

Lynette reaches behind him. "I need to remove it. You won't heal with it in your flesh."

"Lyn, No!" Kyros screams as lightning flashes and thunder crashes once again, this time striking the sword that pierces his skin.

The pulse of lightning shocks Lynette, and she's violently thrown away from him.

He's on fire; everything is burning. The strike would have killed any mortal, but not Kyros.

"What did you do? What did you do!" Cary screams, rushing to

Lynette's side. "This is all your fault," he spits out bitterly as he rocks her body in his arms.

"Look in the mirror!" Kyros replies, even as grief overtakes him.

With a mighty push, Kyros screams and pulls the enchanted blade from his chest. Warmth pulses as his body oh-so-slowly knits itself back together.

Rising to his feet, Kyros stalks over to his enemy. "Get your hands off her! She's my wife, not yours."

Perhaps there's still time for me to save her. She begged me not to change her to an immortal until after our daughter had grown, but it will be her demise.

"She was your wife," Cary says, his voice defeated.

Kyros roars, and the ground shakes beneath his feet. "You will pay for this, Cary Astoria. If it's the last thing I do, you will pay in blood for your petty jealousy and pride."

Kyros' fist cracks into Cary's face, but he only laughs before spitting out blood.

"We got her!" another voice rings out, followed by a child's wail.

Spinning, Kyros' eyes search for the newcomer.

My daughter. I need to save her.

A glint of gold sparkling in his peripheral is the only warning Kyros has before a net is thrown onto him. It brings him to his knees, and immediately, all power flees his body. His chest wound leaks golden blood from where it didn't completely seal.

"You coward. Face me like a man," he screams at Cary.

Cary turns, cradling Kyros' daughter in his arms. Her arms flail as she screams, breaking the god's heart. She has no idea what transpired, that her mother was taken from her too soon.

"I want you to live knowing that I have what's yours—what should have been mine. You will never see her again."

"You better hope I die, because as long as I draw breath, your days are numbered. I will find you and tear your beating heart from your body."

A shiver goes through Cary at Kyros' words—his vow.

"Throw him into the pit," Cary says.

The golden net holds Kyros completely helpless. Every bit of his power is snuffed out. Kyros watches his enemy walk away with his only child, his heart cracking in his chest, even as anger incinerates his insides.

I will find a way back to her, if that is the last thing I do.

Overwhelming pain wracks Kyros' body before his vision goes dark.

BACK IN MY OWN HEAD, I fall to my knees as pain courses through me. At this point, I don't even know if it's mine or his. Tears stream down my face, and I start to retch.

A hand on my shoulder brings my eyes up to his. There's a cold fury in his gaze. "Surely you see I must take my revenge. It is long overdue."

Overwhelmed with grief, I only nod. "Whatever you need, Father."

Before I can react, he's latched onto my throat, sharp fangs piercing me. I scream in surprise, and Kian's distant cries barely register.

"What's happening? Why does it hurt?" I gasp as he drinks and drinks from me. My strength is waning, and I slump down, the sun god's arms holding me up with surprising strength.

He tears away, my shimmering blood gleaming around his mouth. But no, it's okay. He said he needed this to get out. Surely he didn't hurt me on purpose.

The sun god bites into his own wrist and thrusts the bleeding wound toward my mouth. "Drink, daughter."

I hesitate, the golden blood a foreign thing, but the scent of it makes my mouth water, so I open for him. He pushes his bleeding wrist up against my lips, and my tongue laps at the blood, the taste an explosion of sensations. Kian's blood is smoky and savory, but the sun god's? It's like being burned alive in the most pleasant way. My insides light up, the blood almost too sickly-sweet, but I can't get enough.

Without warning, my body starts to convulse on the floor of the pit as his blood continues to flow into me. The pleasant burn turns to agony, and I'm lost to pain. When I finally come back to myself, I have no idea if it's been minutes or hours, but the sun god stands over me.

"What's going on?" I mumble.

My body feels strange, like it's not my own anymore. The power buzzing through my veins is almost unbearable in its strength, and yet I feel weak.

"Rae!" Kian yells. "Please tell me you're all right. What's happening?"

"I'm okay, I think," I call back up to him, my throat raw. Had I been screaming?

"What's going on, F-father?" I ask again.

Kyros looks down at me, a tinge of regret showing in his eyes. "I'm sorry it had to be this way."

"What do you mean?" I ask, a frantic feeling growing in my chest. "What did you do to me?"

"It was the only way."

"What do you mean?"

"The only way I can leave is if another god takes my place, and you were my sole option. Only demi-gods can become full gods through the exchange."

Like being doused with the coldest of waters, panic sets in as everything becomes clear. *I'm a goddess.* "No . . . no . . . you can't mean to leave me down here."

"If I can find a way out for you, I will, but I've been down here long enough. There is vengeance to be had." His voice is cold, unfeeling. "I need to get back to her."

Her? With sudden clarity, I realize my mistake. In the vision, I thought he meant me . . . he needed to get back to me . . . but I was wrong.

"Please, you can't abandon me here," I beg. My mind can't even wrap around the fact that my father—the sun god—used me . . . he tricked me. Once again, I was lied to, but I'm lying here, weak. Helpless. I have no idea how to use my new powers.

"I won't forget what you've done for me, daughter."

The sun god crouches to the ground, and with strength I can't even fathom, he launches himself up and out of the pit.

The air shifts around me as he disappears from sight. There's a shimmer, but then the light I conjured blinks out, leaving me in complete darkness. Distantly, I hear Kian's shouts, but nothing registers. I try to clear my head, but I'm still lost in the fog of transformation and betrayal. Willing my power to form another ball of light, my heart sinks when it only sputters weakly, shooting out sparks before disappearing into nothing.

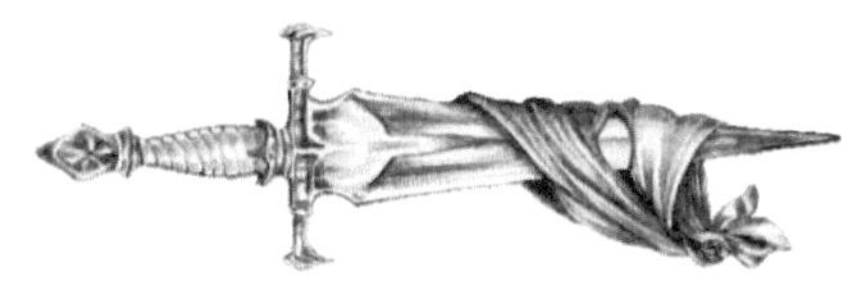

Chapter Fifty-Two

KIAN

The sun god comes flying up and over the edge of the pit through a shimmering barrier I couldn't see until now. This can't possibly be happening. I didn't hear everything that transpired, but I heard enough.

He lands hard on his feet, the cave floor shuddering beneath the force.

"What did you do to my wife?" The words come out in a menacing growl as I stare down the sun god, the one I've been searching for and thought could save my realm.

He straightens, nonchalantly brushing dirt off the rags he wears. Despite the obvious weakness in his body, he is still to be feared. "Watch your tone, son of Silenius. I am still your god."

"How could you leave her down there? Your *daughter*?" I grasp for answers, but the god's visage is cold and ruthless.

"The only reason I do not drain you where you stand is for *her*," he replies, looking down his regal nose at me. His eyes flick to the binding mark on my arm, barely visible in the dim light he exudes. "They should have never bound you."

"What? I don't understand?"

The god growls, and with immense speed, he has me pinned to the wall of the cave. "Now that she is a full goddess, your life is bound to hers through your marriage bond. I cannot kill you without killing her. You were never meant to be bound!" he roars.

I start feeling lightheaded from the god's grip around my throat, but no, I can't pass out. Rae needs me.

"Luna is a meddling fool," he barks out. "This has her written all over it."

Confusion flares in my mind, but I'm seeing spots and my breathing starts to sputter. With a sound of disgust, the sun god lets go, and I slump to the ground, losing consciousness as the cave goes dark.

"KIAN!"

My name on her tongue startles me awake with a fierceness. I scramble to my feet, groaning as my hand flies to my throat and the bruises that are certainly darkening from the god's inhuman grip.

"Rae!" I gasp. The room is pitch-black, and I'm afraid that if I'm not careful, I'll end up falling into the pit with her.

"Kian, are you okay?" her weak voice echoes up the walls of her prison. "Gods, please tell me you're okay."

I drop to my hands and knees and cautiously crawl forward to the sound of her voice. "I'm fine, love. Are you?"

A strangled cry reaches my ears, and it breaks something in me. "We never should have come. It was all a trap. He lured me here with his power, and I didn't question it," she says, her voice dissolving into sobs.

"Love, I'm so sorry . . ."

When my hand hits air, I stop and fumble around for the pack that has to be nearby. Relief courses through me when my fingers close upon the leather strap, and I drag it closer. There has to be something in here I can use. Rifling around, I find a small box of matches. They will have to do.

The match scrapes against the stone floor and flares to life, and I hold it up over the pit. The light is barely a spark, but after the darkness, it's something. Though I can still barely make out Rae's form lying at the base of the pit.

"Rae, my love, I'm here," I say. "What can I do? Can I pull you out?"

She sniffs. "I don't think you can, Ki. He made me take his place. I'm as trapped down here as he was." Rae wraps her arms around her knees, curling up into a fetal position.

The match burns out, and I curse as the flame singes my finger. Within seconds, I light another one.

"There has to be something," I plead, but who I'm pleading with, I don't know. The god I worshiped above all has failed me and ripped away the woman I love.

"You need to go," she says weakly. "He's hungry . . . Sera and Alex . . ."

"I can't leave you here alone."

The match sputters out, and I light the next one.

"You must. I would never forgive myself if they died because of my impulsiveness."

"This is not your fault, Rae," I try to assure her. "You're not responsible for his actions."

She barks a bitter laugh. "That's kind of you, Ki, but I never should have given myself to him so freely. I should have known better."

I squeeze my eyes shut. The truth I don't want to admit to myself is that there is nothing I can do from here. I need assistance, but the thought of leaving her alone breaks my heart in two.

"I'm going to get help," I say. "Watch out. I'm going to throw my pack down for you, all right? It has a little food and water left."

"Okay." Her voice is weak and resigned.

I light the final match and carefully take aim, listening for the thud of the bag.

"Don't forget about me," Rae croaks out, and I want to yell and scream at the unfairness of it all.

"I could *never* forget you." I almost choke on the words. "Hold on, love. I'll come back as soon as I can."

I stumble through the dark with hands outstretched, seeking the passageway back up to the falls. Each step away from Rae is a knife thrust into me, over and over. I might as well have ripped my heart from my body and left it behind.

BLINDING sun beats down on me when I emerge from behind the falls. Gone is the cloud cover we came in under, which can only mean one thing: Kyros' power is back.

Dread fills the pit of my stomach when I don't immediately see Alex or Sera. If the sun god got to them, Rae would be devastated. She wouldn't be the only one.

"Alex! Sera!" I cry out, praying to the other gods that they've been spared.

I run down the path we cleared, calling their names repeatedly. I don't see any bodies, but still . . .

One moment, I'm running, and the next, a force takes me to the ground, filling my mouth with leaves and dirt.

"Would you stop screaming?" Alex whispers harshly, his body covering mine.

"Thank the gods you're okay." I groan. "Now, get off me."

Alex rolls away and springs to his feet, and I push up to my knees.

"Where's Rae?" Sera's frantic voice cuts in.

"Kyros tricked us," I say as I brush the dirt off myself and stand.

"I knew something didn't feel right," Sera grits out. "When that asshole came flying out of the falls, Alex and I ducked out of sight as quickly as possible. We can only hope your screaming didn't draw his attention."

"It's a good thing you hid," I reply, ignoring the dig at me.

"'Ducked out of sight'? Ha, that's one way to put it. Sera tackled me into the bushes." Alex huffs. "What in the hells happened in there?"

I shake my head. These two . . .

"He made her take his place." I run a hand through my hair. "Rae is a goddess now . . . but she's trapped."

Sera and Alex stare at me, mouths agape.

"I did not see that coming," Alex says.

"How do we rescue her?" Sera demands.

"As much as I hate this, we need to find Lord Astoria." Sera oddly perks up at my words. "He was responsible for putting the sun god away the first time, so perhaps he knows what dark magic is holding Rae captive now. He's our best hope . . . but the problem is, Kyros has a vendetta against him, and I'm not sure if we can make it to him before the god does."

"Shit," Alex and Sera say in unison.

"You're telling me. I left some food and water for Rae, but we need to get back to Elsmont as quickly as possible."

Alex and I march back into the jungle with Sera trailing behind.

THE HUMIDITY IS a million times worse with the sun out in all its glory, and we are sweating, panting messes when we finally make it back to the beach. We only have drops of water rations left, and Sera looks wan, her steps no longer sure as she favors her injured leg.

"Are you okay, Sera?" I ask.

She gives me a withering look, but there's also a glint of . . . guilt? "I'm fine, Your Highness. Let's just get to the boat."

Without a word, Alex swoops her up into his arms.

"What in the hells are you doing?" Sera cries. "Put me down."

"Don't be ridiculous, Sera. Your leg is killing you. Let me help," Alex says, eyes straight ahead as he walks. "Besides, you're only slowing us down."

I wince. *Wrong thing to say, buddy.*

Sera crosses her arms and huffs.

Idiots.

Glancing out to the water, I startle at the small boat skimming through the waves, heading straight toward us.

"Uh-oh, we've got company," I say, wondering how we should proceed. Is it angry fishermen coming after us for our boat theft? Though with their aversion to the island, I find it highly unlikely. "We need to get back to the boat."

"No shit, Ki, but there's no way we're going to make it before they get here," Alex grunts, sweat beading his brow.

He might be putting on a good front for Sera, but I can tell he's exhausted after all the hiking we've done today. I'd offer to help but know there's no way he'd accept it.

"Let's pray to the gods they're friendly," I say as we continue to walk toward our stolen vessel.

When the boat gets close enough to see some of the men's faces, Alex sets Sera onto her feet, but she refuses to look at either one of us. "Well, we're either incredibly lucky, or shit is about to hit the sand," he says.

I turn to face the boat, and none other than Lord Astoria is at the helm.

"YOU LEFT HER THERE ALONE?" Lord Astoria yells before throwing a punch straight at my face. I easily block the blow and knock him off-balance. We quickly filled him in on the sun god's betrayal when he landed, and he's not taking it well.

"Do not forget to whom you speak, Cary," I growl. "Nor let us forget whose fault this is. Was it not you who trapped Kyros here to begin with?"

Cary straightens the lapels of his coat, chin high, ignoring my accusation. "Do you have any idea what you've done, princeling? Any idea what you've unleashed on our realm? You think things are bad now, but mark my words, it's only going to get worse."

"How in the hells did you even know we were here?" I ask. "And how do we know if we can trust you to help Raelyn?"

"As for your first question, I have my eyes and ears in the palace," Cary scoffs. "Though it appears I was too late to stop you from making a potentially realm-ending mistake. And secondly, Raelyn is *my* daughter. Of course I will help her."

I grit my teeth, trying to remind myself that he's our only option right now.

Lord Astoria arrived with two men I didn't recognize, but just then, the third comes to shore after securing their vessel.

Dylan Fucking Havordshire. I let out an almost hysterical laugh. "What in the realms were you thinking bringing *him* with you? Why would I allow him anywhere near my wife?"

Dylan gives me a wide berth, and I note fresh swelling and bruising around one of his eyes. That wasn't my doing . . . His jaw, however, is a little crooked despite the healers' best efforts. He's lucky he can talk.

Cary looks almost abashed. "Despite his deplorable actions toward my daughter, which he's assured me he will continue to pay penance for, I need him here."

I'm feeling quite murderous. "You have some nerve, Cary."

He glares at me. "She was meant to be with him! Everything was arranged, and you had to muck it all up by courting her seven years ago."

I shove those memories down—I need to focus on the now. "Can you help us get her out?" I demand, changing the subject. "Can you break whatever spell is holding her there?"

Cary shakes his head, and something in me breaks. "That pit has been here for millennia. It's meant to contain gods. I only knew about it because Kyros let the information slip. Why do you think he was on this isle to begin with?" Cary spits out. "He's happy to paint me as the villain, but it was *he* who came here with the intent to trap a god."

Sera throws up her hands and grumbles, "You men and gods are all mad."

"Watch your tongue, servant," Cary says.

"Do not speak to her in that tone," Alex cuts in, rage coating his words. "Speak to her again with such disrespect, and I'll have *your* tongue."

Cary is spitting mad, turning his attention back to Sera. "Don't think I'm not aware of what you did. Delaying your message so I wouldn't get here in time."

Sera stands her ground, refusing to respond, and I'm filled with a sense of dread . . . betrayal. Alex looks between Sera and Cary, confusion muddling his features.

"What did you do, Sera?" I ask.

"What I had to," she replies, face hard and unyielding.

Alex looks like he's about to explode, but we don't have time for this.

"Cary, you're the one Kyros wants, and if you care about Rae at all, you will be the bait to catch him."

"We should wait til nightfall," Cary replies. "He's too strong with the sun out. But you're right, catching him is the only way to save her."

"Where should we lure him?" I ask.

"Back where it all began."

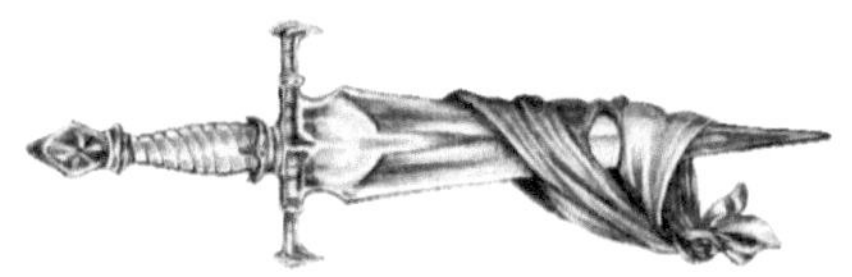

Chapter Fifty-Three

The sun sinks below the horizon, and the drastic change in temperature is jarring. As much as I'm loath to thank him, I'm grateful Cary brought extra water and rations for us.

Sera volunteered to keep Rae company by the pit, and despite all the questions I have for her, I don't believe she means her harm. Truth is, her betrayal benefited us; if we'd had to travel back to Elsmont to find Cary, Rae would have been alone that whole time, which is unfathomable. I'm angry but . . . relieved? Either way, I don't fully trust Sera, which is why I sent Alex to accompany her.

We spend the rest of the day hiking up to the highest point of the island. The craggy mountain peak is devoid of life—char marks streak the small plateau. Cary's men strain as they heave a large trunk in front of where Cary and I decided to set up an altar.

"This will work to summon him?" I ask, pacing back and forth once the altar is completed.

"If he's out for blood, as I imagine he is, mine will surely call him," Cary replies.

"What's in here?" I ask, nudging the trunk with my foot.

Cary kneels to open it. "There are limited ways to subdue a god . . . and you're lucky I have some pieces in my collection."

I swear as he reveals the chest filled with a golden net and three enchanted blades.

"Father would have cleared your debts and then some if he knew of these," I say. Was it foolishness or fortune that he hadn't?

"These are priceless artifacts, princeling." Cary sneers.

I clench my fists at my sides. If this bastard calls me "princeling" one more time, I'll give him a taste of the Shadow's wrath.

"And you're so sure he'll fall for the same tricks a second time?" I raise a brow. Shockingly, I'd gotten Cary to divulge bits and pieces of how he'd trapped Kyros here twenty-six years ago as we hiked through the jungle.

"Beggars can't be choosers, now, can they?"

We're fucked.

Cary directs his men to hide themselves and the net behind an outcropping of rocks, and Dylan readies a fire by the altar. Reverently, Cary hands me one of the enchanted blades before sheathing the other at this side. The last, he gives to Dylan, who holds it in his uninjured hand, and I roll my eyes. The man is not worthy to carry such a blade.

"Be careful with that," Cary chides me as I test its weight.

I jab it at him, and he jumps away, cursing.

"Show some respect, princeli—"

With a practiced maneuver, I have the razor-sharp blade mere inches from his throat. "I highly recommend you stop calling me that." I tut. "Speaking of respect—"

"Would the two of you stop messing around?" Dylan interrupts, standing in front of the altar. "We're about to summon a god who very well might kill us, and you're bickering over there."

Withdrawing the blade from Cary's throat, I step back. "As much as I hate agreeing with the asshole, he's right. We need to try to work together."

Dylan mutters something under his breath, but he's not worth my energy.

Darkness has completely fallen, the only light coming from the moon, the stars, and the crackling fire burning bright by the altar.

I follow Cary and stand before it, wondering how long he's going to wait to summon Kyros.

Before I can react, Cary grabs my palm and slices across it with a blade, Dylan jumping in to keep me in place.

"What in the hells?" I yell, the cut throbbing and burning as he squeezes my hand over the blazing fire.

My blood sizzles and spits, shooting off sparks that float up into the night sky.

"Gracious goddess Luna, we beseech thee to hear our plea," Cary prays, still squeezing my hand painfully over the fire. "Accept this offering. Blood calls to blood."

"Have you lost your mind?" I hiss as I finally manage to yank my hand away from him and Dylan lets me go. "This isn't what we agreed upon! What makes you think she'll answer? None of the gods have answered in centuries."

Cary looks to the sky, holding the bloody blade aloft in offering, ignoring my words. "Gracious goddess Luna, we beseech thee to hear our plea," he repeats reverently.

I step back from the altar, trying to quell my fury. I shouldn't be surprised that Cary went rogue. Tying off the wound with a piece of my shirt, I debate whether I should return the favor and start slicing into him.

A gasp out of Dylan has me spinning around, looking for danger, my blade raised. "Up there!" he says in reverent awe, pointing toward the sky.

What looks like a glowing star is falling toward us, growing larger with each passing second.

"What in the gods' names?"

Cary falls to his knees then prostrates himself before the altar, and

Dylan quickly follows. Unease has me holding my ground as the light draws closer. Did his prayer actually work?

A flash of light almost blinds me, and I fall to my knees, blinking rapidly to clear my vision.

An ethereal voice, smooth as silk, speaks: "My child, you called?"

I lift my eyes and am met with a creature so divine, no words could truly do her justice. Hair as white as the moon cascades in voluptuous curls that fall below her breasts. Her pale skin is on display, adorned only with a diaphanous cloth that drapes her hips. Eyes of cold, glowing steel meet mine, and she takes a step closer.

"Blood of my blood." Her voice drips with honey. "How wonderful to set eyes on you after all these years."

I duck my head, still in complete shock that the goddess Luna stands before me. "I'm honored by your presence," I reply, daring a look up at her again.

Her countenance is almost overwhelming to look upon, and I lift my hand to shield my eyes just a bit.

A sparkling laugh leaves her mouth as her light dims. "Apologies, dear one. It's been oh-so-long since I've been to your realm. I forget how frail you are."

I try not to bristle at the insult, but she's not wrong. I'm speechless in front of the goddess who is said to have started my family line centuries past.

"Thank you, my lady," I sputter with little grace.

"*Now!*" Cary screams, and I gasp as a golden net is thrown onto the goddess, instantly taking her to the ground.

An unearthly scream comes out of her mouth, and I cover my ears as Dylan stabs her in the stomach, pinning her to the ground with his enchanted blade.

"What the hells, Cary?" I yell. The asshole kept me completely in the dark.

"What is this treachery?" the goddess screams, golden blood leaking out of her wound.

"I didn't trust you not to give anything away. Better to keep you innocent in this," Cary replies.

"Release her!" I shout at him. "What have you done? Do you wish to call more calamity upon our realm?"

"Do you want to save your wife or not?" Cary grits out.

I lunge toward the goddess, but Dylan blocks me. Cary's other men stand guard on either side of the goddess, weapons at the ready.

"This can't possibly be the way." I stare at him incredulously.

Cary lets out a wry laugh. "I should cut you some slack, Kian. Some of this knowledge is not written in the history books."

I frown, turning to him. "Explain."

Cary looks around almost nervously but speaks. "Men should not dare to interfere among the gods and their games."

"Stop speaking in riddles."

Cary points toward Luna, disdain in his eyes. "You are probably aware of the longstanding feud between the sun and moon." His lip curls. "They have cycled through hate and love endlessly over the ages."

"Yes, I'm aware of that much. What else is there?"

Blowing out a breath, he continues, "Luna and Kyros were in a cycle of hatred when he visited our realm three decades ago. Lynette, Raelyn's mother, and I were courting when the sun god made his appearance. It was without pomp and circumstance. He glamoured himself as a mortal and inserted himself into court." Cary grits his teeth. "I do not wish to dwell on that time, but needless to say, Kyros—he called himself Cyrus at the time—stole Lynette from me. How could I have even tried to compete with a god? Though I didn't know what he was at the time."

"What does that have to do with Luna?" I ask.

"She was furious with Kyros for coming to our realm. The gods had agreed to keep their distance, and he was breaking their own accord. She thought to balance the scales, to lure Kyros away by making him jealous and involving herself in court. She interfered somehow . . . with your bloodline. I'm not sure what she did exactly, but it was while your mother was carrying you."

My brow furrows and my lip curls in disgust. The gods are more screwed up than I ever could have imagined.

"Didn't you wonder why I was able to summon her with *your* blood?" Cary scoffs.

"But there's nothing special about me," I protest. "I'm no demigod. What could she have done?"

"No, you're not, but you're still of her bloodline." Cary tuts. "And for some reason that is beyond me, her interference caused you to be drawn to my daughter—your presence awakening her gifts."

"What is he talking about?" I yell at the goddess trapped beneath the net.

Her eyes glow with fury, but surprisingly, she answers. "I fed your mother my blood while she carried you. Not much, but enough for it to change you—just a little. Have you never noticed you're just a little bit stronger and faster at night? More agile?" She gives me a knowing smile before it turns to a grimace.

I shake my head, unwilling to accept the words she's saying.

"Of course you'd be drawn to Kyros' child." She laughs, but it hinges on hysteria. "You are two sides of the same coin—each other's salvation and ruin."

I lunge toward her again, only Cary holds me back. "Tell me how to save her!" I demand.

"Free me, and we'll talk," she replies.

"Don't listen to her," Cary says. "There's nothing she can do for Rae. She would never willingly take her place."

"Then why did you summon her?" I grit out.

A blood-curdling roar rends the night sky, and I ready my stance, sword drawn.

"That's why," Cary says, a nervous gleam in his eyes as he draws his own enchanted blade.

My body poised and on high alert, I turn to the dark jungle. Of course he'd show as a lion.

Cary's men surround Luna while Cary and Dylan wait near the altar. That leaves me standing on my own to meet Kyros. While I feel exposed, I failed to mention to Cary anything about Kyros' inability to kill me without killing Rae . . . I suppose we both have our secrets. Despite Cary's words about wanting to protect her, I have yet to see him put action to them. Hiding her away and drugging her is hardly protection in my mind. That is control, pure and simple.

My heart jumps into my throat when the largest lion I've ever seen leaps into the clearing, hackles raised, a menacing growl rumbling through his body.

His golden eyes scan the perimeter, and when they land on the captured goddess, his lips curl into what almost looks like a smile.

"Kyros, my love, free me!" Luna calls out, her voice pained and breathy.

I stand warily before him, wondering what he's going to do, when Cary shouts from behind me, "Kyros, an offering."

Spinning around, I gasp when Cary shoves a surprised Dylan in front of Luna. I duck out of the way just in time as Kyros pounces on him with a mighty leap.

Collapsing to the ground under the weight of him, Dylan's body convulses as the god swiftly drains his blood. Cary's other men flee in terror at the gruesome sight. Dylan was a piece of shit—it's hard to feel sorry for him—but being eaten alive . . . I shudder.

"Let's make a bargain, Kyros," Cary calls out. "I hope the sacrifice of my man shows my sincerity."

Damn, he's cold.

"My life in exchange for hers." Cary points his sword toward the goddess, who hisses angrily, gold blood pooling around her abdomen.

I'm about to erupt with rage, when to my relief, he adds, "And you must use the goddess to free your daughter."

The lion drops the remains of Dylan's body and turns to face Cary, who's holding his sword up in surrender.

The air around the lion shimmers with a golden glow, and in seconds, the god stands before us. No longer clad in rags, he's draped in the finest gold. Skin no longer sallow but radiating with life. His back is to me as he takes a step toward Cary.

Cary's eyes avoid mine, and I wonder what he's thinking. Knowing the plan ahead of time sure would have been a hells of a lot more helpful than just flying by the seat of my pants here.

"We meet again," Kyros purrs.

Cary blanches but appears to hold his composure as he stands his ground. "Well? Is it a bargain?"

I dare a step toward Kyros, trying to keep my feet light and silent.

"What makes you think you have anything to bargain with, old friend? You can't seriously think a snack would be enough," Kyros scoffs. "From where I'm standing, I have the advantage here. I can finally have my revenge on you and punish the goddess to my heart's content."

"I've missed you, darling," Luna coos. "I can't wait to play." She makes eye contact with me over his shoulder, and I freeze, wondering if she'll give me away. Luna winks, and I release a breath, continuing my stealthy steps toward them.

"Silence, Luna. I'll deal with you soon," Kyros growls.

"Surely my summoning the goddess here and wrapping her up like a present in addition to my sacrifice is worthy of some boon," Cary says.

Kyros only laughs and stalks closer, knocking the enchanted blade away with his hand as if it were nothing. "You think to best me when I'm in this form? Perhaps you were my match with a sword in my mortal form all those years ago, but you'll never get the better of me again." He grabs Cary around the throat and lifts him off the ground. "Will you beg?"

Clearly none of this is going to plan, but Rae is all that matters now. I thought I needed the sun god to save my realm, but we'll find another way. We have to. I will not doom my wife to spend the rest of her days in a dank pit. Does that make me a selfish bastard and a terrible prince? Maybe so, but I'd see the world burn before leaving her to rot. Perhaps Luna's right: she is my ruin.

On silent feet, grateful for the apparent stealth and skill granted to me by the goddess, I close the distance to Kyros and plunge my enchanted blade through his torso.

Chapter Fifty-Four

RAELYN

"Are you sure you're okay?" Sera asks for what feels like the millionth time.

"I'm fine . . . just a little uncomfortable."

And devastated. Broken. Betrayed. It's starting to feel as if none of my parents ever cared about me; I was just a means to an end for all of them. To my adoptive—or should I say thieving—father, I was a means of revenge. To my real father, I was a means of escape. All so he could be free and find his way back to perhaps the only true love of his life—my real mother. Will he try to steal her from the paradise of Celestia or find a way to join her? I don't even know if such a thing is possible, but the gods' ways are mysterious. I suppose I'm about to figure that out . . . if I ever make it out of here.

Light flickers above but hardly reaches me, though anything is better than the pitch-black I sat in for hours and hours. When I heard Sera's and Alex's voices, I cried with relief. Perhaps I'm too harsh on the sun god. I was only alone here for a few hours and felt madness creeping in—he'd been trapped for nearly three decades.

My mind goes back to the memories Kyros showed me. My mother's love for me had felt real, but she'd chosen Kyros in her final moments. I want to be angry at her for leaving me alone to be raised by a controlling asshole, but if I'd been in her place and that had been Kian with a blade in his chest, would I have chosen differently?

"Talk to me, Rae," Sera calls down. "I can feel the spiraling from here."

I close my eyes, leaning against the wall of the pit. "Tell me a story, Sera. One like you used to."

"Which one would you—"

"It's time, Sera," Alex interrupts. "You need to tell her. I doubt you have much of an imagination anyway."

A soft "oof" comes out of Alex, and I desperately wish I could see them. Did Sera punch him? My lips quirk into a half-grin. I hope she did.

Footsteps stomp away, and the light grows just a bit dimmer.

"Scare him off?" I ask.

Sera peeks her head over the edge. "He's taking a break or something."

I shake my head. "You know, Sera, I don't understand why you have to be so mean to—"

"Shut it, Rae. I don't want to hear it," she interrupts.

"What does he want you to tell me?" I ask, a pit forming in my stomach.

"Why we came back."

"Why *did* you come back?"

She takes a deep breath. "Lord Astoria is here. They're laying a trap for Kyros to try and free you."

Hope and panic flood my body. I'm terrified that something horrible will happen, but staying here indefinitely sounds unbearable. "Why didn't you say so when you first got here?" I ask.

"I was trying not to worry you. Better to deal with one thing at a time."

It feels like she's hiding something, but I'm so tired . . . and panicked. Worrying about Kian . . . *and* Cary despite my anger toward him.

"Fine. But I really do need a distraction even more now. I feel so helpless down here. Tell me one of the stories about the fae girl in the realm with two suns."

"If you insist." Sera clears her throat. "Once upon a time, there was a beautiful fae girl with long, golden hair and sparkling violet eyes . . ."

That sounds kind of like Sera . . .

"She was wandering through an enchanted forest in the realm of Lunesai when she came upon the most beautiful pool of water. The water was unlike any she had ever encountered before, because when she looked into its depths, she saw other realms instead of the reflection of the one around her. Every day, she would visit the water, staring into it and dreaming of adventure. One day, an enchantress wandered by and warned the girl not to get too close. 'They'll whisper to you, daring you to get in, but if you do, you could be lost from your home forever.' This terrified the fae girl, for she loved her home and her family, but still . . . the pool called to her. It became an obsession. She would forgo chores and time with friends, continuously drawn to this magical pool in the forest. One day, she sat by the waters, reading, when the water started to ripple and churn. So startled by the occurrence, she jumped to her feet, dropping the book. She watched in horror as it slid toward the pool, as if it had a mind of its own. She couldn't lose that book! It was her mother's favorite. Without thinking, the girl lunged for it, but she was just one moment too slow. The book slipped out of her grasp and into the pool. A cry of despair left her lips, but the girl had made a grave error. As she reached, her fingertips had grazed the water, and an invisible force latched on and pulled her in."

I'm lost in the tale, even though I've heard it before. Somehow, this part feels even more sinister after what happened to Sera in the lake.

"The fae girl was trapped within the magical waters, falling, falling, falling . . . Realms swept past her, and she feared she would be trapped in that endless abyss for eternity until, finally, she stretched her hand toward one of those lands and was spit out onto a field of flowers. Dazed and confused, she looked to the heavens, hoping for just a moment that she had somehow made her way back home, but there was only one sun in the sky. The fae girl wept and wept, for she was in a strange land with no way home."

A deep, overwhelming sadness fills my heart at the tale. "But she does make it home eventually, right?" I ask, trying to remember how the story ends.

Sera's voice is resigned, almost sad. "No, Rae, she never did make it home."

"What happened to her?" I ask.

Sera props her head on her arms as she looks down into the pit. "She wandered the realm, using a glamour to hide her ears, learned the customs and language, and found a kind family that took her in as their own."

"I don't remember the story being this sad," I say, looking up at her.

"Well, perhaps that's because I tried to make it a happier tale for you, but this time, I thought you were owed the truth."

Confusion flares through me. "But it's a story, right? None of it is true."

Sera runs her fingers along the edge of the pit. "I'm sorry, Rae. I'm sorry for so many things . . ."

"What are you saying, Sera?" I rise to my feet, if only so I can see her just a bit clearer.

She brushes her hair behind a distinctly pointed ear. I must be imagining things.

"What?" I shout, then start to pace. "Are you telling me you aren't from this realm? Are you fae?"

Sera utters words in a lyrical tone in a language I have never heard before, but wait . . . My mind flashes back to when she regained consciousness after almost drowning, the nonsensical sounds coming from her mouth. Damn.

"What in the actual hells?" Alex's voice echoes through the cavernous room. I second his sentiment.

I stop my pacing and look up, a white glow emanating around the pit.

"Sera, what in the realms is going on?" I can only take so many more betrayals before I truly crack.

"I've been studying the runes since we got here, and I think I finally understand what they're saying. They're an ancient fae enchantment . . . and there's no way Cary can help us without Kyros' assistance."

Alex swears again, and Sera turns, muttering something I can't quite hear, but I'm sure it's snarky.

"Wait, so what does this mean?" I yell, trying to get Sera's attention again.

"It means I might be able to find a way to free you, but it will require a sacrifice."

Alex finally steps into view, his glower terrifying to behold. "What do you mean, sacrifice?"

Sera winces. "My ancient fae is rusty to say the least, but all magic comes at a cost."

"Who pays the price?" he demands.

She looks down to me before turning to face him. "Whoever breaks the enchantment takes on the burden of the sacrifice . . . or maybe its 'curse'? I'm not completely sure."

"Absolutely not," Alex says at the same time I say, "Forget it."

All the hope that had risen in my chest slowly but surely deflates. I have to trust that Kian and Cary will find me a way out. I won't sacrifice my friend, even if I'm hurt that she's withheld something so major the entire time I've known her.

Sera places her hands on her hips as she glares up at Alex. "You cannot tell me what to do. You're not my master. Besides, why do you even care? You've made your feelings toward me clear."

"I can't lose you, Sera!" I exclaim. "Please, I don't want you to do this. Do you even know what you'd be risking?"

Sera holds her head high, straightening her posture. "There's not much you can do to stop me from down there."

"Sera, please. Let's give Kian and Cary time. Gods willing, they can convince Kyros to return."

"She can't stop you, but I'm not beyond removing you from this place by force," Alex growls.

"You wouldn't dare." Sera points a finger at him. "How do you know I won't go ahead and curse you while I'm at it?"

Can she do that? I know next to nothing about the fae. It's been millennia since any were known to exist in our realm.

Without warning, a burning pain slices through my stomach, and I scream.

"Rae!" Sera yells. "What's happening?"

I drop to my knees, my hands pressed to my abdomen, golden blood leaking out around them. "I don't know." I gasp. Oh no. Oh no . . . Kyros said—"Kian!"

"That's it," Sera says. "I don't care what you think. I owe her after everything I've done. I will pay whatever the cost."

My vision blurs as pain overtakes me. It requires all my strength to keep my hands on my stomach to staunch the flow.

Distantly, Sera chants in that foreign language, and the runes light up the cavern as they glow brighter and brighter until there's an explosion of light and a heavy weight lifts from me.

"Sera? Alex?" I cry. "What's happening?"

"I'm okay," Sera says, and I breathe a sigh of relief, but what was the cost? What sacrifice did she pay?

"How do we get Rae out?" Alex asks. "She's nearly bleeding out down there. I don't think she can climb the rope."

"I need blood," I say weakly.

"Lower me down!" Sera yells at Alex while tying the rope around her waist.

It feels like a blink—I'm fighting to stay conscious—but Sera's worried violet gaze meets mine, and I want to cry.

"I'm here, Rae," she says calmly as she ties a tunic around my waist. It's painful but seems to help. "Now that the enchantment is gone, you should be able to heal yourself after you feed." She slices her wrist and holds it up to my mouth.

I couldn't resist if I wanted to. Instinct kicks in, and I gulp down the tangy, earthy blood. Strength returns to my body, and the bleeding slows, but fear for Kian takes over, and I pull back before healing completely.

"We need to get to Kian. Kyros said we're bound, and he's hurt."

Sera frowns. "They said they were hiking up to the highest peak, but I don't know where the path is."

I wrack my brain for all the studying I've done on the gods and their powers. The problem is, I'm not exactly sure what I am? Some lesser sun god? Something new? With sudden clarity, I recall reading about gods having the ability to transport themselves through will . . . Is there any chance I have that gift?

Shakily, I rise to my feet, wrapping my left hand around the glimmering marriage bond, and direct my thoughts to Kian. I remember the sensation of willing my light to do as I bid, but this time, I will the buzzing power within me to take me to my husband.

Light brightens around me, and I step into it.

Chapter Fifty-Five

RAELYN

I blink, and I'm standing on a dark, rocky plateau. It takes a moment for my mind to catch up with everything before me—a burning fire, an altar, a golden net holding a bleeding . . . wait, is that gold blood? Is that a goddess? Where's Kian?

I stifle a gasp when I spot Kyros standing above Kian's limp form, ready to plunge a golden sword into his already bleeding body. I can scent him from here, and a howl leaves my lips.

Kyros spins to look at me, confusion marring his features. "That's not possible."

With a hand pressed to my middle, I rush at him, screaming, needing to do anything to get him away from my husband. My eyes catch on an abandoned sword behind him, and at the last second, I slide to my knees, ducking underneath the blade Kyros holds aloft. To my relief, my fingers close around the hilt. Doing my best to block out my pain, I spring to my feet behind the god and swing the sword with all my might.

The clang of metal on metal reverberates up my arm, and I gasp at the speed with which Kyros has outmaneuvered me.

"Daughter, put down the sword," Kyros says placatingly, withdrawing a step. "We can finally be a family after all this time. I'll take you to her . . . to your mother. I'm sure she would be overjoyed to see you."

"Don't listen to him." Cary grunts from where he lies on the ground, trying to push himself up.

My eyes dart between both of my fathers and then to Kian, who lies far too still on the ground . . . but I'm alive, aren't I? He has to be okay.

"Come, daughter. Put down the sword," Kyros repeats. "Let me have my revenge, and then we can be a family."

I hate that there's a part of me that wants to listen to him. The little girl who felt unloved by her mother, the girl who always felt different, the girl who sought a father's approval above all else. But my eyes flash to Kian on the ground. Kyros was ready to make a killing blow, *knowing* it would also kill me.

"Such pretty lies, *Father*," I retort, readying my stance. "I will never trust you again."

Kyros' golden eyes burn as I swing at him, trying to get him away from Kian. "You'll regret your choice, daughter. I won't make such an offer twice."

I fly at him with a vengeance, and we parry back and forth, but I can't quite get the upper hand. I'm faster, more agile than ever despite the aching hole in my gut, but he's stronger. The clang of our swords rings out through the night, and a faint cackle comes from the direction of the mysterious goddess. I can't afford to lose focus now. I need to stop him.

"You think I want to go with you?" I grit out, punctuating each word with another slash or thrust of my sword. "You tricked me! You brought me here, and instead of being honest and asking me to take your place, you deceived me. Did you ever love me more than you loved yourself?" I cry as tears roll down my cheeks.

Kyros looks unmoved as he swings at my legs, and I barely jump out of the way in time. "You can't possibly understand my love. I'm a god. Wait until you've lived millennia. Then we'll speak again."

I scream, and it's my undoing. Kyros knocks the blade from my hand and holds his to my throat.

"Perhaps I should decide for you. I'm sure your mother would love to see you," he muses, then frowns. "How did you escape the pit?"

"A fae broke the enchantment," I reply.

A low growl emanates from him. "Damn. Now I have to figure out what to do with Luna."

My eyes dart to the goddess under the net. There is no way in hells . . . Luna? The goddess of the moon?

Kyros runs a hand through his hair in an oddly mortal way before his face hardens again. "You have caused me much grief, Raelyn. Perhaps I should just end you now."

I stand my ground, not willing to show weakness, even as I break inside. "Do what you must."

Kyros retreats a step, withdrawing the sword from my throat. His muscles bunch as he pulls his arm back, ready to thrust it into me. I squeeze my eyes shut, but the killing blow doesn't come as I'm shoved out of the way. I catch my balance before I fall, my eyes flying open to Cary standing in my place, a sword plunged into his chest.

"No!" I cry out. As angry as I've been, a part of me will always love the man who raised me.

"You fool," Kyros spits at him. "You've only delayed the inevitable. With you out of the way, what's to stop me?" He closes the distance between them, pushing the blade in to the hilt. "You've lost, Cary. You failed."

Cary chokes, and blood sprays from his mouth, but he smiles an odd sort of smile. One of acceptance and . . . cunning? "She will always be *my* daughter." His eyes dart to mine, and he whispers, "I love you," right before he plunges a golden dagger into Kyros' heart.

"*No!*" the trapped goddess wails.

Kyros blinks in shock. Once. Twice. His free hand goes to his chest, and then he collapses. An explosion of light shoots out of his body, heading straight for me, and I scream as it hits me with a fiery heat. Knowledge of the realms floods my mind in an overwhelming rush, and I grasp at my head in agony. It's so much . . . too much.

I'm on the ground, staring up at the night sky, unable to move, when smoky grey eyes meet mine. I want to sob in relief as Kian pulls me to his chest, holding me tightly as I allow all my tears to fall.

"Love . . ." he whispers. "It's okay. We're going to be okay."

"Are they really gone?" I ask, even though I already know the answer.

"Kyros' body disintegrated into ash," Kian says. "Cary is dead."

I squeeze him, and he flinches. "Gods, are you okay?" I pull back, searching for the wound on his abdomen, but it's sealed shut. Thanks to our connection?

A low chuckle comes out of him. "It's not so bad anymore, surprisingly."

Loud sobs grab my attention, and I twist to look at the weeping goddess. "I have so many questions," I whisper.

"Let me just say, the gods are incredibly screwed up," Kian replies.

"Watch it. Apparently, I'm one of them now."

Kian cups my face in his hands, examining me closely. "You're incredible, Rae. You saved me."

I shake my head, even as tears pool in my eyes. "I didn't do much . . . Cary sacrificed himself for me . . . for us." I take a breath before continuing, "I'm grateful to him, but at the same time, he was a terrible father."

Kian squeezes me to his chest again. "It's a complicated thing, to love one who treats you poorly. It's okay to have mixed feelings about it all."

I take a deep, shuddering breath, shoving those thoughts away for later. "We should probably deal with the angry goddess."

"You're right."

Helping me to my feet, Kian wraps an arm around my waist, as if he doesn't want to let me go, and we make our way over to the golden net.

"Is that Dylan?" I gasp as I take in the barely recognizable body and shudder at the gruesome display.

"Yep," Kian says. "You can thank Kyros and Cary for that."

Gods, I hope I can burn the image from my brain. I do not wish for him to take up any space in there ever again.

"*What did you do!*" the goddess shrieks at us.

"We did nothing," Kian says diplomatically. "Cary is the one who killed Kyros."

She screams again, and I want to throttle her.

I kneel down before Luna, allowing the goddess in me to shine a little brighter. "Kyros is gone. His power is now mine." As I look upon the goddess, I'm filled with a sense of knowing. Flickering images of her history with Kyros flip past in my mind. Gods, Kian was right. Incredibly screwed up.

Luna glares up at me, showing surprising strength in spite of the enchanted blade pinning her to the ground.

"I will free you if you swear not to take out your wrath on this realm," I say calmly, coldly.

"And if I don't agree?" she grits out. "You can't keep me here forever."

"What's one more dead god?"

She laughs almost hysterically. "Foolish baby goddess, you can't kill me."

I frown, looking to Kian, and he shrugs, clearly not understanding what she means.

"Kyros' ashes would imply otherwise," I say.

"Go ahead. Stab me. See what happens."

"I do not wish to play games with you," I grit out.

"All I will say is that Cary must have truly loved you for his blade to strike true," Luna says. "It takes quite a sacrifice to kill a god as ancient as Kyros."

My heart skips a beat, and I glance at his body, an odd grief threatening to overtake me, but I swallow and shake it off.

"There are very few things that can permanently contain a god, and by the sound of it, you just destroyed one," Luna coos.

"But I have a fae who is more than willing to reactivate the wards," I say, hoping to all the other gods that she won't call my bluff.

Luna looks at me suspiciously, her starry eyes trying to bore through me.

I clear my throat. "Do we have a bargain? You will not harm this realm?"

Luna sneers at me but then nods. "We have a bargain. I have no desire to return to this gods-cursed realm anyway."

"A blood bargain," I say. "One you cannot break."

Surprise flutters across Luna's face. "You're learning, baby goddess. Fine."

She swipes a finger through her bleeding middle and holds up the shimmering substance to me. With a grimace, I gather some onto my finger and put it into my mouth. Magic surges through me, and I know her oath is binding.

Grabbing the hilt of the blade, I yank it out of her and am rewarded with an ear-piercing shriek. Kian carefully removes the golden net, and she rises a little unsteadily to her feet. She is striking to look at despite her disheveled appearance.

She licks her lips and sniffs the air. "You don't mind if I have a snack before I leave? I smell cowards."

I raise a brow at Kian, but before I can think of a response, the goddess is a blur of silvery light disappearing into the trees.

"What in the hells was that about?" I ask. "Oh gods, what if she goes after Alex and Sera?"

Kian shakes his head. "I'm pretty sure she's tracking down Cary's men who helped trap her."

"Should we stop her?"

"Personally, I wouldn't want to get in the way of a hungry goddess."

"I'm glad she didn't ask for proof that Sera can remake the wards. I don't even know if that's possible."

Kian's eyes widen. "Sera? I have much to catch up on, it appears."

"Do you think Luna will stay away? I'm still figuring out how this all works."

"I don't know anything about blood bargains, but if she somehow finds a way to break it"—he wraps his arms around my waist, pulling me into him—"I believe I know a powerful sun goddess who will fight to protect her realm."

He rests his forehead on mine, and I glow with warmth. His belief in me makes me want to prove him right. Kian presses a kiss to my forehead, and I melt into him. He's my strength and my wings.

"What do we do with all these things?" I pull away and gesture toward the enchanted net and blades. "Surely we can't just leave them here."

Kian frowns. "I don't really care to lug them down the mountain in that heavy chest."

"I wonder if I have enough power to travel again . . ."

He quirks a brow. "Travel?"

"Ah, you were unconscious when I arrived. I got here by stepping through light somehow. I don't fully understand it, but it's a goddess thing. I'm not sure if I can bring anyone with me."

"Well, it's certainly worth a try." He grins.

Kian places the enchanted net and blades back into the chest after setting fire to Cary and Dylan—it's the least we can do. They'll forever remain on this cursed isle.

Kian turns me to face him, his hands gently cupping my cheeks. "Are you truly all right? I can't even imagine what's going on in your mind right now."

"I won't lie and say everything is fine, but with you at my side, we can face anything." I lift my right arm, the golden mark shimmering in the moonlight. "We're eternally bound. You're stuck with me, my prince."

A grin splits his handsome face. "There's no one I'd rather be stuck with."

I rise to my toes, and he crushes my mouth to his in an all-consuming kiss. I thread my fingers into his unruly hair, pulling him even closer. When our mouths finally part, I whisper, "I love you, Kian. Let's go home."

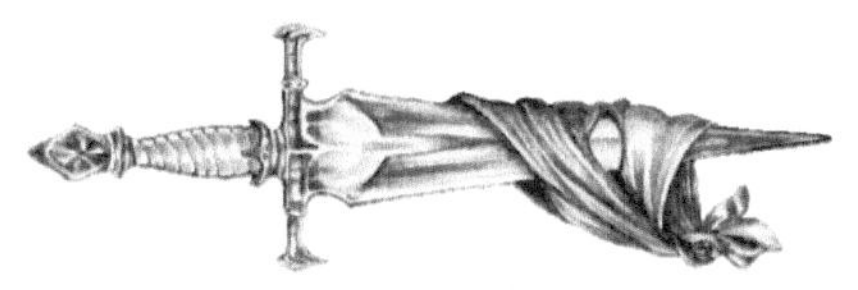

Epilogue

KIAN

1 MONTH LATER

The trial of Lady Olivia Astoria has finally arrived. The king was not pleased when I insisted on bringing her in, but he finally acquiesced; proof of a plot against the late Lord Astoria was the final straw. I know Rae can't wait to close this door of her life.

Rae still has nightmares, and I desperately wish I could erase them. She also feels responsible for Sera's curse. When we met Alex on the beach, Sera lay limp in his arms; only, it wasn't Sera . . . I shake my head. Alex has been a mess, and of course, Sera continues to push us away during the day.

We forgave her betrayal once she was finally able to explain the binding oath Cary had placed on her. He'd abused his knowledge of her fae heritage to use her for his own gain, but still, things have not been the same.

Deciding to keep Rae's new goddess status a secret has been difficult, to say the least, but she insists it remain that way until she gains full control over her gifts. It's still a little too early to tell, but reports have trickled in that this season's crops have made a miraculous recovery, and we're looking at a more bountiful harvest than we've seen in years. The Shadow just might need to go into early retirement . . .

Rae squeezes my hand as we rise for the king's entrance. "What do you think he's going to do?" she whispers.

"Gods, if I know," I mumble under my breath. "It completely depends on what mood he's in."

The king sits upon his throne, and everyone takes their seats on the uncomfortable benches. I swear they were made to torture us at these hearings. With a motion to the guards, Rae's stepmother, who looks quite worse for wear, is dragged into the throne room. Her clothes are filthy, and her blonde hair hangs limply around her haggard face. The dungeons did not do her any favors.

"Mother!" a high-pitched female voice shrieks from the right, and I groan as I notice Rae's siblings being herded into the room and held off to the side.

Rae stiffens beside me. "I don't know if I'm actually ready for this."

I squeeze her hand again. "I've got you, love."

The prisoner is pushed to her knees before the king, and he frowns upon her.

"Lady Olivia Astoria, you've been charged with assaulting Princess Raelyn, plotting the murder of your late husband, Lord Astoria, and the questionable deaths of your previous husbands. Do you have anything to say for yourself?"

"I never killed anyone," she simpers, her head bowed.

"Will anyone speak on your behalf?" the king drones on, bored.

The room is completely silent until Rae stands, placing a hand on my shoulder. "I'll speak for her."

"You may come forward." The king motions.

Rae looks like the goddess she is, draped in green and gold. Her hair falls in gentle waves around her face, and as inappropriate as it probably is, all I can think about is slicing the gown from her body and wrapping that hair around my fist so I can—

My father's voice breaks into my daydream like a pail of icy water thrown over me. "What do you have to say for her, princess?"

"While I have no love for my stepmother, I do not wish her dead." Rae speaks clearly.

"What would you have me do?" the king asks.

"Your Majesty, I do not pretend to have all your wisdom and knowledge . . ."

I try not to snort. She has far more than he ever will.

"But I believe it would be just to strip her of her title and wealth and send her to work in the farmlands."

"I beg your pardon?" Lady Astoria raises her voice, a note of panic in it. "I wouldn't survive out there!"

The king has an amused grin on his face. "I like the way you think, princess. I approve of your suggestion with one caveat." The entire room seems to hold a collective breath, waiting for his judgment. "Send her to the borderlands, to Paiden. I have no desire to lay eyes on her again." He looks to his advisor, Ethan. "Make it so."

"No!" Lady Astoria shrieks. "Please, Your Majesty, have mercy!"

"Get her out of here," the king commands, and the guards drag her out. Good riddance.

"Your Majesty?" Rae asks.

He turns his attention back to her. "Yes, my dear?"

"What will you do with my brother and sisters?"

"Ah, yes, I almost forgot. Well, as they no longer have parents, spouses, or any estate to speak of, would you like to take responsibility for them?"

Rae rolls her shoulders back and shakes her head. "No, Your Majesty."

Chessa starts to cry rather loudly, and Erika sends a seething glance in Rae's direction. What did they expect? They abandoned her. Rae owes them nothing. They don't even share blood.

"However, I believe my father has a distant relative in Sillamae. Perhaps they can be sent there."

"Perfect," the king says. "Well, if this unpleasantness is over, I'd like to get to my dinner." He rises from his throne and is escorted by his guards out the side door.

Rae returns to my side, sliding onto the bench. "I'm so glad that's over."

I press a kiss to her forehead. "You and me both, love."

"Do we need to join your father for dinner?" she asks.

"Absolutely not." I grin. "I have plans to unwrap my dinner in our wing."

Rae's cheeks tinge bright pink, but her eyes glimmer with desire. "Lead the way."

Grabbing her hand, we swiftly make our exit, only to be stopped by Rae's sisters and her sulking brother. Erika and Chessa stand with their arms crossed, bodies practically vibrating with anger.

"How could you?" Chess whines. "No one wants to live in stinky Sillamae! You have everything you ever wanted. Why can't you make space for us?"

Rae narrows her eyes. "What? You want me to give you my room here the way you stole mine at the manor?"

Erika shoves past Chess and puts on what I think is her best attempt at an apologetic look. "Listen, Rae, I'm sorry for how we handled things at home. It was wrong of us to take advantage of you and allow Stepmother to treat you that way."

"Out of everyone, I thought you and I had something of a relationship, a friendship, even," Rae says to Erika. "And yet, the minute it became inconvenient, you left me to rot." She taps a finger on her chin. "Should I call the king back and have him send you to Paiden with darling Stepmother? Backbreaking labor is quite character-building."

Chessa gasps. "You wouldn't dare."

"Watch me."

"I hope you're happy," Erika says, voice dripping with sarcasm.

"I couldn't be happier," Rae replies and squeezes my hand.

I take her cue, and we briskly make our way out of the throne room.

"Do you mean that?" I ask, so fiercely proud of the beautiful goddess at my side.

"Is life perfect?" she replies. "No. Do we still need to figure out Sera's curse situation? Absolutely. But I have you. We've got this."

Unable to stop myself, I pull her into a quiet alcove and capture her mouth with mine. My tongue teases the seam of her lips, and she opens for me, her body relaxing, so pliant and willing for me to have my way with her. She tastes divine, and I will never grow tired of kissing her. Rae hums happily into my mouth as I devour her, one hand gliding down her body while the other finally wraps itself into her glorious hair.

"Ki." She groans. "Our wing. Now."

"As you wish."

And then the Sun and her Shadow disappear into the night.

THE END.

If you enjoyed this story, please leave me a review!

Tales of the Forsaken Realm will continue in Book 2, where we learn the cost Sera paid and the curse she must overcome.

Coming 2026

Acknowledgments

First, I'd like to thank God for His unending patience, grace, and the passion to tell stories. Without Him, I wouldn't be able to do any of this.

To Justin—I know I already dedicated this book to you, but I truly couldn't do this without you. Thank you for putting up with the late nights and messier house so that I can follow my dreams. You are my biggest supporter and it means the world to me that you love my books too.

To Rachel—book number 4, can you believe it?! Are you sick of me yet? You have taught me so much, and I'm forever thankful that you help my words shine bright and make sense. I'm so grateful I found you on IG back in 2023 and that you took a chance on some baby authors and made us believe we could do it, and now you believed in *me* enough that I could write one solo too. Thank you for everything and for dealing with my random freak out text messages at 2 am. Get ready for book 5!

To my Alphas—Lisa, Holly and Megan. You all made this book so much better. Thank you for reading my unpolished prose and helping me take Kian and Rae's story to the next level. Your unhinged reactions gave me so much life and joy!

To my Betas—Eva, Lauryn, Leslie, Michelle, and Willow. Thank you so much for helping me fine tune TSAHS! Your feedback was immensely helpful in making sure I got the story where it needed to be. I appreciate all the comments and love.

To my Street Team—You all are the best! Thank you for sharing my posts and art and helping get the word out for TSAHS! I couldn't do this without you. I love getting to share sneak peeks of art with you.

To Lou—my very first Patron, thanks for cheering on my story from the beginning. :)

To some of the wonderful new friends I've made this year who have helped keep me from spiraling about deadlines or brainstormed me out of plot holes, thank you Sarah and Juliette for helping me survive this wild season and for getting conned with me. ;)

To my MTP family—2025 has been a wild one, but I'm so glad I got to meet quite a few of you in real life (if only it had been under better circumstances 🥲), but I couldn't do this without you! Thanks!

To Valerie for the kick in the arse I needed to believe in myself and write a book on my own. Writing *The Stars Would Curse Us* together gave me the courage to keep pursuing my dreams and continuing my publishing journey.

Last, but certainly not least, to some of my dearest found family—🤍🤍🤍—so grateful to you ladies for all the love, the rants, and the endless support.

About the Author

Stephanie's passion for literature ignited at a young age, shaping her into an insatiable reader. Her love for writing began with crafting short fictional tales and poetry during her childhood—a spark that only intensified as she delved into writing stories for her college newspaper while pursuing a degree in Broadcast Journalism. Stephanie's sense of humor shines through her writing, infusing her work with witty banter and endearing characters. She resides in Maryland with her musical husband and four rambunctious children. When she's not sneaking in a writing session, you can find her nose stuck in a book or baking goodies for the family.

Check out my website: silverflamebooks.com

instagram.com/stephdevourerofbooks

facebook.com/stephaniecombsauthor

tiktok.com/@stephdevourerofbooks

patreon.com/authorstephaniecombs

Also by Stephanie Combs

The Stars Would Curse Us Series

co-written with Valerie Rivers

The Stars Would Curse Us (Book 1)

The Stars Couldn't Break Us (Book 1.5)

The Stars Could Save Us (Book 2)

More from Midnight Tide

The Seventh Sister by M.A. Brown

Balance the Scales

As Above So Below

Stolen away to the dark shores of the enemy kingdom Ertha's thrust into a tangled web of political intrigue and deadly secrets that leaves her wondering who she can trust. The otherworldly right hand of the king, who is her keeper? Or the soldier she healed who has vowed to protect her at all costs?

When it becomes clear she wasn't just taken by chance–that there are much more powerful entities with their hands steering her fate—she's forced to confront that nothing is as it seems, not the men who protect her, the world she knows, or even herself.

Available Now

www.ingramcontent.com/pod-product-compliance
Lightning Source LLC
Chambersburg PA
CBHW031201010826
48971CB00013B/1209